THE DARK LEVY

Ten Tears Chronicles
Book 1

BY: ALARIC LONGWARD

TABLE OF CONTENTS

THE DARK LEVY

For my darling wife, once more.
For Lumia and Arn, for making me smile every single day.
For my cousin, who has read every book of mine.
And for the forgotten gods.

A WORD FROM THE AUTHOR

Greetings, and thank you for getting this book. The follow up to this one, **The Eye of Hel** will be out in the Fall 2015. Also, a sister series to this book, Thief of Midgard and the first book in the series, **The Beast of the North,** is already out. I humbly ask you rate and review the story in Amazon.com and/or on Goodreads. This will be incredibly valuable for me going forward and I want you to know I greatly appreciate your opinion and time.

Please visit

www.alariclongward.com

and sign up for my mailing list for a monthly dose of information on the upcoming stories and info on our competitions and winners.

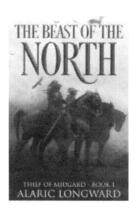

OTHER BOOKS BY THE AUTHOR:

THE HRABAN CHRONICLES – NOVELS OF ROME AND GERMANIA

THE OATH BREAKER – BOOK 1

RAVEN'S WYRD – BOOK 2

THE WINTER SWORD – BOOK 3

BANE OF GODS – BOOK 4 (COMING 2016)

GOTH CHRONICLES - NOVELS OF THE NORTH

MAROBOODUS - BOOK 1 (COMING WINTER 2015)

THE CANTINIÉRE TALES – STORIES OF FRENCH REVOLUTION AND NAPOLEONIC WARS

JEANETTE'S SWORD – BOOK 1

JEANETTE'S LOVE – BOOK 2

JEANETTE'S CHOICE – BOOK 3 (COMING LATE 2015)

TEN TEARS CHRONICLES – STORIES OF THE NINE WORLDS

THE DARK LEVY – BOOK 1

EYE OF HEL – BOOK 2

THIEF OF MIDGARD – STORIES OF THE NINE WORLDS

THE BEAST OF THE NORTH – BOOK 1

QUEEN OF THE DRAUGR – BOOK 2 (COMING EARLY 2016)

GLOSSARY

Able – a French Ten Tear and Albine's brother.

Albine – the French girl and one of the Ten Tears and Able's sister.

Aldheim – the jewel of the gods, home of elves and the First World of the mortals, Aldheim is a beautiful world full of adventure and uncanny beauty.

Alexei Donskoi – a Russian Ten Tear, Dmitri's, and Anja's brother.

Aloise Bardagoon – wife of Almheir Bardagoon, the Regent's wife, a lover of music and a lady in dire need of Shannon's help.

Anja Donskoi – a Russian Ten Tear, Alexei's, and Dmitri's sister. The brains of the outfit.

Asfalon Bardagoon – son of Almheir Bardagoon.

Bilac – a Fury Whip of the Dark Clans, jailor, and teacher of the Ten Tears.

Cerunnos Timmerion – formerly the Regent of Aldheim, the defender of the land.

Cherry – a strange, mute member of the Ten Tears. Guardian of Shannon.

Cosia – a Fury Whip of the Dark Clans, jailor, and teacher of the Ten Tears.

Dana Crowther – utterly powerful member of the Ten Tears and Shannon's driven sister.

Danar Coinar – lord of the House Coinar, devious and driven.

Dancing Day – the waters of Freyr's Tooth and Spellcoast. Dangerous and pirate ridden.

Dmitri Donskoi – a Russian Ten Tear and Alexei's and Anja's brother.

Elder Shannon – Shannon's grandma, and a priestess of the old ways.

Euryale – the snake headed native of another world, Euryale is the captor of humans of earth, the creator of the Dark Levy, the mistress of her house of gorgons, and she has many devious plans. One of the First Born, just shy of the gods.

Eye of the Crow – Hel's eye, her sole contact to the lands and beauty she once knew, before forced to be the caretaker of the dead and the Rot.

Ferdan – Elder Shannon's overly religious friend.

Filling of the Void – the beginning of everything, when ice of Nifleheim's rivers and molten bridges of lava mixed in the void.

Fanged Spire – once the palace of Cerunnos Timmerion, now home of Euryale.

Freyr's Tooth – the northern part of the elven kingdoms.

Ganglari – servant of goddess Hel, shape shifter, and a lord of Helheim.

Gjallarhorn – god Heimdall's fabulous horn, used to open and close all doors.

Grey Downs – once the island seat of House Timmerion, ruined by the Lord Cerunnos in the **year of Sundering.**

Hand of Life – goddess Frigg's gift to the quarrelsome elven lands of Aldheim. Also called the Second Light, counselor of the Regent. Hand of Life was always thought to be an elven female, but Shannon proved the theory wrong.

Hel – goddess of the underworld, keeper of the dead.

Hel's war – the war goddess Hel unleashed at the theft of the Eye of the Crow

Himinborg – the great city of House Safiroon, close allies of the House Bardagoon. Himinborg guards the only land route to the Freyr's Tooth and the noblest lands of the elves and hosts the sundered Gate of Svartalfheim. Lord of the House Safiroon is Talien Safiroon, an ancient, masterful Spell Lord.

House Bardagoon – led by the Regent, Almheir Bardagoon, they rule over the majority of the holiest elven lands of the Freyr's Tooth.

House Coinar – the southern house and fourth in Aldheim, fabulously rich of trade and raids. Foes to the north.

House Daxamma – the Holder of the Southern Passes, the high elven house commands more land than the other four great houses. The house stands in the mountain range to South Aldheim, where few elves venture since the Sundering. Often considered savage and less noble than houses of the Freyr's Tooth and northern Spell Coast, Daxamma are deeply distrustful of the Regent and the other higher houses. Enslavers of humans, Daxamma use them freely in their armies and are ever the arm and muscle of House Coinar.

House Safiroon – The second house of Aldheim, they hold the southern half of Freyr's Tooth, the holy continent just north across straights from Spellcoast. Himinborg is their fabulous capital.

House Timmerlon – formerly the first house of Aldheim, the house fell into ruin in Hel's war.

House Vautan – the third house of Aldheim, they command the northern tip of Spellcoast and are allies of the Bardagoons and Safiroons.

Jotun – ice or fire, the giants hate the gods.

Lex Cyburn – one of the Ten Tears, the conciliator, and the one who loves Shannon.

Ljusalfheim – home of house Bardagoon, the first house in the northern half of the elevated continent of Freyr's Tooth. There stands the Hall, Freyr's Seat.

Maa'dark – Gifted Hands. Spell casters who can see and use the power.

Markax Daxamma – lord of House Daxamma, uncannily tall and less wise than other of the five, nonetheless a lord of much power.

Medusa – Euryale's and Stheno's sister. Lost in Midgard.

Niflheim – land of primal ice, home of the nine frozen rivers and Hel rules the land, in addition to Helheim that is located in this land.

Ron Cyburn – one of the Ten Tears and a thug.**Saa'dark** – Dead Hands. Sacrifice of worth to gain power.

Serpent's Run – the sea-lanes near Vagabond's End, rumored to host a great serpent.

Shannon Crowther – the human Hand of Life, healer, and a miracle in Aldheim.

Shinna Safiroon – the eldest child of Talien Safiroon, Shinna is to one-day rule Safiroon holdings. She is to marry the eldest of house

Bardagoon, Asfalon Bardagoon, to cement the alliance between the two houses of Freyr's Tooth, the noblest of the elven houses.

Silver Maw – armor of the Hand of Life.

Skills – the power of creation often grant those humans entering Aldheim skills that are not spells.

Spellcoast – the vast continent of the elven nations.

Stheno – Euryale's sister. The one she is trying to restore to her.

Svartalfheim – the land of the dark elven and dwarven races.

Talien Safiroon – as old as Almheir Bardagoon and Danar Coinar, Talien has ruled the southern half of Freyr's Tooth for thousands of years, shrewdly navigating the schemes of House Coinar and Daxamma, guarding the north for the Regent and his allies to the south, House Vautan. He is the father of four elven boys and one daughter, Shinna Safiroon.

Thak – a fire jotun, a giant.

The Dark Levy – a levy of the troubled of the earth to travel bi-yearly to another world, where they discover who they really are. A device of Euryale seeking for something specific.

The Gates – the ways gods built to cement the Nine together. Lost since Hel's war.

The Houses – elven lands are divided into thousand houses. They compete fiercely and challenge each other into a game of power. The top five command the loyalty of the rest and this division makes up the power division of Aldheim.

The Nine – the nine worlds the gods claimed at the time of the Filling of the Void.

The Sundering – the tumultuous event of the closing of the gates after Hel's war.

The Tenth – the land of the Timmerions, our earth, the world elven houses tried to make for themselves, hoping to be like the gods. Home to the Dark Levy, humans whom the Timmerion's once manipulated so they could touch the power.

Trad – house Vautan's fabulous capital on the Spell Coast.

Ulrich Cyburn – an Austrian member of the Ten Tears, foe of Dana.Vagabond's End – pirate islands of the Dancing Bay.

Vanir – gods and goddesses allied with the Aesir.

Wild's Coast – after the Sundering, the eastern Aldheim was thrown to anarchy. Few know what is taking place in the formerly glorious elven kingdoms.

.

'The Eye of the Crow,
from Hel's face shorn.
The gods are gone, for the Horn is lost,
and both will be found at a great cost.

An awkward fool,
will dance with the twisted ghoul,
the Cold Hand shall seek the tools,
and argue over love's curious rules.

The Pact of the sister is fulfilled,
the false god wickedly thrilled.
The Horn shall blow,
freedom for those below.'

- Frigg's Prophesy -

MAP OF NORTHERN ALDHEIM

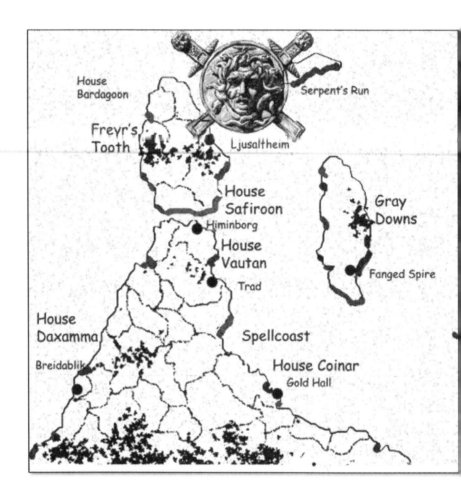

PROLOGUE

This is the story of two sisters, one dark and outwardly happy, the other red of hair and lost; sisters so different yet bonded in love. Yet, despite their differences under the light of the sun, in the silence and deep of the night, they were equal in suffering, both haunted by secrets half forgotten.

In that, they were not alone. There were others.

This is the story of the sisters' descent into struggle and danger; a story of lands beyond our memory and the hidden road full of wonders. It is not a road for everyone, for it is called the Dark Levy by its mistress, and only those who carry the curse, the blessing some few would call it, can heed its call.

The sisters found the Nine Worlds.

These are the words of Shannon, as spoken hundreds of years after the events that took place across the realms. She was a human of the Tenth. Then she changed.

Listen.

PART 1: THE SILENT WORDS

'Yfed y gwaed dy gyd-ddyn.'

Dana.

CHAPTER 1 - Ynys Môn, Wales, year 1815

We hiked up the hill after my sister. She was whooping and running up the track with our old guide, and I cursed softly. Damn her.

I was not happy, but Dana was obviously ecstatic as she skittered after the oddly boulder-like sailor on the rubble-strewn, mud-plagued route up the hill. Her bright yellow shoes were slipping on the slick mud, which covered the solid Welsh hillside. Our parents were not content either, despite the fine weather. It had been raining that morning, and everything was glistening wet. Mother echoed my curses, for the disgustingly happy Dana would look a mess when we eventually returned to the flowery valley and Grandmother's ancient, odd tile house. Despite the hardships, Mother and Father resolutely puffed their way along, despairing of the path up the ancient hill, a near obscure, almost forgotten track that was bravely fighting against a horde of invading weeds. I followed them; trying to enjoy the bright, clear weather and the shrill cries of birds one could hear above the distant hammering of the sea against high, craggy cliffs.

It was hard to enjoy life that day. Then again, I had had trouble enjoying anything for long years. I shook my head at Dana as she waved at me, but I attempted a smile. I managed it, but it was almost painful.

She was sixteen, eleven months younger than I was and acted like a damned ten-year-old. To imagine she was my sister? Impossible. Sometimes she seemed like a light-footed, merry wood spirit of our old Welsh stories, where I felt like a moss-covered boulder forced to roll along and after her. She had a knack of enjoying life, quaffing it down with gusto and thirst, which was annoying, occasionally. I had begun to hate cheerful people, and Dana was far too cheerful that day.

We were close, despite my annoyance with her. We had always been close, but there were differences in our character. From an early age, people had noticed how brilliant Dana was at everything. She was outgoing and seemed genuinely interested in anything people spoke with her about. She had a knack for making anyone feel special, no matter the topic. Yesterday, I had seen her speaking with the old Colonel Hayes about Napoleon's return from Elba. She knew nothing of the subject, not a thing, but the colonel was left smiling. Perhaps he had entertained fantasies of marrying her. She had plenty of suitors.

People. They loved her, and the ease she navigated myriads of different personalities and interests was admirable and sometimes, to me, a bit dishonest, for I felt like she was cheating. Surely she pretended to be interested in them and their stories. She pretended, that's it. I didn't. I could not. They all thought she would end up a politician, though of course she would not. She would marry and be content with making babies. She would marry well. She laughed happily like a child, sang like a lark, danced like Kathleen Bailey in our village, which is very well indeed. In short, she did everything exceedingly well.

The truth is I was jealous of her. She didn't only excel in everything she tried; she was prettier than I was. She was petite and beyond beguiling, her pouty lips were full, her oval face framed by long, dark hair that was so thick and wavy one had to resist tugging at it. She had sensual laughter, her eyes twinkled with blue fire, and her face was that of the angels. And I had freckles, was tall as my father and clumsy as a drunken elephant. I've never seen a drunken elephant or an elephant at all, but I'd imagine we would get along famously if I did.

Not that I was ever drunk, for I didn't really enjoy feasts. I was thought weird. Crazy, even.

I shook my head at her. She had again stopped to wave at me, beaconing me to hurry. She grinned; she did that when she was challenging me, silently urging me to fire up and take her bait. A competition, that's what she wanted, perhaps to determine who gets to the summit first. A simple, innocent thing, indeed, sisterly competition, yet I did not hito. Never did. I was never a challenge for her and never wanted to be. She looked briefly disappointed, even after years of similar disappointments, and I shrugged as she turned to run on.

Damn her. I hoped she would not break her foot as she hopped over a fallen tree, balancing on it briefly.

I sighed.

No, I was not like Dana. God knew what I was.

I swiped hair off my face, spitting at some strands in my mouth, hugging myself as I made my way to a drier patch of grass. What was I? What would I be? What had I done? Not much. That last question I could answer. Not much at all. Unless suffering was actually doing something. That I had done plenty of.

I had always suffered.

Everything was a strange struggle. I was not sure why, but there it was. It is true I was selfish, for there were so many people who lived with poverty and pain, who were ill with some incurable disease. There were plenty of those. Our medicine left so many people without answers and hope, yet I was physically healthy. People had no homes and endured abusive parents. At least I had a wealthy home and loving parents. I smiled briefly at Charles, my father as he was rolling his eyes at a patch of slick muck before us. He wore a heavy woolen coat, which was spattered with mud. I shook my head. It does not work like that. We don't care about the others, not as deeply as we should. We tell them we are sorry should they share their misfortunes, but we aren't really. We are only happy their suffering is not ours. And so, despite all that was good and even splendid in my life, I still suffered.

The reasons for my suffering were strange. I did not understand them, not really. There was more to it than being shy. My misery was profound, unfathomable, and so hard to bear. I wanted to enjoy life. I really did. I did envy Dana her pretty friends and the frequently changing, hugely handsome boyfriends. I wanted all of that as well. I did not wish to be unhappy, but it was impossible to be anything else. The misery ran deeper than the seemingly mundane issues any young woman might go through. For a long time, I had questioned happiness. Was it something of a myth?

The closest I ever got to the answer was in a dream.

I could not fully remember the dream, but I remember I had been happy. You know you can die in a dream, right? You can fly like a hawk or fall from great heights. I dreamt I was happy. It was a carefree, brilliant feeling of utter contentment. I was sitting on a horse, of all things. The wind was whistling, and there was not a soul in sight, and that is all I remember, except for the blissful joy of contentment, of a purpose. Oh, I yearned for that feeling when I woke up, for months I did. I would dream the dream later on, but that memory of freedom stuck with me, and so I knew the difference between what I did not have, and what I thought Dana dld have. There was happiness out there, just not for me. I wanted the dream, but no, waking up I returned to the world where I had no plans nor will to make any and felt restless and lost except with Dana. Always had. I was lonely but could not find any friends.

Dana was my salvation.

Despite her many impressive skills and the many friends and sullion, she always found time to be with me. She would help me when I was sad. Sometimes she forced me to the beach with her and there she laughed and dodged the waves while I smiled at her from the shallows. Occasionally she appeared in the salon, where Father was training me with a sword. He had no son, and I wanted to learn and so he had taught me with a longsword. I was clumsy, the weapon heavy, but it was the one thing I truly loved. There she faithfully cheered me and complimented my progress. How she charmed others, she charmed me. I loved her. She was my sister. Is. She was my anchor to life.

But she could not save me from myself. I was so unhappy and didn't know why, then.

Soon I was being excluded, even ridiculed in the village. I think that was inevitable, though, while being a brooding sister of the most popular girl in the village gave me some protection, there are always those who don't belong and they get the short end of the stick eventually. There are always the odd, crippled members of the pack that others shun and mock. I never thought I would be one of them, despite being a recluse. I tried to take part, occasionally, at least. I took part in celebrations, in church activities. I smiled at people and listened and spoke when I had to, but that did not stop the curious, critical beasts from smelling my weakness, from smelling my issues. I am not sure when the heavy brunt of daily mockery began, but at some point people started avoiding me and I stayed in our home as much as I could, studying Father's many books. I remember one time, when I was speaking with a child I did not know, a nice boy who asked me for directions at the market. People stopped to stare at me strangely, some snickered and others whispered to their friends, and I knew I was the target of their amusement. I was eleven, I think. I ran away in shock and checked if there was something stuck on my back. Mud? Hay in my hair? Pig shit on my shoes? There was not.

It was Shannon they laughed at.

Shannon amused them. My voice? My looks? Just something about me made them savagely cruel. It happened mostly behind my back. They never really confronted me, but they were always whispering when I could not see them. Soon, by the time I was fourteen, they called me crazy, whispering just loud enough for me to hear them. Not all did, of course. Those who did not know me spoke to me kindly, but the ones I saw every day, people we socialized with, met in the church and at weddings and celebrations … they drifted away from me. Dana was my relentless champion.

She got the family in trouble when she punched a boy called Michael for calling me a mad cow. He was from a mining family that hated our wealthy farmer family anyway, and Father only switched her rear for it.

I loved Dana for that. And Father for his mercy.

Dana told me to ignore it and that everything was fine. She could not understand my issues, of course, but I often napped in her lap and felt happy there until Father came to take me to my own room. Before that, she would comb my hair and speak with me. 'Shann. You gotta find a way to live this life. You just have to. I'm not going to be around forever.'

'I know. I will. Sure,' I told her, knowing I would not.

As it turned out, I was not crazy, but I shall speak more of that later.

Soon after the first incident, even Mother and Father began to think there was something wrong with me, and I overheard a discussion between them. Mother wanted to send me to live with her mother for a year. She lived two days away on the coast. Grandma refused, saying I was too young.

This went on until I tried to kill myself.

That took place on June 15th, 1813, two years to the day before our trip to meet Grandma. I was fifteen, and I'd had an argument with Mother that left me boiling with sorrow and anger, and my head was rippling with thrumming pain all that evening. I remember

I felt hopeless and lost, alone and despondent, and the pain had been so terrible. But there was more. I had seen something frightening and strange in the reflection from my window. I remembered little of what that had been. All I remember was that it had been terrifying. Perhaps I was mad. Yes. I was, I thought then. In the end, I got up, walked to the grain shed and found a pitchfork. I placed it under my chest and thought about the end. I leaned forward, felt the tool pinch painfully and then it broke under me. I fell in hay and dust, and ran home. I never tried that again. I had scared myself shitless, but the thought did lurk there behind my eyes every day after. The dream. The happy, careless dream. I daydreamed of that dream. Perhaps I had dreamt of being dead, and there was peace and happiness there.

It was an encouraging thought.

It was a scary thought.

The truth was I would not be able to hang on for fifty years, feeling so unhappy. I knew it. I would seek death again. One day. Dana would not have to worry about me then.

I massaged my forehead as I strode up the hill. Two years to the day. And I was feeling strange again, miserable as hell. I had changed those past two years. Usually, I had suffered the silent and barely audible mockery, my growing feeling of inferiority and hopelessness with stoicism and sullen acceptance, but ever since the clumsy suicide attempt, I had grown more aggressive.

Dana. I needed her. Yet, I was growing more hostile, more upset at her. I would snap at her, and that day, I wanted to run to her and stop her from … smiling? From being happy. I felt she was betraying me. I nodded to myself. I knew the reason. I was afraid I would lose her. While we were nearing the time in our lives when we would have to go our own ways. She would marry. She would move. I would be a spinster and a recluse. And she did not seem bothered about it. She loved me; I knew that, for she had comforted and been there for me all our life, but she had always told me she would not stay to do so forever. I was responsible for myself, and she was right.

I feared the changes about to take place in our lives.

'Come on, Shannon!' Dana shrieked as she turned to me. 'You can't be too tired, yet!'

Tired? I felt a tug of rage. My head was suddenly throbbing, as though there was a painful, twisted vein writhing inside my lobes. I glowered after Dana, briefly admiring her delicate features and then cursed myself for it. God, what was wrong with me? I felt something was coming, a storm was rising, and I feared it.

The wind blew as the old sailor turned to look back at us. He scowled, his hairy face not quite sporting a beard, but more like tufts of coarse hair twitching in annoyance as he looked on at our slow progress. I felt his eyes on me. There was something annoying about the old bastard as well. Ferdan, he was called.

Drunk, and Grandma's friend. An annoying idiot, I thought. Dana did not seem to share that feeling, for she was tugging on his frazzled sailor's coat sleeve and he grudgingly followed her. I nearly slipped, going on one knee. Charles, my tall, wide father grabbed me, his strong arm pumping out, snake fast. I flashed a brief, dry smile at him and trudged on, adjusting my shawl.

I wanted to go down to Grandma. She was watching over Rose, our four-year-old sibling, and if Rose let her, she would have dinner ready. Elder Shannon. She was my mother's mother, an old hag; some might call her something out of old Irish fairy tales. She always articulated her words carefully. She smelled of the old people, with old clothes wrapped around her rotund body, covering most all but her hands and her wrinkled, fat face. She lived in her weather-beaten house on the rugged, ancient island of Anglesey. The family visited her, even if Mother did more often, for she was old and Bridget, my mom worried about her. Father did not mind the trips. He was moderately wealthy, our farm did well enough and could run itself for a few days.

We were the Crowthers. I was Shannon. She was Dana. As she reached the top I looked at her and for a strange moment of clarity, I knew things would change soon.

Dana reached the top.

CHAPTER 2

Ferdan was a grizzly old beast. He smacked his hairy lips, ignoring my father's crowd as the smelly wrinkled man tried to wrap his dirty arm around my shoulders, but I ducked away from the old bastard and looked at the sights. I sensed he was surprised, hurtfully so, but I was grumpy and not willing to acknowledge it. 'It is a grand one, is it not?' he asked after awhile with his thick drawl. Charles grunted. He had the same origins as Mother did, rooted there in the frontiers of Wales, Scotland, and Ireland, and we respected those strong roots. They followed us faithfully, we dragged them behind us like a natural burden, never letting anything change us nor cut these roots, and so they never actually broke. Looking at the rugged, ancient sights around us, it was easy to understand why.

The sight was indeed grand.

More than grand, familiar in ways we could never fathom, as if a thousand generations of Crowthers and McGannons, Mother's family had stood on this very hill, staring dreamily at the surrounding waters and ancient stones, and we could dimly feel what they had felt.

Looking northwest, one could see the Irish Sea, blue and silver alternating like dull fish scales, the waves traveling lazily across the boundless horizon as they always had. The old man looked that way with a wistful leer, for he was once a sailor in His Majesty's service and now a fisherman, creature more of the waves than the hills.

To the south and east, the land spread out. Down there, on the valley below a hill they called Mynydd y Garn, there were myriad emerald green valleys, some with yellowish, okra-colored stretches, flowers and small woods and pastures lined with hedges or old, stubborn stonewalls. The houses looked cozy, well tended, there were spots of gray and lazy blue water. A sight to please the eyes, no matter where the eyes came from. The English loved the land just like the locals, and many a wealthy farmer had moved in in the past decade.

'Look, Shann, there's Grandma's place!' Dana said with annoying eagerness, and I nodded and squinted that way. There were hills, barren but for the lush grass and a few incredibly tough trees, and nestled between two such gnarled trees was a house made of dark, red bricks. It was a large house, where we fitted well, and we all wondered how elder Shannon kept the place in repair and milked the two fat cows she kept.

The old man stepped next to Dana after my rejection and placed his dirty hand on her shoulder, squeezing it 'Aye, there it be. See? The farting cows? Specks of birdshit from up here. Hah?' he said, and Dana just grinned at him. Here, again, she managed something I could not.

'Charles, where's Ireland?' I asked, turning my back on Dana. I did not call him Father. Never had, and I knew it sometimes hurt him.

He pulled me next to him, pointing at the faraway ocean. The wind blew and long strands of my thick red hair flew to my eyes. Father helped remove them. 'There, pretty one. Over there. Far but not so far,' he grumbled.

Bridget nodded. 'Not too far, dear. That's where our family came from. Right across there,' she said wistfully. 'He was a Norseman and went to Ireland to viking a bit and then they came here. He found a girl and built a hall. Became a chief of a local tribe. So they say. Who knows for sure?'

The old, gnarled man moved with Dana to stare at the sea. 'Your grandmother knows, if any. Hook, the old bastards called this island, especially the Norsemen and Danes when they had an itch for a bit of robbing. And they did have that itch often, perpetually. They would sail from the north, see, there? Across there, hugging the coasts with their bleeding, fat traders and lithe drake ships full of rancid, bearded rapists and cowardly robbers, especially after the Irish didn't let them rape and rob at will, and they lived here in the islands. Killed holy monks, the heathens,' he said while spitting. He glanced at us, realizing he had potentially insulted our ancestors and finally spat again in embarrassment. 'No offense to your ungodly relative, of course. I am sure he was a nice man and raped only rarely.' He smiled gleefully at his own sarcasm, and Father bristled at him. Dana giggled at his brazen tone, but I did not.

Ferdan was madly religious. He hated Protestants and those who believed in the old gods with an unsurpassed gusto, and his holiness was curiously mixed with utter coarseness, and in my upset state his words aroused me, and I could not keep my mouth shut. No, I lashed out and some wicked part of me rejoiced. 'Didn't they think the damned monks were the heathens? Weak men? Unable to fight for their gold?' I asked him.

Mother nodded though her eyes betrayed the shock at my tone. She made the sign of the cross and waved at me, and then she sighed as I looked away from her. Her short dark hair was blowing slightly in the wind, and she sounded worried as she spoke. 'Shannon is right, even if she is out of line. We have Norse blood in the family and yes; they were not bothered by fears of foreign gods, only swords and spears set against them. They had little use for the repentance and the demands of our Christian God. They did not demand much from their gods, at least beyond their immediate and everyday needs. They had their high Odin, and powerful Thor and so many others, and those gods asked for little, except for men to live bravely. Nor did they hate any other gods and those who believed in them; not those Celts still worshipping their old ones, not even the Christian one. They came here for the gold and the land and even, perhaps, for some dangerous adventure. The rich churches were just too juicy to ignore,' she said, echoing my grandmother. 'They wanted riches, our relatives did.'

Ferdan spat again, his mouth dry of spittle and stared at me. 'Be they damned relation to you or not, they were bloody thieves, savage murderers and filthy slavers they were, and God hated them. He does still, see? As much as he hates the French and Lutherans. But this place is special, and terror to the old gods and their misplaced servants.' He pointed at the green space not twenty yards away.

Charles snorted, his long nose dripping. 'See what, Ferdan?'

The man eyed Father carefully. 'Know the history of this place? Eh? You were visiting here since forever, but I never brought you here.'

Mother nodded carefully, her small face pinched with worry at the tension between her husband and the fisherman. Father shrugged. 'Nah. We visited here when they were young.' He nodded at us. 'Just didn't ask you along. We know something. Fairy tales and stories. Sad tales. Why?'

Ferdan laughed deep, a phlegm-filled rasp that made me

shudder. 'Aye. Fairy tales. Well, them fairy tales ring true in Ynys Môn, so they do. The heathens in the ships? Your ancestors? They came later. There be people living in these here islands for thousands of years, and it was here where the old gods were finally banished from our lands. Here. On this hill. The Danes and the Norse were but serving echoes when they arrived.'

Father took a patient breath. 'The Romans? Was it Paulinus? He was a heathen too, wasn't he? Killed the druids or something.' I nodded. Father had a modest library and I loved the stories of old times. Elder Shannon was ever speaking of the old myths and gods.

Ferdan snickered and gestured around himself, making a circle. 'God works miracles, Charles my boy. Sometimes men like Quintus Veranius and Suetonius Paulinus, and their hard, heathen legions hold the sword smiting down the bastards. It is proper the snake eats itself. Over there died the last of the great druids of yon past. The knowledge died with them, the door was closed and the lies were gone and so we only have the Lord Jesus Christ, and his father, our one God.' He stopped and still pointed at a particular spot on the rocky ground.

'The door?' Charles laughed drily. 'How mysterious.'

I shrugged as I eyed the patch of ground. There, below, was a flat stone the size of a man's head, apparently natural and uneven. The stone felt out of place on the windy hill, small stones were strewn about it, bearing marks of time and the beatings of heat and rain, but it felt peaceful. Old, sad, and holy and somehow, Ferdan's mockery made me angry as if he was an enemy disrespecting a bravely fallen hero by pissing on the face of the corpse. I was enraged; fell into it so quickly, so very easily that day, having worked up frustration, and my head hurt dreadfully. I wanted to inflict pain, to be spiteful. I turned to Ferdan, snorted in derision, and his eyes narrowed with a warning. 'You speak of our old gods, yes? Perhaps they are as real as any other ... '

Ferdan turned on me in anger, and Father placed a hand on his chest. Charles scowled at him. 'She is seventeen. She is Christian like you and I. She just has opinions and ideas. You will treat her with respect. And keep your hands off the girls.'

Ferdan eyed him, grinding his brown teeth together, but eventually he nodded as father removed his large palm. 'I said the door was closed. That door led to hell. I know there were beings once in our fine world, demons really, who served their selfish needs. Cerunnos, Taranis, Manannan, there are stories glorifying them as gods, but demons they were. These are filthy names reeking of blood, and the druids suffered for their sins, I am sure. Hellfire, at least, was eagerly awaiting them. The pretenders, these gods were but mad spirits. Just like Odin and Thor and such of the Northman, or what the Greeks and Romans worshiped, or the Mayas, the Egyptians. All fools serving evil. You speak of things you know nothing of. We are fortunate to have our true God, the real God, the one creator of all, and not the angry, selfish spirits that run around the cosmos creating havoc. Read the Bible, redhead.'

I smiled at him like one would to an utter fool. 'Bible? Yes. I've read it. I'm a Christian, like Father said. I go to church. But I'm sure all the ancient religions had as much right to claim ...'

'God created man, girl!' Ferdan spat.

'Which god?' I said and grinned at my heresy. 'Look, I'm just saying ...'

'Ours!' he glowered. 'How dare you! Your soul, girl. Think of your soul!'

'Yours? Were you there? Look, there was a book that said that the spread of Christianity has cost hundreds of millions of lives. Pagans, yes, but lives still. Sometimes, that is just impossible for me to understand. They were innocent lives. Most were. Or are you saying they went to hell and deserved it?'

'Perhaps they did?' Ferdan growled.

Dana stepped in. 'Shann, come on. He is right ... '

'Dana shut the hell up,' I hissed, and she did, squinting at me in surprise. I was surprised as well. Mother put a hand on her mouth, and I sneered. 'Come on. Why do we have to listen to this disparaging old fool...'

Father raised a finger. The wind blew suddenly, bringing moist alr from the coa as we stood there silently, breathing hard. Then, after a while, Ferdan spoke, tired, not angry, his eyes looking at me warily. 'No matter the faults of the Bible, everyone should cherish the message, the good and the generous tales and the lord of hope hidden in the texts. Hundreds of millions died for Jesus? Perhaps. But that is the fault of the men, not of our God. And be there a God or no God out there, I'd rather have a fanciful, tale of good than the evil pretending god bastards trying to flay my soul, drain me of hope and purpose. Your grandmother healed me when I was thirty. Lung issues, nearly died, so I did. I helped her later. We have a bond of trust. I know she speaks about the old things. Aye? I know it. I see her in you. Yet you must be careful. You mock God and, of course, you don't think he is real. Yet I think you believe in the others.'

'I believe in God, yes. But I believe there is more. And you call this miracle a "he." A man?' I sneered. 'I believe, but I do not know what is the truth. Nobody does.'

He shook his ragged head. 'It. Her. Do as you will. I will believe. But do not mention the demons aloud, do not call for them, nor equal our God with him. The Romans came here to kill the heathen druids. They mostly did. And here, the greatest of them died by the swords of the legions. Aye. As willed by God all mighty. With them, the false gods all but disappeared from this world we live in. Few can call them now, even if they might still reach out for us. Some smatterings of evil remain, but not much. The age of Christ truly began that day, here, in Britain, no matter if he ever even existed. His message is a better one than anything before or after it. Beware of the alluring voices these demons sing with, especially the female ones. You, Shannon? Beware your temper, and your interest in such matters, for if I deemed them dead, I meant dead to our happy world. No matter the evil we do, they were worse. You are too interested in these things, I think. You should talk with a priest.'

Ferdan turned to go, his eyes feverish as he regarded me. He took the winding path down, and I swallowed the words I had been thinking about. Mother shuddered and pulled me around. 'What the hell is wrong with you? Why irritate him more than you already did? He has known you for a decade.'

I shook myself free. 'I have disliked him for a decade. I don't care ...'

Father shook his head at Mother. 'Mother is right, but I don't want Ferdan touching you. He is a greasy old sod. All sailors are strange. Dana, you too, stay away from him. Now, let's enjoy this view and try to behave.' His eyes glanced my way, but I was unhappy as I gazed at the spectacular view. They enjoyed it, but I still felt unreasonably upset and stared at the place the old fool had claimed the druids died at with their old gods. Odin. Our relative had prayed to him, perhaps. He had been a free man, strong, striding to claim his place in the world by the strength of his ax and his bravery. I shuddered. That was what I needed. An ax and courage to shape me some freedom, to make a place for myself. With Dana? I caught her eye, and she smiled. Yes, perhaps with Dana. Odin. God, all-father, they had called him. The god who demands little but bravery and an attempt at a life well lived.

Such thoughts were intriguing. Ferdan was right. I believe in God. I did. I hated and loved him, but sometimes I yearned to believe in something that was wild and full of life, not constricting and wrapped in the fear of death. When Grandmother spoke of them, the old ones, I felt close to them. I felt there was something else to this world of ours, something we had forgotten, as if we were husks devoid of soul, just grinding on, forgotten, lost souls. I went to the spot where the druids had supposedly died, kneeled and overturned a small rock by the large one. Here, they had perished, Ferdan said. The old priests, the ones who knew what we had forgotten.

I felt a need to put my hands out like the druids had likely done, palms up, and eyes closed. Had they truly worked miracles here?

I loved history and mythology, and so I dug the names of the gods out of the recesses of my memory. 'God, Odin, Thor, Tiw, Freya, Freyr, Frigg, Sif and the others, hear me. I, Shannon believe in all of you,' I whispered. 'If even one of you is real, save me,' I added and got up unsteadily. I felt a strange tug in my breast, a fluttering feeling of panic, perhaps, but then I thought I had imagined it. Dana was watching me, her face pinched in a curious look, and I knew she had heard.

CHAPTER 3

We marched down the hillside, sweaty and itchy, tired to the bone, and got to the valley only after the sun had set. We hilted the severely eroded rubble road for the brick house, and Mother was making plans for a trip to the moors, up in the north where her uncle lived. I loved the thought of such sights. Moors. They were rolling and foggy, seemingly endless as time, shattered by crags and decorated by clear lakes. Dana was humming close to me, and I knew she would smile like the sun if I looked at her. I did not. Instead, I put my hand on hers as we walked in the cooling night. She squeezed it and I answered, happy for a moment. Some drowsy birds were chirping in the dark, mournfully calling out for spouses they likely did not have, or perhaps, just tired of having one. Coming to elder Shannon's own road, we passed the finely crafted wooden arches around the ancient rock walls, entwined with vines that emanated the fragrance of jasmine, even in the dark. Then we smelled lamb cawl and knew the dinner was ready, despite Grandmother having had to herd Rose around.

Beautiful intro: drowsy birds chirping in the dark – love it!

We came to the door, an oil lamp swinging in the slight breeze, and Dana was strangely allured by it, leaving it swinging even more crazily, and I stopped it as I passed. The door was slightly ajar, and we could hear Elder Shannon singing with a rasping voice as she was setting the plates and Rose was explaining her drawing to her. Probably she had drawn on a wall with ashes, leaving a horrid mess behind. I smirked. Grandmother had a way with her and much more patience than the rest of the family. We went in through a doorway that was crumbling at the edges, the plaster gone from the walls. The pine floorboards creaked as we came in, Dana rushing ahead. 'Hi, Grandmother! Rose!' A shriek as our sibling rushed out, and I heard potatoes scattering on the floor. She grinned at Dana, squeezing her ferociously, her long, blonde hair bouncing madly up and down.

'I ate already!' she said, turned to us and rushed to me. I grabbed her and let her kiss my cheek, and then she went to Mother, who snatched her up. 'And washed my teeth.'

'You washed your teeth? Not Grandmother?' she asked with some amusement. 'How ...'

'Yes!' she piped in.

'I'll take you up and to bed and wash them one more time, just in case,' Mother said with a grin.

'No! Not ...'

Grandmother popped her fat face into the foyer. 'Hi, lovely Dana! Did you enjoy the sights? Rose, go with Mom. Brush the teeth. The powder is in the desk.' Rose nodded and did go with Mother, singing happily. Grandmother was a miracle. What we could only accomplish by cajoling and begging, often accentuated by a raised voice, she managed with a smile.

Dana walked to the elder Shannon, grabbing her hand and she was soon constantly chatting about the excellent sights of the afternoon. She called Ferdan an exceptional guide. My brief happiness was gone, and I cursed her under my breath, for my headache was throbbing angrily. Father grabbed my shoulder and pulled me around. 'Let it be, love. She is not trying to annoy you, she's just happy.'

'Must have gotten all the damned happy genes in the family,' I told him savagely.

'Still, let her be happy,' Father said abrasively. 'You have been terrible for months and months. Today? The worst day ever. You have the problem, not she.'

'I do,' I agreed and nodded them away, stumbling with my jacket. 'But that Ferdan ...'

'Shannon!' Grandmother yelled, wisely interrupting my explosive answer. 'Come and help us out, dear girl.' I calmed immediately, and I felt like Rose must feel when she did her magic.

'Sure thing,' I managed without a smile and went to the kitchen that was simple plaster walls adorned with beautiful if faded azure and red flower paintings. Grandmother smiled at me knowingly, as

Dana was chatting amicably. She was still praising old Ferdan's guidance as if to annoy me and then we carried out a bowl of herb-sprinkled, delicious stew.

Soon, with Rose sleeping soundly, we ate and Grandmother was listening, occasionally asking questions while smiling. Her face was fat and bloated; most of her body was entirely covered. She was armed with keen, coal-like eyes that seemed to take in everything. I stared at her and she stared at me, and it seemed she was struggling with something, which was unusual since she seemed the most carefree person in the whole world.

'How long are you staying, love?' she asked Mother when Dana was finally quiet. 'There will be an exciting market held by the Red Lamb, down in the village next week. Food and ale. Soldiers will be drunk, but there will probably be some good deals to be made. Your grain and my contacts? Cannot lose.'

Mother was nodding, making calculations in her intelligent, organized head. 'We sell everything we have to the army as it is, but it might be useful to check the fair out. If the war ends, who knows if they will buy?'

'Napoleon is doomed,' Father chipped in. 'We should prepare.'

'Ferdan will set up a table, and I'll make some kidney pies and tarts ...' Grandmother was saying, and that's when my head throbbed, my hands twitched with pain. Grandmother's eyes turned my way, and I swore there was a flash of pity in them.

They all turned to stare at me. I fixed my eye on Grandmother. 'Why are you friends with Ferdan? He's a gross bully. Filthy as a pig. I bet he talks about fish guts, the quality of his farts and the quantity of the ale he guzzles down daily in the Codir's Tavern.'

'Shann!' Mother said. 'That's enough. Grandmother's known him for ages. Behave yourself.'

Grandmother was nodding sagely, while placing a calming hand on Mother's arm and raising another finger to silence Father. 'He is a bit coarse, love,' she confided in me with a kind whisper. 'A tad fanatic in his old, set ways. He was in the war. Fought in Trafalgar, he did. But he has respect for me, and I for him. You should pay attention to his stories, not his opinions.'

'I liked him fine,' Dana said. 'He is nice enough if you don't ...'

'You batted an eye at him,' I spat. 'The bastard probably thinks you wish to bed him. He likes to squeeze you, run his filthy fingers over your shoulders, and you purr like a slut.'

'Shannon!' Father yelled, getting up. 'What the hell is the matter with you? Can't you behave? Apologize! Such words ...'

'Ferdan is soo great!' I mimicked Dana and threw a napkin on her plate.

Mother shouted: 'Get up and go!'

I did get up, not looking at their eyes. I felt near unquenchable rage swelling inside. I tried, hoped to stem the tide and to apologize, but I could not. 'I'm just so sick and damned tired of this crap. I wish someone died so we could stop the polite shit talking and endure sorrow in silence for a change!'

'If you do not like our happiness, go to bed,' Mother told me thinly, barely keeping her tone under control. 'Will do well for you. And us.'

'You know, Mother. I never liked you,' I said and saw that hurt like a cut by a knife.

'Shannon,' Father said softly, perhaps afraid I would say a similar, terrible thing of him. 'Please ...'

I shuddered, rubbed my face and took a staggering step away. 'I'll sleep alone, so take Dana with you, and perhaps Ferdan,' I said, while Dana was quiet, her eyes appraising me carefully, in total control of her pretty self. My eyes scoured Mother, who did not look at me, but at Grandmother, and I think she nodded at her. That was strange, and I felt robbed as they ignored me. I stormed up the stairs and ran to the sparsely furnished guest room. I pushed open the creaky window, the moonlight filling the room with its pale light, and curled up on the bed without undressing. I felt sick, and I cried, and I did not understand what was wrong with me. I heard them laughing downstairs, content and happy, and that made me feel even more terrible. A part of me wanted to go and apologize to Mother and Dana, to all of them really, but I could not for it was only a minuscule part of me.

I fell into sleep, sort of, full of nightmares.

At some point in the night, an owl hooted outside the window. I woke up with a breathless startle; my head throbbing painfully. I gazed at the squat bird that took off from a dark bough, hooting again as it went away in search of a rodent. I massaged my head and wondered if I had a stroke. I could not lie still, or breathe properly. I sat up in a panic, feeling nauseous and climbed out of the bed, stumbling in the dark for the door. I opened the heavy thing, yearning for cool water. I made my way to the end of the hallway, cursing softly in pain and fear. I stumbled downstairs, struggled to the kitchen. There was no hot water to be had, but I wanted none. I found a bowl of water, lathered my face with the blissful, chilly drizzle, enjoying every second of the beautiful relief.

It was only a momentary relief, for the insidious stabbing pain conquered the fresh pleasure of the water and came back with a renewed force. It all reminded me of the shitty evening two years before, the night I had tried to kill myself. Judging by the furious pain, this bout was going to be terrible.

I leaned down, whimpering, vomiting briefly. I moaned and put my face against a wall, where there was a tall mirror and I stood there, eyeing myself. I thought I looked like a lost ghost, a dreadful stranger. My mouth distorted into a gaping maw, my eyes were sinking into my skull, and the sound that came out of my terrified mouth was not of this world, but rather like a whisper from a deep well. That was the face I had seen in the window that day I had tried to kill myself. I remembered it then. I stared at the mirror in the near dark while trying to close my mouth, but instead it opened wider, and I sobbed in terror. I could neither stop the sound coming from the impossibly open maw nor look away.

Then, a grave-cold hand grabbed me and dragged me away from the mirror, and guided me out the door. In the haze of pain, I stared at the figure. Its great bulk was moving cumbersomely, yet with energetic purpose. I let her guide me for it was Elder Shannon, her eyes betraying deep worry. She gazed at my face, she was wondering at my pain, and I swear there was a bout of panic in that look. She was pale, very pale, and her fear made me even more terrified. We stumbled through the paths in the woods, moist grass wetting my dress to the knees and then suddenly we stopped. She spoke to me kindly as we sat on a mossy rock with a light stream running near.

Birds, especially some nightjars with their churring calls were still active in the woods. The crashing ocean waves could be heard across the hills and woods as Grandmother soothed my ears with a willow voice of comfort. She spoke to me in the language of the old people. 'Bydd yn iawn, cariad,' she said easily, stroking my hair, pulling me onto her lap. There was no warmth in me, or in her. Her fingers were ice cold in the night as my wondering mind tried to grasp the meaning of her words until I got it. It will be all right, indeed.

The moon was high when I felt a bit better, improving little by little, gazing up at her eyes as she smiled. The odd voice was gone, and I touched my face tentatively. It seemed normal.

'What the hell is wrong with me?' I asked softly, not expecting an answer.

Yet, she had one. 'Stop cussing, girl. It's your own fault. You called them by your name and they heard. Did you not? And I didn't even have to tell you how. You knew already.'

'What?'

'When you were up there, you told them you are ready,' she said and took my face between her hands. 'You are called back, love.' She smiled sadly at me. 'It is the day. That particular day. The hour of the Dark Levy. I have never answered their call and only once made the summons.'

'Called where?' I asked, miserable and confused. 'Summons?'

She shook her head as if the answer was impossible to provide. 'You are one of the many, my child, and there are many hallowed places like ours all around our world. You are not alone,' she told me while raising me to a seated position, and I felt sorry, for I was two heads taller than she was, and I had been likely crushing her. Her face was pallid and strange.

I snorted softly; afraid my head would again flare with pain. 'Yes, there are plenty of people who are mad. Like old Edna in our village. Drools and giggles. Nothing unusual about that, is there?

I'm mad, Grandmother. They all think so. I'll just fall deeper into madness. It's so scary. They'll put me in some horrible asylum and fill me with sedatives. I bet it won't be long when I cannot speak or piss like normal people. I'll sit in my piss and never notice. I'll be giggling in some unwashed room with a dozen other crazy bastards and nobody will care.'

'You are not mad, girl,' she said with a sad smile. 'No, it is not that. I know that now.'

'I'm ill, then. My head hurts, and I saw something in the mirror.' I was sobbing, for I was terrified. 'Was not the first time, either.'

She nodded at me. 'Sure, there are people who are truly mad, or indeed have a deadly disease, but this is in many ways more dangerous. There are people locked up in forgotten prisons and hopeless asylums for having what you have. And it will get worse.'

'I know it gets worse,' I told her miserably. 'It's worse than it was two years past.'

'I know, love. I told you. I've seen it. I've had it. I have it.'

I stared at her carefully, but she was serious. 'Had what? Have what? Exactly?'

She took a deep breath and shook her old head forlornly. 'I was always agitated when I was young, much like you, forever tired with the mundane, ordinary, boringly tedious life, with all my life, in fact. I was petulant and unreasonably angry when my head hurt, especially at this date every two years, but it was more terrible after

I was a teen, especially then. I did not know what to do with my life, what to reach for and why. I was always so very unhappy. I never found peace from the depths of depression, my child.'

'You?' I wondered.

She nodded 'Life seemed ... wrong. Sometimes too hard. Especially on this very day. It is a special day for us, even if you have not called them by your name. It is hard, but I've managed to survive so far. Once I also called them by my name. I was told to, by my father, Patrick.'

'You are always smiling, and you enjoy your life,' I told her bluntly, and she laughed merrily.

'No, I was and am faking. Life grew a bit easier as I got older as if they no longer thought I was of use. But this very day used to be hard, always so, even without the call. Often, I drank myself senseless for this evening. There is a reason for all of this pain and confusion, but I am not sure if you wish to hear it. But yes, you must hear it.'

'Not sure? Yep, I'm ready to hear. I'm so tired of living like this. I do not wish to ...'

'Kill yourself?' she asked sadly.

'Yeah,' I told her, my voice withering. 'Have you ever thought ...'

She nodded carefully, smoothing her dress. 'Ferdan saved me, girl. I hung myself, and he came in just in time and helped me, for he is a good man, indeed, despite his obvious faults. He could have just let the pagan hang, no? I had a child, our Bridget, later on. I endured and gave life and care and enjoyed what I could.'

'You survived for Mother?'

'Yes. No,' she said. 'Both. I had a position to fill. A priestess, if you like.'

'Look ...'

She put a finger over my mouth, and I went quiet. 'My father expected me to keep up the tradition, but I had half decided not to. There are many families like ours around the world, but we are growing fewer. It's just too hard a burden to carry to survive until old age. And it might not be a bad thing for the families of the Dark Levy to die off. It is dangerous, I think, to heed the call. I vowed not to involve you in it. I have been watching you for years. I worried about you, hoped you could pull through this without me. I had sworn to myself I would not do anything to push you to the promised escape of the old ways. But I changed my mind this evening.' She looked mildly uncomfortable, and I stared at her. 'I spoke to someone, not an hour ago and hoped to help her cross over like my father helped others of our family cross. I thought she would indeed benefit from the call. She is harsher and hardier than you. You lack something she does not.'

'What don't I have?'

'Ruthlessness,' she said with a small voice. 'She is ruthless, and I think might do well when she goes. Oh, I was right. She is ruthless, more than I thought. But she is a bit mad as well and that actually surprised me.'

We sat there for a moment or two, and I saw she was struggling with herself, biting her lip and wringing her hands. 'You hung yourself?' I asked for I did not believe her.

'Here,' she said softly as she opened up her high-necked tunic. An angry rod and white ooar glarod in tho moonlight, marring hor throat crudely. 'It is hard, Shannon, to be enveloped in constant, strange pain, always angry, always confused. I do not wish for you to suffer such a fate, at least any longer than you have to. I think you won't be able to live with this thing like I have.'

'Why do we have this ... thing? What is ...' I began, staring at the terrible scar around her neck, but she shook her head.

'What is it?' she mused. 'It's the most natural thing in the world if you are lost. It is a yearning that cannot be fulfilled. Have you ever seen a captured bear in a cage? Have you? Of course you have. There was one in the fair the other year. Was it happy?'

'Happy? No, it wasn't. It looked sort of confused, nervous, agitated ...'

'Sometimes aggressive, other times sluggish, most of the time just entirely uncaring of his life as he walks around that little world restricted by bars. Such creatures live, barely, breathing in and out, their life holding little meaning. They run in circles until their paws and joints give up,' she said and added: 'they are like us.'

'You and I?' I asked her, fascinated.

'The few unlucky fools like us, yes. Don't you feel like something ...'

'Is missing,' I added quickly, wondering at her face that was white, so very white and strange. She was frightened. We stared at each other for a long while. 'But what is missing?' I asked afraid of her answer.

'Our soul,' she answered. 'Or part of it. Our purpose is gone, Shannon. We yearn for something that was once. It is a power. A primal force and it is no longer with us. Like a captured wild animal yearns for freedom, we yearn for our true connection to the power we should have. It is almost a divine power. I do not know if it is Ferdan's God, or something else, but some of us felt it, once. We used it. And we still remember it. It was part of us. Part of some of us, at least. Most humans didn't see this power, but some few did.'

I stared at her for a moment, looking at her strangely vacant eyes. 'Grandmother, I ...' I began but went quiet and sat still, unsure of what to say.

She sighed and gave me a sideward glance, careful not to startle me as she ruffled my hair. 'I know nothing, love, nothing is certain. But there are stories in this family, so there are.'

'There are a lot of stories in the family, Grandmother,' I grumbled.

She laughed with a clear voice. 'Yes, but it is an old family.

Stories tend to accumulate, love. There are many families like ours, all across the world, as I told you. Many of them know the old stories though few speak of them in public, only in private to those who are affected. They speak of the power we lost. And while there might very well be the God, the stories also speak of lesser deities. Gods in their own right, perhaps.'

'Does that old, rancid sperm whale know the stories?' I asked sourly and thought Ferdan had sneaked up on us for a night bird was startled to frenzied flight near us. We stared as it flew and Grandmother patted my hand.

'He believes in God, love, in sweet Christ and thinks the salvation is something one can grasp at by being kind and charitable, even to old heathens like me. At least he hopes it is so, so very hard he does. I hope he is right. Surely there is a God to look after our souls? He also believes there are evil creatures men once worshipped. He knows I have seen them.'

'So tell me,' I said. 'What do you mean, you have seen them?'

She smiled. 'Grandfather told us about the gods when the others went to hear Father Andrew preach of love and Christ and how women are the Devil's own sweethearts. That priest was drunk, love, always during the sermon and once drank down all the wine meant for the holy communion, and later fell over old Gracie as she was confessing her many sinful thoughts.'

'Isn't that done in the confessional?' I asked with a small giggle.

'Yes, he fell through the screen and over her and shat himself. Gracie thought he was the Devil taken and she died a month later of the fright. Father Andrew put her to the grave,' Grandma said with a bemused smile, and I held my hand across my mouth, trying to stop laughing. After a while, I managed to calm myself.

'And? What did Grandfather tell you?'

She smiled and adjusted her scarf. 'He, my grandfather sat us down around the fire pit in his old, moldy house, hoping to avoid Grandmother Mary's keen ears, for she was a terrible gossip. He told us something came out of something, and there is no way for us to understand it.'

'That's it? Something came out of something?' I asked and quaffed, despite the lingering ache in my lobes. 'Grandma ...'

She waved her hand at me. 'Shannon, it is certainly not human, no. Something came to fill the void. Is it God? Perhaps not. Perhaps God came before it, though I think the lesser gods were born of it, this power. It has life, but no face. It was and is the power that gave birth to everything. It created the materials and ingredients of life, the building blocks, indeed. The rest, all the architecture and the various products are made by something else, lesser, more simple gods, perhaps, but not like the God we hope will give us a raise or a better husband, and eventually, a blissful spot at his heavenly table. That God, Ferdan's God, ours salvation is a greater mystery. This power, Shannon, is like a huge unseen sun, source of energy and life and we once saw it. In our head. That we no longer do, is driving us mad.'

'That sounds so vague,' I said.

She waved her hands. 'It is vague. I shall not dwell on God, Shannon. I will just speak of this this power. It was the beginning and not only of this world. I know there are worlds out there as well and I know there were creatures we called gods living in them, shaping them. We worshipped them, indeed we did. Patrick's stories say they are much less wise than the benevolent saviors we read about in our hopes of salvation. Some stories say these lesser beings made all the men as well. In their image? Perhaps. But that is disconcerting, love, for we are terribly flawed.'

'Grandmother, there is no way for you to know this,' I told her sternly. 'Or for the Great Grandfather Patrick, for that matter.'

She squeezed my arm. 'I have seen this power. Felt it, rather. That one-time grandfather helped us call the creatures of these worlds in our name, and we had to decide if we wished to go or to stay.'

'Seen and felt the power,' I said softly as I glared at her. 'Gods? You are serious?'

'I am serious enough, Shannon,' she whispered. 'The power? It is glorious. It is real.'

'You are not some kind of a conspirator, Grandma?' I asked. 'You want to go back home?' She was speaking, but no voice came out, and I wondered for I felt I saw through her for a moment. Then soon, she was whole again. I was mad, that was it.

'Of course, I am! Even the paranoid have enemies. But this is the truth, not a lie.'

'Grandma,' I held her hand. 'There are no ... creatures of other worlds. Soon you will claim there are giants. Science ...'

She grunted and swished her hand in agitation. 'Read your father's books, love, but do not think all the answers can be found there. Even the Bible says there were giants once, sons of Anak, over thirty tribes of them. And more ...'

'Grandmother, I am not sure how this helps with my headache. It makes it worse, in fact,' I winced. 'You are just talking nonsense and all of it means as much as Ferdan's words. This story of yours is like a hangover. I've never had one, of course, but I've seen Father after he comes home from the pub. You are supposed to help me, but you are frustrating me.'

She nodded. 'I said I have seen and felt some of these things, Shannon.'

'What kind of things?' I asked suspiciously. 'You said you had to decide if you wanted to stay or leave? You stayed, apparently.'

She leaned forward in sorrow. 'I would not, could not do it. And now you might have to decide as well. Had I not had Bridget, you would not have to risk so much. I cannot bear to have put you in such danger.'

'Do what?' I asked her with growing impatience, and she hesitated.

She took a ragged breath. 'There was a moment in my life everything seemed clear for one fleeting moment. I did not feel anxious, not lost in the least. It was this very date, and I was young. And I saw this wonderful power. I felt it. There were once gates to our world. They are still there, though what Ferdan hoped for, but they do not function without a call and something else. There are people who still know the old rites. I never told Ferdan this, but not all the druids died up there, oh no. He suspects we are kin to them, but he is not sure.'

'Gates? From where?' I asked, perplexed. 'I don't understand. What are you saying?'

She slapped her thighs. 'Where they lead, I know not.'

'Grandmother,' I breathed.

She patted my hand. 'Something happened somewhere, Shannon, and we were abandoned here. We lost the connection to this power. Ferdan thinks the death of the heathen priests banished the creatures that ruled here once, but I think there was a war or some calamity, out there somewhere, and something terrible happened. We worshipped the lesser gods still, and some of us, the very few, those whom these flawed gods had granted special gifts went near mad by being denied the source of life, the power. It is what I felt and saw, that day when my brother left. For a briefest of moments I did. It is the power of light and storm, primal and eternal. It is what all life and matter are made of. I think it can be ... harnessed.'

'Like magic? You could cast spells?' I asked with a small smile, yet utterly mystified by her story.

She smiled with a yearning. 'I remember it well. The power is unfathomable, and I think that magic, miracles can be performed by touching and pulling at it. It is the opposite of the void. I felt the fury of power unexplainable. Fiery flames of eternal fires I felt, the nature's original forges.' She smiled and her brow was glistening with cold sweat. 'It was brilliantly bright and utterly dark, and yet so natural. It makes me cry to think about it, the glory of it. It was there; I finally heard it and could nearly ... play it. Touch it. Pull some of the flame and heat to me, but it was so hard, so very hard to understand what to do with it. It was like an ever-shifting, mad harp with millions of strings to play with. Yet, it is said some of us simple humans once tapped into it, creating wonders and miracles. That was before something happened and before the gates were closed, but this one ritual we still know, and it lets us travel and when the gate is open, you can see the power.'

'Let's go inside,' I told her earnestly, and she shook her head.

'No. Our family were of these high humans. Of the men and women the Romans killed up there. Of those who could still perform a summoning ritual. Especially this very night, they could send a call and then heed one from the other side, no matter the sundering. And it is still possible. For there is still something out there looking for us. And the reason why we are so agitated and lost, Shannon, is that we can still sense that power. Our minds know there is this magnificent force, but are unable to touch it. It drives us crazy.'

'Summoning?' I asked, mystified.

'It is quite simple, Shannon. Grandfather gave us a choice. We could go, but some might stay. One would have to stay at least, to learn the truth from him, to continue the line and to care for the family that suffered.'

'You stayed?'

'I stayed,' she agreed. 'Though it was cowardice, not nobility. The summoning requires something unusual, but I never had it in me to perform it, nor take part in it. Not fully. Happily, I never had to think about performing the summoning before. Bridget, your mother, is somehow spared this condition. But you are not. I knew this two years ago, for I called for them to you, and you were called back.'

'You caused that terrible thing to me? Two years ago? No! Of course you didn't!' I yelled at her, furious. 'I tried to ...'

'Bridget knows and kept an eye on you. She nearly failed and we almost lost you. But yes. I am to blame. I went up there and called the gods in your name. I told them you believe in them and so they answered. I had to know for sure you had this same thing, for there are other strange things going on with you. But now I know about them as well.' She smiled benignly. 'You are too weak to live here with this condition. You have to go.'

Mother knew? I shrugged and hugged myself. 'What could you not do? Something your brother did? I don't understand.'

She waved her fat hand. 'It is simple. There is more than the call. There is the key we have to ... turn. Patrick called it "the Unthinkable Act." And it is, to an ordinary human. It's about blood,' she told me softly.

'Blood?' I asked with a voice that should have left her no doubts about the fact I thought she was mad as hell.

'Blood. Blood is the key. Blood connects the people, the races, the gods and the worlds together over distances and time.'

'You don't mean to say we are some kind of bloodsuckers? Grandmother!'

She looked confused. 'We are, in a way. The old stories are but echoes. All of them get their fiber from the legends. Echoes are curious things, Shannon, for an echo to be heard, someone must have shouted a long time ago. This is not a story of bloodsuckers, but our family's story. I once saw this entire thing take place. I really did. I told you. It is no unproven theory, but a solid fact. I was there when it was opened.'

'A gate?' I half-smiled at her, my head throbbing. 'It's a

wonderful story. But an unlikely one.'

'Yes, a gate. My brother went through it. Patrick thought I would go as well for he was still young and thought he might make more children to take his burden and priesthood. But I could not. I stayed. He died a year later.'

'You had a brother? Michael?'

'Yes, Michael. He was a sweet boy, but he had it bad in here. He had so many problems it was hard to fathom, Shannon. Much more severe than yours. When things got bad, he nearly killed people, especially when he grew older. So, Grandpa did the deed, and Michael followed his instructions and ... left.'

'Where is he now?' I asked, feeling uneasy. She seemed strange and perhaps dangerous and somehow she was not totally present.

'He is gone, Shannon,' she said, wiping a tear. 'I was afraid, Shannon. What lies on the other side? I know not. But I saw and felt the wonder while he left, as I described. No matter what awaits there, dying slowly here might not ... might not ... ' She hesitated and sobbed.

'What?' I said, grasping her hand. 'Grandmother. I do not believe you.'

She pulled me to her. 'What did you see in the mirror?'

'Nothing,' I whispered.

'You saw a monster. A creature of alien lands, terrible and

familiar at the same time, but certainly it Is not from here, Shannon. It had small, beady eyes, a mouth to devour a baby wholc. It is the thing that always answered the summoning, every second year. And you belong to her Dark Levy. It's an old name; none know who named us thus. The night Michael went, I saw this thing in the very same mirror you did, for we had called them. They sense you, out there. They call back for you. We must beg for them to come. And I think you should be gone, Shannon. You will die of misery and pain if you are not released. Even if you are not as ruthless as she is.'

'What do you mean?'

'That you could possibly leave this place, Shannon. Something is grasping at you like it was for me. It is inhuman. Is it evil? I know not,' she whispered. 'But you have a choice. And you have a duty.'

'How would I leave? If I believed you, that is. Blood?'

She took a deep breath. 'You will see. One is enough, so Patrick said. There is no need for more than one. And she is certainly capable of doing the deed. I could not, not ever.'

'More than one what?'

She smiled wistfully. 'You two are old enough. I told her about this as well and did she ever surprise me. She will be as Michael was and your Great Grandfather. As ruthless. She will show you how. You will be surprised. Don't be afraid. Don't worry about your parents. Bridget knows about this, of course. She was spared the curse.'

'Follow her?' I asked her mystified. 'Lonely?'

'Dana,' she whispered, her face wrinkled with worry, then sorrow. 'I will miss you.'

'Dana?' I sputtered and nearly screamed. 'What does she have to do with this?'

'You love her,' she stated.

'Yes, of course I do. But ...'

'But eventually, you have to find your own way. You might, yet. But she will be there and you have to remember, Shannon, that she cannot protect you forever. She has her own fears, and she is reckless as she tries to find happiness. She will change, I think. She will think you weak. Find your own way. Love her, but not without a care for your own soul. She found her real self this night, perhaps you shall as well and both will be different and at peace, in the end.'

'She doesn't have this!'

She shook her head with misery. 'She is like you. She suffers as much as you do, keeping in control, every day and night, outwardly elegant and happy but not so inside. She too cries in the dark, just like you do Shannon, for she hears the willow voice of the power calling for her. She is very, very persistent and strong, disciplined and logical, I think more than most, but I think you will find your strength at some point, as well. She went up the hill this night, for she did what you did and saw what you saw in the mirror, and I spoke with her. And she is more, much more practical than you are. Yet, no matter what she does, always remember there is a spark of light in her as well. She did not wish you to know these secrets. She tried to stop me from telling you. But she could not. Now you have to go.' Her eyes were haunted.

'She left without me? It cannot be, she is ...'

'Not happy, she is miserable,' she told me brusquely. 'She warned you that she will go. She thinks you won't have the strength to follow, and she is going without you for she cannot bear to stay. I think you can do it. Do it rather than die here. Your duty is to make sure you find a life for yourself. Your mother will understand. She is my daughter. Your father won't. They will miss you.'

I shook my shoulders to relieve the ache. 'But should not one of us stay, like it was with you and Michael? If we both go ... Grandma. This is so mad.'

'There is Rose,' she said softly. 'She has this.'

'No!'

'Yes,' she said. 'For her, go. Don't go for Dana. Go for yourself and poor little Rose. Find happiness, Shannon, no matter how weird it might be. And your duty, love is to keep Rose safe. If it is a happy place, call her one day. If not, make sure she stays here. That is your duty.' She got up and walked away. I sat there and watched her go, and she made no sound as she walked through the bushes. Then I got up and hiked to the road, one that would take me much farther than I ever hoped.

CHAPTER 4

The trip to the hill took much longer than I remembered, and my feet were hurting. My skirt was moist from sitting on the ground, and I shivered with cold and fatigue as I made my way forward, begging I would not run into any people who were returning home from a local pub. I felt nauseous. I was tired and hungry. I shook my head as I thought about Grandmother. She had seen what I had seen? A creature in the mirror? Her words of the strange power and the gods were haunting. They were hammering at me.

And Dana. She was going without me?

More, she claimed Dana was suffering from the same malady I was. For some reason, that made me happier. She had pains, she was depressed, and she was tormented? Like I was? It was never evident in her, not in the least, but she was always better than I was, in most anything. Perhaps also in hiding the pain and confusion? Perhaps, just perhaps she was as unhappy behind all the masks she put up for her friends and family. Grandmother claimed she was faking.

No.

She must be wrong. It was not possible. I shook my head. I would go up the hill to see what she had been talking about. It was a crazy damned idea, I decided and I cursed myself, stopping in my tracks.

I should go back.

Yes, Dana was asleep in the house. Surely she was, I would speak to Mother about Grandma in the morning, for Elder Shannon would need help. She was going crazy, surely. She could move in with us. I glanced up to the hill that was bathed in moonlight. Nothing. I could hear the sea hammering the faraway rocks and shuddered in indecision. I turned to go home. Then, I caught movement. Birds were flying around there on the hill, disturbed by something. My foot took a step forward. Then another. Towards the hill, not the house. It was not all fables, was it not, what she had said, what her family spoke around the fires? My family, I reminded myself.

I had seen a thing in the mirror.

I had.

It scared me to death. However, she had seen it as well. So she claimed. Moreover, I had made a call for the gods as well, had I not? Had Dana? Grandma said she had. And one day, poor Rose would suffer like we did. No, I had to go up to see if Dana was there, indeed. What if she was up there? And what was that about a deed Grandma could not perform, not before and not now, but Dana could? Blood? Blood was the key. I took a painful breath and ran on the slippery road, and soon my thighs were fatigued. If she were up there, I would get her, whip her shapely ass raw if she resisted, and I would get her home, no matter what happened. I doubt she would love me after, but she had no business walking around the silent, dark land alone, no matter if she was the golden girl of the family. Damn her. Anything could happen out there. There were soldiers in the village and most were thieves. And rapists.

I looked at the desolate hillsides and giggled. No. They were all passed out. She might slip in some deer shit, maybe.

I sobered as I arrived at the track leading up the hill. I cursed bitterly and headed up there, happy I had slept with my clothes on. It was chilly, nonetheless without my jacket and scarf. The mud was worse with the moist dew of the night covering it. It was slippery, squishy, and soft under my shoes, and I groaned as some wet, freezing cold muck made its way to my socks. Then, I despaired once or twice, unsure of the direction. The road was a joke at best, but the sounds of crashing waves kept me going. After what seemed like ages, I went through a copse of light woods, past a somewhat familiar mossy boulder, and stopped, for I was there.

Dana was not in her bed. She was there.

And she was not alone. Ferdan was standing by her, indecisive, fidgeting.

Dana had indeed made the call as well, and none of it was fables. She was sobbing on the field of grass; by the ancient stone we had seen that afternoon. She was hugging her shaking knees fiercely. Her dark hair was swathed in shadows, and she was twisted on her side, her frame brutally raked with harsh sobs. She was going up and down, up and down, like something was kicking her. Suddenly, she was reaching forward, trying to grasp something I could not see. Her hands twitched as she pulled herself to a seated position, and I saw her face, and my heart stopped. It was horribly distorted. She was croaking, her jaw apparently dislocated, the mouth was huge and yawning, her eyes beady and small as she was trying to speak, gibberish really, like a wind blowing through a dark tunnel. Her eyes betrayed terror. She was hollering in pain, in stabbing pain. I felt pain growing in my lobes as I stared at her in horror.

Ferdan went kneeling next to her, cursing softly.

'I thought you were smarter than your sister, lass. Much more like your sick grandmother, aye? Trying to avoid these things. I told you all the druids died, but it seems you learned different, eh? You should not have come here, no. I'm happy you sent for me. I came just in time, aye?'

'Help me,' the echoing, hollow voice whispered.

Ferdan kneeled before her, grasping at her. 'You have to bear it.

I will take you home, and you will bear the pain. Do not heed them. No. You cannot reach them unless you do ungodly deeds, anyway.'

'Ungodly ...' she was whispering with a mad, thin voice, her huge mouth stretched wide.

'You are not like that, no, you are not,' he said brusquely. 'Your grandmother is not like that either, and I think she wants you to go home, so she does. I will help you.' He grasped her shoulders and tried to lift her. 'I helped her once or twice with this thing. Calm, calm, lass. I ...'

With that, I found out why Grandmother had thought Dana was ruthless. She had known Dana as she is, not the perfect young woman with a carefree giggle, but she had seen glimpses of her soul, seeing her own troubled brother in her.

They had killed a man on the hill the day Michael disappeared.

And so would Dana.

Blood was the key, she wanted to escape, and behind her happy smile there was a tortured girl screaming for a release. Dana's hand was shaking as she looked up to Ferdan. She hesitated as she massaged her head, the pain in hers similar to what mine had been when I woke up, but she was indeed capable of a murder. Her impossibly open mouth breathed a sigh of despair, her eyes hardened from small points into fiery coals. Her hand flashed forward, a bloody kitchen knife sharp as the light of the sun pushing forward as Ferdan gasped and tried to pull away.

He could not, being old and slow and so the blade was entwined in his belly, sticking out weirdly from his fat mass, and his face betrayed shock. He screamed like a child, and so did Dana, as she fell forward. She was sobbing in fear and rage, but her face was no longer her own, but twisted in a sinister grimace, feral and mad, and whatever creature was calling her, it was not a creature I was willing to meet. I could understand why Grandma had forgone the trip.

I shook with fear as I looked at the perfect sister I had known all my life. She did not seem familiar, no, squatting over the dying man, her face distorted and dangerous. Her skirt was bloody, her shawl ripped.

Ferdan cried as he tried to push away the squirming, slavering Dana, who managed to grasp the blade, and then she wrenched it sideward, opening up a terrible wound with a shaking hand. Ferdan howled and begged for mercy, Dana answered weakly, unintelligibly, shaking over him on her knees, her hands letting go of the blade's handle. I shuddered as I went forward, grabbing a thick stick from the mud, not knowing where I found the strength to do so. 'Dana?' I said softly. Her face turned towards me over her shoulder, and she looked like a naughty child caught pinching a biscuit. The creature disappeared from her face. The evil mouth closed with a clacking sound of teeth banging together and revealed the scared face of a girl I knew.

I trembled in fear; so did she.

'Shannon,' she said with her own voice, frightened, touching her jaw and face as if disbelieving she was back to normal. 'Stay back,' she continued, with a rasping, suffering voice.

'You murdered him,' I stated while staring at her in disbelief, my voice breaking. 'Or is he still alive? He is, isn't he?'

'It is the only way, you see,' Dana blurted, speaking quickly, with a quivering voice. Her eyes were deep, bottomless with fear. Then, she growled and her voice changed. She was trying to sound arrogant. She was belittling the crime. 'I did it. For a purpose. All these years of acting, Shann. You needed me like a puppy needs a hug. I felt sorry for you, for I knew what you suffered. You were weaker and weaker each year, weaker than I was. I could force myself to excel, even with this … thing. I challenged you, Shann, every day. Tried to make you a fighter. I tried to help you. I wanted you to overcome this darkness, to fight with me and to follow my lead. To find strength somewhere.' She gagged, nearly throwing up and fought to regain her composure. 'Instead, you shriveled. You just gave up. Grandmother knew I would be able to do this. She told me how to do this. I did. I killed the dirty son of a bitch. For me. Do you hate me for it? Resent that I did the hard part?' She shuddered as she stared at Ferdan's body. 'I am doomed, no matter what we find out there. But there was no choice. I was losing my fight as well. I hate this place.'

I slumped as I watched her and felt sorry for her. Never once had I suspected she might have needed my help. I took a step forward. 'Let's think about what to do. We could hide him. None would think ...'

'No!' she screamed, and I stopped abruptly. She was breathing harshly, trying to collect herself, and she managed it. 'I said I did the hard part. I'm proud of that, not afraid. I do not need you covering my tracks. It's done. Don't try to fix this. Please do not. I've fixed it, and it is not something we can undo. Ferdan, he was our gift. Mine. I have unwrapped him. The Unthinkable Act, Shannon. I performed it. I won't go back now.'

'You are possessed,' I told her with tears.

She laughed in agreement. 'Possessed? So are you. We are cursed. From birth, Shann. Nothing happened to me. This was always coming, I was always waiting for this night and you? You were always suffering, withering. I didn't want you here.'

'Why?' I asked while taking a step forward. 'Because you think I'd fail?'

'You were always so weak,' she said without hesitation. 'Useless? I love you, but ...'

I swallowed the sudden rage. 'Grandmother said this night and the future will change us. Perhaps I shall be strong as well? Stronger?'

'I ...' she began and sighed. 'I don't want to look after you if it's not so.' I took another step forward. 'Stop,' she growled, and I did, not knowing who she was. She thanked me with a nod. 'Shannon. Do you want to go? Really?'

'I don't know? I doubt it works,' I said weakly. I was terrified, to be honest. I thought of Rose and losing Dana and nodded.

She looked resigned as she shook her head at me. 'If we meet out there, you must be prepared, and it's possible I won't help you out. It's possible I cannot. Not every time you need it. Understood? I feel I shall have power, and I shall go after power. I'll do it ruthlessly. I have already begun,' she said and glanced at Ferdan with a hint of dismay playing on her face. She shook her head again and then, suddenly her face distorted, and she grimaced in stabbing pain. She howled like an enormous wolf, and I took a step back as she scrabbled around Ferdan, crablike. She panted and stopped, her eyes regarding me. 'If you stay, forgive me,' she said with a terrible, hollow voice, stopping, holding her hand out weirdly, stretched and strange. 'If you fail at this task I'm about to perform, try to cope in this shithole. They will tell you are mad, and perhaps you are, but take care, love.'

I shook my head in bitterness. 'I need you.'

'I needed you, sometimes,' she said unhappily. 'I am going to leave. I told you this many times.'

'If you go, I shall go,' I told her desperately. 'I promised Grandma.'

'Her? When? How? That is impossible,' she said, looking bewildered and shaking as the pain conquered her. 'Never mind. To us!' she laughed and ripped out the blade from the wound. 'Yfed y gwaed dy gyd-ddyn,' she yelled with a trembling, excited voice. Then she put her full lips on bloody wound and drank.

I retched and looked at her in disbelief, wondering at the wild face, smeared with blood. She slurped, gagged, and shook her head as she came out of the wound. She was twitching, confused, still swallowing the warm liquid, near suffocating as she was trying to cope with the last of it. She got up, taking uncertain steps. She turned her back on me, raised her hands out to her sides and I swear to all that was still holy and whole, she was wrenched forward. There was no sound, no movement on the top of the hill; she just flew forward, her body lingering in the air, for the slightest moment. Then, the air before her went dark, stars disappeared and for a small, glorious moment, I felt rushing ice rumbling through my being, the distant roar of the inferno, all mixing together at the edges of my consciousness. I was happy; I was free of all the confusion in my life, the depression and felt like a small god myself. It was the power Grandma had described, I thought as I tried to make sense of it all. This was what I had been missing all my life. It was a clear, powerful, pure thrust of power, eternal and mysterious and still a power of utter clarity, and never before had I felt such bliss. I touched something wonderfully strange, laughing as I fell on my knees. It was flowing around me, inside me, sneaking to my very core, the icy sheets of power that were somewhere far, yet so close and I heard the roar and crackle of the distant fires.

Then, in the midst of my bliss, I remembered Dana and saw something had come for her indeed. White as bone, hands with absurdly long fingernails, black and sharp, came to sight. Then the mighty arms shot out, four of them springing from the air, the palms opening up towards the sky. One hand turned towards Dana and held a bright golden metal bracelet, simple and delicate. Dana's mouth opened in a blissful scream and without any hesitation, she thrust her hand forward. The white hand gracefully slipped the bracelet on her wrist, where a bright light flared. She screamed. Her clothes burnt away in an eye blink, blue fire consuming them, and for an instant she was naked.

And then she was gone.

So was the flowing ice, the over-powerful, incredible force, the brief happiness, only leaving the ever-familiar anxiety and misery.

I was alone.

I took deep, panic-filled breaths. Dana was gone. It made no sense. There was silence, uncanny silence as if everything was postponed for a heartbeat, as if something was still waiting out there. Even the wind stood still. I shook my head heavily, feeling at a loss. She was gone, and she had done something terrible. I took careful steps forward, eyeing Ferdan's body, looking around for

81

anyone who might be out there lurking. Nothing.

Dana had killed him.

She thought it her right, Ferdan a gift. She had drunk his blood and then been snatched by a savage force. She had been writhing in pain and then screaming, so very happy, likely all of that at the same time, and so had I, for a moment. Like a god. Yes. That's what I had felt like. A god. No, not like a god. Someone who can speak with the god. Grandma had talked about it, and I believed her now. That was the force that gave birth to everything. Inhuman, yet familiar. I had thought of touching it, pulling at it. I cursed and envied Dana as I went carefully towards Ferdan, who was not moving. I smelled a strange fragrance of crushed roses and jasmine as I went to my knees next to the old man. He was still alive, in terrible agony, paralyzed with it. I hesitated, remembering what Grandmother had said.

One was enough. One death?

'Shannon,' Ferdan groaned. 'Dana … your sister.'

'She is gone,' I whispered, my head aching. 'I don't know where.'

'Imagine I survived Nelson's mad tactics and twenty years at sea only to die to a wee little girl. Your grandmother is not mad, you know,' he grimaced, shivering in his terrible pain, and he laughed with a wince. 'Of course, you know. You saw the bloody thing. She is far, far from mad, Shannon but did she know this would happen?

That Dana needed me for such an act? I'm disappointed in her. In both of them.'

'Perhaps she betrayed you. Grandma. Your creator did not help you,' I told him, unsure why I mocked him, a dying man. I felt immediately ashamed.

He grimaced again, his eyes probing me with worry. 'What took her was evil. It's still lingering here, isn't it? You are not cruel, just confused but you seem ...'

'I am sorry, Ferdan,' I told him and held his hand. 'Truly I am.'

He sighed. 'I told you. You said hundreds of millions have died for our God, for the lessons of love and compassion. It's all worth it, if this is the alternative. It is quite natural for a man to hope for a kind God, Shannon, hope and beg that there might be just one merciful God who actually cares enough to spare the poor sods dying in shit here in this miserable place. I know as I said, of the other creatures that used to inhabit this world. Your grandma told me something, and I know she is of the old blood, even if she tries to hide it. What Dana will discover is not going to make her happy, for they are not all benevolent, not by far. Just look at me, and what they demand of us,' he snickered and then wept in terrible pain. 'We are tools. Just tools. Your grandmother thinks it is a terrible thing to be cut off from those beings, and probably it is for your family, leaving you listless with desire. But I think we should rather enjoy a benevolent religion than be slaves again to things who care nothing for us. Even dying is preferable to that, Shannon.'

'I understand. I am sorry, Ferdan,' I told him, crying, for my head was throbbing, in terrible pain. 'But I felt something. It was wonderful, Ferdan. I don't know what it was. Perhaps it was some strange source of magic. I loved it. And you fear it, I guess.'

His eyes glowed with hope. 'You should fear it and the things out there, as well. Yet, perhaps you are right. It is wonderful you said?'

'Absolutely wonderful,' I told him sadly. 'Just so damned beautiful. Unexplainable.'

He nodded heavily. 'And you felt this …thing?'

'Yes, when the gate was open,' I told him with yearning.

'Do you wish to follow her?' he asked as he saw my face, my yearning. 'Try to look after her? And yourself. You need to change your life.'

'Yes! And no.' I hesitated. 'I will change. I know it. But who is she? She murdered you, stabbed you. She was not Dana,' I sobbed. 'What is she?'

He clapped my hand weakly. 'Don't think about her. Yes, she is different. Now think about Shannon. I said it would be best to die, rather than meet the old beings. What do I know, what indeed? In there, you might find some peace from your inner demons though perhaps you will find real demons, as well. Here, you will suffer and wither. Your grandmother has been coping, but you two do not look like you might make it. There might not be a Ferdan to take you down from the noose in time. Go and see what it is like. Learn to fight. Yfed y gwaed dy gyd-ddyn.'

'What?' I asked.

He shook his head. 'The old way, lass. Drink the blood of your fellow man. This is how they sacrificed, Shannon, in hopes of traveling. Dana knew this, apparently.'

Grandmother. She had told her. She had also known I was not mad enough to kill and bleed a living thing, not even Ferdan, but perhaps she thought I would be able to drink the blood. Something was whispering to me, coaxing me, with strange, silent words, urging me on inside my head. It was not speech, it was something different. I had an urge to obey, to please the creature I had seen. I felt my back arching, my head spinning and saw Ferdan's eyes widen in terror. I knew my face had changed for I could not speak, my jaw was a mass of pain, my eyes were hurting.

'I am so sorry, my girl,' he whispered and turned his face away, taking his blood-soaked hands from his wound. I shrieked, cried like a madwoman. I briefly fought what I was about to do, but all I thought about was peace. No, not all. Peace and Dana. Of Rose. And of great opportunities. And escape. I saw the glistening, bleeding wound by my hands, felt something tug at me. It nearly threw me around, and so I gave up, sunk my face in Ferdan's wound and lapped at the flowing blood like a thirsty dog, feeling his slick skin and fat and muscle in my mouth. I retched, but my mind instantly cleared.

The key had been turned.

I stood up, my arms were flailing madly, and I found myself flying up and staring at a dark, round gateway. It was still, cold, bitter, and yet inviting. The power of ice filled me again, tumbling, forceful and strange, a torrent of clear energy, and the giddy feeling of unusual clarity filled me. I forgot about poor Ferdan, and I took a deep breath, for I knew something was about to happen. Then, the four pale white arms shot out from the emptiness before me. One dark-nailed, thin hand held a bracelet. I shook in fear. It was unfair. Hearing and seeing the strange power, the promise of freedom, one would never refuse anything. Not even a strange bracelet held by a monster. I put my hand forward. The thing clamped the bracelet around my wrist, and it locked quickly. The hands grabbed me, the palms were dry and hot and the arms pulled me in as I felt cold, so cold, and my clothes just burned away to nakedness.

To darkness.

Then light.

I fell and tumbled, feeling dizzy. I saw bright, odd stars, two moons, one red, one white, and I felt water and ice rip through me. I felt a stone roof over me, then it turned to a stone floor, and I fell down. I was far from home.

PART 2: TEN TEARS

'A woman, a human like you? No, I am not a human. Never a human. Not even quite.'

Cosia to Ron

THE DARK LEVY

CHAPTER 5

I t was an uneven floor. I remember running my hand across it, feeling around, rubble moving under my fingers. I tried to get up, managed to get on all fours, and there I stayed, retching and weeping, for I was totally disoriented and confused. I gazed around at the deep shadows and high, uneven ceilings and heard water dripping. Then I remembered the bracelet and saw it was hanging around my left wrist.

I also noticed the bracelet was changing.

It was growing thin, sort of melting like butter; it was altering and turning into puddles of silvery golden metal. It did not drip to the dust but stayed on my skin, and I tried to scrape it off on the rubble beneath me, for I was afraid it would burn. It did not. At first. The puddles twirled on my skin and then things got really weird, for they grew sprouts, thin silvery lines running up my wrist and then my arm, producing elaborate, beautiful, hauntingly intricate lines with an increasing speed. I rolled onto my back, staring at them in horror, sobbing as I vigorously tried to rub them off. Then I attempted to grab the shoots, but there was nothing to grab, as if the silver streams were not real, only a vision.

But they were more than real.

They began to burn.

It felt like they were burrowing into my skin, into my arm, digging deep, burning into the muscle, entwining around the veins, then sliding to the bone below. I howled, I did, I screamed and sobbed and raged in fear, and I was not alone in such pain. Many other voices joined me in the screams, not near, yet all around me. That gave me brief, strange comfort. The pain tore at my arm until it stopped very suddenly, and I could only take deep, shuddering breaths, semi-conscious, still feeling something adjusting all through my arm, from my elbow to my fingertips and all the way to the bone.

Then, the silvery twirls glowed dully and the pain went away.

I sat up, experimenting with my hand. If the thing had not been so scary, it would have been so damned beautiful. Under the skin, over it, somewhere in and out of it the twirls stayed put, silvery blue and sort of metallic. I ran my finger across my forearm and then I noticed the rumble of something that I instinctively knew to be ice and the distant roar of fires, and I forgot the terror of the strange, mutating bracelet.

It was not something just anyone could notice, no, it was the power Grandma had spoken about. I heard it, felt it and somehow even saw it. It was like a new sense, one I had been denied all my life and suddenly, it all became clear. I sat there, butt naked, wondering at a torrent of eternal force as old as time and found I could perceive its finest details if I put my mind to it.

It was not like magic in the books and stories told by the old folks, no.

There were no batwings, no spirits were needed, and neither wands nor Incantations were required.

It was just there.

And some could manipulate it, use it, and connect with it. Others could not. Yet, as I now know all too well, it makes all the difference on how you are trained to use it. You might be coaxed to explore it and to do it on your own, but it can kill you, or those around you. One can spend several lifetimes studying it, and you will but scratch the surface. I had felt it briefly when the portals opened and now, it was around me, calming and sensible. I sensed there was a fierce fire, a roar of ancient inferno, a river of molten, old power, like a distant echo somewhere, but much more powerful was the roar of frigid, pure waters and the rumble of primal ice. It was there, very close, and I raised my hands instinctively to pluck at it, touching it, running my fingers through it, hoping to draw some of it to me. There were millions of ways to exploit it, I decided, more than millions, I added as I attempted to grab and pluck at some of it. It was like drawing at a cotton ball, though I was sensing more than seeing the streams running across the space from it to me.

I felt an overwhelming need to mix one part of the frigid waters of the vaporous, freezing mists and some of the ice mounds tumbling down to the eternity. I felt a need to make a construct of intricate, rare beauty, and I did it, creating a strangely familiar weave of icy power, and then I was pulling at it with all my force.

The frigid force filled me so quickly I stiffened into a frozen icicle and I screamed with surprise and pain.

I was drawing quick, panicked breaths, and I pushed it all out, feeling a refreshing breath fill the room for an instant, but it was refreshing only for a moment as I suddenly felt exhausted and slumped on my knees. I was not hurt, though. Even my arm stopped throbbing. My mind was again exploring the power, but somehow I pushed away the instinct, the forces that were beautiful to feel and see, yet possibly lethal to use. I was shivering uncontrollably and got to my shaky feet. 'God, my God,' I was saying, rubbing my arms and chest, for I had just touched something I knew was more than likely the beginnings of all life. I shivered for a while, cursing the darkness.

But I noticed it was not so dark anymore. My eyes turned to my arm. It was sparkling with silver radiance as if my magic had turned it on, made it alive.

In the glow of my strange sigils, I saw I was standing in a cave and there was a doorway, rough, natural, perhaps. I also remembered I was nude and that I had heard other people screaming. I cursed again, feeling self-conscious, and then I giggled, wondering how the mind can worry about such things when you have just witnessed a murder, lost your sister to a dark maw and then, your mouth full of warm human blood followed her to an alien world of wonders where you touched the god and experienced a magical bone tattooing without any anesthetics. I stared around the room and noticed bits of rusted iron, an upturned mining cart. 'Damned mine?' I wondered as I rolled my hand across the rubble. Then, I saw a statue toppled onto its side.

I scuttled forward to stare at a half-buried face. It was a man, I thought, but perhaps not, for there was ethereal beauty in the face, nobility and perfection you could not deny. It was wearing robes and perhaps a bit of armor, chain across its chest, and a helmet with long horns, sticking out to the sides. 'Cerunnos?' I wondered, remembering the Celtic god few knew anything about, the lord of the horns. Obscure knowledge, I surmised, but something I had loved. Perhaps it would be of use in my new world. I straightened and stared at the face. It was not human, no. Too perfect. Likely had no human concerns either.

A scream. Thin and full of pleading.

'Dana!' I yelled and ran for the doorway, trying to see what was down the tunnel. There was nothing, no sound of a living thing, no movement. Not even an echo. There was only the blip of dripping water, which was streaming down wetly from the gloomy walls, I walked to it and pressed my face to the rock, letting some drip to my mouth. Was I alone? No. I had heard people scream. And just now? Or was it only me? I was reputedly mad, was I not? Even Dana thought I was strange. I hesitated and wiped my mouth, happy for the cold drink that tasted somewhat sulfurous, and took steps forward toward the dark tunnel sloping downwards. It looked dank and dangerous.

Below me, something moved.

A reddish light was bobbing, up and down, crazily. I saw a girl, a head shorter than I was, with clipped, roughly cut hair and a thin face staring around, looking at the dark shadows behind her. She was naked and scared and she nearly fell as she ran off. She disappeared from sight, apparently turning a corner.

It was another person. That was all that mattered.

I made my way down, cursing the rubble-strewn slippery ground. I whimpered as some broken stones rolled under my feet, nearly twisting my ankle. I grasped at a boulder and shrieked as I saw another stony face, old and strange with broken features and hugely thick hair, a full mouth and a scar across the chin. I pushed up and decided I had no time for discoveries and games and ran down. 'Dana! Anyone!' I screamed. The tunnel was slippery and dangerous, water trickling down the stone in maddeningly cold rivulets, but I ran heedlessly. I was shivering, sure my lips were blue, and then I rounded a corner and fell, spilling on the stone, the way slick and smooth, plunging down into the darkness. I shrieked again, sure I was to break a bone, perhaps more. I tried to keep my feet out in front, then for the obvious reasons, being nude, I struggled to slide on my hip, but I went around and around, spitting water and for a moment I thought the water was red, and I had hurt myself. Then, it turned bright again and the mad ride went on for a while. I was sure I would be crushed, but only until the slippery stone gave up the wild decent and I rolled into a hall.

This room was different from the near natural tunnels.

I got up on all fours, and in the eerie light from my strange sigils; I saw a tall rounded cupola, a floor made up of chiseled stones, depicting wondrous things, probably ancient. There were fragile mermaids, flying lizards, what I took to be some sort of dinosaurs and bears of gigantic size, hundreds of different kinds of animals, and animals I had never seen. There were men on lizards and even horses, and then there were beings being worshiped, that much was clear. These creatures were large, yet with limbs like men, happy and boisterous, perhaps good-willed and generous by the kind looks on their faces. The beings were being basked in adoration. Hordes of people were bowing to them, and leading them was a tall man in a horned helmet. The horns were like that of the statue I had seen. I moved on. One brilliant carving showed a man with an unruly beard, white and long, his shoulders swaddled in a faded red coat and in his head there was a twin dragon helmet. He bowed to a beautiful woman of lithe limbs. I crouched as I eyed the mysterious sights and then finally walked around the huge place, shivering. I wondered if I could touch the fires lingering in my mind, for I was freezing, but the ice was tumbling so loudly through my head, I decided not to try. I contemplated on touching the ice again, more carefully this time.

Suddenly, I felt something strange.

I felt as if someone was touching the same strands, pulling at the power of the fire. I saw what was being pulled and combined, clumsily I thought, and I realized this was being done behind me. With a yelp, I turned to stare around at the room, and my eyes fixed on a figure standing immediately behind me.

There stood a boy, my age. He was nude, his arm burning with fiery red sigils. He was blond and long-haired, all grin with a thick jaw, and he had tattoos on his chest and sides, of ravens and skulls. I realized he was staring at my breasts, and I covered myself up with a blush. He grinned sheepishly and indicated his nakedness, and I blushed as well, for he was not a bad looking boy. 'Not much we can do about it, eh? I'm Lex. Lex Cyburn. You speak English? Yes? Or no?'

I frowned. He had an American accent. 'Shannon,' I said with a small voice, for I had ever been awkward with people.

'You from New York?' he asked happily, his eyes never leaving my body.

'No, I'm Welsh,' I told him.

'Damn! English! I guess we are at war? We were last year, probably this year as well. You are not armed?' He stretched his neck to see behind me.

'I'm Welsh,' I said icily. 'And I don't want to shoot you. Unless you keep staring at me like that.'

'Sorry!' he said, lifting a hand in the air disarmingly, 'I'm from Boston.'

I frowned at him. 'Have you seen anyone else around?'

'No, not really. But I guess I'm happy to see you! Do you feel it?' he asked, his eyes gleaming. 'The … power? I just knew there was something here. I knew it! They did not lie back home.'

'No, they sure didn't,' I stated sourly. 'Where are we? Any idea?' I asked, staring around the room, hoping for a place to hide. He was totally shameless as he spun around, whooping, and I blushed again as I stared at his round ass. Damn American.

'Goddamn. I don't know, but I wanna have some answers to this tattoo on my arm, eh?' he smirked, showing his dangerous looking red arm. 'Have you tried to touch it?' he asked.

'The thing on my arm? Yes, of course. It …'

'No, no! The power. See?' he concentrated and sweated. He was still touching the flame side of the power, holding some parts of it, and uncannily, I could see what he was doing. He pulled at simple parts of the flame, quite recklessly and filled himself with that power. Soon, from his hand a tiny flame sprung forward, weak, then too strong as it blasted away, and he shrieked and fell back, laughing as the flames burnt away from him, ending in a tumbling ball and scorching the ground before him.

It felt warm and wonderful, and then I cursed him before I knew what I was doing.

'No! There are carvings there! Precious!' I shrieked, taking steps forward.

His good mood evaporated in a show of incredulity as he leaned down. 'OK. Yeah. Are they important?'

'I don't know. Maybe? They are old.'

'Ah, you don't want me to wreck the precious past. You a history major in college or something? You look smart. Well, you look great as well,' he said with an infectious grin.

'No,' I told him, blushing furiously as I chased the grin away.

'Me? I didn't do much studying. Terrible at school. The family traditions demanded my attention. And my boat. And ...'

'Got it,' I told him imperiously and regretted it, as he looked mildly hurt. 'I was terrible at school as well. This ... thing made it hard to study. But I do love history.'

'Bookworm,' he grinned. 'A gorgeous one. Well, now you can study all you want. We are free. Just imagine. We've been missing this all our lives! How could we ever manage it?' He was massaging his palms, I smiled at him tentatively and even gratefully, for I was warm again.

'Best not burn off anything either of us would miss,' I chided him gently.

'I won't burn it off, don't worry,' he winked, and I blushed again at his insinuation. Then even he looked embarrassed but kept grinning 'Sorry, you know Americans. We don't have any manners. You a noblewoman?'

'I'm a farmer's daughter,' I told him sullenly. 'I meant these clues to our whereabouts,' I growled and rubbed my temples. 'I tried to pull the power, but it nearly killed me,' I told him. 'It feels strange, like a million tons of grinding ice running down a frozen river.'

'I feel no ice,' he said dreamily, 'but the flames roar so loud. It is glorious. Ice, eh? That's strange. So damned strange.'

I nodded and wondered at his words. 'I can sense the fire, somewhere, but it is so weak.'

'Like a damned inferno, girl,' he said. ' I wish to learn how to use it.'

'Who,' I asked him carefully, 'did you kill to get here?'

He opened his mouth and shut it, then looked down. 'I ...'

'Never mind,' I said, looking at him warily, then around me. 'I am not sure I enjoy it here.'

'I'll miss my dingy,' he told me softly, his good mood subdued. 'Swan.'

'Your what? A swan?' I asked, thinking him mad.

'A boat, my boat,' he stammered. 'I'll miss it. But little else. We had these stories in the family, of blood and madness, but it's not mad, is it? It's just ... right. Uncle told us we would be given a choice one day. It was yesterday. He wore these robes. It was in the woods some twenty miles off Boston, really creepy place. He bent on this altar, which looked old, by the way. You would have hugged it.' I gave him the evil eye, and he took the hint. He rubbed his face and shook it vigorously. 'He worked with us. He was a thief and a bully. He had stolen from the brotherhood. My uncle asked me to bring this particular guy along. There, he told us what to do, but only if we wanted to. Then he called our names and these strange gods. I was scared shitless. I understood why he wanted me to bring the guy along soon enough. He killed him, just like that. Didn't see it coming, neither did Joseph. Uncle did it quickly, thank God. Then he told me ... you know. My face. It sort of twisted? Not sure how I managed to do the next part. The bloody deed. But I ... did it after ... It was not pleasurable, not fun, definitely would have had a cold beer rather than lick at the steaming blood. But I think nobody's going to miss him.' He looked away and I knew he felt bad about it.

'Did he have a mother? This thief? And what brotherhood were you talking about?'

'We all have mothers,' he scowled. 'But his was a bad one, a whore. I suppose she won't miss him. Maybe.' He looked away, unconvinced by his own words. 'And he was a thief, yeah. That is important. You steal from your own, anything can happen.'

'Never mind,' I told him, tired of the pointless discussion, and looked around, hoping to find something to cover myself with.

Lex shook his head. 'I know what you mean. Really. Shannon, relax. We are here. We can't ... you know, worry about everything right now. Did someone do it for you?' he asked, looking embarrassed. 'It's the only way ...'

I shuddered and was about to tell him about Dana. I shut my mouth and thought about it. No, I didn't want to tell anyone. They would, perhaps, hold it against her. 'My grandma killed a man. My sister went and drank from the wound. I ...'

'Followed,' Dana said as she walked to us from the dark, her lithe body glistening with water and sweat, a fiercely red brand burning on her arm like live flames, much stronger than the one on Lex's arm. The fool boy whistled softly. 'She followed me. My sister drank the blood Grandma spilled, and here we are.' She walked to me, tall and dark and finally grasped at me, laughing wildly. I sobbed and grabbed her furiously back, holding on. 'We are free,' she said and leaned to whisper in my ear. 'You lied for me. Perhaps you are different here, after all. Canny and useful. Try to keep in control, though. Let me run this.' I nodded uncertainly at her words. I was not sure I liked the new, conniving Dana. Nor did I trust her as I had. And yet, I loved her.

'Free?' I told her with a small, trembling voice. 'This is not home. Nor safe. Everything safe is gone. No police, no laws. We don't know if we are free.'

'We make the laws!' she said happily, as if to a child. 'We don't have to pretend, for once, and that is worth it all,' she giggled. She grabbed my head again and put her mouth to my ear. 'For once, there are no throbbing pains in the night, no chains of expectations, nobody to look down at us if we fail, and we can make our own rules. None shall mock you here, think you are crazy. If you don't act it.'

'Is she crazy?' Lex asked with a grin, having eavesdropped.

'She is,' Dana smiled, and I pushed her. She grasped my arm, staring at my eyes. 'We are free! Everything, Shannon, is just right. For once. Forget the old world. Can you feel the power? We always had it! Can't you see that? We were gold chips buried under sand, Shannon, back at home. Here, we will enjoy!'

'You did not want me to follow you,' I told her bluntly.

She sighed and tilted her head. 'It's time we grew apart a bit, Shann. I don't want you to be so dependent on me. Here, I wish to do things my way. I told you. I want to be free and happy. And not worry about you. Nor do I want you to worry about me.'

'You killed ...' I began to whisper.

'I did,' she whispered back, forcefully. 'Stop it. Forget and be happy.'

'I second that,' Lex interrupted having heard that part, walking closer. 'She's right ... wait.'

From the corridors, more lights shone. They looked eerie, then like bubbling red flashlights, and then figures showed up. Two were creeping carefully forward, a reddish glow around their forearms, both were dark as night. They were a boy and a girl, perhaps twelve, black and handsome, the girl's hair long to her calves, the boys curly and wild. One said something softly in a language we did not understand. It was the girl. 'I bet she doesn't understand English,' Lex whispered. 'Wonder where they are from.'

The two stopped to stare at us, and the girl was fidgeting. I saw she had been crying and looked lost. The boy looked at her miserably, but shrugged and grunted and came forward to stand near us, on guard. The girl hovered nearby and we all stared at her. 'Who are ...' I began, but Dana nudged me. More reddish lights shone in the corridors, and a group of people arrived. Two were wolf-like men, in their twenties, bald and thin, one girl, perhaps our age. They stayed on the side, eying us warily until the girl, a tall blonde cut with shapely breasts waved her hand. 'Privet, druz'ya.'

'Oh boy,' Lex whispered. 'Is that ... Heard it from some sailors. Russians?'

The girl grinned and shrugged.

'Yes, da!' Dana chirped and thumbed me. 'They are Russians I'm sure of it. Shannon, and I'm Dana Crowther. From Wales.'

'Lex Cyburn,' said the American boy, eyeing the girl with a lecherous grin. 'An American.' The Russian girl noticed his lingering look but brazenly flaunted her shapely body by bowing slightly.

She made elaborate movements with her hands, pointing at her chest. 'Donskoi! Anja Donskoi.' She pointed a finger at the two men and spoke at length. We all looked at each other, confused.

The black girl sighed and spoke. She pointed a finger at one of the bald boys. 'Alexei. Dmitri has the crooked nose. She says he broke it on a toilet door, drunk. They are her brothers both, and she is their unlucky sister. They are from St. Petersburg.' I noted they all had slightly slanted eyes. I had heard Russia was a big country, and they looked exotic.

'Nice to meet you,' Dana grinned and eyed the black girl. 'Your name?'

'Able et Albine,' said the boy. 'Nous sommes de Marseille.' The girl shrugged.

'She won't answer?' Lex asked curiously.

'I think they are French,' I stated. 'From Marseilles.'

'Where?' Lex asked.

'From Marseilles,' I told him. 'It's in France. That is Albine.' She scowled at us. 'Right?' I asked.

She nodded

'French?' Lex asked Albine, who nodded. 'And you know English? And Russian!'

'Obviously,' she said morosely. 'Albine.'

'Albine,' Lex whispered, giving me a strange look. 'A kid still.'

'Dangerous children both,' I told him as I smiled at them encouragingly. They had killed someone to be here, perhaps.

Dana nodded at her while making subtle signs for me to be quiet. 'We ...'

'You lied,' Albine said with a thick dialect.

'What?' Dana asked.

'I was listening out there,' she whispered. 'About your grandma sending you here.'

'I did not!' Dana said. 'This is no way to speak to someone you just met, is it? What if I called you a thief before even asking your name?'

'You might, but I know you lied,' Albine said, but apparently regretted saying anything. She shrugged as we stared at her strangely.

The Russian girl said something with a small smile.

'What a strange bunch we are,' Albine said with a bored voice. 'Her words. But I agree.'

We stood there, uncomfortably silent for a while, wondering what to say and what to do next, each of us nude as the day we were born, their arms burning red and mine with silver. Lex, apparently unable to sustain the silence grunted. 'So. Do you think we are still on earth, after all? It all looks strangely familiar. The stone looks like rock back home, and there are no giant fungi ready to consume us. Nothing weird like that, eh? Surely, an alien world would look different, no? Like somewhat strange, at least?'

'There was a weird statue and this floor? It looks bizarre,' I said. 'And we have not seen anything yet.'

'No,' Dana said. 'We are far ...'

'Yes,' Albine answered at the same time, and the two stared at each other, shrugging. 'Perhaps we are still on earth?' the girl asked. 'How could we know?'

Then we knew.

The room shuddered. A doorway opened, and past the shuddering door, there was a corridor with a bright, burning light. The light filtered, snaked to our hall, illuminating the room slowly. The door was taking its time, ripping itself open, very slowly, thin dust blowing and billowing through it as if it had not been used for years. The light was brighter now, but something was passing through it. A shadow, flickering and iridescent was moving there, coming forward as we squinted. It walked, that much was clear, and it had a dark, swathed cloak around it, covering much of its face and body save for long, shapely white legs, ending in elaborate golden shoes. Its hands were at its sides, the fingers moving and light was playing on the fingertips. I felt it was touching the power, the fiery side of it, and I guessed that was what made the light. I wondered at the elaborate strings she was weaving together with ease and saw more lights spring forth from her hands. They were red and white, floating around the room. The figure glided forth and stopped before us, and we huddled instinctively into a group. The dark hood turned and stared at each of us in turn. What it was, I knew not. It was small, shorter than we were, moved smoothly as water across the stones, and yet seemed somewhat human in its ways.

'Lady,' Lex began with a trembling voice, for it was obviously a woman. The thing shook its head, and the hands groped the air. Fiery light and the subtle fire mixed, and I felt her pulling at the power and creating a complicated pattern and suddenly, streams of light engulfed us. Then, nothing.

'Can you understand me?' said the woman's powerful, singsong voice.

'Yes,' Dana said with apprehension. 'You ...'

'She speaks her own language,' said Anja with wonder. 'And so do we.' We turned to stare at her. The language was ours, and we realized we had not spoken English, but some other, far older language.

'Welcome all,' said the woman, the voice beautiful and enchanting. 'I am called Cosia. I already know your names. And the gift of speech is yours for good. It is the universal language of the world.'

'Where the hell are we?' asked Able softly, the French kid.

'I would like to know as well,' I added.

'What did you say?' the creature asked, her voice full of amusement.

'We,' I said and put a hand around Able, who looked supremely startled, 'would like to know where we are.' The swaddled female snickered, and I decided I did not like our host. The Russians were tittering as well, and I scowled at them until Cosia's hood turned that way. Then she looked at me again, and I did not enjoy the look.

'Lady ...' Dana grunted and half stepped before me. Cosia turned to look at her. 'Forget her. I guess we would all wish to know where the hell we are.'

'Where?' Cosia said. 'Why, you are not with Hel. You are all alive. Come, you three, join your fellow students.'

'Students?' Albine mouthed, but we all turned.

We turned to find three more people. Two were brutally tall men, one dark and the other redheaded, and they grinned at the same time. There was something similar in them, a swaggering confidence and arrogant expressions. The last one was the short girl with thin cheeks, the one I had seen running, and I saw she was, perhaps, a teen with a short mop of black hair, looking strangely at the lot of us. All had reddish symbols playing along their arms.

'That is Cherry,' said the red-headed man with a thick voice. 'And I'm Ron. That's Ulrich. German.' The latter grunted, powerful arms folded over his chest, eyeing the lot of us.

'Austrian,' Ulrich corrected him. 'From the Alps.'

'Can she speak for herself?' Albine asked irascibly, nodding at the girl. The French girl was looking for trouble.

Ron stared at Albine with disdain. 'No, I named her. Cherry is a good name. Her hollow cheeks are pink and red like those cherry tree blossoms, you know? She does not speak. Not a word. We tried. Change your tone.'

Her cheeks were indeed red, and she was not making a sound or showing any emotion. A survivor, I thought, used to desperate situations.

'Mute,' Dana grinned. 'Now, where are we?' she asked Cosia with some impatience. 'And what's this about being students?'

Cosia swept her hand around the hall, and the many strange globes of light began drifting around. I noticed the floor and the walls were indeed covered in beautiful drawings and script. She took a deep breath. 'All questions will be answered in time.'

'But surely you should tell us now,' Dana demanded, and I nearly pulled at her to shut her up. She noticed it and shot me a venomous glance, and I stopped my hand, but she nodded at me, and I suppose she understood my concern, for she asked no more,

'As I said ...' Cosia went on with a warning note in her strange voice.

'You heard her,' Ron shouted and nodded at Dana. 'Tell us where we are. And what the hell are these things around our arms. It burnt like shit when they attached themselves to our bones. And I didn't ask for one, by the way.'

Cosia shook her head, her voice now cold. 'It's always like this with you humans. Always so many questions, always demands for exact, logical answers. You lot have lived in that filthy mine colony of yours for too long, I think. You have grown arrogant as beggars of Brygga and ignorant as savages, making a mess of epic proportions. All of you think you are born with rights, entitled to answers and silly freedoms you enjoyed before. Your gods left you and now you are the gods? Hah! Once, you were tools. And tools you are still. You are this year's Dark Levy. That is all you need to know. Now shut up.'

Albine, the black girl, gritted her teeth. 'We are no tools, you hooded creep. The Dark Levy? Sounds like some form of slavery to me. All of us are seeking peace, harmony, and what we found was pain and more questions. People died to get us here! In here! You say we are not entitled to answers? What are these things on our arms?'

'You came willingly,' Cosia whispered. 'You let her take you.

Your families sent you here, your names were whispered, and so you are ours.'

'Our aunt forced ...' Albine began.

Anja pulled at her shoulder and whispered, 'She made some damned impressive lights just now, small girl. I would not aggrieve her.'

'No, she is right,' the loud Ron said in Albine's support. 'Tell us something, at least. You seem human, but ...'

Cosia snickered, no longer a beautiful sound, but grating and inhuman. 'A woman, a human like you? No, I am not a human. Never a human. Not even quite. All will be made clear to you, as I said, as I promised.' She stopped and was apparently amused after the sudden burst of anger. Her voice regained the beauty and singing quality. 'But I shall humor you. Know you did not find peace or harmony for years to come. You are the property of the Shrouded Serpent Merchant House, and as for the Bone Fetters in your arms? They are there to make you property, slaves if you will, and ours to be exact. They will make sure you will not try to embrace those silly illusions of freedom and rights, the lies you were unfortunately born with. You will obey us. You will do so until we sell you. Or eat you.'

Stunned silence followed.

She nodded, apparently surprised at the lack of expletives. 'This world and the Nine are a heaven for the gifted. Those who see the

Shades rule all things, living and dead. You are amongst these lucky ones. By that fact, you would expect reverence, riches, and servitude from others, those who are not so gifted. Even in this world, where the many noble houses rule the land, there is no house unless a maa'dark rules it. Maa'dark, the Gifted Hands are holders of vast lands and honor and always feared and respected.'

'And we are not?' I asked her.

She bowed to me slightly. 'You are a saa'dark. A Gifted Slave.'

'We are ...'

She shook her cowled head. 'Stubborn. All humans are, and you are not the only ones we have seen enter this room. No, no. Understand this, if you know nothing else. We are of the maa'dark. Perhaps not of this world, but of those who see the Shades nonetheless. You call us the Gifted Hands or just mistresses. We are as free as you can be in the Shrouded Serpent Trading House, obedient ladies of the Dark Water and Deep Murk Clans and of our mistress, your owner.' She stopped to stare at us and then lifted her hands in a sign we should rejoice. 'Yet, be happy. You are special. No human was meant to be a maa'dark. That you are is a twist of nature and the crime of the lords who used to own this land we now occupy. This might not comfort you in your thralldom, for you are not only stubborn but also arrogantly foolish, yes, but you will be useful and less uppity soon enough, yes you will. But, above all, always remember that human is the least of the intelligent races. Now, rebel away. I rather expect you to.'

With that, she shook her cowl off.

Her skin was bone white. Her hips were wide and shapely, her legs well-sculpted and muscular. She wore a leathery, dark loincloth that covered her privates and her breasts were covered in some sort of chain mail, dark and supple. Silver and golden hoops beautifully ringed her arms. Her face was rather human, near enchanting with delicate bones. She had a smooth brow and shapely mouth with dark lips. Yet, the eyes were bright and yellow, like jewels, emotionless and harsh. Her hair was hugely long, dark, and vibrant. I stared at the hair more carefully. 'My God,' I said. She did not, in fact, have hair. The slithering strings were thin dark snakes, mesmerizing and alive, apparently looking at all of us, wary and spiteful, moving like a deadly sea of weeds. Cosia grinned, and we froze, suddenly aware things would not work out as Dana had hoped they would.

Cosia was oblivious to our stunned silence, her finger ticking at each of us, counting us, taking account of each of us as if memorizing something we could not understand. 'I am no god to be honest, but to you, perhaps I am. This is, my young, foolish friends, the Grey Downs, our war-torn refuge, once the gate to the Tenth world, the abandoned one, which is, of course, as you guessed, yours. It is our land in a world few dare call anything their own, and we will keep it. It is, lovelies, an island refuge, once the jewel in this

114

world, so keep that in mind if you plan to escape. You see the Shades, yes, but no application of the Fury nor the Gift have been found to this day to allow one to fly through the air, and I would not try to swim, should you get the chance. Consider this your school. You will be schooled here, indeed. I ...'

'What the hell are you talking about? You own us? Let us speak to ...' Albine blurted and Cosia turned her way, shutting her up though only barely, for Albine was making small, angry sounds. The female's eyes shimmered in the magical light, going from yellow to white and her thin, elegant eyebrow arched. I pulled Albine back, and then Cosia regarded me. Her eyes went to my silvery sigils. There was some brief hesitation on the face, and then she lifted a finger.

'There is something very peculiar, oh so strange about you. Come to me,' she murmured, and I felt her spin some ice and air and a force grabbed me tightly, air curling around my legs and arms, and I was pulled by the power, ending up on my knees, unable to move. 'Such a spell allows you to be drawn and pushed briefly, my students, but also held as she is. Observe.' She tightened her hand, and the spell she held curled around my midsection, making me sob in breathless panic until she grinned and let go. I was drawing pained breaths and stayed still. Curiously, I saw what she had done, what wondrous, strangest bits of ice she had pulled and merged together with air, and I felt a brief rage and

THE DARK LEVY

considered hurting her with a similar spell. I glanced at Dana.

She shook her head carefully.

Cosia lifted my face from the chin, her hand strangely warm, and she leaned to examine me. The hundred snakes, dark as night, also turned their eyes towards me. Albine took a hesitant step forward, but one of the Russian boys put a hand on her shoulder. She ripped herself free, but Cosia seemed to pay the quarrelsome kid no attention, still staring at me. 'You are a curious one, are you not?' she ran her finger across the embedded markings in my arm, the one she had ominously called the Bone Fetter, and it tingled. 'Strange color, is it not? Never seen the like, and I have seen plenty. But we will see, very soon.' She snapped her fingers, and the bonds around me renewed and twirled me around and threw me painfully back at Dana's feet.

'Respectfully,' Ron said darkly as Lex helped pull me up, 'we are no slaves.'

'Not in the least bit,' Albine agreed with a childlike growl, and we all felt she grasped at the power.

'Ahh, here it is,' Cosia giggled. 'Violence.'

Sweat trickled on Albine's face as she was trying to find something to use as a weapon, some clue on what to pluck at, what strings of the strange power to combine, how to weave them together. Her arms twirled as she shook, making a brave and dangerous effort at drawing hot winds and fires to her. Now there was a near scorching wind whirling around her, buffeting us all, building to a terrible strength. Ulrich, the Austrian boy, tried to grab her but flew on his back from the gust and the rest of us toppled like wheat inside a tornado, our nails scraping on the intricate floor carvings. Albine was shrieking, and we could all **see** by the look on her face she was terrified. Cosia, however, smiled and snapped her fingers once again. Albine's sigil flared. A simple, dull ring gleamed on Cosia's finger, and the wind died instantly, and Albine fell on her knees.

'I can't hear it!' she sobbed as Able came to her, scowling at Cosia. 'She shut me off.'

'She shut us all off,' I said softly, feeling bottomless sorrow, not unlike an addict staring at a toilet where the drugs had twirled but a moment before. It was not like it had been back home, where something seemed to bother you all the time, driving you crazy, but here there was only craving, disappointment, and anger at being thrust aside. The Bone Fetters were our true jailers, I decided. We could never leave if we lacked our powers. Cosia stared at me, and she nodded as if knowing what I had been thinking.

'The mistress controls the Fetters, a mighty First Born and our lady. These rings give us access to her right to deny you the Shades. And she received the right to your obedience when you accepted the gift,' Cosia said with a small smile.

'And where is the mistress, then? Why send a minion to treat with us and not come here to face us herself?' Ulrich growled.

'Face you?' she chuckled and shook her head with pity. 'She does not treat with you, no. She is above you like Mar is, the star of the world. Neither that nor she shall you see for long months and only should some of you prove worthier than the others, shall she give you an audience. Cheer up, toads. Consider this service something you must give in order to repay us for escaping the Tenth. There, you would have withered away. Here, you shall serve, but also smile, occasionally,' she smiled sweetly as if to show us how. She had fangs.

'Give it back to us!' Ron demanded but settled down as Cosia's beast eyes turned his way, and her singing voice laughed happily. 'You took our ...'

Cosia bowed mockingly. 'So I did. Yet, I just told you. You gave us the right in order to travel here. It's the price for the trip. Also, you are but children in this art. Do you think we would let mere humans run around, seeing the Shades, using it at will and with no control? Madness that would be, would it not? Did you not see what the young fool just did? You humans often learn a spell or two the first day you feel this power, but that does not make you an adept at their usage. Letting you run around empowered thus, it would be dangerous to us, dangerous to you, dangerous to the Grey Downs and the lands around us. You would caress the fire of the Shades, and no doubt, very soon you would be pulling carelessly at the many strings you should not and releasing powers you do not understand. Even before releasing anything, some of you would burn up splendidly after absorbing too much of the power. No, no. It is no game, girls and boys, no. It is a delicate art of conserving your abilities, knowing what you can hold, how much and when, what to weave, when to release it and how. The power we call the Shades and the result of a spell, if it is the destruction you seek, is the Fury. If it is a beneficial and kind spell, it's called the Gift. Neither kinds of spell-hurling are a game, no. Yes, you are slaves, dear ones, for your sake as well as ours. You are precious, delicate slaves, who are worth their weight in gold and silver, and we are loath to lose any, even if such a lesson will do you good.'

'Will?' I breathed.

We eyed her, grinding our teeth together. 'Mistress ...' Dana began.

Cosia cut her off. 'Mistress? Some of you learn quickly, no? You will be here for two years, learning the rudiments of your powers. Then we shall sell you like chunks of ripe mutton to whoever wishes to bid on you. And there will be many if we train you properly. Oh, you will have uses, you will.'

'Will you treat us well?' Ulrich asked reasonably. 'At least tell us this much.'

She shrugged as if thinking about it. We stared at her carefully, and finally she seemed to snap out of her thoughts. 'Well. I could lie and have before. I think I shall be honest this time. It is no world for humans and certainly not one with such powers. There will be dangers, but perhaps it is no worse than what you had back home. You escaped the troubles in your old lives, many of them with the laws and rules of your pitiful lords, but know there are no worlds without laws. In your sad, misguided land, you lived in frustrated pain and forever confused, but in here, you will be useful. You will at least know what you lack when you cannot see the Shades. I promise you no kindness, a trait for humans, at least occasionally. But there will be little confusion, as we will tell you what is required, and the pains and hurts you will suffer are all easy to understand. You shall, in any other thing know this one law. Obey. Then, one day, perhaps, you shall make your own decisions. If you survive.'

'If we survive?' Alexei asked with incredulity. 'What kind of a school is this, exactly?'

'A school for the strong,' Cosia grinned. 'And you are only as useful as you are strong. It is a school to prepare you for a world that dislikes you. This class needs a name.'

'Where are we, exactly?' I asked. 'Grey Downs, I get that much, yeah, but what is this world?'

She ignored me. 'Wait,' she said. 'There are ten of you?'

'Eleven,' I said. 'Unless you count differently from us.'

'Shut up, girl, you awkward fool,' Ulrich spat.

Dana spun on him. 'Do not threaten her. Nor insult her.'

'She isn't ...'

'Silence,' Cosia said softly. 'So One is too many.'

'You summoned us!' Anja spat. 'Why summon the wrong number?'

Cosia shook her head empathetically and the snakes waved in unison. 'I said one is too many, not that there is a wrong number of you. Sometimes we get twelve for a class, other times eight, but the rule is, one will not make the cut. While I said we are loath to lose you, it is so you have to understand your place. It is a lesson, and it is a valuable lesson. Call it the awakening, your scourging, if you please. It is meant to teach you things will be different. You, despite your troubled past, have lived guarded lives. Volunteers?' Her eyes flashed around. 'Well?'

We stared at each other, not fully comprehending what she was asking. Lex took a step forward.

'You?' Cosia asked, tilting her head.

'What? No!' Lex told her with a nervous wave of his arm. 'Why not just send one back? They will suffer there forever, lost to ... the Shades and die prematurely anyway. That's a lesson for us, no?'

'And you would like to be sent back?' she snickered. 'No, you cannot go back to your pathetic Tenth, your earth, the cesspit of House Timmerion's mining colony. It is not part of the Nine worlds, and the gods did not craft the gate to it. No, it was created by former lords of this hall, eager to attain what the gods had, their own dominion, independent from the Lord Freyr. Arrogant bastards. This gate is different, not governed by Heimdall's horn Gjallarhorn. Its secrets are mostly gone. Our mistress discovered the way they had moved back and forth in the beginning before the Tenth was given a permanent though secret, gate. She knows the spell to summon the Dark Levy every other year, even without the high gate. Without the gate, we cannot send anyone back. That knowledge was lost with the fall of House Timmerion and the disgrace of Cerunnos Timmerion. You are stuck here, that's the story.' Cerunnos, I thought. He had been a mortal? Someone who tried to reach and grasp a world for himself? My mind spun, and I nearly did not hear what Cosia was saying. I found her eyes on mine. 'No, no, none shall go back. And the lesson is to be given, nonetheless. Mistress so orders. So, one of you is just too many and which one shall it be?'

'You mean one of us is to ... die?' Lex asked incredulously. 'Truly? This is a joke, right? A damned cruel joke, but just a joke?'

'Yes,' Cosia said quietly, the snakes hissing. 'And no, I am not jesting.'

'Which one?' Ron asked brutally. 'The one you like the least, mistress? The least useful one? The weakest one? Take the Frenchie.' His eyes settled on small Albine, then he saw Cosia looking at me. He grasped my shoulder, smirking like a simpleminded school bully, sensing weakness, immediately ready to pounce. 'Or take the addled one if you must. Despite her looks, she seems to be a burden we don't need to carry. She is the weak one. Just take this one.'

Ron was making a claim for the leadership of a bunch of slaves, and the look he cast about was brutal and aggressive. I ripped my shoulder free of him.

Ulrich shook his head. 'Wait. I ...'

Dana sighed, apparently resigned to take my side. 'I say take the one who keeps talking. Take the ape here, the fat, foul-mouthed piece of shit.' Dana pointed spitefully at Ron, and the large man reddened, taking a step forward. He was not fat, of course, but thick with muscle. It made no difference for Dana had sweetened the insult with a smile and a tilted head, and like bullies, he was not one for words.

'No, we must not bicker ...' Anja began, but Cosia clapped her hands together. We went silent.

Cosia was ticking her nail on her tooth. 'I see you lot are going to need a lot of discipline. I'll take the one who is the weakest, of course,' she said happily as if discussing breakfast arrangements. 'But not at face value. So. Let us see. You all see the Shades, the power that makes us more than those who do not. One spends a lifetime learning spells, of Fury, the force for destruction, of Gift, the gentler arts. The masters of this world teach their students slowly, gently, coaxing their minds to see the right ways and paths, the braids and weaves of wondrous creation, and they have such time to spare. In our world, where we come from we do not teach anyone like that. It is too slow. For us, the method to learn spells is another spell, one I master. It's rather more dangerous and uncomfortable that taking your time. It is painful, harsh even. And it can only be cast on those who are weaker than the caster. You all qualify in that regard.'

I hesitated, for could I not see all the spells they wove?

Cosia continued, 'Some die from such teachings, as the master forces his will over the students, thrusting aside the natural guards of the victims so perhaps if that takes place no further lesson will be needed. Yet, you humans are hardy, much stronger than the finer beings of this land. Now, I shall give you the one spell you will need this year. You have discovered some on your own, already, and will in the future. Such is the way of the Shades, it sometimes teaches the students who grasp the Shades for the first time, but this spell will be what you shall use for now. Now, be strong. I shall not be able to see to your minds, but I will grasp and harness it, like a parent holding a naughty child by the hair, and you will look and learn the spell I shall cast after.' She snapped her fingers, we could see the Shades, and we all laughed with the force tumbling in our minds, making us whole.

It was a pleasure we enjoyed only for a moment.

Her hands moved, and I sensed she was making a delicately

complicated spell. She was touching fire and ice equally and then, suddenly, we could all feel her mind grasping at us and we, in our blissful moment of joy had no chance to resist. She was forcing her will on us and strangely, we could all feel she was forcing our eyes towards what she was doing. It was a crushing, soul breaking feeling as all our fibers resisted the spell. Someone was whimpering, another was screaming, and we all fell to our knees and fought, instinctively but weakly. It was impossible. She was beyond our strength to resist, she had no need for subtlety, and was well used to the game. She thrust inside our heads, and we all found ourselves visitors in our own body as she dragged our minds to stare at what she willed.

'Gods, let it be quick,' I prayed, for it hurt so badly. We were dimly aware of her arms pumping crazily in the air as she was murmuring softly. In my head, I saw she was forcing us to reach for the power in a certain way. I dimly heard the roar of ancient fires as she showed intricate ways of plucking at that far away energy. She showed us what to reach out to and what to combine. There was a bit of heat here, some flame added to the mix and a touch of roaring noise, then she was combining them very delicately, pulling and braiding the fire, the heat and the noise, binding them together to throw a spell out of her fingertips. We saw thick, angry yellow weaves of fire burst away, making their way to the wall.

Then she released our minds, leaving us sweltering and covered in sweat. Albine was breathing hard on the floor and was dragging herself up, so was one of the Russian boys. Ron was massaging his forehead and the girl called Cherry was whimpering.

Cosia nodded at us as we stared at her in stupefaction and then at the far wall, where she had built a thick wall of flames, sizzling and burning cobwebs in a fantastic show of deadly art. The flames were thick, near sentient and fierce as they spread up and down, left and right. 'Imagine that teaching performed on one of the less hardy races. You humans are resilient, that is true. You saw what I did. This is a way to make a simple wall of fire, deadly, of course, but simple still. Most spells are much more complicated and to hold you for so long at this time as to teach you, would break you. You will grow stronger and next year we shall teach you more. Remember, none of you will be anything but weapons. You will all learn useful spells here, mostly for the simple art of destruction, and some of you will specialize in more … focused spells, but it will all be about fire for that is all you few human saa'dark can see anyway.'

I shook my head and opened my mouth, but thought better of it. I could see ice. It was so close, and fire so far.

Cosia furrowed her brow at my confused look until I looked down and then nodded, her fires disappearing, leaving the fiery art of slowly burning cobwebs spreading on the far wall. 'Now, one by one, make a wall of fire over the yonder wall.' She pointed to her right. 'You, girl.' She pointed at Albine. 'You tired yourself with your buffoonery, so you had better hope to impress, even if it kills you. I care nothing for children; will give you no special treatment, even if younger ones are quicker learners than the older ones. Quicker, but also too delicate, we have seen before.'

Albine scowled at her and then turned to look at the wall, brooding and angry. Able was whispering to her, but she was paying no heed. Perhaps she was contemplating on throwing the wall at Cosia, but her predator's eyes flashed and the French girl nodded, knowing better, for now. She had some sense, then. She murmured, her brow was sweating, and her hands moved. I saw her pulling at the spell, trembling with exertion. Finally, a thin gout of fire played at her fingers as she shook even more, staring at the power with round eyes. I saw she was not doing it right anymore. She was beyond tired, shocked by her glowing hands. She was trying to fix them frantically. She managed it, nearly spent. She grimaced, shirked, and I felt her draw in much power. Then the fire burst out, uncertain and sputtering. There were slow gouts of fire weaning out of her fingers, moving towards the wall, where they exploded weakly on impact. She slumped, whimpered, and fell. Cosia smiled like a benevolent parent. 'It is hard. But good, though not superb.'

The Russians stepped forward, eyeing each other warily. The two bald brothers began moving their hands, swearing softly as they consistently failed. They were doing it wrong until Anja stepped in between them and grasped their hands, squeezing them, and then letting go. That calmed the boys, and I saw them all pull at the powers. Their hands glowed, fire burst forth in uncertain lines and together they built crisscrossing, shuddering, mad, thick waving lines of fire that hit the wall and sputtered man high, burning with blue and green flames. Cosia nodded at them, staring as they kept at it and wove a long wall of flames, full of holes and flaws, and then it collapsed with a strange whistle.

'Interesting,' she said. 'Since we often get families here, I know siblings can make each other stronger and more focused, but you have more finesse than most your kind. Next. You. Blond dolt.'

Lex stepped forward, apparently hoping to beat the challenge quickly. He was roaring with anger, pain, and he wove the spell surprisingly well, and from his hands burst forth a thick burst of fire that turned to smoke and cinders before hitting the wall. Some of the flames danced wildly around the room until Cosia scowled and cut him off the Shades. Cosia pointed at Ron. God, but I was afraid of that one already.

Ron walked up and pushed Lex aside brusquely, holding his hands out and so smoothly, so skillfully as if he had always done it, he wove the spell and stretched his hands out. Bright lines of thin fire shot quick as lightning across the room and there they expanded. He managed a wall that was fierce, but some of it burst back towards him as he did something wrong after all, and we all fell back as the flames licked between us. Cosia was staring at the performance, her eyes grading us imperiously. Ron would surely make the cut. I noted Dana was fidgeting nervously as Ron shrieked with a victorious roar, pointing a subtle finger her way. She had made an enemy.

Ulrich shrugged, stepped up, and failed utterly. Ron was whispering to him, and Ulrich was nodding, doing it again. He cursed, and I saw he was gathering, just totally the wrong powers. So did Cosia, who stepped forward angrily, but then a fierce face emerged from the floor, breathing gouts of vapor. A hand was appearing beside the head, which was now scowling at us, and we all took steps back as the cheeks of the thing puffed out; apparently ready to do something fatal. Then the face went away in an eye blink as Cosia cut Ulrich off. 'An exceptional show! Fool. Such mistakes can kill you. This is why you will need lessons. Painful ones.' Cosia spat and pointed a finger at Cherry, who walked forward cautiously, timidly.

She was calling for her spell. I saw her pull at fires entirely different from what had been taught. She was skillful, powerful, and deft as if used to such work. She grinned.

And disappeared in fumes.

Cosia's face lit up with a grin. 'Well done.' She snapped her fingers as she cut Cherry off from the Shades, and the thin-faced girl fell to the ground behind Cosia. She had tried to escape through the door and was backpedaling from the angry hostess. 'With some discipline you shall be most useful, little one. Though next time, you shall do as you are told.' Cosia smiled, harnessed the power and brought a spell of Fury forth. The mute Cherry actually made a sound. Or rather, she shrieked in pain for blue flames danced on her back, leaving angry red welts as they drove her back to us, on her fours. She was sobbing in pain, and I grabbed her away, hissing as one of the hot flames danced around us, before disappearing. Her back was angry red and some black skin hung in small tatters. 'Go on,' Cosia told us, uncaring of Cherry's pain, folding her arms beneath her breasts. Able stepped forward uncertainly, but Cosia pointed at me. 'Shannon they call you? Throw a firewall over the wall.'

I hesitated and let go of Cherry, who was whimpering at my feet. I stepped forward and took a deep breath. I saw the Shades and grasped at the flames, but they were far, far from me as if they spoke a different language. Cosia's dark eyes twinkled as she saw my struggle. I managed to pull the power, just a bit but lost it, for it was slippery and distant. I felt like I was trying to lift a truck. I gave up and in a panic reached for the ice instead, gasping at the tumbling force of freezing waters and icy winds. They filled my being. I did what I had done before, held my hand out, weaning and weaving a gentle combination of power, not as strong as before. I let it go. It burst out, feeling like fresh ice flowing around me, and I looked around.

Nothing. Nothing happened, and the rest looked at me askance, some in relief, Ron definitely very happy by my apparent lack of skill.

Cosia nodded, her snakes hissing softly. 'It seems this Ron is right. Your Bone Fetter is lifeless. There is an issue with you. So be it,' she said coldly.

She was gathering power for a spell. The others swiftly moved away from me.

All but Dana.

She glanced at me in fury and then she stepped forward, interrupting Cosia. My sister harnessed the Fury, her hair flying around her head. Crouched and trembling, she wove a gout of fire that flew from her hands, both hands, thin and thick lines both twirling and playing in the air, then splashing to ignite the hall's far wall, roaring to life, blackening the stone and the carvings with exceptional heat. She kept the firewall there, terribly concentrated, and by the look on her glazed eyes, mesmerized. Then she glanced at me and winked, sweat running down her forehead. 'Enough,' Cosia said, at least a bit impressed.

But Dana was not done.

An offshoot of fire danced away from the wall, racing for us with near intelligent, malignant purpose. We scattered, yelling warnings as the flames filled the air, and we all saw how the flames reached for Able. They danced across his thigh and up his chest, trying to choke him, and I grasped at him, pulling him away. I saw Dana mumbling under her breath, her face twitching with concentration. She was doing it on purpose. She was sweating in anger and pain of holding the spell of Fury, but with her last shreds of strength, she threw the cheated gout of fire at Ron, who had been standing behind Able.

Ron's eyes popped out of his head and he screamed as the infernal spell engulfed him, he hollered and clapped his hands on his flaming torso as the heat tore at his hair, setting it alight, his flesh bared by the clinging, living heat. The stench was terrible. Dana fell on her fours, panting, but I saw she was excited as she eyed Ron. The man was running around, screaming, and scraping at his blackening flesh until he fell on his knees. We all could see Dana's flames clinging to his meat, and then his bones, and he fell down on his face with a sickening crack. He was dead. It was clear. He was gone so quickly we could barely understand it. Ulrich screamed in unholy rage and ran for Ron, going on his knees next to the smoking skeletal bones and meat.

'Shit,' Dana whispered. 'They're related?'

'Don't think so. Or perhaps?' Anja answered coldly. 'But you ... piece of shit.'

'It was an accident,' Dana said sullenly, but I saw the glint in her eyes. She climbed to her feet. Cosia walked forward and gazed at Ron's corpse, probing it with her foot. She snapped her fingers, and we all lost the power. We were all staring at Dana, who held an austere, concentrated poise, her hands behind her back, her breasts proud. Ulrich sobbed and got up on shaky feet, wiping his face and mouth with the back of his hand. He turned and saw Dana standing there. Then he charged.

Cosia intercepted him, her leg shooting up from the ground, lightning fast, and Ulrich was on his back, nose bleeding, groaning. Cosia's sword was on his chest. 'You will not attack her, you filth. She did what she had to do. She saw your … brother? Yes, your brother was challenging her for the leadership of your miserable band, for the meaningless title of the most powerful. And so, she took the chance. I applaud her.'

I stared at Dana. Had she saved me or made herself the apparent leader? Perhaps both.

Ulrich was breathing harshly. Cosia leaned on him, her snakes brushing his face. 'If you think you have nothing else to lose, you are wrong. No?'

Ulrich growled; a death-like mask of hatred plastered on his face. Finally, he gave a single nod. Cosia grinned. She turned and walked around us, stopping near Cherry and me. I wiped tears off my face as the demonic woman crouched next to me. She ran her fingers across Cherry's back, and I noticed the skin was smooth again. Cosia gazed at me with interest and saw my tears. She picked one off my cheek.

'Your name shall be the Ten Tears. The first one has rolled down your cheeks, and one is gone. This class now comprehends the value of their lives, and so I think you are ready to begin your road. For some, it will be longer, for others, it need not be, and more tears shall roll until it feels natural as breathing to lose people you know. I think you might prove to be mostly a useful bunch, saa'dark. And interesting. Thank you. Dana?' The yellow eyes scourged my sister.

'Dana, yes,' she breathed, exhausted.

'Dana,' Cosia hissed, 'I shall keep an eye on you. You show potential for many excellent rewards. Welcome to Aldheim, Ten Tears.'

CHAPTER 6

M ore females like Cosia entered. Their eyes were yellow like hers; most were short and sturdy, well proportioned. They were armored in supple, dark chain mail, looked callous and deadly and curiously, all sported differently colored snakes coiling around their shoulders. Even the type of the snakes seemed different, for some were thin, others fewer and thick. The women all carried simple whips, and on their belts, there were stubby, short swords. 'Knights and goblins next?' Dana asked with a snicker and gazed around our group, as the others were still staring at her with both hatred and distrust. Gone was the strange, hopeful joy we had briefly shared as we met each other, nude and innocent and at the beginning of something new.

I grunted. Dana had not been innocent. And now, everyone saw her as utterly ruthless. Who knew what they had done, but by the looks they were flashing at her, none had killed before.

She had. She had killed. More than once. My sister.

'Dana,' I said slowly. 'You killed him. Did you do it ...'

'A mistake,' she said with some forced humility and regret and turned to look at the other students. 'It was a mistake, that's all. No matter what the snake woman claims. And you should not complain, sister, for you were very fortunate.'

Ulrich said nothing, his eyes dark and burning in his skull. I felt animal-like fear as I looked at the broad Austrian. But Anja had no fears about speaking up. 'Bullshit,' she said with a sweet smile, and her brothers growled. 'You went straight for him. You went for him for your sister.'

'She did,' Albine agreed and even Cherry seemed to sniffle supportively.

'Yeah, and didn't Ron's … spell, that shoddy excuse of a fire explode and nearly kill us? We had to dodge those flames, all of us. Mine failed as well.'

'Shoddy spell?' Dmitri said spitefully. 'It was as powerful as yours. Call me paranoid, but I think that is probably a part of the reason you did that bit of murdering. And yeah, he made a mistake of some kind. But you did not. Yours was crafted with skill and guided by devotion to your sister, and my cynical side thinks you wanted no competition like Ron. You made no mistake, girl.'

'I did, boy,' she hissed and Dmitri rolled his eyes. 'Why keep questioning it?'

'You are not speaking truthfully,' Albine said with finality, and Dana stared at the small girl with frustration.

'Perhaps I did make a mistake,' Dana said coldly. 'Perhaps I should have roasted the meddling French girl or perhaps even you,' she told Dmitri.

'Perhaps you should have,' he said angrily, pushing her. 'I never killed anyone for profit!'

'Hey!' Lex said. 'No touching the girls.' He pushed Dmitri back, and the two faced off.

Alexei was comically trying to step between them as our hosts stared at us mutely, with growing impatience. Dana smiled thinly at the argument. 'Look.' Alexei pointed a finger my way as he squeezed between the two to face Lex. 'That girl should not have made the cut,' he said darkly. 'She can't cast a spell or couldn't at least, for some reason. You don't get second chances when you fail. You should be out. And that sister of hers is a killer. And she is here with us.'

'You are talking about her as if she should be dead,' Lex sneered. 'We are not applying to any damned military school. And yeah, it's terrible he died,' Lex said, but for some reason I thought he might have grinned, 'but it's not her fault. Had that ...' his eyes wondered to Cosia who was staring at us, '*thing* told you your sister would die because she cheated and helped you two nervous shits with your failed spells, would you have stood there like a lump of shit? No. Now shut the hell up,' Lex insisted, and I noticed Cherry was holding my hand. I squeezed it, gratefully. 'You shall not hit a girl as long as I stand here. Don't turn into animals. She is alive and shouldn't feel bad about it. And we should hate the ones who did this to us.' Lex's eyes scourged Cosia.

Cosia hissed, and we stiffened. 'Silence, saa'dark. Stop your powerless yapping. You've had your fun. Now we shall all move up, and you shall stop this argument or you shall dance to the whips until one more falls. Keep your rotten mouths closed, you whimpering children unless you cannot be civil,' she yelled. 'Dress in these.' Thin robes appeared on the floor and we warily grabbed them. Albine was struggling with her hem, for she was short and so was Cherry, but soon we were a sullen, huddled group of unwilling slaves and students, adjusting the strange garbs. The robe was not very practical, and indeed not very warm, being thin. There was no footwear. Cosia nodded. 'No boots for those who would run. Your feet will bleed, and you will be easier to sniff out.'

'What are we going to ...' Anja began to ask, but a whip slapped on the floor before us, silencing the girl.

'Silence, you damned fools,' said one of the newly arrived snake women. She was tall and muscular; her snakes were bright yellow and orange as were her eyes. Her face was tattooed with red and dark twirls, with dark smudges in the middle of her cheeks, looking like a skull's eyeholes. 'Move up, lively now, girls. And call me Mistress Bilac. I'm the Fury Whip of the Dark Water Clan and Cosia's partner in putting you in your damned places. I'm not nice as she is.' She turned to go.

'Damned to hell,' Lex murmured, and we followed them, all of us turning to look at Ron's corpse, save for Dana, who followed Bilac. Then we were past the doorway, into a medieval-looking passageway, complete with sputtering torches. Apparently, the snake women did not use magic for everything. They guided us to a door and Ulrich passed it, kicking it savagely. Cosia's fingers twitched around her whip, but she did nothing for now, nor did the other guards. There were some four around us, armored and wary, none speaking, but just coaxing us up a wide set of stairs. The tall, muscular snake woman with yellow serpents was leading us up, and Cosia came last. I stumbled a bit, stepping on my robe's hem, and one of the women danced after me, her whip slashing the wall near me. Cherry pulled at me, blanching, her small face pinched with fear, and Lex stopped to support me. Able was walking before us, and I smiled at him as he smiled at me, apparently grateful for trying to spare him Dana's flames.

'Happy you made it,' I told him, for no spell had been asked of him, and he smiled back.

'You OK?' Lex said, gazing at me and then at Able. 'You feeling fine?'

'Fine?' I grinned tiredly. 'No, not really. Are you? We are ...'

'Prisoners,' he said. 'It's pretty wild, isn't it? But at least they have a plan for us. That's the first ever for me, having any sort of plan, even made by someone else.' He smiled inanely and then glanced back at Ulrich and up ahead at Dana. 'Look, despite everything, you have friends. OK?'

'Right,' I told him silently. 'I've never had friends, you know? Only a sister.'

'Really?' he grunted. 'Why? You don't look impossibly ugly. And you seem twice as smart as I am.'

I rolled my eyes at him and shrugged. 'People don't like me. I don't like them. Whenever I made the effort, people snickered at me, mocked me, and thought me a freak. I don't know why.'

'You seem a bit nervous, perhaps that's why,' he shrugged uncomfortably, looking away. 'Not easy to get close to, perhaps? Few make the effort, you know, if it's not easy. If you are not like them. Empty headed.' He smiled at his own flattery, and I gave him a ghost of a smile.

'I am nervous. Is that strange?'

He clapped his hand on my shoulder with relaxed familiarity. 'Well, now you try and make a new start, eh?'

'Hardly an auspicious beginning for that,' I whispered as we both stared at Dana's back. 'Everyone thinks I should be dead.'

'Yeah,' he said and then smiled as I glowered at him. 'Ulrich might actually pray for it, but the rest will forgive you. They're just scared. Try to act cool. Wasn't really your fault, and you shouldn't apologize for breathing.'

'We are all in deep trouble, anyhow,' I said heavily. 'They had one of us killed, just like that. Snuffed out like a candle. What we left behind was far better than this.'

'Damn. If you're always this cheerful, no wonder you're lonely. But I agree all of it sucks. We can't even touch the ... Shades,' Lex said.

'Well, perhaps whoever rules ... Aldheim? Was that the name?' He nodded. 'Whoever that is, has a different name for it and kinder manners. We have to get out of here.' Able stopped before me, and I nearly fell as I tried not to bowl him over. 'Uups,' I said, placing a hand on Able's shoulder, helping him up. Lex and the others stared at me as I spoke to him. 'You OK?'

Able nodded. He did not seem hurt from the flames that had danced very near him.

I heard them whispering behind me. Just like they had before. I turned to look at the two Russian boys who had been snickering, and their faces went slack. 'What?' I asked them.

Alexei grinned at me. 'Nothing. Each to their own.' Anja nudged him, and he looked sheepish. 'Sorry. About that small trouble we had down there. We just ... I don't know. The blondie is right. I know it was not your fault, and we should not have said you should be dead. That was wrong.'

'Fine,' I told them. 'Thank you.'

Anja nodded ahead at Dana. 'I guess your sister is pretty

talented ...'

'She is. Always was,' I agreed.

She was nodding. 'But you see, it's a problem, isn't it? The next time they wish to test us, it's one of us again, should it be a similar test. And you did fail, no?' she continued. 'You see this? It's all wrong, of course. It should not be like this, but it is. I want to be fair, but ...'

Ulrich's eyes met me briefly; his eyes were haunted and cold. 'He is after blood, not fairness,' I whispered.

'Damned right,' he agreed softly but ferociously, and I looked away from him.

I shook my head in regret, feeling cold. 'I had a fresh start here. Now I'm back to what I had at home. That's not fair either,' I told myself. 'Though here people are actually looking to have me killed.'

'We all had a fresh start,' Anja grinned. 'So did Ron.'

Dmitri leaned on me, holding my arm. 'You fizzled. You did nothing. And your sigil is different, no? Are you saying we should all die for that?'

'Hey,' Lex warned him, and Dmitri stepped back reluctantly.

'I said it's not my damned fault,' I growled while pushing Able up the stairs. 'Shut the hell up already. I don't blame you for having no hair."

He laughed. 'Well, that is our fault. You could blame us for it. We are bald because we used to get into fights a lot,' Dmitri said

happily. 'Best not have stringy stuff up there that can be grabbed.'
He leaned over to me. 'Yeah. We are sorry for saying that bit about
you dying. But you had better understand; we won't let that shit
happen again. What just took place? Never again. Your fault or
not.'

I grabbed Able's arm as he stopped to stare at the walls. I
tugged him along and climbed with him.

'Fine,' Dmitri said, looking at me incredulously and bent to
whisper to Alexei, and both shook their heads and laughed until
Anja slapped their heads.

I glowered at them, and they gave me blank looks bordering on
mockery. Nothing had changed. Nothing. I was awkward, on the
defensive, and now the people around me had a cause to fear my
faults. Dana might kill again. If I failed again, perhaps she would.
One bully tried to have me killed; others were hoping me dead,
laughing at me. Dana gave me a long, speculative look, her eyes
strange. Disappointed? Tired? Yes, I had failed again, and she had
gotten into trouble for it.

Why had she? For love, for her? She was different, and I felt I
knew her less than I knew Lex. Or even Ulrich. Him I could
understand, kind of.

We walked up another dusty staircase with wooden support
beams, and water was dripping and flowing from cracks in the walls
in thin rivulets. The staircase seemed to spiral up for ages. We

were soon exhausted and stumbling along. I tried to help the hurt Cherry, and Lex appeared to help me drag her. I eyed Dana, who was walking up the stairs, first of us, far ahead, just behind Bilac, first on any line, as usual. She turned to regard me again, and I stared at my little sister, a ruthless killer. She had possibly saved me. Perhaps, for we still didn't know if Able would have been able to weave a spell. She was ruthlessly determined The mask she had worn all our lives was gone, and I saw her in a new light.

I loved her. Still did. Or did I? Was she something I would learn to hate? Grandma had told me to find my own way. I looked around the group. It would be hard to do that, for they all hated me already. Save perhaps for Lex. And Cherry.

As if reading my thoughts, Albine appeared on my side, whispering. 'Let's forget about you. Tell us about her.' I shook my head and stared at Dana. She had killed for me. Should I tell them she had killed before we came there? Not for me. For her. No.

'She saved me. She is suffering, even if she looks composed,' I said. 'I know her. She's keeping a stony face and maintaining a façade of calm, but she is kind and generous. Has been to me, always. She is harmless as any of us.'

'You don't believe it,' Albine insisted. 'That she is harmless. Is she even sane? To kill so casually? You seem ...'

'Mad as well?' I asked her bitterly.

'A bit,' she agreed, and I heard Alexei giggling at that. 'Perhaps something that runs in the family?'

'Who are you to tell me what I believe and what is true?' I asked, growing angry with her.

'It's her sister, frog eater,' Lex said, exasperated. 'I'm sure she won't betray her trust, no matter how many questions you clobber her with.'

'Frog eater?' Albine hissed, the teen's face screwed in hatred. She nearly pushed Lex, then changed her mind and cursed instead. 'Harebrained pirate,' she hissed at him.

'I was a smuggler, Frenchie,' he answered darkly. 'Never saw the wide ocean. You damned kid.'

'I'm not a frog eater,' Albine pouted. 'And a smuggler is a thief as well.'

'All Frenchies like frogs,' Lex grinned. 'Seen it in Louisiana. Roast them, sprinkle them with herbs and eat them. I know.'

'Come to France, one day, you stuttering fool,' Albine spat. 'We'll roast you.'

Lex opened his mouth to lash back at her, but sighed instead. 'Hey, I don't dislike France. You helped us out in the war and all, but you are like a porcupine. Hard to get close to.'

Anja shook her head as she walked past Lex. 'We are all frogs, and she is right. Dana did roast him deliberately, and I too wish to know more about her.'

'It's over,' I told them tiredly. 'Let it lie.' I was sure Dana would

145

hear what we were talking about soon, should they get even a bit more aggressive.

'No,' Anja insisted, not giving up. 'You are drawing lines between us. We are open and honest. Take us, for example. Yesterday in St. Petersburg, I helped to set up the family store, like a good girl. Later, I stole vodka and drank an excess of other spirits in a strange tavern. Then spent the early night with a strange captain of the guards. OK? I do that. I sleep around. I was unhappy as hell, but still tried to have some fun. The 15th was bound to be bad, and so I made sure I was blasted and knocked out. Then my brothers fetched me, and I woke up to my face being stuffed into a wound of a dead man. Now I am being herded up these stairs by short, murderous women things with worms for hair. They also consider us scum. We are frogs. Likely they could sprinkle us with herbs and eat us too. That's what we are, commodity or dinner. That's what I did yesterday and what I'm doing now and that is all there is to know about me. Us.'

'So?' I asked her.

'So, there are no secrets here. None. Not between this lot. But *she* already lied to us …'

'According to a kid!' I said too loudly. I thought I saw Dana smile.

Anja continued calmly, 'And you are refusing to be part of the gang. This is a world where we have to rethink ourselves. Your sister did already. But she had better think twice about choosing my brothers or me over you. We wish to know more about her. It's fair, and she is not telling. We have to be a team to survive here.'

'As Lex said, you too would have done anything to save your family,' I told her as I helped Cherry hop over a wet stair. 'That's all there is to it. She did this one thing, probably in a panic, and I cannot fault her. She killed once for me, and I'm alive.'

'No, that's not true …' Albine began, but I glanced at her murderously.

'Right,' Anja said, eyeing Albine strangely. 'I agree with the Frenchie. There is more. And you are not right. Had they chosen one of mine, either of the bald idiots? Most of us would have talked about it first,' Anja said unhappily. 'Reasoned with them?'

'Roasted Ron would have been happy to see me dance around in flames,' I reminded them. 'He was not trying to reason and talk about it.'

'She's got a point, sister,' Alexei agreed with a grin, and I liked him briefly.

Anja sighed. 'Never said I liked the guy. But he didn't murder another one of us.'

Dmitri shrugged while picking his nose. 'When Uncle Andrey told us we might have a way to escape our miserable lives before we were thrown into jail, I for one didn't think it would be this weird. The Black Dolphin Prison is probably a dancing celebration compared to this place but had we been thrown there, that shithole, it would have been filled with people like her. Killers. Much less lovely, of course!' Dmitri shouted the last words and Dana, far ahead smiled down at us. Dmitri grinned. 'Shit. Perhaps I just saved my life. Perhaps she will spare me for the last. Even the pirate there sees she is dangerous and ...'

'I said,' Lex hissed, 'that I am and was a smuggler.'

'Don't matter,' Alexei added. 'You look like a pirate. Sort of salty and empty-headed.'

'Takes one to know one,' Lex spat, and I giggled. He went on, 'Coming from two petty criminals who look like convicts or escapees from an asylum, all this is pretty thick. Be careful, or I'll use those shiny, bald heads of yours to shine my rear,' Lex grunted.

'Yeah, we get the asylum thing a lot. Usually from street corner drunks,' Dmitri laughed.

'How did you end up here, captain?' Alexei asked Lex. 'Did you kill anyone? We didn't.'

Lex shrugged. 'I told them already. And no, I didn't kill anyone. Though I did drink the blood, and so did you.'

'You with them, then?' Anja asked him, indicating Dana and me. 'And not with us.'

'Is that the way you want this?' I asked, tired with the whole setting. 'You and us?'

'No,' Alexei answered. 'Didn't you hear us? We asked you to

share something, but you will not. Even we, the less bright ones in the family know we have to stand together. But you have to tell us about her. We insist, in fact.'

Lex spat. 'You Russkies look like you get your hiney kicked around a lot. Let her think for herself, at least for a moment. OK?'

A whip slapped on the stone next to us.

'Move it,' hissed one of the snake-headed females. 'You'll have time to fight later.'

Lex shuddered, releasing his fist and gave Dmitri and Alexei one last baleful look. He whispered to me. 'I wish I had come in two years' time and been spared this awful mad crew. Ten Tears. Damn. Such a weak name.'

'At least you know how to fight back,' I whispered to him with some jealousy. 'I was always just a rag for bullies. Can't handle them.'

'It's easy, just punch 'em until they shut up, or you pass out. Then rinse and repeat until they avoid you, either for fear or for pity,' he grinned. 'Damn, but I wish my uncle had told me more about this. But likely he thought we would be served a banquet and taken to a luxurious spa.'

'I wonder if these shit walkers make life bearable for the bastards back home for luring us here,' Albine spat. 'They promised happiness and joy, and we are handed a fistful of shit.'

'Grandmother sent us here,' I said. 'She hesitated at the

thought.'

'Grandmother or not, you can never tell if they are really honest and cuddly,' Albine said with childish gusto. 'And you lie.'

'About what?' I bristled.

'About your grandmother. She did not send you here,' she said.

'How do you know that, kid?' Lex asked, bewildered. 'You keep calling people liars. Dangerous habit that.'

'She did it,' Ulrich grunted from behind. 'Your sister.'

I began to answer but shut up, glancing at the expectant Albine, hanging on my words. 'Stop hovering over me and help your brother,' I told her, aggrieved.

'What?' she asked and stared at me incredulously.

Lex was massaging his temples. 'We will work this out, later. Well, we are all in the same leaking boat and tired so can we stop fighting. Let her be. What are they?' Lex asked, looking at the deadly beautiful women following us.

'They look like the Medusa,' I said with a small voice. 'You know, from the Greek mythology. There are three sisters, they say, but these cunts seem numerous. I don't know, somehow not as deadly. Killers yes, but not … epic? I read about them in Father's books. He used to study classical texts before he inherited the estate.'

'I wasn't much for school and studies,' Anja crumbled. 'Told you. We worked in a store. Sometimes. Made a mess of it, usually.'

'Aren't they supposed to be evil?' Able asked.

'Yes,' I answered. 'That's right, they are evil,' I said as I placed a hand on his shoulder. I liked him, the least irascible of the people around me.

The Russians laughed softly if mockingly. Able blushed. 'They should be able to ... I can't remember,' he said.

I clapped his back in a conciliatory manner. 'I know. You meant they should be able to turn people to stone with their look. Gorgons are supposed to do that. Says the legends. There was a book—'

The Russians were laughing with tears in their eyes, and Lex looked embarrassed. 'Leave her alone, I said.'

'They hate me, Lex,' I told him. 'Nothing's changed.'

'Never mind them,' Lex said, embarrassed. 'Legends, eh?'

'We can hardly scoff at the legends anymore,' Albine said darkly. 'The Northman and the old Germans had a legend of the nine worlds. She mentioned the Nine, didn't she? And the Tenth. Our world.' I nodded. She was not ignorant, and I rather liked her, despite her calling me a liar every other sentence. And I liked Anja as well. She was right. We should be a team. Dana. She was my sister. Did she want to team with anyone?

'Silence,' said one of the women behind us. 'Two more stairways.'

Up the stairway, there was a simple iron door, which opened up soundlessly. We stumbled through, shivering with cold as a bitter gust of wind whipped through the room. It was a large foyer with a simple iron chandelier swinging in the wind. The walls had formerly been plastered with some red paint, but only fragments remained now. Some of the stones had been blackened. A fire had once raged in the place, leaving it a husk of its former glory. Another door led back down, one up, and there were doors that were open to outside, richly carved, wooden doors with leering monsters as handles. 'This is rather creepy. Not something one will enjoy,' Dana murmured as we saw eerie carvings drawn across ancient wooden doors.

The tall snake woman turned to address us. She was thickly muscular, her arms powerfully corded and her chest covered with heavy golden chains. The skull-like tattoo on her cheeks quivered as she eyed us distastefully, the snakes writhing angrily, echoing her mood. She grinned at us and nodded outside. 'This, Tears, is the Fanged Spire. The tower and the island comprise the Grey Downs and that is all you need to know. You were already told to obey. That means when addressed, you shall answer, "Yes mistress." That is likely the best answer to everything. Go and see for yourself and enjoy it, my urchins, for you won't go out for one year.' She waved her hand lazily. 'Go on.'

We walked to the doors cautiously. They swung in a light breeze as we shuffled forward. The sun was shining brightly in a blue sky, but, of course, it was not our sun, but some other star, and they had called it … Mar? Perhaps it was larger than ours, more golden than yellow. There was a balcony of yellowed and orange stone and a railing of finely twisted iron. We stepped forward timidly. We looked at each other, feeling clumsy, looking around for a danger. Only Dana was brazen as she walked, her arms thrust to her sides as if welcoming the strange sights. We reached the railing and stared at the vast horizon. Around us, an island of ruins, labyrinthine mazes of apparently once fabulous palaces and mansions and rundown buildings spread out. Some had crumbled and fallen; others had likely burnt and even melted. Pyramids and spires thrust up from amidst greenery and golden trees and white and gray rubble. There was moss and vegetation all over, creating a jungle-like appearance in some parts of the ruins, and we all felt it had once looked grand. It stretched far, far to the horizon, the once finest jewel in the world as Cosia had called it. I turned to look up. The white-bricked tower, the Fanged Spire was perhaps leaning a bit to one side, reaching the heights. It was round and squat and on the top, rounded with apparently a golden silvery cupola. Thousands of windows dotted its sides. Birds were flying around it, some huge and white, many dark and small, dipping and climbing, hunting for insects.

Around us, a sea. No, an ocean, I decided, not really knowing the truth.

It was dark blue mixed with brilliant green and gray, choppy with waves that rolled in an endless race to reach some far shores. Not unlike the Irish Sea, but vast, feeling more ancient and far deeper. The tattooed gorgon woman stood near us, staring across the water. 'That hateful sight, students, is the Dancing Bay. It looks peaceful and kind, does it not? In reality, it is where the Houses fight out of sight of their lords and the Regent and where the pirates of the Serpent's Run raid the shipping lanes of the north. There are no ships on the island; nobody sails here under pain or death. Some try, of course.'

She pointed down to the beach.

A wreck was beached on it, still looking sleek and fast, but rotting nonetheless. Others were scattered around it.

The woman continued. 'That's the last visitor to this island. Tried to rescue someone. Fools. As for the sea? Underneath those waves, there are creatures much like in your ball of filth. Were they not all from here? Yes. Yet, there are many other creatures here, those who never left Aldheim. What you have in the Tenth, my lovelies, your sharks, for example, are but little mackerels in comparison to these. I would not venture out there without a sturdy boat, should you get a chance, which you won't. Suffer, my young friends and learn what we shall teach here for two years, and your masters will decide what freedoms you shall have. Call this your home for now.'

'What is the Regent?' Dana asked, eyeing the sea, leaning on the railing with the wind whipping her hair. 'Or who?'

The snake woman regarded her and slapped the whip on her thigh. '*Yes, mistress*, do you remember?'

'Yes, mistress,' Dana said with a bow.

The snake woman laughed with a singing voice, and then she shrugged. 'You will take lessons, soon and get to know the worlds eventually, but the Regent is called Almheir Bardagoon. He rules Ljusalfheim, the heart of Aldheim, in the island continent of Freyr's Tooth. Freyr, who is the god resident in Aldheim. Or was.'

'You have a resident god?' Lex said in awe. 'Freyr? Yes, mistress.'

The orange snakes dipped in annoyance. 'You are an amusing one, are you not? I think I'll flay you and eat your skin, later. But I'll humor you. Freyr is a god. Just that, like any other. There are many. There is one true god to us all and the maa'dark are its true children. You have heard and seen it.'

We nodded, for we had and resented we no longer could.

She giggled. 'Ah, to lose it. I know, I know. But you shall use it daily here though not all the time. You will miss it like a mother, but meet it like a mistress. Be happy, if you can. If not for Cerunnos Timmerion, the fool who took to himself to make his own world, the manipulator of your race, there would be no humans who can see the Shades. Not all do, not even of the mighty, older races. So, you are rare and precious. And very useful to us.'

'Are there humans in Aldheim, and ...' Albine began but went silent.

The serpents hissed as the French girl looked down quickly. The creature was waiting for respect, and the idiot teen did not give it. The whip hovered in the air, and I moved slowly before the small teen. The serpent woman nodded in amusement. 'The Shades do not keep you safe, little one. It cares not for the saa'dark, or one day, with luck of the gods, even if you should be a maa'dark. What humans there are in Aldheim, the Shades care for even less. They live, they breed and rule their own, but they obey. Like you will.'

'Will we meet them, mistress?' I asked. 'The gods?'

She laughed with her sing-song voice and smiled when she was done, shaking with mirth. 'You? No. Why would they meet worms? And the ways are broken, sundered, and there are no gods in Aldheim. His Highness Almheir of House Bardagoon is the Regent, did I not tell you? Forget the gods.'

'Is Almheir a human?' Anja asked unwisely. 'Like us?'

Mistress stared at us in stupefaction, shocked enough not to punish her for omitting the words of respect. 'Human? I just told you. Humans obey. How dare you? You are slaves and useful soldiers. You are the youngest and least graceful of the many races. You must learn this quickly and save yourself some pain.'

'Never,' Albine said stubbornly and moved away from me. The snake female's yellow eyes went to slits, the whip went up and came down, in an eye blink, and I could not help her. Albine screamed and held her face, sobbing and struggling to stand up, and I grabbed her to me, glowering at the violent female.

'You call me Mistress Bilac,' the savage creature spat. 'The Fury Whip Bilac of the Dark Water Clan. We have a gallery for you young lordlings and ladies. Tomorrow we shall begin. It will be hard. Very hard. You will be sorely tested. Every single day, each moment of your sorry lives. Do well, you suffer less. Ask few questions and be patient and happy, or not and suffer pain and punishment. You will see human life is expendable across the Nine, even in Midgard, where your race was born. It is so in your sad colony as well, the cuss pit you hail from, the Tenth. You have seen it. Your race is a mess.' She pointed her whip back inside, and we all turned to go, as I was supporting Albine.

'Help her,' I whispered to Able, who just looked away, and so I cursed him, toiled with Lex, and we half-carried her inside. 'You damned idiots, help me,' I told Dmitri. The Russians were shaking their heads incredulously at us, and I cursed them too. Dana was the last to come and turned to look at the sea, her eyes calculating, brave, free, despite our obvious helplessness. She was making plans, perhaps thinking where she would one day pitch her palace.

The women pointed us to the staircase leading up the Fanged Spire, and they climbed before and after us in silent guardianship. Their yellow eyes glared at us as we made our way up, and it was cold going up the drifty tower, the walls glistening with moisture and tho few torches burning in sconces were sharing no joy nor warmth. They herded us along in the tight corridors, and then stopped us abruptly at the first floor, and we entered a room. It was circular, with old, water ruined paintings covering the ceilings, some high on the walls. There were no windows and some remains of wooden and stone furniture, old as age, the room apparently having been raided and robbed long ago. A small ball of light was burning high up in the wall, amidst the remains of the paintings strange and magical, apparently needing no care.

The room was not totally empty.

It had been converted into a gallery.

Inside were life-sized statues of humans with fantastically realistic expressions, figures by a hundred. We stared at them in stupefaction from the door, even Dana. 'The sculptor is pretty good,' she said.

'Like da Vinci,' Albine added.

'Bernini, perhaps?' I said and grunted appreciatively. She knew something of the art. Perhaps of history as well. I had read a book about sculptures, but she had probably seen the real things.

She glanced at me. 'I actually went to school, unlike the others. We were fairly wealthy. Merchants, you see.' Anja was frowning at the statues. Both bald boys were open-mouthed and wondering, taking small steps forward.

'Get in, girls and boys,' Bilac hissed and booted Alexei, who flew by us into the room. We filtered in after him and stared around. 'Where will we sleep?' Bilac mimicked the obvious question with her singing voice.

'Where shall we feed?' Cosia joined in and added the answer with a grimace of disgust over Bilac's shoulder. 'Here. This is it. You shall relieve yourself in that far corner.' There was some sort of a seat with a hole in it there. 'Soap is there, as well. Brushes for your teeth, paste. When you bleed, clean yourself dutifully with the towels we have provided.' There were no beds, only the cold floor. We were given neither beds nor sheets. Not even a blanket.

Bilac pointed at the far wall. 'That is where you will wash yourselves. Every day.' There was a large stone bath amidst the statues.

'It's empty, and there is ...' I began as I tiptoed to gaze at the far wall and the dubious bath.

'It will be filled,' Cosia interrupted me. 'Every evening, it will be filled. You will eat your dinner here as well. Quarrel, plot or even laugh in a way that displeases us, and we shall come to break bones. This is your home until you earn better. And you shall not hurt her.' She pointed a finger at Dana. 'I'll flail the first one to so much as push her. Endure your losses, Ulrich. There will be more.'

'And how do we earn better?' Dana asked, her eyes glinting with ambition. 'Mistress.'

'Be ruthless,' Bilac laughed. 'Just keep doing what you do.' They closed the door. I shook my head at those words and led Cherry and Albine, with Able trailing us to the corner, and Lex brought me the hem of his robe to daub Albine's face with. Dana sat near me, eyeing the statues as I checked on the hurt teen. The whip had torn her cheek open, and it was bleeding profusely.

Anja was slapping her hands on her thigh. 'You need help?' she asked me.

'Not sure,' I whispered.

'I have some experience with the idiots and their many injuries,' Anja said, but Albine shook her head at her. I kept dabbing the wound with the rag. Anja was walking around slowly, looking bored. 'Well, at least we have these statues to wonder at. Perhaps we can learn something from them.'

'We sure can,' Dana whispered. 'That statue has a similar scar as Albine does.'

I gazed at a figure of a young woman, her hand held out. True enough, it also had a whip mark chiseled on the face. 'Very lifelike,' Lex murmured.

'What the hell is your point?' Ulrich demanded of Dana. He got up, staring at the statues. 'You don't mean ...'

'It was once like us,' Dana said with a slightly nauseous face. 'This one has a bit of robe left.' The statue Dana was leaning on had a sleeve that was brittle and rotting as Dana tugged at it. 'They do care if we misbehave, yeah.'

'Stone?' Anja said, rising up to touch one. 'They can turn people to stone. Like Medusa, what Shannon said!'

'But we looked at their eyes and nothing happened,' I said, horrified as I stared at the statue. She had been fair once, then dead. I felt the urge to run around and stare at all of their faces, but held on to Albine and kept checking her face, swallowing panic.

Albine shook me off and grabbed the piece of robe, holding it on her face herself. Ulrich was up and running a finger across a man's stony face. 'These are minor demons, these women we are to bow to. They mentioned they serve this Shrouded Serpent Trade House and its mistress. I don't want to meet that one. We have to decide what we shall do. Die one by one or make plans to escape. We could have used Ron, he at least knew what he was doing.' Ulrich walked over and went to his haunches before Dana. 'Except for you. I don't want you in my plans. They favor you as if you were one of them. Are you?'

'They do,' Dana smiled dangerously. 'But I am mine alone.'

Ulrich shook his head. 'I'll not forfeit my life for killing you. Not now. But for my brother, there shall be a reckoning.'

'Rather him than my sister,' she told him softly. 'Soon, your brother would have chosen another if he could have. He was eviler than I am. As for your threat? I'll wait. And I shall think of Ron's face as he burned.'

There was a shocked silence in the room, and Ulrich licked his lips at Dana's baiting and wiped his brow free of sweat, a ferocious grimace on his strong face. 'Don't push it, bltch,' the large dark-haired man said brutally. 'For now, we are supposed to work together. But you are a problem. Untrustworthy. Dangerous as shit. Working for your own damned goals. Or your sister's wellbeing, seeing how she failed to call forth any power.' His eyes measured me as if I was a dangerous beast best killed. 'Likely the least useful of us, she is.'

Dana nodded with a dangerous glint in her eyes. 'She is alive. He is dead. They did not say we are supposed to work with each other. Indeed, it might be we are expected not to. Back off, Ulrich. Go and stare at the statues and decide if you wish to attack me. You would make an ugly sculpture, like an ape. Perhaps they would throw it into the sea rather than stare at it. If they don't, I'll sleep at its feet and titter at you.'

'Stop fighting,' Anja spat. 'That is what they want. Let the time pass, Ulrich. But know Dana, we will keep an eye on you.' Both the Russian boys nodded, their bald heads glistening in sweat. 'We saw what took place there. It could have been any one of us. Even if he deserved it.' Her eyes turned to me, gauging me, probing me to build bridges, to be part of the group. I looked away. Dana was my sister.

'We are murderers all,' Dana said with a small voice. 'Soon enough we shall all be killers. You'll see. If you don't already, you are blind.'

'And what was her spell about?' Anja asked Cherry, changing the subject. She came to look at the strange girl, who shrugged. 'You cannot speak?'

She shook her head.

'We are all a bit weird,' I told them defensively. 'Aren't we?'

Anja giggled. 'You sure as hell are.'

'Yes,' I said, used to that sentiment.

Anja grinned and swept her hands around in a conciliatory gesture. 'Don't worry. I am famed for speaking aloud almost anywhere, mostly to myself. People found it weird. My brothers ...'

'We got suspended from three taverns for fighting,' Alexei said happily.

'With each other if we found none bigger than us,' Dmitri added.

Alexei nodded. 'There was this one place, where priests and nuns ran a winery. We forgot to pay once. It was ran by this nun. She was fat but had a kick like a mule,' he said with a grin, indicating a missing tooth by pulling at his lip. I actually laughed briefly as he went on. 'Think we will save the fighting for some later time now. Damn, I could use some water. Or vodka.'

'Or beer,' Lex agreed sullenly. 'You have parents?' Lex asked Albine, who was tending her face. 'Hey, you. Kiddo.'

Albine turned her bloodshot eyes his way. 'No. Orphan. Only had our aunt, but she was wealthy. She was happy to be rid of the trouble of taking care of us, though. Forced us to go, not years from now. She was dying, she claimed, but I think she just hated us.' Albine's eyes turned my way curiously, then away.

'Sorry to hear that,' Ulrich said and walked around, still staring at Dana. 'Is she the only one who has killed?'

'Self-defense,' Dana said patiently. 'For my sister.' I stiffened, fighting the urge to tell them about Ferdan again.

Albine sniffled. 'Aunt killed dogs.'

'Dogs?' I asked slowly.

'Yes, dogs. Mutts. Stray beasts. Nobody said you have to kill another human. I guess your … mentors were ignorant.'

Lex grunted angrily. 'Our guide told me it was the way it had always been done. Then Uncle …' He shook his head.

'Guess they are ignorant bastards, then,' Able said as Albine hissed in pain.

'Don't talk like that,' I told Able, who shrugged, embarrassed. 'Not polite. My grandmother was far from ignorant.' They all stared at me and looked away. The Russians were snickering. 'Dogs, damn it,' I cursed and glanced at Dana, who just shrugged. Ferdan meant nothing to her, apparently. 'Why didn't Grandmother say anything? Not that it was wise to come here anyway.' I looked at my hand, glowing with twirling patterns.

Dana shrugged, her face unconcerned. 'She never liked Ferdan, you know. He was company. That is all. That's why she killed him for us.' I choked for her lie and saw Albine's face twist. Apparently, she thought Dana was lying again. About what part, I was not sure.

'I'm sure she did not know an animal would or could do the trick,' I said heavily.

Able was eyeing my hand. 'The others have a reddish tint in the shackles. Why is yours silvery?'

'I did something wrong, probably,' I mumbled. They all looked at each other. 'Your sister's face is in a terrible shape. I think it might have to be sown.' Albine stared at me as if I had rabies. They were all strange.

'Yeah, good luck with that,' Ulrich said, smiling weirdly at me while shaking his head. He glanced at Lex and Dana ferally. 'Tomorrow, we will know more. As for me? I didn't kill anyone to get here. Did anyone?' The Russians were shaking their heads, so was Dana, and her eyes scourged me. I opened my mouth and shook mine as well, feeling miserable. 'You sure, Shannon?' Ulrich asked, and I cursed.

'We are done with the topic.' I shrugged. 'Let's just concentrate on being afraid.'

Anja nodded with a desperate grin. 'We shall all fear. Every day of the rest of our lives, no matter how long that is,' Anja added. 'Damn, I wonder what time it is. I want food. How long is the day here, anyway?'

'Hope they feed us soon,' Lex agreed, eyeing Ulrich unhappily. 'I could use something substantial. I've had only that mouthful of blood to drink from our sacrifice.'

'As long as they don't serve us Ron,' Ulrich said with a hint of ferocious rage in his voice. 'We will eat well, if we do well, no doubt. They said we are valuable.'

'Those that survive, maybe,' Dana said, looking at Ulrich with a small smile.

Lex crouched next to me, whispering. 'I'll take care of you. Don't worry.'

'I have always looked after myself,' I told him darkly. 'Or Dana has. But thanks.'

'In here, you might need more help,' he said helpfully. 'With your issues,' he added, looking bothered. 'And if you fail again? We shall try to help you.'

Next day, I could fail again. I likely would. And they could do nothing. I nodded at him in thanks.

'Goddamn, I could use a drink, a bottle of vodka or even some water,' said Anja, and we agreed, even I. We sat and stared at the statues. Ulrich and Dana began to walk them through, keeping an analytical eye on the dead and their details and on each other. Agony seemed to be the common factor in the dead, stony faces.

After what seemed like ages, Albine fell asleep next to Cherry and me.

'What is your last name?' I asked Able.

'Doesn't matter now, does it?' he answered sourly.

'Just curious,' I said.

Then, the door opened. It did so silently, almost shyly and very slowly. A face peeked in, then retreated. We shuffled to our feet, staring at the figure we could only barely see. Outside stood a squat, very short and fat shadow with a long, red cap. It stepped in and spoke, guttural like a mountain coughing. 'Well, well,' it rumbled. 'Well bless me but what a sad litter of pups we have here, all tears and no cheers?' It ambled forward, nearly tripping on its long, green beard and snickered to itself as it made its way to the tub.

'What are you, I wonder?' Dana said and smiled.

The thing twirled and put a stubby finger her way. 'What am I? Born of the stone, and hard are my bones. I'm a tomte.'

'A slave like we are,' Ulrich grunted. 'Like us, he has no boots.'

The creature stared down to his feet as if surprised by the claim. He had to move his ample belly aside as he wiggled his toes. 'It is true. They took my boots, tore off my shoots. And yes, I do serve the lovely ladies, straight from Hades.'

'They are beautiful to a blind man, perhaps,' Dmitri said unhappily. 'I once had a girl like them, hair so sticky with dirt it was dangerous to bed her, and I think I got a scar to show for it.'

'That was my girl, brother,' Alexei said dangerously.

'We share everything,' Dmitri grinned.

'Yeah,' Alexei agreed, 'She was poxed.'

'What?' Dmitri asked in panic, and I could not help but giggle. Alexei winked at me, and I didn't dislike them so much. It was that easy.

The tomte was shaking and purring, and we realized it was laughing. 'No girls here, only ears. Pay mind to be careful, young fools, in this most painful of schools. Keep your traps shut or your fingers might be cut. Now.' He ambled to the tub and waved his hands. 'Tap the root and the song, water will come along.' His hands glowed and the clear trickling sound of water filled our ears. We rushed to surround the tub, big enough for two, and wondered at the spring that was indeed filling the tub. The tomte was grinning to himself, his enormous wart-ridden nose shaking and his hulking shoulders heaving with pleasure.

'Skillful, mad thing, no?' Dana grinned.

'Like you, perhaps,' Anja agreed while thrilled as Dana stared at her dangerously.

'Beware, Dana, that you shall not drown in there,' Ulrich muttered.

The tomte growled unmistakably. He poked Ulrich in the belly, and the large young man huffed and folded in two. The tomte wiggled its fingers over him. 'Spell I have, one for warts, perhaps I should let it bloom in your nose, or in your ugly toes?' The tomte was not moving, apparently wishing for an answer from Ulrich.

Ulrich was shaking his head. 'No, I'm fine.'

The tomte grinned, clapped my back, and again wiggled its fingers. 'Nourish the beast and the man, slop for both creatures but no beer or mead.' He dropped something on the ground. A seed.

A tub grew out of the air, wooden and large. It began from the seed, green and small, then quivered and turning brown, it grew planks that entwined to each other. Finally, the tub spat out a ladle. A terrible, mucky sound could be heard, and we peered inside. 'My God,' Albine said in horror. Indeed, the tub was not empty. Inside it was a growing gray mass of slop and definitely no beer. It was the most unappetizing dish we had ever witnessed.

'What in hell's name is that shit?' Dmitri asked horrified; using the ladle to pull some of the gray stuff out of the tub, then let it drop with a sickening, mud-like sound. 'It is like ugly clay!'

The tomte grunted. 'Down in our home, the tomte love to feast, here we have to bow to the beast. Blame your host, lords, and ladies, up there she eats roast. It keeps you alive, even if you do not thrive.' He walked aside with his green beard swishing. The tub was full, the spring stopped bubbling, and Alexei whooped, tearing off his robe and jumping in. The tomte stopped as if catching an important thought. He pointed a finger our way, stayed quiet for an uncannily long time and then grinned. 'I would eat and drink before the bath if you can do the math.' He laughed hugely, stepped out of the door that shut with an audible click, and we stared at the now empty doorway, wondering after him.

'What the hell did he mean?' Albine asked. 'Math?'

'He meant,' I said, 'that the bath is also our drinking water. Nobody should bathe before we have had a drink ...'

We all stared at Alexei, sitting in the tub, a confused look on his face. A series of bubbles rose to the surface, and we tore him out of the water.

The sad excuse for food was terrible, tasteless, and strangely slimy and in the end, we sat in a circle and shared the ladle to use as a spoon. 'Not sure if we can find any common ground, but eating like this? I wonder if they are trying to make us work as a team,' Lex wondered. 'It's a bit like someone taking a bunch of retards into wolf-infested woods with a knife and you must cooperate or die.' None had an opinion on that, and I know most dreamed of even the most simple dish we had ever been served. Anything but what we had before us. 'Perhaps that tomte guy has some way of escaping,' Lex wondered again, determined to break the morose atmosphere. 'God, this is so bad. I want a steak. Or even proper porridge.'

'Yeah,' Ulrich nodded. 'He can summon a river to whisk him away, or perhaps so much food he can kill himself with it. Fat bugger, that's what he was. Whatever he was. I wouldn't share our thoughts with anyone we don't know.'

Dana shrugged. 'Perhaps we should forget the thoughts of

escape until we know what is expected of us. Or perhaps we should just cooperate with them.'

'I bet you would not mind that,' Dmitri grinned.

'Just be patient,' Dana told the man, bravely taking a mouthful of the gray matter, her face ashen.

'I'll go in first,' Anja said and got up, stripped and went in. Lex and even Ulrich, despite his sorrow, both gawked at the girl.

'That's our sister, you two,' Alexei said angrily.

'You pay us to stare at her,' Dmitri agreed.

'Shut up,' Anja commanded them. She hesitated, staring at Dana. Then she nodded at the Austrian. 'Ulrich, want to join me?' Anja asked, and the large man hesitated, stripped, and joined her. Lex looked slightly insulted, and the two Russian brothers mocked him with their long looks. I caught Anja's eye. She was making plans. With Ulrich. And Dana was not part of that. The rest scattered in the room. Cherry and Able walked with Dana and me, and to my surprise Albine followed us.

'Looks like they have an alliance,' Albine told us.

'Where do you belong?' Dana inquired of her sweetly, and with some dislike, for had she not called her a liar?

'I'm on my own. And I don't like the way they mock your sister. And for another reason,' she answered and looked bothered. 'But I don't like you either.'

'Fine,' Dana said. 'And you?' she asked Lex, who was walking over.

'I ...' he stuttered and stared at Ulrich, who gave him a baleful eye from the bath. 'I guess I'm with you. But you ... never mind.'

'I did it for my sister,' Dana told him slowly, sorrow thrumming in her voice, and even Lex nodded at her performance. 'It was not easy. But I won't roll over for them.' She shrugged her long hair to cascade down her shoulder as she gazed at Lex.

'I understand,' Lex said, apparently mesmerized and smiled as Dana's beautiful face beamed up at him. They took a bath together, whispering and even laughing, and I could only stare at my sister, who was playing to win. To survive. Or did she truly like Lex? Perhaps. He was sincere if not overly brilliant. While waiting for their turn, Dmitri and Alexei created a strangely tied ball of torn hems and began to kick it around amidst the statues, whooping.

'The dolts seem indomitable,' Albine noted sourly.

'They are carefree,' I grinned. 'I envy them.'

I was staring at them until they began whispering to each other. One shrugged to the other, and then they turned to us. 'Hey, you two.' Dmitri said happily. 'My brother was wondering if you would like to play. Especially you, redhead. Says you have nice legs.'

'Legs?' I asked him incredulously. 'Is he flirting? Or is he hungry?'

'Flirting. I think. I guess so,' Dmitri said as Alexei could not get a word out of his mouth, blushing. He went on. 'He is always looking for that special girl, but the girls know better. Don't worry about the dolt. How about we just play? You too, kiddo. Even the mute can join. But we don't give mercy.'

'You gonna play? Able? Cherry?' I asked. Both shook their heads. Albine looked away, a tear in her eye. I stared at her, unsure why she was so sad. In the end she waved we away. 'Nobody ever asked me to play,' I noted and liked the idea. 'I was always the last to be picked in any team.'

'We don't have much choice,' Dmitri noted laconically. 'But if it is any consolation, we didn't have any friends either. Real ones. Freaks, the lot of us. Save perhaps for your sister. She seems a survivor.'

'She is,' I whispered, staring at Dana giggling with Lex.

'Call it a truce?' Alexei said carefully. 'Something to do while not thinking about ripping each other apart. Let them make their pacts, and we just do what they say later?'

I hesitated and thought of Grandma, who had asked me to find myself. I ignored Dana's long look and got up. 'Fine,' I said. I avoided Ulrich's face as he was speaking softly to Anja. Tentatively at first, then with vigor, we kicked the ball until Dmitri hit his elbow on a statue as I kicked his legs from under him. He tripped me in his pain, thrashing on the ground, and I fell on his belly, making him throw up the unappetizing muck, and I laughed until my eyes ran with tears, and so did Dmitri. Even Anja grinned at that, gesturing for Ulrich to join us. He shook his head, his feral eyes on me. I ignored him and then even Lex joined us, leaving Dana hesitating on the side, her eyes full of wonder as she was drying her hair on her robe. I knew she had never seen me laughing with anyone.

I had fun. I had never had fun. And it all took place in a tomb full of dead, with people kicking at a rag ball.

In the end, the rest had washed, and I took the last turn and sat in the dark, in the cold water while others found uncomfortable places to lie in. All were silent, but none could sleep. The rags on the statues were stirring in the semi-dark, with some wind apparently managing to get into the room, but it was silent, so silent in there.

'I could use a mattress,' Lex groaned. 'This will kill my back. I miss my bunk.'

'If that is the only thing you miss right now, you are fine,' Anja said mischievously, and we all laughed, curiously enough.

We were divided. Ulrich and Anja on the other side. Her brothers with them, of course. Dana and perhaps Lex on the other. And me. But I had been happy that evening as well. I had people who seemed to like me, no matter what my issues were. Or on whose side they were.

CHAPTER 7

I dreamt of Grey Downs that first night.

Once it had been a mighty fortress and a city of ancient mysteries, and I stalked the hallways, all devoid of life. I glanced at the niches and nooks of the tower, and you could see hints and whispers of old glories. A chest, once etched in gold, and fallen jewels lay abandoned in the shadows of one cold hall, a frame of a picture lay elsewhere, dusted and broken, looted and burnt. Magnificent remnants of letters were still to be seen on the walls, haunting and carved long, long ago in stone, bits of golden and red ink were still evident on the cracks. Stones had been bared beneath ancient rugs and steps bore the marks of thousands of years of wear.

In my dream, I stumbled into a foyer of some lavish, furnished room. Able was sitting there, lecturing a hunched, fat figure. I stared at the bizarre sight.

'Now, it a slaver's hold. One that specialized in the creation of weapons,' he was saying with a voice not his own, rather more an adult than a kid. 'Know, that these arms were acquired from our world, Earth and our descendants of humans once given special gifts by Cerunnos Timmerion, the former Lord of the very hold they are imprisoned in. This took place at the age he, in his arrogance, tried to make himself the lord of the Tenth world and so, in a way, as high as gods. You know something of this, but not all.'

That is what Bilar had told us, I wondered and more. Able was smiling in a self-satisfied posture, like an omnipotent professor, his thumbs under his belt, and I wondered, for he was not wearing a robe, but a white shirt and even whiter pants. He rambled on. 'How this lord, apparently mortal had been able to do this, to grant some lowly humans the access to the powers of creation, is beyond us. Perhaps a spell or an artifact? What do you think, Shannon?' he asked. The hunched figure turned, and I saw Grandma's face.

I woke up, my breath rasping with fear and found Cherry eyeing me with her curious eyes, her thin face drawn nervously in a smile. 'Was I making noise?' I asked her softly. She shook her head, but her eyes looked beyond me. I turned to see Ulrich staring at us from across the room. We looked at each other for a while until he turned away and went back asleep. I noticed I had been holding my breath and fell on my back, trying to steady my nerves. Cherry was still up and I tapped her hand, missing Grandma, Rose, Mother, and Father. I was feeling miserable. Finally, Cherry's hand fell away, her breathing slowed, and eventually I dozed off again, drowsily eyeing the statues around the room. I kept wondering at their pained faces, surprised looks, their young age and wondered how many were still being sought back home.

Some, perhaps. Many, if they took some every two years. Perhaps there were other rooms like this. Gods knew how old they were, those unlucky failures, and my belly cramped with fear, for I was sure to be one. The others hated me. Well, no, Ulrich did, the others mocked me, and some I think liked me, and in my misery, I found I had more friends than I had ever had. Cherry, indeed. Lex, perhaps the two criminal Russians. Albine, sort of.

And Dana. I still had her.

But it would be hard. Had I not failed in most nearly everything I had ever tried to achieve? I snickered. No, I had never sought to achieve anything, not really. And now, the one thing I might excel in, one of the few humans who could do so, the very thing I had so longed for without knowing? Casting a spell and touching the fire to make a spell of ... Fury? Yes, Fury. Well, I was hopeless in that as well. I was one in millions and still a sad failure. I gazed at the silver Bone Fetter on my arm.

I let my hand fall slowly.

Dana. Was she always like this? Able to do anything to get hers? Murder? Lie?

Perhaps. I had always been too busy with my own issues to notice.

God, I thought and rubbed my hands across my face, we were in a fix. Gods, I corrected myself and giggled. The creatures imprisoning us were as remorseless as they were dangerous. They were practiced ladies of the Shades, skilled in arms and brutally adept in the art of terror. They could shut us off the power with an eye blink and likely they knew if we attempted something, watching us like hawks. They were gorgeous in body, inhuman in mind and face, and we were like babes in the care of beasts.

Who was their mistress? A master? No, a mistress, I thought. Surely not Cosia? Certainly not Bilac. They could herd prisoners around, all right, were deadly and dangerous, brutal trainers and merciless guards, yes, but someone had to run the Shrouded Serpent Trade House. And the Dark Levy. Someone had to be the keen brains behind the criminal outfit. Surely this imprisonment was a crime in Aldheim, in any civilized world?

Perhaps not.

I stared at the ceiling, at the shadows for the longest of time, mulling it over. Then, for some reason, I began to feel uneasiness. A shudder went through me, a forewarning of a danger. Just like staring at a light in a nightly sky and imagining it moving; I thought I saw omens of warning in the shape of fleeting, imaginative shadows. I wanted to get up, but despite the feeling of something dangerous taking shape, something I should avoid, I knew there was nothing I could do. I trembled in agitated fear, unable to turn away or even sit up. I gazed at one shadow in particular, one that was hanging near the roof. It was dark, so dark.

I held my breath. I was sure I saw it move.

And I was right, for it was then the shadow on the ceiling turned, slowly, spiraling in the air, one strand turning into a hand grasping at the stone above it. It was a tall and lithe shadow, a womanly shadow that wore a glimmering, silvery tunica, tall boots and a long, voluminous skirt. I saw, in the slight light of our glowing Bone Fetters golden bracelets flashing as it moved and then the face turned my way. It was cowled, but still, under the shadows, terrible eyes shone, bright and white, cold as winter. Those eyes. A shark has cruel ones. I had ever feared sharks despite what people said about the chances of being eaten by one. The truth is, you don't wish to meet such a predator while any part of you is underwater. And so, in that dark, I felt I was a wounded, bleeding bait, being circled by one. These eyes were intelligent, even if they were predator's eyes, accustomed to witnessing death and despair, and I tore my gaze away from them, wondering if I was about to die. My heart hammered in panic as the thing spiraled down to sit on top of a dead student's statue next to me. I stared doggedly to the side, cursing myself for my cowardice as I felt those merciless orbs scourge me. I twitched in terror as a multitude of long, incredibly long, writhing dark snakes descended on the floor, their tongues caressing my legs. They tightened around my calves and slithered under my robes, cold as ice, moving and thrumming across my belly and breasts until they seized my arm and exposed the silver shackle.

Then, nothing. For a long time, not a sound. I found breathing hard but managed to keep from whimpering.

Finally, I heard a hissing sound, and the snakes disappeared. I decided she was still up there staring at the arm I dared not cover. I gathered my strength, feeling the need to prove my worth even by a small measure of bravery, and I glanced up. I saw the lower half of the cowled face, a beautiful chin, smooth, red lips and fanged mouth smiling risibly. Her bright eyes were painful to look at despite the shadows hiding them, and I had to turn my face away.

I felt powers gathering around me, fell asleep and did not dream. I had wondered about the mistress, and I had found her. Or rather, she had found me.

CHAPTER 8

I awoke and remembered what had taken place. I stared at the ceilings of the macabre room, wondering if my dream had been real. Some dust had moved on the statue the thing had been perched on. That part had been real, unfortunately. She had been holding my arm, wondering at it. Likely she thought I was useless.

There was no place for the useless and the weak in the Fanged Spire.

The door banged open. Everyone shot up to a seated position, save for the Russian siblings. Bilac and Cosia entered.

'Breakfast?' Dmitri yawned and noticed Bilac's impatient grimace. 'Yes, mistress,' he said, kicked Alexei up, climbed to his wobbly feet and bowed with a flourish. We followed Bilac's whip, and it was pointing at the door. No breakfast.

We were herded downstairs where more of the snake-haired females lounged in the foyer, some dozen, all hauntingly beautiful save for Bilac, sporting myriad colored snakes. They all stared at us curiously, speaking to each other. They were agitated and quarrelsome, whispering softly but still it was clear they disagreed on something. One pointed at the door. It was open and a huge red moon hung in the sky as Mar was making its way up to chase it away with golden brilliance. We had no shoes and so the cold tiles and frigid stone sent burrowing stabs of icy pain into our bones, but Bilac's whip kept us moving. We were pointed down the stairs, through a different set of doors, next to the one we climbed up the day before. It looked dangerous, and we hesitated, but not for long as our guards kicked and cursed us to the delight of the other ferocious females looking on. We took many flights of nearly lightless stairs to a simple wooden door.

Bilac grunted. 'The feast.' The door shuddered and opened on its own accord, and Anja screamed involuntarily as the gate spoke with a deranged, high voice bordering on panic. We all saw a pale mouth moving inside the plank. 'Welcome, kings and queens of debauchery, to the feast,' it declared until Cosia slapped it and it shut up with a shriek.

We entered, Ulrich kicking it angrily. He had something against doors, apparently. We stopped to stare at the sight.

'Eat,' Bilac hissed, ignoring our timidity and pointing at the corner of the room. We stood on a crude platform, obviously makeshift and wooden though there were some parts of the old stone floor mixed in curiously. The area was spreading far to the left and right, and a wide and formerly grand stairway led down from it towards the dark. We followed her instructions to slouch on a slab of stone. Bread, some porridge, and water were served from simple dark bottles. The food was hard and cold.

'There's no tea, I take it. At least the water tastes familiar,' Anja grunted as she sampled it.

Cosia shrugged. 'This is your first year. You have to deserve the better fares.'

'Told you so,' Ulrich grunted gently as he sat down next to Anja.

'How long are the days and years in this place? Our years ...' Lex asked bravely while sampling the stale porridge. 'Mistress,' he added slowly.

'You were told to obey and to be quiet,' Bilac grunted. 'How many times ...'

'Oh, let us humor ourselves,' Cosia said, sitting on a slab of stone, leaning back. Lex's eyes stared at her full bosom speculatively until Dana slapped him, and I wondered what kind of an arrangement my sister had made with Lex. I felt jealous and cursed myself under my breath. Cosia's yellow eyes twinkled. 'Our day is a bit longer than yours, perhaps, and so is the year, but it is not that different. There are worlds it can be vastly different. Not so in Aldheim. Nor in Midgard. Your Tenth World and their days were molded to echo the days of these two. It is a pale shadow of them, of course, but there it is.'

Dana pointed a spoon at the two dangerous females. 'What is

Midgard, then, mistress?'

'Where your kind were spawned once. It was and is Odin's own world, though he grew bored with it, soon enough. When he did, they brought humans all over the place from that filth spawned shithole. Now shut up,' Bilac spat. 'Spare your strength.'

'Where …' I began, and their snakes grew alert and ready as they stared down at me. Their yellow eyes reminded me of those of foxes, preying on chickens.

Cosia shook her head empathetically and Bilac snorted. 'Ask. One question.'

'Where are the gods, then? Right now, where are they? And what happened to shut the maa'dark of our world out of …' I waved my hand around, indicating the power.

'Shades?' Cosia asked, and I nodded.

Bilac's orange snakes squirmed as she ran her hand over her tight belly. She made a throat cutting motion with one dexterous finger. 'One question. Only one, I said. But I forgive you, for you are fair.' She smiled strangely at me, and I shuddered at her words. She continued. 'There was a war, of course. All the doors are shattered, closed, locked and lost. The one to your Tenth disappeared with the Timmerion family as you were already told.'

'Ages ago?' Albine asked.

Cosia shook her head. 'No. This one took place recently, some ten thousand of your years past. Asgaard was sundered from

Aldheim, Aldheim from Midgard, Nifleheim, Jutunheim, Vanaheim. Muspleheim and Svartalfheim's gates are also closed. We are lucky we can still feel and hear the flames of Muspelheim and the ice of Nifleheim mixing in the Void. Only your Tenth is slightly accessible, at a given date of the certain year, for the gods did not build it. As you know.' Her yellow eyes flashed in anger. 'But Cerunnos Timmerion held the secret to that gate and how he gave men the ability to see the Shades, and he is ... gone as well.'

'What kind of gods are they?' Lex sniffed. 'First, they created the worlds? Yes? They created worlds. Then they lost them. How the hell do you lose worlds? Huh? Mistress?'

Cosia laughed and silenced Lex with a wave of her hand. 'Imagine you, children, a map. A hugely intricate map full of the finest of details, one you could examine all your life. Then, imagine many such maps, one within the other, on top of each other. You can go to one by foot, another by spell and nothing stays in one place forever. The gods explored the very best of the worlds they could find. There were so many, in so many places, so made by the Filling of the Void. There, they crafted and perfected the worlds to their liking, laying claim to Nine of the first and finest ones. And because nothing is constant, they built ways to them, combining all their skills and knowledge to make mighty gateways for all living and dead beings to walk across them.'

'Doesn't still explain why they lost them,' Alexei noted.

Cosia's eyes glittered as she answered. 'They grew complacent, lazy and forgot the maps and their plans and were happy to assume nothing would ever change and challenge them. But things change, and the mortals know it is so. Imagine, little ones, a treachery. One day, the gods find themselves shut in, the horn that opens and closes the gates stolen. They know their precious worlds are there, somewhere out there, but not where they first found them, and their maps are useless. All they can do is stare at the gates and curse the thieves. And, if they are wise, blame themselves for their carelessness. I doubt they do, but perhaps some might.'

Bilac grimaced. 'And the natural question now would be ...'

'Who stole the key?' I dared to ask. 'And what is it? This horn?'

'Enough,' Bilac said darkly. 'You are children and should learn quietly and patiently. Stop asking too many questions that only raise ...'

'What is the key?' Lex interrupted her. 'Come on now.'

'Last warning,' Bilac told him with a leer. 'You are a fair one as well, are you not?' she asked, gazing at Lex strangely. 'Would hate to mar you. Like I did the girl.'

I was startled and ashamed, for I had forgotten to check on Albine's face. She noticed my look, shook her head, and shrugged. It hurt. The face was infected and puffed, and she was not able to eat. Neither was Able.

'Yes, your slitherness,' Lex murmured, and Bilac's eyes flashed. Lex visibly struggled with himself and lost. 'Is it possible to make a formal complaint to the Regent about our treatment, mistress?' He grinned to show he was only half serious, but I prepared to have two patients.

Cosia grinned in return. 'By the Darkness. You are asking for welts. The Regent rules Aldheim. In name only and not this island. We don't consult him on anything.'

My sister swept her hair behind her back and jumped in. 'Mistress? What is the Regent? A slithering beast of some sort, a bulbous, fat greased lizard or something we might know by looks to be such a high, noble thing as to rule a vast land?'

Cosia shrugged, her snakes weaving around her head dangerously. 'There are men and beasts aplenty in Aldheim and both are crude and uninteresting to the higher people, like us, the Dark Clans. Make no such comments to your betters, girl. Slithering beast indeed. As for Aldheim? Elves rule the land. They ruled the Tenth for a time. They are shifty and treacherous, power-hungry and crueler than a bone breaking shark.'

'Elves?' Ulrich asked in stupefaction. 'The pointy eared things? Short and slim? There are stories of them in Europe.'

'Pointy eared?' Dmitri added. 'Nude and tiny!'

'No way!' Alexei chortled.

'Elves. The outwardly noble and beautiful lords of the land, yet indeed cruel things,' Bilac corrected. 'And they are just as tall as you are. And not nude! You do not believe in elves? Not even after witnessing our glory?'

Alexei spat and turned to Dmitri with a grin. 'They are calling elves cruel,' he whispered unwisely. 'Only a heartless monster would make us eat that slop served last night '

Cooia winked at him, and Bilac nodded heartily. 'You just lost the chair game. You know this game, do you not? It is an elven invention, though there is no music here unless screams and the slap of whips on shuddering skin and flesh,' Bilac hissed. 'One question; these were the instructions I gave you, and there has been far too many already. And you forgot the law of obedience and the proper way to address us. But you are understandably excited, and so you shall live.' She gestured and the air twisted and grasped Alexei, ripping him off the ground, his last bite of bread flying in the air. He screamed as the wind tore at him, spread-eagling him, and he flew to Bilac. It was the same spell used the day before, one of the ice and winds, and I felt it, knowing it well. 'Kiss, small brother,' the fiend said and pressed her lips on Alexei's, and the snakes bit him all across his face. He screamed in pain, and as Anja and Dmitri sprung up, Bilac's animal-like eyes followed them. The Russians did not move as Alexei writhed in her embrace, whimpering, then he slumped.

'He going to live?' Anja asked bitterly, her hands clutching her rope.

Bilac snapped her fingers, and the boy fell to the floor, shuddering, bleeding and dazed. He threw up, his face puffy and raw, marked by dots of blood.

'Is it poisonous?' I asked nervously. 'The bite?'

Bilac grunted. 'Yes. But you should be happy mine are sweet and orange and yellow. Not like Cosia's here,' she said, casting a baleful look at Cosia and her dark snakes. 'He will recover. He is paralyzed, the fool and cannot scream, but the pain he suffers makes him scream inside his head.'

'How will he train ...' Anja began, gazing at his brother in distress. I noticed Dmitri pick up Alexei's bit of bread and push it slowly into his own mouth. He saw me scowling at him, and he shrugged, swallowing the hard thing.

Bilac kicked Alexei so hard, her chainmail jingled. 'He won't today. Let him suffer there.'

'Today, the rest of you shall train,' Cosia said. 'As we will train each and every day.'

'One day, we shall no longer train,' Anja said coldly. 'We shall be free. Just pray we won't meet you out there. Mistresses.'

They giggled at her fury. 'Truly?' Cosia asked. She thumbed a ring on her finger. 'And if we do meet, you had better learn some powerful spells, girl, for such a battle is a terrible one, no game for children,' Cosia breathed, with pity. 'And we shall eat well if you do.'

'Did you eat Ron? Make a feast of him?' Ulrich asked darkly, casting a furious gaze at me and Dana. Albine looked down as well, sorrowful and pained, and I nodded at Able to go to her. He did not, his face nonchalant.

'Enter the feast,' said the door happily, apparently only concerned about ancient celebrations.

'Your friend,' Cosia snickered, 'roasted him far too well. We do not make soup of bones nor gnaw at marrow. Yet, we would have, had he not gone up like a torch. You will learn not to spit on rare dishes in this Fanged Spire, our tower, boy. Silence, or join him.'

Ulrich growled, trembled, and Anja placed a hand on his mighty arm. He looked at the hand and shook his head, indicating he was trying and remained silent.

Dmitri climbed to his feet, shaking and cursing, approaching Alexei. Cosia flicked her hand in approval, and so he and Ulrich dragged Alexei to the side. His face was swollen and raw, filled with bite-marks, and he was whispering weakly. 'I tell you, there was love in that kiss, fiery love,' he told them bravely as they reluctantly left him there. Cosia pointed a whip down the stairs, and we abandoned our empty bowls, all still starving.

'Go!' Bilac spat.

They guided us down the long, dusty stairs. It was gloomy and dark in the cold chamber. Cosia grasped at the Shades, plucking at the roaring Inferno and the familiar balls of light flew around us, burning over our end of the vast hall, hovering in place, a few of them twirling around each other. Parts of the floor had fallen down to the abyss, and the wind was howling through the holes. It was an old hall, the ceiling high as the hills, so tall, in fact, I found it hard to understand how it fitted in the tower. The depth of the hall was also strange, for while the fiery balls lit it well, casting shadows far and deep into the unknown depths, surely there had to be and end to it. It was like a stadium. It was, in fact, the remains of a feast hall.

And a feast.

The floor was full of broken, rotting furniture and burnt pieces of wood. There was a massive, still standing table stretching to the far shadows. Scattered on the table were broken vases, plates of curious sizes and shapes filled with bones and mold. And there were skeletons, parts of them, some holding broken weaponry; others still dressed in tattered finery. Some had heads, others not. One enormous skeleton was sitting on a rotten chair, holding its own head on its lap. Many others were lying strewn about the room. 'The old War Hall of the Timmerion family,' said Cosia reverently, then laughed. 'He made it less grand on his final hours. Sit.'

We sat, they kicked us into a line, facing the room, and we waited.

Bilac eyed us spitefully. 'You will be taught to respect the

Shades. You will learn to harness spells of Fury, to bring forth destructive forces with precision and savagery both. That is your function. Fire, and only fire, since you are limited so, and cannot grasp at the ice.' I stared at them briefly. I had grasped at the ice. I had. I barely felt the fire. Is that the reason I had failed? But I remained silent.

Gosia picked up the onnnah lii i liiiiils iii iliiiiy uunooo in the huge room. 'Casting such spells requires the right way of combining strands and streaks of the old fires, of finding just the right paths of braiding and weaving them all together. You saw this yesterday, vermin, when you were taught the simple business of calling forth a wall of fire. Some did badly, others did what they wanted, and yet others still did nothing.' Her eyes sneaked for me. 'Fire is a fitting tool for war, and we shall not teach you many of the lessons for the Gift, the beneficial spells, the ones for amusement and happiness. You shall not create fire dancers, flames of many colors, and the visions of the future and such. No. We shall not risk your lives to teach you such spells. I told you this yesterday. No. Only spells of Fury interest us and these you will learn next year, enough of them to make you proficient killers and, of course, you will have a spell of defense. You will meet maa'dark in combat, perhaps, who spend and waste their days wondering at the Shades, trying to learn many useless spells for such sport. It is a profession of many of the students in the Spell Hold, louts, to learn spells by fragile and slow experimentation. Gods only know how many and what kinds of spells there are available, and indeed the maa'dark of the worlds have only touched the surface. But you will be focused on a few and will know what to do with them. Do not stray.'

'I'd love to study the power,' Albine whispered softly. 'And not learn of the Fury. Only of the Gift.'

'Indeed,' Cosia said, 'but none of the Dark Levy are given the choice. None. You are the least of the races, the youngest, rash and the most foolish. You will be weapons and not scholars. That is all, and that is what you are suited for.'

'And elves are maa'dark, mistress?' Dana asked.

Cosia pointed at her with her whip. 'Yes, many of the nobles of the elven houses have the honor, though not all. And some commoner elves find the Shades and are then made nobles for the house they served. Also, there are many creatures across the Nine who are maa'dark, but no humans. You are freaks, thanks to house Timmerion's strange experiments in the Tenth.'

'So, if this is so, mistress,' Dana asked, eyeing the dangerous women bravely, 'then what use are weak humans to eleven nobles, who, no doubt, are far older, more skilled in deadly application of the Fury and the Art of the Gift? Won't we just fall like leaves, should we ever be used in war? No matter if they waste their time with useless spells. They do have more time to spend in study, no?'

Bilac grinned. 'Yes, if you were used in an open battle. They fight wars. There are a hundred houses of the nobles, and everyone vies to climb the ladder. Maa'dark are needed for their unique skills. You will know yours very well. And you have an advantage.'

'They don't know we are dangerous,' Ulrich grunted.

'Yes,' Bilac nodded approvingly. 'They don't expect danger from a human. Imagine a house your lord will attack, for whatever reason. You will be scruffy and carrying bales of hay, looking innocent enough, smelling of dung, and perhaps you'll drive a wagon. Then, when unloading such a load, you hide yourself amidst guards and slaves, and perhaps you will slay a critical enemy in the dark of the night, or clear a gate for an invasion. And still, after doing this, they might not know there is an enemy amidst them. Take this spell your rat-faced friend invented,' she pointed at Cherry. 'The stealth? That will be very useful.'

'We are to be murderers,' I stated flatly.

Cosia shrugged. 'Yes. Such as you are precision weapons, meant to perform tasks, useful in so many ways. You will have uses. When you meet spears and swords of your master's enemies …'

'Spears and swords?' Albine laughed, for apparently she was a slow learner or had a death wish. Perhaps her wound was making her delirious. Or, she was just a kid. Likely all of that. I grabbed her hand, and she shook mine off, twisting her lustrous, dark hair into an angry bun. 'A proper battery of Napoleon's cannons would blast your bones to the sea in an eyeblink. In seconds. A volley of musketfire would make you far less arrogant.'

Bilac stepped forward and slapped her so hard Albine fell on her back, holding her already ravaged face with shuddering pain. Able spat on the ground but was spared a slap. I stirred instinctively, but Cosia pointed a finger my way, and the message was clear, even if her eyes never left Albine. 'You invented such weapons when you lost the Shades. Your science took the place of the most sensible, rational part of your lives, your gods, and their magic. Scientists, politicians, and priests. Those witless, untalented wastrels mimic the power of the maa'dark, and they elevated science and false religion over magic to suit their own needs. Yes, we have heard of your technology and your fabulous arms, but take a thousand maa'dark and they could enslave the lot of you again. There are spells that would leave you blind, your weapons useless, and you the unhappy victims of simple swords. We live simple lives here, but the many wondrous spells of the Fury you could not handle, should you fight Aldheim. Consider yourself lucky, girl, to learn what we will teach you.'

'I don't believe you,' Albine said stubbornly, sobbing. 'Our lives are shit, and you call us lucky?' She was feverish, I decided, the wound on her face raw.

Bilac pulled her up. 'Life is shit, girl. Best make sure yours Is blessed with the occasional bliss of touching the Shades. So learn, human, for you are one of the lucky ones indeed,' Cosia said, 'Now, one more thing.' She eyed us strangely.

Bilac waved a hand lazily at us. 'As it happens, humans have another advantage over the elves. Some of you do, perhaps all, though not all find their specialty.

'We taste better?' Dmitri mumbled. 'In mint sauce.'

Cosia ignored him. 'Some of you will have skills. Not the spells some of you nearly discovered yesterday, but ... different.'

'We have never had any skills,' Lex snickered. 'Mistress,' he added.

'We are wastrels,' Anja said. 'Never been of any use, mistress.'

'That is true in the Tenth,' Cosia said, staring at us. 'Here, some, if not all of you have a special skill or even more. And these skills are strange and wondrous as if pulled from the Shades itself. The last batch of humans had a boy who could run through walls. We are no scholars of the White Halls or the Spell Hold, but the Dark Levy is often granted something useful when they arrive. And this is not something the Bone Fetters will block. It's ingrained in you. Perhaps this is something Cerunnos Timmerion did with your families, long past.'

'Could it be anything, mistress?' Anja asked, a small smile on her face.

'The Shades is the limit,' Cosia said. 'Who knows. Often they are little things, like this one girl who could create and control smoke. Another could withstand flames fairly well. Few are skills that are even more powerful and most are humbler. There are uses for any of them. Some will not find theirs, ever. Few have none, perhaps. So we will be keeping an eye on you. And if you discover such skills, tell us. It might make your time here more pleasant.'

'If I learn how to create vodka?' Dmitri muttered. 'Sure I will tell you.'

'Did the boy who knew how to run through walls survive, mistress?' Ulrich asked darkly.

'Of course not,' Bilac spat. 'He fell through the floor, and we only recovered his head. This is why we are training you. To grow you.' Bilac nodded at our thoughtful faces. 'So cheer up. It will be a painful road for you, yet, the maa'dark of this world do not have these skills. And so, perhaps, some of you are worth a ton of gold indeed and will find a place for yourself, eventually.'

'I wonder if Ron had a valuable skill,' Ulrich growled. 'Worth fortunes, perhaps?'

The females giggled. 'In truth, we don't care if he did,' Bilac said. 'His death was profitable as well, and we do not worry about losses and failures. We celebrate successes. So, we shall see. Not all of you will make it, and your skills and powers will die with you. Now, pay attention. Your lives will depend on it. One of you is gone. More will follow. The fewer of you survive, the higher the prize that will be paid, for they will be hardened and strong saa'dark. And so, you will learn to breathe.'

We stared at her.

Cosia waved her hand, and the globes twirled around us. 'You will train in weapons, dear friends, for even a maa'dark will sometimes be hurt and too tired to see the Shades and harness the spell's Fury. You will need to survive when it is so. This year, you will learn endurance. Stamina. You will learn to hold and gather power, so much more as to make a difference. For the maa'dark who can fight the longest is truly worth many of those who weave the mightiest spells only once.'

Cosia grinned. 'And so we will teach you.' Her ring glowed. Our Bone Fetters burned, and our heads filled with the power of creation. We witnessed the spectacular roar of the original fires and the grind and crunch of the ice and water, all cascading to the Void, where life was born. We touched the strings that made up the mysterious power; our hands and minds ran across the elusive force. It was a supreme effort to pluck at the power, the millions of strands and apparent chaos, for we barely knew what to do, and so we all just sat there, not doing anything but admiring it, drinking it, our eyes closed. I remembered all the spells I had heard and seen to the day and imagined how to pull them. The tomte's water spell flickered in my mind, the spell they used to push and pull us about as well, but this was when Bilac slapped her whip behind us. 'Harness the spell of Fury, grasp the fire as we taught you!'

I felt the others fill with the power, the firewall spell we had learned the day before, and I tried to grasp at it, as well. I knew the path, basically, pulling at the flame that was fiercely hot, only taking so much of it and tried to add heat and vapors, the roar and smoke to it. I pulled at all these elements, so far from me, felt sweat drip from my brow, but it was like pulling a dead horse, a bus with punctured tires, a weight so heavy I felt physical pain to my chest. I was dimly aware the Bone Fetters on the arms of the others were burning fiercely. Mine was silvery and still.

Finally, I let go and slumped forward.

Cosia crouched next to me, her snakes twisting around my hair and neck. 'No?' She raised my arm and looked spitefully at the silvery things. 'Inspire her.'

A whip danced on my back, and my eyes shot open with the pain. I screamed but power latched onto my hands and knees, and I stayed put. 'Grasp it, you useless bitch!' Cosia yelled. 'Can't you see it? Take it! We taught you this! The others can! They make mistakes, no doubt, but they can! Once taught, you can never unlearn it, and I guided you, Shannon, and I know you know the path!'

'I can't,' I screamed in pain again as the whip lashed across my shoulders, ripping at my robe and flesh. The others stared at me expressionlessly; sweat glistening on their faces. Most were displeased, I noticed, save for Ulrich, who was staring at me with a small grin, hating me for Dana. The whip flashed across my back and buttock, the end of the whip curling around my belly. 'Stop!' I yelled, but that only urged them on. And so it went on. It went on until I felt blood trickling across my back, and I slumped, half losing my grip on consciousness. The pain was terrible, pushing me to murky depths of agony.

Then I remembered the ice I had grasped at.

I heard the rumble and grind, so loud, saw the bright frozen rivers and pulled on the cascading ice. It was so close and joyously easy to take and pluck at, and I did what I had done twice before. It was a complicated weave. I was pulling at icy elements from the very edges of the Shades, then from the brilliant middle, deep inside the cascading ice and combining them efficiently and into a beautiful weave. The freezing ice filled me. It filled me with seemingly boundless power, and I released it with a shuddering breath. I felt cold shivers, like a fresh wind cleansing everything around me, and the pain ebbed away. Albine gasped and held her cheek.

Flames danced across the room crazily as the students released their power and gaped at me. Cosia waved her hand, the ring glowed, and the flames went away as they were all shut away from

Shades, and one of the burning globes hovered near me.

'She healed herself,' Cosia breathed. 'I told you so. She healed that one yesterday.' She nodded at Cherry.

'She healed Cherry yesterday?' Dana asked curiously and with a hint of challenge, though there was a tremor of fear in the undercurrents of her voice. I did not know it, but the whipping had been so harsh my back had been shredded. Pieces of sliced skin had been hanging down my back amidst the ruined robe. Cosia was pulling at the ragged, still bloody robe, her fingers running across my back.

'Smooth. Like baby's backside. What do you see when you grab the power?' Cosia crouched before me, her yellow eyes slanted with curiosity, the snakes playing and some entwining around my hair, keeping my head in place. 'Speak, or they will make you wither. They carry poison, girl, the sort you will regret for long hours before your acidic demise.'

'Mounds of ice, whirls of snow, glaciers falling, the tear of bitter winds,' I said, still held by the snakes. 'The fire is there, but far, far away.'

'Ice?' Bilac asked in a hushed tone, crouching and touching my shackle. 'Humans should not be anywhere close to the ice. None can sense it. It was devised so by the mad Cerunnos. So that's why she cannot do this.'

'What does that mean?' Dana asked with worry and suspicion. I gazed at her, terrified as I was bent on the ground by the air spells. I tried to calm her down, but she was frowning at me. Was she jealous?

'It means we cannot teach you. And that you are dangerous. And precious. She is the one,' Bilac said reverently.

'Yes, it is her,' said a soft voice from the top of the stairs. It had the same singing quality as did Cosia's and Bilac's, but it also had a power, a commanding presence that left you subdued. Let her be. She will attend me. Send her out.' We all turned to stare up the stairs, but there was only the door.

'Yes, mistress,' said Bilac strangely, softly. 'Well, I'm sorry, girl, but you will go up there.'

Cosia pointed at me while staring up at the door as well. 'Go and prosper, the awaited, special one.'

'What?' I asked as the female gave me a small bow.

'Special and the one indeed,' said the strange voice softly. 'And you shall not hurt her again. Unless she tries to escape.' A power rushed over me, and I was shut off from the Shades, left in the dark like the others. 'Come,' the voice coaxed me, and I turned to look up the stairs. I walked up slowly, my legs trembling, acutely aware of the many eyes on me. I passed Alexis, who was on his elbows, staring at me feverishly. He grinned at me with encouragement, and I returned it, for he moved his hands and head freely, smugly placing his arms behind his head, relaxing, apparently faking his helpless state. I had healed him as well. Cosia and Bilac were herding the others into a solid line.

Then, the door opened.

There, swathed head to toe in a dark red voluminous robe was a female creature. The cowl was alive; the thick, dark snakes alive under it, and some of them were slithering down her arms, across her chest, twirling and entwining her body, and around her waist. I tried to move my feet, but it seemed like terror was emanating from the creature before me, My heart was beating wildly. I was covered in cold sweat and fought an urge to kneel. She chuckled, her voice hollow and rasping. 'It is right, human girl, to bow before me. You are not the first mortal to do so, nor shall you be the last.' I did, and she stared down at me, measuring me. She was not as tall as the other snake women, the gorgons of the Dark Clans, but far more dangerous, it was clear. She seemed larger than life, wiser and ancient as the stone beneath my feet. She seemed inhuman, and I had a feeling she was a creature of both cunning and primal urges, and she was undeniably, without any doubt, what we would call *evil*. She was careless of morals and callous, I thought and I knew it before she had really said anything. She sighed and walked up to me, walking around me, a sulfur-like stench filling my nostrils. I was afraid, so terribly afraid for reasons I could not understand. 'I am called Euryale. It is just one of my names, but there are others you will learn of. And you are Shannon of the Tenth. And the Hand of

I ife. The first human I have heard of to hold that title. Surely the only one in the long history of the Nine and of Aldheim, especially.'

Hand of Life? She crouched before me, and I was forced to gaze at her. 'Yes, mistress.'

'Euryale,' she said, and her full red lips twisted into a smile. Her emerald green and icy white eyes were flashing from under her cowl as she gazed at me from the murky depths of her robe. I felt pain behind my eyes as she looked at me and I turned my face down from the eyes, but her hand shot out, icy fingers holding my chin painfully, and I kept my head up. 'A scared little saur you are. A doe, perhaps you know this animal? Yes, scared to the bone, to your sweet marrow, indeed. And that will not do. You must not fear so, lovely Shannon. You have a destiny.' She smiled, the full red lips suddenly feral for she had long, dreadful fangs. She shot forward and embraced me, and I shrieked. I felt her pulling at ice and frigid winds, twisting them together in a furious, violent way and a dark hole opened up behind her. She fell back to it, and the darkness swathed me in a cold grip. She held me, I twirled around with her. I was not sure if I was standing, which way was up and which was down, and finally I fell to the floor of a richly furnished, deeply cushioned, vast chamber. 'This is the top of the tower, the heart of the Fanged Spire, human girl. Once but a guard captain's abode, now my humble home. Sit.' Her long nail pointed at a plush chair.

'I have bled,' I told her with a small voice. 'I would ruin it.'

'Blood washes off, girl,' she said as she slid into a huge, leather-bedecked chair of her own, her shapely, powerful legs stretching out. 'Sit. I rarely have guests here and would not wish to seem unpleasant or unkind, nor a selfish hostess.' From her cloak, two pairs of arms flexed out, one grabbing a splendid goblet, another an elaborate, red bottle, a third thrumming its fingers on the armrest and the last one gesturing at the chair. Gods, she had four arms. It was the creature that had pulled us away from our former lives. She opened up her garment and underneath she was clad in a golden black tunica ending mid-thigh, entwined in silvery flowers. 'I will keep my head covered, girl. You have heard of the Sisters, no?'

'I have had history lessons, mistress,' I said, and I had. As history was the one thing I rather excelled in, and I knew about the three gorgons. 'Which one of the three are you? Or are you something else? You are a gorgon, I think, but ...'

She apparently smiled, lying back on the vast chair. 'Gorgon? That means terrible? Do I look awful to you?' She stretched her beautiful, powerful body, her four arms on top of each other on the armrests, except the one that was mulling the bottle and the liquid inside slowly, around and around.

I hesitated as I stared at the multitude of glistening snakes, swaying on her shoulders, back, and hips. 'It is not, perhaps, for a human to say what is beautiful and what is terrible in Aldheim. Yet, one might look like a rose and still have thorns. But I apologize for the word gorgon and shall call you ... a Sister?'

She snorted and poured the liquid into the goblet. She placed it on the side and grabbed another goblet, filling it as well, chuckling to herself. She gestured, my arms got goosebumps as the cup flew my way, and I had to be fast to snatch it. She gestured at me as if complimenting my reflexes. The silvery Bone Fetter was twinkling in the dim light, and her eyes were running across it. I noticed there were candles burning on the desk, not far. I was drawing deep breaths, keeping calm. After some time had passed and she was done with her scrutiny, she spoke, languidly. 'It has ever been so the Bone Fetters react to humans like this. Red is the fiery color of the power of the fires and should I put one on an elf, as I have, it is always silvery, like yours. Thus, I suspected you are the one.'

I nodded, holding the goblet, not sure if she wished me to drink or not.

She went on. 'As for the gorgons? The myths of the humans? They are fairy tales to you, yet they are echoes of the past, not just fables. You humans are creatures made by Odin and his brothers, and we were all born in the Void. What took place in the Tenth, I shall not speak of. Cerunnos made a mess of things, he did, and so now you people are divided and confused. Yet, no matter what myth you think of, be it Greek, Chinese, Mayan, Roman or Celtic, they all lead to one truth,' she said with a feral smile, tilting her head curiously. 'You have so much to learn if you are to serve us.'

I sat still and decided to go for it. 'I am confused by ... Aldheim.' I nodded at her desk, where fat candles were sputtering. 'Our world might be a mess, you have no technology. You apparently have no firearms and rely on the ... Shades for everything.'

She smiled. 'Shades, yes. On everything. I hear you hesitating when you call the power Shades. Not all the races call the power the Shades. It is how we see them, the ever altering streams of power. But the elves call it the Glory, for they are high-minded and noble, ever decorating their lands, houses and even thoughts to make life seem grander that it is. Others have different words for the Shades. Use what you will. I will not be offended. Just do not call it the Shades if you speak to an elf. As you will. They will not appreciate you if you do.'

'Yes, mistress,' I agreed. 'But ...'

She waved a hand, one of the four. 'As for Aldheim and its apparent backwardness? One of you had this discussion with my servants just now,' she said languidly. 'While we seem ... medieval? Yes, that is the word. Medieval to you, is it truly so your technology, your factories and ships and science and theories on everything make you mightier and happier? No.'

'I don't think so,' I told her softly and fidgeted, then spoke out. 'It does make us seem more intelligent, though. Or advanced.'

She laughed happily, her voice ringing with mirth. 'Ah, my! More intelligent, more knowledgeable? Have you not seen the Shades? The Shades is intelligence. The beginning and the end. That is the truth your ignorant scientists and priests seek. You humans! You have never heard of the Nine, and some part of you still thinks you are the center of the vast universe. Is that an intelligent way to go about your life? You know now, right now, more than all your priests and skeptical scientists combined.' She ̷̷̷̷̷ ̷̷̷̷̷ ̷̷̷̷̷ this world is no better than yours.'

'It's not?'

She shook her head sadly. 'Think of it this way. A world without the gods and the mighty ones, the lords of the Shades to hold the sway over the mortals, a land ruled by those who covet nothing more than power always ends up shattered and unjust. Some will have most of the wealth, much of the health, most of the land and the heaviest fist. Most of those who lack these things suffer and live in squalor. It is so in the Tenth, it is so in here. And I wish to change all that. We need the gods. We lost them, you see.'

'You wish to bring the gods back?' I asked her in stupefaction. 'Nothing more?'

She shrugged. 'Make no mistake, while I am one of the First Born, ancient and wise, I too covet riches and the hunt. It is in our nature. Yet I too wish to make amends, having caused some of the problems that led to the Sundering,' she said heavily, looking down, remorseful. 'Like it was in the Tenth and still is, war rages in Aldheim.' She leaned closer, her eyes intense, 'And should I manage to bring the gods and goddesses back, we could reclaim peace for Aldheim. Perhaps for the Tenth, even if the gods never visited it to begin with. Wars are decided with a spell and sword, the Old Way, the honorable way. Gods would see to it. That is not as they are fought in Aldheim and in the Tenth currently. Treason, cowardice, and schemes are the trademarks of the lords of these lands. Gods would bring justice back to us all, and conflict would be honorable again.'

I looked at her dubiously. 'As Albine said, I doubt they could take the Tenth. Our Earth.'

'No?' she asked with some mirth. 'Let us say the elves find a way and go and retake the Tenth. They would rebuild the gate and their armies, a hundred thousand, perhaps more would rush in to lay claim to the land, swords and spears glittering. You would prepare to fight us, attacking us with your many fiery weapons and yes, you would smash an army of a hundred thousand spears to cinders. Of course. Eventually. Yet, the truth is they would not march an army of spears against your cannons and muskets, no. They would send unseen assassins to slay your leaders, others to adopt their faces, for your leaders have no defense against the Fury and the Gift, and so they are like children. Then, we would turn one against another and should we really wish to fight a battle? We would send a few clever, shadow-walking maa'dark to turn your cities into burning husks, your ships into broken pieces of expensive junk. Your lands would be sunk mysteriously.' She leaned forward. 'Shannon, those who have nothing, the simple ones? The poor and suffering masses? They would adore us. They would worship the leaders we would replace and should the elves reveal themselves to the lands? Show their powers? The poor would love the maa'dark, worship the godly, mighty powerful ones like they would any celebrity. They would see stories and myths walking amongst them, we would charm them, and they would bow to us. Soon the vermin would accept a life without their silly, foolish rights. They would abandon the soulless ways and false beliefs. Science is a beautiful thing, but the Shades is the basis of all science, and seeing the masters of science at work would change their heart, yes. I would be a queen in no time.'

I grunted, not convinced. 'You? You started speaking of the elves taking the land and then you speak of your reign.' She leaned away, waving her hand at my question, and I felt uncomfortable, for she might be right. Such creatures could easily sway the masses of the poor of the Tenth. Of Earth, I cursed myself.

'Us. Elves. Anyone. I was speaking of bringing the gods back and the justice with them. Don't get stuck on semantics.' I agreed, not wishing to aggrieve the creature anymore. 'Drink.'

I tasted the wine carefully. It burned exotically and warmed my guts quite wonderfully, and I could not help but smile. 'Thank you. Mistress.'

She whispered, her green eyes flickering under the hood. 'You are welcome, my young friend. You asked me who I am. I told you my name already. Anything else you wish to know?'

'I ... everything. I only remember there were Three Sisters. Everyone, well, some know the story of the Medusa,' I said. 'And of Perseus. He killed Medusa, no?'

She smiled. 'Everything? That would fill more books than in yonder shelf.' She nodded at the one end of her curving room, where a hundred thousand books of various makes and sizes were swaying on the shelves before a tiny, sturdy desk. A glowing book was open in the midst of it. She snapped her fingers to draw my attention to her. 'I am Euryale, sister to Stheno and Medusa. I am the Queen of the Grey Downs, Hand of the Night and also called the Devourer by the elves. I have other names, for I am old as time, younger than the gods, but only just. I am a lost soul in Aldheim, most of all.' She looked down, I felt immense sorrow fill me, almost with throttling intensity, and I had to remind myself she was a slaver and a mistress of murder. She looked up, sighing like wind in a tunnel. 'Now I make a living here, this world that is not mine, not truly. I am a trader as well as a queen, of course. While I take pride in the fact that Shrouded Serpent Trade House is a wealthy house, feared and respected across the Spell Coast and the Dancing Bay, the northern straits even, and I suppose you might call us pirates as well, I am still unhappy.'

'Pirates?' I asked.

She waved one of her hands as if it was a matter of no consequence. 'Oh! We do raid, but so does everyone else, for the sea is where feuds are settled while the Regent holds the peace in the lands. I am not loved, Shannon, by the elves, but they tolerate me for they have no choice. I have powers they cannot overcome and so, some trade with me, as well. Particularly those in the south.'

'They told us you have no ships here,' I said.

'Pirates need no ships if they have me,' she grinned.

'You trade us,' I told her bluntly.

'Amongst other consumables,' she giggled and leaned back.

'Consumables? It is a ... strange world,' I said, clutching at the cup of wine.

'Strange, strange indeed,' she said. 'But not strange like yours, where only the dead know the truth.'

'The dead?'

'Those who die and travel to Hel's abode,' she told me. 'Your heaven and hell combined.'

'Devourer?' I asked her with a nervous voice, deciding to change the subject. 'What do you devour?' Then I cursed myself, for the subject was no better, likely.

'Why, the living!' she laughed, tapping her four forefingers on the arm rests. 'I don't feed on stone nor the plants. I eat the flesh of my hapless foes, and I hunt for the challenge, for what else is there for a queen to amuse herself with? Do not your nobles kill for fun? Your kings wage wars and dream of blood? Yes? While you named our kin for our errant sister Medusa, we are gorgons indeed, terrible creatures born of the Shades by the shores of the frozen Gjöll river, flowing in the freezing world of Nifleheim, home of the flowing ice. To see my soul, to gaze into my eyes, Shannon, is to gaze at the beginning. Few mortals can survive that.'

My head was swimming. 'Have you ever hunted in our lands?'

'In your Earth? The Tenth? No, it was Timmerion...'

'I know, the elven lord of this place attempted to make it his, his own world and took his people and slave humans to mine, and ...'

She snapped her fingers on all four hands at once. 'I see Bilac and Cosia are gossipers,' she said with some disappointment.

I nodded. 'You should punish them severely,' I said and grinned against my own judgment.

Euryale roared with mirth and then waved a hand at me as I was also chuckling. 'They stole me the pleasure of telling you this, but then, they did not know you are special or suspected it. But no, the Sisters have not visited it. Nor the gods. They sometimes quarrel over some world with the other gods and we have hunted these strange lands, but ...'

'Other gods?' I asked her, drinking the last of the wine, feeling the burn all the way down my toes.

'Of course, there are other gods. While Odin's ilk molded and claimed the Nine after they grew tired and bored of lounging in the Void, wondering at their powers, other gods have claimed their worlds, as well. Like the Vanir with whom the Aesir made an alliance. But there are many, many other first-born lords out there. The Shades or the Glory or whatever it is called by the thousand races is common to all the living creatures and those who can, use it for destruction and creation. Odin's god's rule the Nine, they made and molded this world, created the elves and the men and occasionally they do war over other worlds. That is their sport, and the hunt for glory and war is what they love. Your world, Earth, was rich in minerals, gold especially. Perhaps the gods would have eventually found out what Cerunnos Timmerion was doing, and would have come there, building gates and ways for themselves. As for the Sisters, we never went there, though, as you see, I know about the Tenth. The Dark Levy is what I created from the shreds of knowledge Cerunnos left here, his simple gate forgotten and lost. I dived to the stacks of the books full of elvish rituals and ways of catching you lot, and found that at that precise date, and if the priests whispered your names aloud, it was possible for me to reach through the space and time and take you.' She smiled happily, though there was not much happiness in the discussion. 'I would have loved the Tenth. For a time, at least. I would have hunted the races of men and elves and even the giants Timmerion was spreading over the land, happily I would have for no gods watched over them. There are, I know, still beings you humans would not believe exist out there in the Tenth. I think only a few of these creatures survive, hiding, occasionally feeding, waiting for the ways to be repaired so they can leave. Few humans remember the Nine. Children's stories, your seekers call them.'

'Seekers? You mean the scientists? Those people who dabble in all sorts of explorations and theories?'

'Them, and others. Storytellers, politicians, priests. Those who seek answers, mostly to bolster their own position and ego. The rest of you are just lambs,' she snickered. 'But I know the old secrets, and thus, you are here. As for Medusa? Our sister is lost, but it took place in the world of Midgard and yes, Perseus was real, but I doubt she is dead. This Perseus could never slay one of us. Not permanently, at least. It takes a god's weapon to do so, and no mortal can get a hold of one. But do not dwell on the question of slaying us, human girl, or I shall get suspicious.' She winked at me, and I reddened and bowed my head.

I took a deep breath and spoke quickly, blurting something unintelligible as my nerves were wracked. I stared at the beast-like woman before me and decided for the first time ever I had a real reason to be nervous. I looked around the vast room to calm myself. 'So, you called me the Hand of Life.'

'No questions about the gods, their mercy, and heaven? Usually you of the Tenth are so confused about your afterlife, you always deny my words and call all this nonsense, especially the parts about the gods and your past. You babble about your books and theories from where you came from.'

'You wish me,' I began, then straightened my back, 'to ask if there are gods, and they are merciful? Grandma told me they made us in their mold, but they are terribly flawed. So I just assume it is so.'

'Yes, they are,' she agreed with humor. 'Go on.'

'I'm going to assume we created the merciful gods in our own imagination.' Ferdan's words echoed in my mind as I aired them. 'We made them the image of what we thought right and worshiped an ideal we could not reach ourselves. I will also assume the gods care for their sport and their power, and they get bored and are grumpy like any. They are celestial beings and cruel. They are jealous of their possessions. Perhaps some are not, but most are beyond our understanding. I am like them. Afraid, angry, jealous and only sometimes kind. I'll expect nothing good from them, and so I might be surprised now and then, should I meet some one day. This is how I feel. Yet, you say they would bring us justice. Is that likely?'

'It is better to be ruled by bored gods than simple mortals,'

Euryale said, impressed. 'An omnipotent tyrant can make all mortal onoo seem small In comparison, yet a god is a god and you worship it, for you have no other choice. They might make things better for most, bring some light to the dark. At this time, I wish to see them returned. Perhaps it's a mistake? Perhaps they will remake the Nine, and not bring justice but sword and spell?'

I rubbed my forehead. 'What is the Hand of Life?'

The creature was quiet for a while, then ran her fingers across her arms as she wondered about me. 'First, you seem scared to your core, afraid of the shadows, terrified of the future, of your companions, most of whom think you strange, but that is nothing new to you, is it?' I shook my head. 'Then, you suddenly gather strength, tired of my games and deny a lifetime of lies and demand to know what I want with you?' She snickered. 'My, but you must be the one.'

'What, mistress, am I?' I asked her again, clutching the goblet of wine as I feared her answer.

She smiled ferally. 'You are a very special one, Shannon. One I have waited for a long, long time. You are the sole reason I have any interest in the Tenth, to be honest. I have been fishing for a myth and found it. All the ingredients of a miracle are here. You are a human Hand of Life, not an elven one, and the one who will help me.'

'I will?'

Euryale looked startled for a moment and then continued with a surprised tone. 'Yes, of course you will. You will do anything I ask. You will, for you fear for your sister as you should. Let us speak about what I need you to do,' she added. 'Drink. Ah, here.' She noticed my cup was empty and forlornly looked at the empty bottle. 'Does not matter. Fill up the cup.'

'What ...' I began but was interrupted.

'Fill up the cup,' I heard a gruff voice grumble, 'into a fine wine it will add up.'

'I ...' I noticed the goblet was full again. I gazed around and saw the tomte grin from the shadows, having filled my cup with a spell.

'Nox is a tomte,' she said with a languid smile. 'They come from another world, just like we both do and are especially excellent in all magic that nourishes and aids. He belonged to another, but now he serves me.'

'The slop he serves us is hardly appetizing,' I complained softly.

'Yet it teaches you to endure the misery. For usually the Dark Levy is a miserable lot, having lived soft lives inside a pampered shell. Yet, as for you, I think you will get a better fare here, with me,' she smiled.

'I shall visit you often, then?' I asked, dreading her inevitable answer.

'Yes,' she said, and I drank and went quiet.

She endured the silence as she looked at me calmly.

'I am not sure,' I eventually ventured, 'I would be comfortable eating well while the others ladle shit into their mouths.' Dmitri and Alexei would not hesitate, I knew.

'Ah, humans and their morals!' she said. 'And should you eat mutton in thick gravy here, drinking that,' she pointed at the goblet, and I felt guilty for that as well, 'then you would still have to eat your portion of the slop below, for you would not wish to get caught enjoying while they suffer, at the very least.'

'Perhaps,' I allowed, feeling shamed.

She leaned forward, her arms flexing under her ample breasts. 'So enjoy and eat both the feast and the slop. Yes. As to who you are? You are the first human I have heard of that can listen to the eruption of Hvergelmir, the tear and flow of the mighty spring of ice, the rime-crusted eleven rivers of our homelands, the eternal streams of Niflheim that feed the Void. You hear the frigid rush of Gjöll and the others, you listen to the grind of ancient ice and oh! It's so easy for you to grasp at the power. More, not only do you hear the ice, you see parts not meant for the mortals. Humans are exclusive to Muspelheim's fiery roar, most adept at the pure power of destruction and mayhem. You have a bit of god inside you, girl and so, I have a need of you.'

'Yes, mistress. A god?'

She breathed heavily, and there was a victorious gloat in her voice. 'Goddess, rather. A rare thing you are. Much awaited by me!

Understand this, Shannon. There are powers no mortal has mastered. One is the skill of the flight. We can pull and push at mighty, massive things, but none can truly fly across the sky like a god. We can travel, but not fly. The Arcane Council has studied that spell for millennia in the Spell Hold and with no success and many silly deaths.'

'We can fly in the Tenth,' I leered at her briefly and then looked down. 'There are these balloons.'

'*You* cannot,' she frowned. 'Your machines can. But there is more, and listen to me. Only the gods and some of the First Born in their infinite power and wisdom can reverse decay and death, and they know the ancient, original spells that were born with the time. These beings can see deeper to the Shades than mortals. It is theirs to control life and death.'

'But I ...'

'You, Shannon, bear this burden,' she said intensely, her eyes burning. 'As gods do not grant any of their creation eternal life, and as the elves, the highest of their creations suffer from maladies, injuries and are forever scheming against each other, then Odin's wife, the meddling Frigg bestowed a mighty gift to the mortals of Aldheim. She is a gentle soul.' She spat and sneered at the thought of Frigg, and I think I learned to love Frigg by her words, and so easy was it for her to restore my faith in the gods.

I gave nothing away, but just nodded. 'Yes, I see.'

Euryale continued. 'She saw the elves, quarrelsome, arrogant and thought to meddle in Odin's and Freyr's affairs for she loves the mortals. She bestowed a gift on one female, only one at any given time and primarily a female, for you and I both know, Shannon, that females have the wisdom males can only gawk at. Of course, two girls holding such power would make them terrible rivals, for women hate each other.'

I giggled dutifully, thought of Dana and myself and hoped it was not so. We would both have power in Aldheim, apparently.

She went on. 'She gave the power of wisdom and counsel and the miracle of healing to one mortal being across the lands of Aldheim. She decreed it so that this mortal female is to always counsel the mortal lord of the land, the jewel land of the gods, Aldheim. For while Freyr rules, or ruled the land, there was always a Regent, the highest elf of the First House to run the daily issues and solutions to the many ails of the mortals. So it was, and so she always stood high in the counsels of Aldheim, and she would be seen as the proof of favor to any house holding her favor. Indeed, she stood with the Timmerion House for ages in her armor of silver. One died, another was born, and so The Race was devised, for any house finding the new Hand of Life would rise to the lead. Yet, for millennia, it was the Timmerion's, every time. Since the Sundering and the fall of Cerunnos, the House Bardagoon, Lord of Ljusalfheim, where Freyr's Hall stands have held them.'

I was interested, despite myself. 'Cerunnos Timmerion was the last of the Timmerion clan?'

'Cerunnos Timmerion was and for thousands of years, held the Hand of Life next to him in high esteem, though I dare say she did not know about the Tenth. Now, of course, there is no House Timmerion,' Euryale smiled as our faces were very close. 'Now, there is something I need. Something only the Hand of Life can fetch me. And you happen to be that one.'

'How is it I am one? Is it because we came from Aldheim initially and are maa'dark, no matter our heritage? Because Cerunnos gave us this power? That only in the Tenth, there are human maa'dark ...'

'Saa'dark,' she reminded me. 'Yes, that was my theory, now fact. Humans of the tenth come from here. That means the Dark Levy are from Aldheim, some were altered to hear the Shades, they are maa'dark, and I was right, for they fulfill Frigg's pact,' she answered with a relish. 'The elves assume it must be an elf to hold this honor, but all the old texts I have scourged,' she nodded at her vast, high bookshelves, 'suggest Frigg gave this power to anyone of Aldheim at the time of death of the last Hand of Life, anyone who could see the Shades. Elves are arrogant, foolish in their arrogance and so; they are prone to make mistakes. I deducted it would be possible for one of you to be the Hand of Life. So, I went to work.'

'Work?'

'Yes,' she agreed with a fanged smile. 'Work. I created the Dark Levy as I told you. The priests still called out to Timmerion and the gods. I began to accept their calls. I called back on you humans, the ones still out there. I failed so many times and despaired. Centuries rolled past.'

'But if there is only one Hand of Life, that means one has to die in order to ...'

'Elves are long-lived. Far too long-lived. You see, the lords of the elves are forever competing at holding the favors of the Hand of Life. As I told you, when one dies, a frantic search begins, and it's a turbulent time called The Race. Yet, Almheir Bardagoon has been successful in snatching this personage to him for many, many times. I have slain most of them. Not all, but most. The last one died some seventeen years past, in the service of the Regent. The Race has been on for all that time though none dare challenge the First House and its powerful allies in the north, even in the absence of the Hand of Life. And here you are. You are seventeen. You can heal. You can miraculously mend wounds. And now, a mortal, a human has confirmed what I always thought possible. It is possible for your kind to have this mighty power, as well. It is incredibly rare, no doubt, for there are so few of you, but it is possible. You are Frigg's chosen. And you, unlike an elven Hand of Life, will follow my will.'

'What ...' I began to ask and shut my mouth and then opened it up again, 'You killed them? How long does an elf live?'

'The high ones, for thousands of years,' she grinned. 'Of course, I cannot wait for such a long time. So I am called the Devourer.' She leaned close to me, very close. 'I have had many fine kills while hunting for the Hand of Life. You wish to know what happened to the one?'

'Yes,' I said carefully, not daring to rob her of her apparent pleasure of telling me.

She tilted her head as if relishing the memory. 'I sneaked to her chamber, Shannon, in the deep of the night. They guarded her, of course, but even the elves have weak moments, they grow complacent and bored and develop habits one can eventually use to one's advantage. The guard died first. He loved a servant, and I used the servant to distract him, after threatening the servant with the loss of her family. Distasteful?'

'Yes,' I said softly.

She nodded. 'You have human morals. Perhaps that is useful, perhaps not. In any case, the guard and the servant died, entwined in passion, and I took the guard's face. I gained control of the room she was sleeping in, blocked the door, and there she was, on her bed. She was fair and beautiful, sweet as a young flower. She awoke to my presence and battled me, using mighty spells of guard to cover herself in flames and ice. She called spells of destruction to slay me. She did this for a while at least, destroying the hall but

224

not me. In the end, I left her head on her desk as I fled, and her heail was in her mouth.' She was looking at me with curiosity as if finding nourishment from my terror and unease. 'How does that make you feel?'

'I guess,' I breathed, 'you are one evil ... mistress. But I suppose that would mean the elven nobles you oppose are good and generous, and I suspect they are no better than you towards us.'

She grinned. 'Bitch? That is what you likely wanted to call me. You are growing braver. Take care not to become too bold. Yet you gave a sagacious, anciently wise answer, human girl. Nobody is kind to you humans. You are slaves, it is so and has ever been so. You rule your own, but someone always rules over you. Everything is subjective, Shannon. In the Tenth, you slaughter, exercise ruthless prejudice on the less fortunate of the humans and destroy nations and tribes you consider enemies because they believe in different stories. And yet, despite this evil, you can judge others.'

'Yes,' I told the beastly creature, deciding to keep the discussion simpler, despite yearning, burning to learn more.

'Now,' she continued, 'the Hand of Life is precious to the Regent. She is the gift of a goddess. She can heal ails and sorrows and such a gift can even make your enemy crawl to you. I saw Danar Coinar, the conservative, ruthless and arrogant enemy of the north crawl to Almheir Bardagoon to beg for his son's life after a war of the House Volant's succession. He begged and was granted his wish. The High Council of the Five always quarrels, the south blaming the north for many things they consider sins, the north, being strongest and well allied hold the south at bay. Usually, the Regent finds the Hand of Life easily and without bloodshed. This is so, for few families, those who find their newborn, have this unique gift wish to give her to the southerners, the Houses Daxamma, and Coinar, but rather to the splendor and riches of the north. It is for the Regent then to hold her on their side, trying to keep the precious gift safe from the evil of his foes and my clutches. Yet, the Hand of Life is unique in other ways than her power to heal and counsel. There is a great schism in Aldheim, and that is due to the Sundering.'

'Tell me about the Sundering,' I whispered.

'Soon,' she answered, placing a cold finger over my lips. 'It is so, that only the Hand of Life could restore the gods. The south, fervent in their religious madness urges the Regent to use the Hand of Life to fetch an item, a very particular item. The Regent fears to lose the Hand of Life. The Regent had been loath to let the Hand of Life take this dark road, keen to keep them alive and at his side. Only these holy ladies hold a spec of a godly power, they are the only ones who can enter the seat of Freyr, the hall of Ljusalfheim. And there is something lurking in that chamber, Shannon, something that caused all of this chaos in the Nine, and it still holds something I could use. We all could use. The gods as well.'

'And I am to go and fetch this thing?' I asked incredulously.

'Yes,' she agreed. 'Goddess Frigg had a vision the day she decided to create this great gift and it is known to me.'

'I am no high caster of Fury, nor am I even an elf. Should I go to … Ljusalfheim and be accepted by the Regent, the elven nobles even, would he let me try this deed?'

'I will make it so he has few other options,' she told me casually. 'And it will be very hard. But what else can you do? The gods are heedless and lost, you only have me, and together, we can restore the balance. The charge Frigg gave to the Hand of Life, Shannon, was to heal the ails of the land, and this ail is in need of healing. The hall is guarded, human girl and my friend, by spells that only the Hand of Life can pass.'

I stared around the room, my mind whirling by the many implications of her words. I would die. I was sure of it. I let myself get lost in the sight of the room. Many wondrous apparatuses lined the desks, some apparently unused, covered with a fine layer of dust, many statues leered or stared at me from the shelves. I spied the huge cabinet, made of dark stone, hosting thousands of small statues. Another like it loomed on the far wall and next to it was a covered, oval-shaped mirror. Euryale smirked. 'Many are magical. The Crafters made them thousands of years past. You are all I thought you would be. Curious and intelligent. I have waited for so

227

long for you.'

'While killing those human saa'dark who do not have my skill. Selling off to slavery the others,' I stated angrily though I kept my face away from her.

She nodded heavily. 'Yes. While slaving your kind to the elves is good business, I have ever hoped one day the Hand of Life would manifest out of the gate. It was my theory, and I was right. You can spare the others to come this fate. Perhaps you can restore their sanity as well if the gods return.' I often felt I had been one of the most shunned people in the world, and now a woman with snakes on her head claimed I would be a god-powered speaker for the elven world and could change all the Nine. And the Tenth. 'Are you all right, human girl?' she asked, with a hint of annoyance in her voice.

'Yes, mistress,' I told her with a small grin. 'I love irony, that is all. I am sorry. Are you sure of all of this? What if I can just heal and found a spell none have ever found before. Perhaps it is a skill? And now, I am being set up for something I will ruin entirely.'

She cocked her head at me, wondering. 'Skills are humbler things. Rare and precious, but smaller in many ways and usable even with Bone Fetters. Worlds are full of exciting creatures, some nearly as old as the worlds themselves. We were all born when the ice and the fire filled the Void and the gods appeared to create the Nine. Since then, none has healed, save the gods and the Hand of

Life. None. The others cannot see such depths of the Shades. Even I cannot. You can see powers you might think anyone can touch, but few can, in fact. So. There is purpose in this, Shannon, and that you can heal, it is beyond unique. But I do not trust even such odds, but ask the fates. Hear this. It is the old prophesy by Frigg.' She suddenly grasped something behind her chair and pulled forth a man's head. It was half rotten, the jaw was horribly burnt and twisted, the hair gone to the bone, but I saw it was Ron. I felt breathless terror as she was calling for powers, and I saw the ice and wind twirl in a somewhat repugnant way, touching strange vapors at the edge of the ice. She was hissing at the head, caressing the charred lips and then she gave it a dry kiss.

The eyes fluttered open, the tongue lolled out, and the face took on a confused look. Euryale smiled at me. 'The maa'dark, especially the elders like me, know many spells, my lovely Shannon, and your friend gave me some help as I have forgotten the old prophecy. He fetched it for me when I was chatting with it last night. Hear it.'

'He was not my friend,' I said with a small, scared voice.

The head was not offended, but spoke dryly and haltingly.

'The Eye of the Crow,
from Hel's face shorn,
the gods are gone, the Horn is lost,

both will be found at a great cost.

An awkward fool,

will dance with the twisted ghoul.

Cold-Hand shall find the tools,

and argue over love's curious rules.

The Pact of the sister is fulfilled,

the false god wickedly thrilled.

The Horn shall blow,

freedom for those below.'

'Silence, my dear,' Euryale whispered to Ron who was smacking his dry, dead lips, and I felt a moment of confusion as I nearly offered him a drink. It was a damned, talking head. 'Silence and be quiet. Sleep now, and go to Hel.' She kissed Ron's face again and regarded me with amusement as she lay the head before me, her delicate lips smeared with some repugnant blood and rotten flesh. She licked it off, and my belly churned. 'It is no Mimir's skull, no, and the hints it can give are tenuous at best, but this is an old poem. Tell me, are you an awkward fool? I think you are. Did they not call you such? That Ulrich? It is no coincidence. Hand of Life. Those are holy words, given by Frigg in her hall Fensalir when she gave a part of her to gift the first elf with this duty.'

I bristled at her amused tone and drank the wine to the end. I hesitated and leaned forward to place the now empty goblet on top of Ron's head, and she looked at me curiously. 'I feel the fool, sometimes, mistress. What is asked of me? Exactly. And what does the cold-hand mean? And the rest of it?'

She leaned back, looking strangely haggard. She waved a hand. 'The rest? Cold-hand? I know not, dear. We shall see. Consider it an adventure. And so, I shall tell you of the Sundering. The worlds are not balanced, girl. We are cut from the gods and it is so because the gods did not pay attention when they made the elven nations. The pointy-eared, black-hearted bastards wanted more than the Tenth. They wanted this world for themselves, as well. Or rather, House Timmerion, the First House of Aldheim, the lords of the Grey Downs and vast lands of the Lost East wanted it. Like they wished for the Tenth, so they schemed to get the grand jewel. Cerunnos Timmerion, the eldest arch-mage of the land, the first elf and slayer of dragons, the maa'dark of the First Light was not content with his splendid wealth. He sat at the feet of Freyr in Freyr's hall, in Ljusalfheim, the home of House Bardagoon, but he wanted the seat, not the pillow at his master's feet. It was his fault, his and his court's.'

'There was a war?' I inquired.

She nodded. 'There is ever war with the elven noble houses. There are thousands and most feud in silence. Other times the massive wars of the major house fill the land with death, but this was a different kind of a war. There was a war that began when Hel, daughter of the demi-god and giant-friend Lok was cast from the heavens and torn from her father's bosom to care for the dead in Nifleheim; a punishment for Lok's many crimes. Before that, she was a happy girl, a slip of a girl really, dancing in the flowery meadows of the Nine. She visited Aldheim, time and again and danced under Mar and the Two Hounds, our star and moons and was more beautiful than millions of stars on a bright winter night.'

'Hel? Truly?'

'Yes,' she said, and I noted a brief moment of grief in her voice. 'Then, suddenly, by Odin's wrath she was misshapen and unhappy, doomed forever to shoveling the rot of those who died ingloriously or of sickness. She was the caretaker of the mortal spirits and in care for the deceased evil and the despicable weak. Her flowers were gone and so was her dance. She was given death to look at, dead to care for, a bed of rot, a throne of skulls. There she sits, brooding and vengeful, mad, perhaps, ruling the rebellious dead and the reclusive ice tribes of the elder world of Nifleheim and oh, she is a queen most terrible in her anger. Then there was the business with Baldr, for Lok wished for revenge, for Odin's revenge, and not even the gods know where that started.'

My heart fluttered. 'I have heard of this. Lok killed Baldr by trickery?' I asked, intrigued. 'I think Grandmother once told me about it!'

The gorgon leaned forward. 'Yes. Lok was bitter to Odin for the insult of taking his children from him, even if Odin punished him in the first place for his meddling and scheming against the gods. In vengeance, there is no beginning, Shannon, only the end when one cannot retaliate anymore and gods, girl, can do it for a long time. Yet, a fool of a god, the blind one Hodur, who was fooled by Lok, poisoned Odin's son Baldr. None had time to heal him, nor to get to him. The Nine Worlds shook at the high god's anger, for Baldr's spirit did not linger in Valholl, but by Odin's own degree flew to Helheim, where those go who die ingloriously of age or disease. The bright god had not fallen in war nor bravely, for he cried in hurt and pain and soiled himself as he went. So, Odin sent Hermod, his servant to fetch Baldr back.'

'Hel must have enjoyed this,' I murmured. 'Did not Hel ask for all things dead and living to weep for the poor, beautiful god, and if they did, he would be restored?'

Euryale laughed gratingly. 'Oh, she did. I saw it. She made Hermod wait and seated Baldr so this could be viewed by all, still in his soiled clothes. Imagine the insult. So, when a giantess Thökk refused to weep for Baldr, Hel condemned him to remain with the dead, it did not sit well with the Aesir and the Vanir. No.'

'You saw this?' I asked in awe.

She hissed and then she was laughing. 'We saw it. All the

denizens and us, the First Born of Niflheim saw it. Oh yes, we did. And so, in our greed we agreed with what Freya and Freyr, the cursed Vanir sisters and rulers of this land suggested. We stole the Eye of Hel, also called the Crow's Eye. The one thing she treasured beyond Baldr's imprisonment.'

'How did you steal it?'

'She knew me,' she said quietly, looking away. 'She was misshapen, sad and alone. And I showed her compassion.'

'You were friends?'

'More!' she said unhappily.

'You pretended love for her?' I asked with a small voice.

'Pretended ...' she whispered, looking down. Then something changed in her, and she shook her head empathetically. 'Yes,' she said. 'And when she was not expecting it, I used her blade, the Famine to cut it off. I fled as she hollered in excruciating pain. I managed my escape, by magic and guile, and as Freyr instructed, I gave it to Cerunnos Timmerion, here in Aldheim for safe keeping. The gods were to bargain for Baldr and we were to receive ...'

'Riches and land here,' I concluded. 'Surely this place is warm and wealthy, more so than a glacier.'

'I hate the cold,' she grinned. 'And so, I took her eye. And fled the land of the dead and gave it over.'

'What did it do?' I asked as she shifted in her seat. 'The eye. Crow's Eye. For it was surely precious.'

'It allowed her to gaze at the realms. The poor girl was lonely, as I told you,' she said unhappily. 'The only device she had for seeing what she once loved, and I took it.'

'They reneged? The gods? No. The elves did, of course.'

She laughed. 'Yes, they trusted their foolish servants far too much. They trusted the Eye to Cerunnos Timmerion, their mighty Lord, the First Light, Regent of the land. Yet, the elf had other plans. There are masterful elven maa'dark, casters nearly as powerful as the gods and so they are arrogant. Oh, let us be fair, perhaps Cerunnos had a reason to betray Lord Freyr. After the theft, Hel unleashed a swift, brutal war in these lands, as you see when you gaze out of the window. Across many planes, in fact, searching for the eye. Many of the finest elven cities are built around the gates of the gods. In the east, the Lost East, the elven city of Aggarnor was surprised to meet the grinning legions of Hel's armies, Jotuns of Niflheim, white dragons of the glaciers and many other beings rushing through the gate into the heart of their city. Hel's minions and mercenaries sacked the whole of the east, then sailed across the Dancing Bay, destroyed Cerunnos Timmerion's hold here and were finally fought to a standstill in Himinborg by the valor of Cerunnos Timmerion, heading all the elven armies. Yet, the gods were slow to muster Asgaard, bent on negotiating while the elves suffered. Hel's minions burnt and killed and brought rime ice and bitter winds across the lands, leaving rubble, iced cities, butchered houses and burnt citadels in their wakes. Perhaps the gods enjoyed the spectacle? Yet, Hel was no fool to trust her armies. She sent her servant, the wily Ganglari to Asgaard, pretending to give Baldr back and by incredible feats of lies, Ganglari stole the Gjallarhorn of Heimdall. I hope they flayed Heimdall for his lack of care, the god of vigil. Faugh! That horn is the key to the gates. That horn opens and closes all the gates, dear. Ganglari stole it and had it blown across the lands and all the gates were closed, the gods trapped in Asgaard, the fools betrayed. All the gates were closed, save the one from Niflheim to Aldheim for Hel wanted to destroy the land, regain her eye and to keep Baldr.'

'And where are the relics now?' I asked..

'Ah, you have a taste for the old stories, you do,' she laughed. 'The elves still served Freyr, his sister Freya and even high Odin and on the god's behest, they made a pact with Hel she would get her eye back, should she leave their land at peace and return the horn. Oh, they met Hel's servant Ganglari outside Himinborg and that is when Cerunnos Timmerion failed. He dreamt of victory. Of more that the Tenth. Of Aldheim, one without the gods, who had been trapped. He held the grand, fabulous eye, Hel's fateful eye and stared at it and then he showed his true color. He refused to give it over. Oh, the rage! Hel sent the remainder of her armies, her giants and legions of the dead at the high walls of Himinborg and while the elves eventually prevailed, enduring significant losses, Hel was cheated again. The elf grew bold. He had even grander plans by now. Cerunnos now had the Tenth, Aldheim, and he thought of taking the war through the gate to Helheim, to Nifleheim. Finally, after petrifying losses on both sides, Hel had the horn blared and so the last gate was closed. So it stands today. The elf holds the eye, Hel the horn, and the gods hold the grudge, no doubt.'

'And you?'

'I?' she stretched, her many fingers rapping the wood mightily, the claws making small marks on the hard wood. 'I am stranded. Delegated to the role of a merchant. My sister is Hel's prisoner. We loved the gods, obeyed them and now, due to the elven betrayal, we are as sundered as the gates. The gods cannot reward us for our thievery, so we are also cheated. And the land suffers for the elves without the gods are like humans. Nasty and bitter.'

'If the elves could drive back Hel's armies, how is it you survive?'

She laughed, bitterly. 'Well, Shannon. I have a secret, one that makes me very, very powerful. They do try, occasionally, to bring the war here, especially if I have taken something of theirs.' She smiled. 'But Grey Downs is hard to take. I have sunk many, many ships around its waters, so many the sharks and monsters of the deep have learned the feeding is good on these shores. I'm more than I seem, for I have a secret that gives me great strength with the Shades. So they endure me, fight their own wars and trade with me when they need weapons to use against each other. Which is often. And I? All I want is to restore the gods. And my sister. And the gods' reward, for Freyr owes me.' She was moody and forlorn, seething in anger and then sorrow.

'I am sorry for your sister.'

'Sorry?' she roared, her mood changing direction like a wayward tornado. 'We are the night terrors, Shannon. We have devoured thousands of your kind, destroyed nations and kings of men across the planes and the worlds. I am the elf eater. The Devourer. We are not to be pitied. We are duchesses of Niflheim and beyond human remorse. But I want her back. And that means the horn has to be rescued.'

'From Hel?' I asked.

'From Hel. And she has to receive her gods cursed Crow's Eye, her only treasure, her fine eye in order for the horn to be released,' she said heavily. 'Then, the gods may return, punish the guilty, and I shall be reunited with Stheno. We shall find a home as we were promised, no longer a prisoner on this accursed rock, dealing with filth and slaves, eating elves and men I find boring to crack open anyway.'

'But how can one reach Hel, even if one is to find the eye?' I asked, ignoring the part about cracking open men as dread made me shiver. 'The doors are closed.' She disappeared, her shadow whisking along the floor and the chair.

She appeared at my side, whispering. 'There are ways, my love. But as you said, we shall need the eye.'

'And I truly have a part to play in this?' I asked incredulously. 'This is the duty the Regent is loath to give his Hand of Life? A dangerous mission? You said something is trapped in Freyr's Hall. Is this where ...'

'The Eye is in the hall, yes. For Cerunnos Timmerion stole something that belongs to the goddess of Rot and perversely, his trophy corrupted him. He is still there and so is his court, the ones he spared. He left many of his family to defend this citadel when Hel's armies sailed, getting rid of his mighty daughters, but he took his fawning advisors, and they are all dead and living both now. And none can enter unless they are touched by the goddess, charged with the preservation of Aldheim. And you are.'

'I am to go there and ...'

'You will dance with the ghoul, for it is an undead, terrible thing that has taken Freyr's Hall, and only you can defeat it. You, the awkward fool.'

'I ...'

'Shh,' she hissed. 'You are a healer, love. You, a human woman are the Hand of Life, a creature Frigg gave the elves as a favor, a healer and an advisor, though, in truth, little heeded, for elves love war. You will be loathed for your ancestry, but also loved for the elven Regent will have a need of you. Oh yes. Trust me with this. And you likely ask what you will receive, should we make a pact?'

'Yes, but surely I shall die!' I yelled as she grasped my chin, her fangs near my face, her arms grasping at my robe as she pulled me to stand before her. I looked away from the fiery eyes as her four hands gripped me and removed my robe.

I shivered as she gazed my nakedness up and down. I'll free you. You shall be the first and the only human saa'dark to be made into a maa'dark. You will be allowed to walk without the Bone Fetter, this magnificent shackle. The doors will be open, gods will fill the worlds and life will change. Perhaps we will find a way to send you home if you wish? Perhaps your muddy ball will again see the Shades and even the gods will find it. In short, you may go, you may stay, but you will be powerful and free. You will walk or you will run, at your own speed, exercise your own will, and go where you wish. And you may take your sister with you, yes? A sister for a sister, eh? Blood is all.'

'What do I need to do?' I asked, nearly pissing myself for her evil eyes were burning with maniac hope, a whiff of desperation, her breath reeking of blood. 'I am no match for a … ghoul, surely. Not even if it is blind and demented. I am powerless.' Her hands caressed my naked sides and shoulders, gently, and I could feel my heart beating against my chest.

She breathed her warm breath on my face. 'I will teach you what you need to learn. You will learn to hold power like your friends do, you will learn to fight, and you will be something, Almheir, the so-called Regent, will need desperately. A noble and wise Hand of Life you shall be, no matter your race. He will need you, and he will let you attempt to restore the gods, for times will be desperate, and he shall have trouble that can only be averted with the help of the gods. You shall begin the road by learning, by excelling in this power. Fail at that, and you shall regret it. And so shall your sister. Every day, you shall be here, and I will school you. When Almheir Bardagoon has taken you, you will find and retrieve the Eye of Hel, and I shall use it to recover the Gjallarhorn, and we both will see our sisters.'

I nodded. 'I agree to this pact,' I whispered.

'Ah, I agree as well. But I shall make sure you are also properly motivated,' she said and grinned. The snakes flew out in a threatening manner to surround her, looking like a living cloak of darkness, throwing back her hood and cowl, and for a briefest moment I saw those ancient, terrible eyes. She was a writhing, living beast of nightmares. Her mouth was impossibly stretched, like ours had been when she had summoned us, her soulless eyes were like fires of the hottest inferno, and I felt the outsides of my eyes petrifying. I wrenched my gaze away. She fell over me, her fangs tearing at my shoulder, and I felt drained, unable to even scream as I felt some part of me being whisked away. The snakes slithered around me, holding me still with brutal strength. I whimpered in terror and fear as she fed on my blood. I swooned and shuddered, fighting the urge to try to run as her snakes caressed and licked my breasts, but I refused to scream. Struggling would be futile, perhaps mortally so.

Finally, after minutes had passed, she was done, breathing hard, her face calm, and I turned my face to stare at the blood trickling down my breast as she straightened. I fell to a seated position, staring at my ragged shoulder and I swooned, terrified, weak and nauseous, to my side, feeling as if I was dying. There was a throbbing, seeping pain in my chest. 'What I gave you, Shannon, will one day slay you. It is called the Rot, and elves know it well. Only I can cure yours. You cannot, not that. It's as old as the gods and the Hand of Life has always failed in trying saving herself from it. I know for I have experimented with your dead predecessors. Why? I know not. But you can heal it from others. This I have also seen. And you will. You will see. Fail or rebel, Shannon, and you shall regret it. This is my pact, one not based on trust, but fear. Terror and fear of death have ever worked wonders with those who are too honorable for their own good. Now, heal the wounds. Touch Gjöll and her sister rivers and weave your spell. The Rot will remain.'

I felt the Shades were suddenly available to me, and I

desperately grasped the familiar strings and filled myself with energy, weakly and slowly, still in shock, but then I managed it and released it. The festering wound closed, but not all of it. I did it again, tired beyond exhaustion and did it once more, and felt the pain go away.

'Good, superb,' she said hollowly as I began to lose consciousness and saw her eyes glow. 'You will live, perhaps, and we shall all get what we desire.' She was grasping at power, the portal opened, and I felt dizzy as she traveled with me through the shadows and shades and finally lay me down in our hall. The creature disappeared through the dark hole, and I felt her pulling at the power, casting a spell as she hurtled into some other room. She cut me off the Shades.

What had she done to me? I felt my shoulder, it was cold and numb.

Yet, despite the terror of the creature, I had a mission.

.

CHAPTER 9

I slept, dreamed uneasily and woke when the others came to the room that evening. Dana ran to me, lifting her robe's hem. 'Shannon?' she shrieked. I rose from my stupor and eyed her as she crouched before me. The rest gathered around, staring at me curiously, Ulrich, with an unmistakable look of disappointment playing across his face, most of the others with doubt and bewilderment evident in their eyes and smiles. Only Cherry plopped to sit next to me, with a shy grin. 'You look strange,' Dana said, running her finger across my face. 'Sort of drained.'

'Who was she?' Ulrich grunted.

'That is our real mistress,' I told them weakly. 'And she will teach me for I am different.'

Dmitri grinned. 'She is right in that.' I gave him an evil eye, and he shook his hands. 'I mean it in a very endearing way.'

'In what way?' Dana demanded, dropping her hand from my face, and I stared at her in astonishment, for just the briefest of seconds and for the first time in our lives, I was sure she was jealous of me. She blushed and shrugged, annoyed. 'They said you hear the ice but not the fire and what does that mean? I cannot hear and see anything like that. None of them can, either.' She nodded at the others.

I gazed at Ulrich whose fist was balled. I shook my head. 'It means I have powers the first people of this land ... will appreciate.' I glowered at the large man, and Lex saw it and stepped in front of him. The two men stared at each other until Anja pulled Ulrich away. I shrugged thanks to Lex, who grinned at me affectionately, and I worried about him, for while he was brave and quarrelsome, Ulrich seemed the more powerful of the two. I spoke to Dana softly so the others would not hear. 'She has plans for me. The rest of you will be made ... *useful* in a more direct application of power, the Fury, but there is value in what I can do and so she is hopeful for the Dark Levy is all a sham. She profits from you, yes, but she wants more. She has been looking for me, for thousands of years. I fear her. She is a real demon. But I do not know what else I can do but to obey. I only know I can heal and that is unique. Well, I can do that somewhat. It is terribly draining to gather such powers and then to release them, and I'm likely doing it wrong and sloppily. There is a lot to learn. She will teach me.'

'What is the mistress like?' Alexei asked curiously, trying to hear what I was saying, for he had not gone with Anja and Ulrich and Dmitri pushed after him.

'You do not wish to meet the mistress, no, and do not ask about her,' I said with a shudder. I trembled as I thought of her face, as she bit and fed on me. Dana was thoughtful, calculating and she stared around at the others.

'And you hold the access to her, the gatekeeper?' Dmitri smiled, his eyes glinting. 'Are we to keep away while you play with the mistress? Suffer and starve, while you ...'

Cherry scowled at the boy, and I calmed her with my hand. 'No, do what you will. Don't blame me if you do not receive power and privilege, but pain,' I told him bitterly, massaging my shoulder. She had drunk my blood, for God's sakes. Why was the shoulder so numb? The Rot? I fought the urge to look at it.

'But she will teach you?' Dana whispered to me.

I leaned forward, whispering back. 'She will teach me. And it will be dangerous, not a party at all. I am doing my best. For both of us.' I sobbed and held my hand, and the rest looked disconcerted at my reaction.

Dana smiled widely and leaned so close the others could not hear her. Able came to sit with us, trying to eavesdrop, but could not, likely. Dana ignored him. 'It's you and me against the worlds. But we never did work well together, did we? In fact, you never worked at all. So now I am to trust you with my life?'

I clapped Able's cheek and smiled at him, and Dana glanced at the boy with apparent annoyance while the others looked uncomfortable. I shook my hair free of my robe, searching for words. 'I needed you, Dana. I had no other friends, only you. I loved you, for you tried to help me, and I know you loved me. I do love you, despite what you did, despite the fact I now sometimes wonder if I ever knew you. You never needed me, but here, now, we need each other. We have to learn how to appreciate each other. As equals.'

She smiled at me, glancing at Cherry, whose face was unchanged as she studied ours. Lex was hovering nearby, and Ulrich had gone to sit by a statue of some poor dead girl, his eyes never leaving us. Dana looked back at him and whispered. 'He is a paranoid bastard. Got to be careful with the damned, strange fool. I trust Lex. I suppose she is your lapdog?' Dana nodded at Cherry.

'I don't know what she is. Friend?' I suggested, raising my voice so she could hear me and gazing down at her. Cherry nodded. At me. Not at Dana. 'And I think Able here is fine with us as well. Not sure of Albine?' I stretched my neck to gaze at the dark face of the child, as she was sitting by the door, staring at me.

Dana shrugged and came so close she was hissing into my ear. 'We will see about ... them. Good. We have a few, Shannon, who will survive this, or at least help us to do so.'

'Dana ...'

'Us. First and foremost. We shall grow stronger as we go on, and it will be so that we shall walk out of this place. Trust me, you can do whatever she asks. If things get hard with this crew, you must trust me with the harsh decisions. You were always the one to wither under pressure, and I am not like that. You know this. Let us work together, grow and complement each other's faults. Obey me and we will be free.'

'I … We shall, Dana,' I told her earnestly. 'I suppose I have to learn. I suspect I will.' I rubbed my shoulder, wincing at the thought of the murderous she-beast. 'I shall learn to be …'

'To be practical?' she said gently. 'I was practical with Ferdan. He was the key, I turned it to gain our freedom from the pain, if not from servitude, and it gave us a chance at a new life. And it might all be worth it, Shannon. This is not home. This is a new world, and we can carve a piece of it for ourselves. Simple. Live or die. Remember that when we make our way forward, OK? We have to be strong, you have to trust me, and I have to … trust you. Even if you have ever been weird, even after we came here. Really weird.'

'I'll try.'

'Be practical. Like I was with Ferdan.' Her eyes flickered to Ulrich. 'And Ron.'

Ron's dead head came to mind and I took a deep breath and tried to forgive her, to accept her words as wisdom. 'I do not know if it was practicality or viciousness, Dana, but I will have to learn both.'

'Learn both, for we need to change ourselves if we are to survive,' she whispered. 'I shall share my secrets with you from now on, and you shall share yours, and it will be all right. And don't get too close to them.' She smiled at Cherry and the others and then looked deep into my eyes. 'Sisters.' She stared at me, and I felt angry with her for a moment. Yet, she would die if I failed. She had ever tried to help me. I nodded.

'Sisters,' I said and gave her my hand.

'Good,' she agreed, and we hugged under the baleful eyes of Ulrich.

The tomte entered, grinning at us. Under its wrinkled brow, I thought I saw some other emotion playing in his old eyes, likely pity. We stared as the creature ambled forward, filled the tub with clear water and served us another tub of slop. The rest groaned and shuffled over to eat the thing, save for Albine, who was miserable, and Able, who went to lay on his side by her and slept. The tomte shuffled past me, staring at me, and it stopped. It stood there for the longest of times as if lost until it smiled gently. 'Many secrets does the tower hold, up, and down, and far below,' he said softly. 'One day call for Nox, friend, and he shall guide you through to the dead end. I feed it, and you will meet it.'

'What?'

He left me gawking.

I shrugged and stared at the shadows all around the hall, hoping Euryale had not witnessed the event. Apparently Nox did not love her, and he might doom me as well, if he was not careful. Then I forgave the tomte, for I found I had a fat sausage on my lap. I smiled in gratitude. I thought of eating it alone, I admit but walked over to Albine and shared it. Able did not have any, sleeping tightly, but Albine did, eating ravenously, her misery less for a while, staring at me while I was nudging at her brother who just turned to the other side. So young. Kids. Lost both. They were so strange, never speaking to each other, and I guessed they must have gone through some terrible event in their history. Close and apart, both. We ate until Alexei whistled and nodded at me, and Cherry and I got up, despite Dana's words not to get closer to anyone. We kicked the ball of rag around vigorously, the boys giving us no mercy, and I took the bath late, only to find Alexei had not taken one yet.

'What?' I asked him, in the middle of undressing.

'Ah, well, shall we share?' he asked with a nervous grin.

'Why didn't you take one with Dmitri?'

'He is ugly,' he noted.

'He is your identical twin,' I retorted.

'His mind is twisted, I meant. He might be handsome as a god, but he is retarded and farts in the tub,' the boy said happily and undressed. I sighed and climbed in with Alexei, who was blushing vigorously, apparently attracted to me for some reason.

'What now?' I asked him as our legs entwined in the bath. I felt I was blushing as well.

'I can wash you?' he suggested and saw I was scowling. 'Your hair?'

'Sure,' I told him and dipped my hair to the water.

'I had a girlfriend,' he began as he washed my hair with water and some strange soap the tomte had left us, 'but she was a bit too stupid, to be honest. And greedy. I gave her to Dmitri though she didn't know it. Don't ask. We are twins, you see, and they don't know the difference.'

'This the one with the pox?' I giggled.

'No,' he said sourly.

'Are you sure she didn't know? His nose is broken,' I said. 'Perhaps she wanted to switch?'

'I ...' he stammered and glanced at his brother balefully, his hand in my hair until I splashed water on his face. 'She spent all the money I had stolen from Uncle, so perhaps that's punishment for him. She sucked him dry as well. I mean of money. Now, I have no girlfriend, obviously. But if I should have one, I'd be happy to share all I have for I have nothing, and there is nothing to spend it on in here anyway.'

'You trying to ask me something?' I said as I gazed at Lex speaking with Dana, and she was laughing. Lex's eyes met mine, and he frowned.

'I ...'

Gods, but Lex was handsome. I got up and placed a hand on

Alexei's. With some regret, for I had never had a boyfriend, I smiled at him. 'I need a friend, Alexei,' I told him morosely. 'But who knows? Later.'

'Thank God. Gods. Whatever,' he exhaled, a bit disappointed. 'I'm a terrible boyfriend. Probably would have gone for your sister in the end.'

I dunked his head under the water and then tore him up, for he stayed there and I had to cross my legs. I liked him, for, despite my awkwardness and their occasional mockery, he treated me like a person.

Dana and I slept next to each other. I stared at her as she snored slightly. Euryale had promised us freedom. Dana had agreed, and we would work to attain it. We had a plan. A dangerous, deadly plan, one that likely would get us both killed, but it was a promise, and it takes very little more to give one's will to live back.

Yet, I looked around the room. I stared at the poor child Albine. At Able, the strange boy who barely spoke and one I realized was even more shunned than I had ever been by the others. None had spoken with him, nor invited him to join the discussion. I stared at the strange Cherry, who was seeing nightmares, and at Lex, the stalwart, a foolish boy whose smile made me blush. I glanced at Anja, who worried about his brothers, and then at the two idiots, both of whom I called friends, for some reason. Alexei especially.

Curse him, for I had been tempted to say yes to him. And Ulrich. He had lost his brother. He hated me for it. I could understand him, at least sort of. He was hurt. Bitterly so.

Dana was the only one truly dangerous of the lot. And Euryale. And I was allied to them.

I tried to sleep, but it took a long time to do so, and what I saw were nightmares of Grandma, telling me to find myself.

PART 3: THE FLAMING HEART

'You know what I am offering. I say all or none.'

Anja to Shannon

CHAPTER 10

That first year we survived.

In the mornings, we would wake up early, shivering and cold, getting up under the stone eyes of the dead. Our predecessors were there; reminding us life is precious and happiness fleeting in Aldheim. The smart ones learned quickly to get up before the beasts got in. That was a useful skill as you had the time to piss and stretch. Ulrich and Anja did, I did, though never Alexei and Dmitri, who would have to hold their damned bladder all morning, complaining miserably about the problem until Cosia or Bilac gave in and let them relieve themselves. We would invariably shuffle down to sample the frugal gruel and soon, after but a few months not one of us held any extra weight. People had birthdays, which Anja somehow managed to plot for us, and the celebration was always modest. The one having it was given a spoonful more of slop and congratulations. I turned eighteen, and Lex giving me a kiss on the cheek was the best present I had ever had, I realized. The boys were growing long, scraggly beards, and Alexei's and

Dmitri's hair grew as well, and they developed a grudging respect for me, for I found I had a taste for practical jokes. While Anja was often their victim, I managed to steal and hide Dmitri's rope at least once, making him frantic for one night at least, terrified of having to go naked to the training. They played the vicious game with the ball of rag, once tripping Lex so badly he was sore for a week. Ulrich and Anja were close, and so were Dana and I, with Able and Cherry hovering near at all times. Albine still stayed out of the groups, silent and grave, and I let her be.

After a few months of this, seeing no one else but knowing there were others in the Fanged Spire, at least one class before us, our whisperings in the evening were those of envious people. If there were other people training on the other levels, students further along the hell than we were, they surely did not suffer as we did, at least from hunger. Occasionally, when we were allowed to see the Shades, I could feel there were others doing so elsewhere, near, not too far, but that was the only evidence of a life outside our seclusion.

I was special.

I would sit with the others in the War Hall of Cerunnos Timmerion and wonder at the wreckage Hel's army had done there. I puzzled over who the dead were, the daughters of Cerunnos amongst them, no doubt as Euryale had claimed. I wondered how they had died, and my daydreams never invoked sharp reprimands nor savage kicks the others received for their laxness. I was protected. I would massage my shoulder, wondering at the numbness and cold, but otherwise, I did not suffer the welts and pains.

While Bilac and Cosia were around, we made few jokes, spent little time risking the unnecessary punishments. When we could, we rested, even when someone was getting whipped or beaten for inevitable mistakes, for harnessing the spells of Fury was more exhausting and draining than anything we had previously known. The two females forced us beyond our abilities, often leaving us heaps of shuddering pain. We gathered the energies; we held them, gathered even more until our fibers were throbbing with pain. The aftermath of doing that often felt like a limb gone dead from the lack of blood, but the limb was your mind, and you could not easily remedy it. No. The excruciating pain just went on. For the two bitches, the brutal training was probably not cruelty, but a way of life, suffering as normal as farting. They switched or whipped the others if we did not grow quickly enough to meet their expectations and those expectations might change daily, even hourly. Ulrich was convinced they were schooling us for a very violent career, and we would be grateful for it in the end, but I did not feel grateful, or happy.

They were training us for war, that was true, and after Ulrich's words, I wondered what kind of a world we would see out there.

One full of ruins? Or wondrous and full of beauty? That is if we should live to see it. Euryale told me elves were senseless and cruel, and I feared them.

However, I feared her more.

I often stared at the Bone Fetter entwining my arm, the silvery, pulsing light holding us prisoners and wondered at Euryale's promises. She was a dangerous thing; old as time and few of her motives and thoughts were something a human would indeed understand. Her word? Worthless? Likely. She, or rather it was a shifty beast. She wanted her sister, the gods, and their cheated reward. Or something else, something more? She was not to be trusted. Cherry was. Lex, perhaps, he was straightforward and kind. Dana, was she? Perhaps. Our relationship grew as the months went on. She would speak to me, about things we had never spoken about, about the future and our plans for freedom though she did not talk about the past. We had acted all our lives and getting to know her was a curious, interesting experience. She was a perfectionist, that much I had known, but she used to have fun on the side. Now she did not. She did not take part in the discussions or the play of the evening, things that kept the rest of us sane. Everything she spoke about, everything she did, led up to her goals, and things she had planned for as long as she could remember. Now they were our goals.

She wanted to make it through the Fanged Spire. She wanted to be free. I gazed at her as she said that. What was free to her? Was it a roaming existence, learning of the worlds? Perhaps. Or was it something like Euryale wished for? Riches and power? All she spoke of was freedom. She held me close. I was the key to that. She was my sister.

I owed her. She had killed Ron for me.

I had been horrified by what she was able to do, but she had been loyal to me, despite her drive and issues. I would trust her to look after me in the future. I would do so as well, I decided. What else was there? For her, I endured Bilac and Cosia, hunger and cold and the constant snickers of the others, even if I loved them. Their mockery was painful, the jests still there for reasons I still could not grasp. Happily, they also liked me fine, most of the time. They were as much freaks as I was, in one way or another.

I said we learned to hold power.

We had seen hints of wondrous things, bits of magic, spells of fire and airy shackles. There were Cherry's disappearing act, Ulrich's fiery face spell, and Albine's cinder storm and I, of course, saw the spells Euryale had cast. In fact, I remembered all the spells they had cast so far, saw and quickly recalled the way they were constructed, but in the training, they demanded only one thing. Every morning we sat in a line, Lex, Cherry, Dana, and me. We were to the right of Ulrich, Anja, Dmitri, and Alexei, all gathering power, harnessing the spell of Fury. I called for the healing magics, wondering at the ice and the rime, freezing water and withering wind I was holding, Frigg's Gift. Hand of Life? Healer and advisor to elven kingdoms? I snickered. Hardly.

But we all learned to hold more and more of the power, and what seemed tedious and strenuous, limiting and insulting, even, was nonetheless as important as endurance is for a marathoner. We had the ability, the guts to dwell in the unknown, deep waters of the Shades, but we were children in the art of spell casting.

We had to grow.

That was to be our primary duty that first year. Bilac and Cosia kept us down in the shattered war hall for hours and hours. It was punishing in ways an outsider could not witness. We were always concentrating, holding and caressing the power inside, always to the very limit, then pushing the painful limit further and were not readily allowed to release it. It was like holding a dangerous serpent. It felt like walking a line above the clouds and ever so dangerous, for at some point you had to let go of the energy, and often you were too tired to let it go safely. Once, Alexei fell forward as he struggled, and gouts of rebellious fire burst forth, leaving Anja with singed hair and scorched skin. I healed her, and the others eyed me carefully, their faces expressionless, and so did the two lesser gorgons. I realized they all, even the jailers looked at me with respect. That was something I had never had.

The price for the respect was Euryale. In the afternoons, she whisked me away from the door.

She did what Bilac and Cosia did. She made sure I ate first, though. I had succulent meats with a delicious, salty sauce and a drink of sweet nectar after, but she was far more brutal than Cosia and Bilac. She pushed me, not by words, but by using the spell Bilac and Cosia had used, entering my mind, forcing me beyond what I would have dared. She pushed me to grasp more and more, to go ever further, and there were days I passed out in agony and I bled from nose and ears, for sometimes she went too far. 'You can do this,' she told me after I woke up, 'and you can heal the damage.' She would sit there and see to it I did, heal myself. 'I see what you do when you grasp the spells, to a point. You see parts of the Shades none others do. I was right.'

'Yes, mistress,' I would tell her. I did not feel special. I felt like a victim of a brutal assault. I would finish the food, push back from the food with scared jerks, and she would teach me. Every day. Yet, every day, I would hold the power of the ice, the tides of the frigid rivers. I would wonder at the sheer beauty of the brilliant power, wishing to see the nine rivers of Niflheim. Every day, with the others and with Euryale, I grasped the familiar spell of healing and held it though I was ever tempted at trying to discover new spells, new ways of pulling together compelling, interesting effects. I was hungry to probe and sample the power that was our birthright, but she would make sure I did not.

'First, you have to grow familiar with it. Do not dive into the dark waters, Shannon, before you know how to swim and even dive. Many die if they do, others live but are never the same again.'

'Yes, mistress.'

So it went on, for months until we could no longer count. We bathed in the evenings, endured the stench of excrement, ate the damned terrible slop, played with the rag ball when we had the energy, even with Ulrich occasionally. I spoke much with Able, wondering at Albine's silence and Cherry's glinting eyes and endured Dana's calculating looks as she stared at the people I had grown to like. She was thinking of ways to survive, and I was trying to remember we were to do so even at the expense of the merry Alexis and sad Albine. And Cherry, who was ever with me. We would occasionally play games before we fell asleep, and Cherry taught me to dance though we had no music. She had quick feet, and she showed me intricate dance steps, one foot shooting in front of another, then back. She giggled at my clumsiness until I got it right and rolled her eyes when I pretended fatigue was to blame. We also scratched a chess game on the stone and used pieces of rubble and wood to play though she was far better than I. I rarely stood a chance for more than thirty minutes, and even then I tarried to stave off the inevitable. She still did not speak but slept next to me, her hand around my waist while Dana was nearby on the other side. I would untangle Cherry's short hair as she did, wondering about her story. Able would sit and smile at me as I finally fell asleep, and I liked his gentle smile.

Gods, I prayed. Where are you?

They did not answer.

Then, perhaps nine months into the training, something happened and the routine broke.

CHAPTER 11

A t midday that day, I again heard Euryale call out. 'Come,' she said, filling the room with her voice as I was summoned to exit the door. Bilac pointed up lazily with her whip, and so I went. Only the door cheerfully greeted me. 'Enjoy your day, young mistress, and do come back.' I was tempted to slap the door for its cheerfulness, but I did not get a chance, for my mistress waited for me beyond the door. She would stand there in the shadows, gather strength, her four, powerful arms would fly to her sides. She would envelop us in the dizzying darkness of the portal, pulling me through alleys of mists and swirling night shades to her chamber. There she once again sat me down, and under her glowing eyes, she forced me to fill myself with the power, more power than ever before. She brutally took me higher and deeper to the power than what Bilac and Cosia ever forced on us. She ran a finger across my hand as I wept, her mind inside mine, pushing me and opening up my consciousness, and I felt older, fey and grim as the thing inside my mind hammered at my limits, painfully raking at me. When she entered my head, I felt the tingle of her intrusion, and I tell you it was not unlike waiting for someone to saw your foot off.

I hurt. Terribly so.

That time, while torturing my mind, even further than before she also spoke to me. 'You have enemies in your group. You have grown complacent and friendly with most, but the enemy is still there, waiting.'

'They don't, I mean, Ulrich does not ...' I said with a shudder, panic welling as I wondered at the power tingling inside me. 'The others mock me sometimes, but I do not think they would threaten me. Even Ulrich has been giving me some space.'

'Well, Shannon, you are a bit strange. You are speaking to yourself,' she said as she pushed at my mind, and I nearly howled, seeing white rime and ice and feeling sort of unglued.

'I don't,' I said. 'Do I?'

'Yes,' she agreed. 'Madness? But that is just delicious, my little human girl.'

I shook my head in denial, hazed by the pain as she forced me even further. Would I know I spoke to myself? No. The mad never do. Why had nobody said anything? Mother. Father. Grandma? Only Dana had told me I have issues. Is that why they laughed at me? Now Euryale told me? How would she know? Of course, she would, she knows everything.

Mother and Father. They had sent me to a shrink, had they not?

Gods, perhaps I was crazy.

'Hold it,' she said, seeing my turmoil. 'See? I tell you the truth when others are content to enjoy themselves with the entertainment of your small craziness. You do not have actors and theater in your chambers, so likely you are the best thing there is. After your games with the rag ball.'

'That is bullshit,' I said angrily, uncertain it was so. 'They like me.'

'Humans are mean little things,' she smiled, 'but think what you will, Shannon. Learn to love them, if you wish. Yet, doubt not there are those who think evil of you amongst those who smile at and with you. Fear him, and them all, actually. Even I have feared in my life. Such fear is an excellent and useful tool for a warrior. It teaches your mind to embrace every breath, to be cautious every second of your life and not spend a moment in idle enjoyment, complacent in false feelings of safety. You will die if you are not paying attention to your surroundings and people. Ever think about what is going to take place, if you let it. Manipulate your future, manipulate your foes. Your sister is like this, I think. But this, Shannon, the spell you hold? It is a weapon. Healing is a weapon indeed. Use it carefully, withhold it from those who hate you, use it as you would a hidden blade. Do not give the blessing freely and only use it if you are about to die. Now, hold it! A bit longer! And if someone comes for you, Shannon, fight. They think you weak, but I see you are not. The wise wait while the rash move.'

'Would they not ...' I asked, for the pain of holding the spell was making me shake with misery, pushing me to tears, 'be careful not to attack me if they thought me strong?'

She smiled. 'No, Shannon. Best appear weak, and then surprise them. The powerful always move boldly if they see a weakling. I remember once, a thousand years past, a time of some turmoil I enjoyed greatly when I was visiting Vaultar, a city for trade near Trad to the west, and there was a prince. This prince was an elf, and as elves go, this one was more arrogant than others of its hugely arrogant ilk. Imagine, lovely Shannon, a face so pinched in arrogance and maliciousness that you could not possibly picture a smile, a grimace of pain or even a yawn in that face. He had the eyes of a pig as well, for not all elves are beautiful, like you, child. A terrible thing that piece of offal. I thought I might sneak into his bedchamber and feed on him, just to see if he truly had no emotions, but I was robbed of the pleasure.'

'Someone dared to rob you, mistress?' I asked, cringing with pain, swooning as she pushed me beyond excruciation. I felt like I would piss myself, my brains on fire.

'No, child,' she chuckled. 'I was hunting him on the roof, eyeing his entourage traveling the muddy streets of the city. I was learning about his personal ways and limits of powers, and while I was flitting from shadow to shadow, an old man pulled a barrel out of an excellent tavern, the Mutton's Root. An elegant place, Shannon, even by the standards of the mortals, that tavern. Nothing like our halls where we lived once, of course, but it had a certain rustic flair I have ever enjoyed. The prince saw the man, an old man he was, his beard long and twisted, eyes rheumy, and he was struggling in the mud with the cumbersome barrel. The elf could have stopped if he had been kind. He could have gone around, had he been in a true hurry. But he was of a different sort. He kept riding, his face pinched like an over-ripe plum. The old man saw nothing from his toils, certainly not a prince of the House Daxamma approaching as he pulled the barrel over and the thing fell on its side, spattering the elf. Oh, he stopped his horse. He looked down at his dragon leather boot, formerly a glimmering, noble thing, now decorated with some red mud. I was sure he was to roast the man where he stood. But no. He pulled a spear. A shiny, sharp elven weapon. And dismounted.'

'And?' I asked, gasping in panic. 'I cannot hold this much longer.'

She chuckled and brushed my hair. 'You are so eager for stories usually, eh? Hold it! Well, what followed was simple. The elf wanted to kill the man, he wanted to bloody his spear for slaying is a thrill all elves embrace, but the old man was more than an old laborer. He was, Shannon, the retired champion of Grinning Blade Company, mercenaries of Himinborg, and the elven arrogance and disrespect for your kind would be costly for the House Daxamma.

The old man was brave. Even if he knew he would pay for the deed with his life and perhaps those of his kin, he did not flinch as the maa'dark approached. Then the elf died with that fine spear in his ass. He was kicking his life away in red mud as the sullen, gleeful humans stared. I was not entirely robbed, for he did look much less arrogant and very insulted, humiliated, and, of course, supremely pained, and so I did find out something about the bastard, after all. House Daxamma nobles die with a grimace, even if they claim they will never flinch in death.'

'What happened to the man?' I asked, white of face, the spell demanding to be released. My fingers were frozen, and I flexed them, and I could not see.

'They killed him, of course, and made the witnesses corpses. Yet, the prince was gone. Be like the old man. Look fragile, like a flower of the Barren Mountains and when their foot comes to crush your petals, let them step on you. The step will be experimental at first. They try you, test the resolve, and make demands of you, suggestions. Then, if you cave in, eventually they will try to crush you. They will either kill you when you do not expect them or push you to dark paths you should never tread. When they try to pluck your life away in these manners, Shannon, slash the offending hand and let them bleed to death. If they wish to attack you one day, like Ulrich inevitably will, best act subservient and let them think you weak. Do so, pretend, and you will finish the nasty business. That way you do not have to look over your shoulder for them in the future. Though, of course, there will always be others. Be friends with them, Shannon. Let them make suggestions and demands, but always remember to keep true to me. Release the spell! But not like you usually do, but at the chair!' She pointed to the side at an old, dusty chair.

And I did.

Icy tendrils of healing ripped from my fingers, dragging me to my knees as I emitted a stream of power so intense and swift the chair flew in the air, shattered to the wall and the fragments whipped crazily across the room. For a second, I contemplated turning the healing stream at her, but she snapped her fingers, and I lost the spell. 'Impressive. You held so much healing power; you could have killed with it, at least by pushing someone over a cliff. And you thought of doing that to me, no? It is in the human nature to contemplate on murdering those you fear and did you not learn it from the gods? Yes. But never make the mistake of battling me, spell to spell. I am more than the flesh you see, girl. And there is always the Rot.'

'My shoulder? It's numb, but ...'

With that, she moved like a spirit for the wall. I must have looked flabbergasted for she smiled. 'Remember what I told you about the Rot? That I am the only one who can cure it?'

'Yes?' I said, rubbing my shoulder.

'You have been marked by a Sister, girl. Here,' she grinned viciously. 'Look.'

She yanked the cover off a painting. But it was not a painting. It was a window. Outside, light was shining brightly with golden color; birds were flickering in and out of the alcove of the window. It was painful to my eyes, a candle went out in the sudden burst of air, and I shaded my sight, desperately trying to see the marvelous light or even a wisp of a cloud. 'Look at your shoulder, girl.'

I did. I peeled the robe back.

And stared.

Around the skin, scars were visible where her fangs had struck me. There were pinkish depressions in the skin, but that did not concern me, for those wounds were healed. Around the wounds, there were tattoos, of sort. Live ones. They were not pictures of mermaids, flowers, or even twirling gothic designs. I saw figures, stick figures indeed, and some obvious skeletons, others something else. Some were moving, others still, some were laughing, their movement jerky, and there were some ten of them.

I blanched and forgot about the light and the birds. 'What the hell is it?'

She waved at my shoulder. 'I told you. It is called the Rot. Only I can stop it, of course, Shannon. Exposed to light, they shall multiply. In the darkness, they do so quietly, slowly and so you have been spared for a longer time. In the light of Mar, or under the

Two Hounds, our moons, they grow active and hungrier. You see they look starved. They are starved and starving and soon, they will begin to feast. I shall not bother you with the details of what they would do to you, no. Yes, I shall ask you this. Have you ever seen a carcass of a beautiful animal and what maggots and ants do to the wound?'

I had. 'Mistress ...'

'Mistress now, yes, yes,' she giggled, not in control of her mirth as she admired the horrible little creatures on my skin. Her voice grated on my ear for the longest of time and finally went quiet as she stared at me. 'It takes a year to advance, Shannon, to the point where they multiply and eat you to death,' she grinned. 'Some months from now, you will begin to bleed, and you shall lose flesh. Darkness has kept you for now. Do not worry, Shannon, for if you keep your part of our pact you shall disappoint them, they shall starve, and I will wipe them away. Remember this. One day, I could be at your mercy, for gods and worlds are not constant and even the mighty can fall. But despite that improbable scenario, you will die a terrible death if you fail me,' she told me darkly. 'And I can bite others.' Dana. She was talking about Dana.

'Yes, Euryale, mistress,' I wept, and she nodded happily, petting my face.

'Now, now. Soon, I shall have a need of you. We shall take a small trip in some months.' Then, she took me away.

I wept in the dark, staring at the skin that showed none of the sibilant figures, hiding in the dark, not one. Yes, I knew they were there, patiently waiting, hoping I would make a mistake, hating their hunger, awakening slowly to a feast. I grasped at my hair, feeling utterly exhausted, and Able sat near me, and I was startled. 'They let you go early?' I asked. 'Sorry, I'm ...'

'Sad,' he said. 'I know you are. I see it.'

I held his cold hand and rubbed it. 'They make demands on us, on me, and have expectations, and their threats are so very hard to bear,' I grimaced. 'Gods, but to face the disapproving relatives and mocking villagers again, instead of her.'

'She is the darkness,' Able agreed and then the door opened and the others entered. They saw me there, speaking with Able and glanced at me curiously. Then I gathered myself and smiled at Dana.

'Are you OK?' she asked, also tired to the bone. 'You should have seen the firewall I summoned today. Even Bilac was impressed, though she will never admit it.'

'I'm happy for you, sister.'

'I think I will be one to turn some heads in Aldheim, sister. With your skills and mine, we will find a way to thrive,' she whispered and I nodded, feeling none of the hope she did. She hugged me gently. 'Remember, obey her for us. The rest do not matter.'

'No, they do not,' I agreed, not feeling entirely honest. Able and

Cherry mattered, Albine as well. I glanced at the Russians, now taking tired dance steps and calling each other morons, and giggled softly. Dana stiffened at that but said nothing. Lex was arguing with Ulrich, and I worried about him, but they separated, angry and spiteful, and I felt lost, for I did not hate them either.

Euryale had told me they would make demands on me. I should fear them. But I didn't. Perhaps I should. I wanted to fear them, for then I would only have to keep doing what I was doing. Obeying Euryale. And Dana.

I went to bath that night, last of the lot, waiting until Anja was done, and sat there silently, rubbing my shoulder. I did so until Lex came and grasped me out of the water. I had fallen asleep, and he lay me next to Cherry, and he stayed there next to me. I was too tired to argue, and I let him.

Could I let them die if that were the price of our freedom?

Perhaps.

Not?

At the end of the year, we would be tested. Yet, my test would begin before that.

CHAPTER 12

We faced some more brutal months. The days were so tiring, so anxious, and we were pushed so far we had no energy to do anything else than eat. Alexei's and Dmitri's makeshift rag ball gathered dust in the corner; we slept the sleep of the dead in heaps, little heeding our welts and hunger. Even Albine curled next to me one night. We learned the power, gradually developing ourselves to hold more and more, and I suffered Euryale's teachings, even if her silence was gratifying. She was pensive at times, then full of energy on other days, then suddenly brooding and finally happy, her moods alternating madly. I thought she grew more and more impatient in her teaching, for there were nights I thought something was broken inside me, despite my healing ability.

Yet, little by little, we could hold power for a longer time, soon, much more of it and a little more effortlessly.

Then, one afternoon, I was not broken by Euryale's teachings, but instead she crouched next to me. She stroked my cheek. 'You can hold twice as much as you used to. More than the others.

Thank me later.'

'Yes, mistress,' I said with a pained hiss.

'Now, heal up, pigeon, for we shall travel the land. There will be an opportunity we must take, people we must satisfy, and your freedom looms that much closer. You will be tested now, lovely one, and the Tears shall be tested a few days from now, as the year ends. Be strong. But first, as I said, I have a need of you.'

'Yes, mistress,' I agreed and she moved with purpose for the end of the room.

There, she was rummaging in a trunk, old with rusted hinges, but what she pulled out of there was not rusty at all. She took out practicable breeches, made of soft, brown leather. A tunic, she produced a tunic out of the trunk. It was a blue and velvety thing of wonder, for it had pearls sewn to its hem and sleeves. As she piled it on my lap, I could nearly weep for the beautiful garments, how soft they felt. She grinned at me. Finally, she pulled out a cloak, simple, dark, and high boots of dark leather. And a belt. It was silvery and golden, the buckle a thing of beauty.

'Sit, sister,' she told me, and I was seating myself on my usual seat, but she huffed and pointed at a place by a mirror. It was tall as a man, oval and dark, framed by dangerous metal carved crows, but as she snapped her fingers, the mirror cleared and the crows shifted to a different position.

I stared at myself.

My hair was wild and long, much longer than it had ever been. My cheeks were slimmer, and there were wrinkles and dark smudges under and around my eyes.

But the eyes themselves were the most different.

On Earth, I had been a wreck. So had most of the others, one way or another. Now, the eyes staring back at me were resolute, steady and a bit resentful, but mostly piercing. Euryale slipped behind me and I tensed, but she laid a hand on my shoulder. You have all changed. You have a purpose in life, be it the growth of your powers or freedom, you all possess confidence and purpose like never before.'

'I suppose that is true,' I said and thought I looked beautiful, despite the wrinkles. Euryale wetted my hair with oily substance as I stared on incredulously. She was humming, her eyes hidden under her cloak, and her four deft hands stroked my hair with the perfumed fluid. Finally, she combed it. 'Did your sisters do this to you when you were young?' I asked, and she stiffened. I noticed the snakes slithering under her cloak and behind her back. Then I laughed, despite trying not to. 'Sorry,' I said as I shook my head.

'Sit still, you silly thing,' she grinned. 'Our heritage denies us the combs though occasionally the snakes do not get along with each other and that can be bothersome. One has to get help during such crises. Once, one of mine got tangled to that of Stheno, and Medusa especially had a terrible time with some of hers.'

'They said she was cursed by the gods. That she had once been a human and ...'

She looked insulted for a moment and then continued, 'No, she was our sister. Forget the myths and listen. We had happy times, eons of them when the worlds were young. Stheno and I would run in the snow, for days, hunting for other First Born, and she enjoyed solitude and contemplation, Medusa,' she said fondly. 'I miss Stheno. Medusa as well. Stheno has the most curious face, innocent and gentle, her eyes strangely subtle, not like mine. She is smaller than I am, but gods know, she could rip through an elven army company with ease.'

'Our amusements were of simpler nature,' I said. 'Mainly just enjoying books for me. Dana had her friends. We all worked hard.'

She smoothed my hair with all her hands. 'We are going to a feast, Shannon. This feast will take place in the settlement of the Six Hills, the city of Trad, capital of the House Vautan. They reside in the northern half of the Spell Coast, just west of here, Shannon. To their north lies Freyr's Tooth, the smaller continent of the highest and noblest of elves. While the south is strict and perhaps cruel to non-elves, like you humans, enslaving millions of them, the north tolerates them even less. In fact, House Bardagoon and the Freyr's Hall and the city, Ljusalfheim are barred to humans. Himingborg, the southern tip of Freyr's Tooth is where House Safiroon allows humans to serve and live, but nowhere else in the northern, holy continent. House Vautan is a sort of a mixing pot of these two extremes. They are nominally allied to House Bardagoon and Safiroon of the north, forever quarreling with House Coinar to their south, the traders and religious fanatics and with House Daxamma, the vast, barbaric house of wilder manners and Guardians of the Southern Passes. In there we shall go. To Trad. And a feast.'

'I shall see elves?' I asked breathlessly as she twirled my hair. 'And a city?'

'You shall, you reclusive, introverted human,' she giggled with her strange, singing voice. 'So much have you changed.'

'The Fanged Spire would turn a hermit into a stage comedian easily enough,' I agreed with her, then sobered. 'I take it there is a reason I am going?'

'Yes,' she agreed. 'They are meeting in Trad. You see, very soon, the great Houses will meet. It is called the Feast of Fates, where they will air all the grievances, agree on which Houses should be punished, which elevated, and there will be other events. Marriages are agreed on there, as well. And I shall show you for The Race is still on and the Hand of Life to be found.'

'I shall be presented like a slave, being paraded before buyers? You are showing me so they know I exist?' I asked unhappily as she was finishing my hair. It was no longer curly, but long and silken, braided in an elaborate twirl around my head.

'You won't have to show your teeth or privates,' she grinned. 'But you shall be shown to the buyer, the one that matters. The only one who can get you to the Freyr's Seat.'

'This Almheir Bardagoon?' I asked, nervously.

'Indeed. Dress up.'

I did, undressing my robe, looking around nervously for Nox.

'He is not around,' she smiled. 'But the tomte see much, and while they do occasionally marry outside their elusive race, he has no plans to do so. He is past the age.'

'I see,' I said forlornly as I pulled on silken underwear with embroidered sides. 'Why is he serving you?' I asked, not sure he was, really.

'Why? I told you he belonged to another and now to me. The tomte serve their masters for eternity unless the master gives them over, and this one did. They make a lifetime commitment to their mistress or master, and I find him amusing, so I'll keep him. He was Stheno's servant. Now mine,' she eyed me as I pulled on my boots. The pants were immodestly tight, I thought, but they felt so smooth, I actually sighed.

'I never cared for beautiful clothing,' I told her. 'But this, mistress, is like a shower after a month of camping in the woods.'

'You are welcome, Shannon,' she said. 'Now, hold.' She opened the door, and Cosia entered. She smiled at me coldly, her yellow eyes flashing. Then she bowed to her mistress, and I felt Euryale pull at powers of the Shades, combining a complex spell of fiery fires and fumes and Cosia's face changed, uncannily writhing. The cruelly beautiful face took on an ageless look. Her eyes were clear and bright as emeralds, green as the shallow, sun-bitten sea and her hair grew into a huge, voluminous cascade of twirls, thick and high, glowing in the dark in a blonde brilliance. 'Good, good. Cosia will get you to the tavern. There, Shannon, you shall sit and enjoy yourself, and you will know when to act.'

'Is that an elf?' I asked in wonderment.

'Yes, that is an elf. Pretty, no?' Euryale told me. 'Now, let us be off.'

'But ...' I began; Cosia shook her head, and Euryale moved like a spirit. She flashed to the mirror and touched it, murmuring a name, releasing spells. The crows on top of it twitched. I felt her force reaching out to the mirror, the mirror reaching out to her, and I saw how it was done, using a powerful, very powerful, overpowering spell of ice. She actually staggered; the mirror went dark as night, and I shirked, for Cosia had pushed me through it.

It did not break.

Instead, I swirled in the dark, saw a speck of fiery light and plummeted for it. I fell to my feet and a pack of cats scattered, running willy-nilly around a white tiled back alley.

I stared at the cats, entirely confused. A large shadow shot by me, and then Cosia grabbed my shoulder, looking around, pulling me into the shadows. She had her hand on a small dagger as she did, wary and nervous, a beautiful, ethereal female rather than the gorgon who had condemned Ron to die. Dana had done the picking, I reminded myself, going for Able first though none had ever blamed her for it. 'Shh,' she hissed, trying to get her bearings.

The smells. They were so many, I felt like a mutt, my nose high in the air. I noticed it was breezy, for some leaves swirled around the corner we stood in, but there were flowers about, perhaps some strange spice, for an enchanting fragrance filled my nostrils. While Euryale had given me meat and bread, there was also a whiff of an excellent stew lingering in the air and so, without asking for permission, I began to walk. 'Wait!' Cosia hissed, but I walked the tiled alley to the end and stopped.

The Six Hills, Trad was beautiful, and it opened up before me.

Mar had set, and the Two Hounds stalked the sky, giving us light, and I admired the seaport of the House Vautan. Thousands of high buildings dotted several tall hills, entwining them in crowns of pearly white and ruby reds, oranges and greens and lights shone on each building. A ring of white walls encircled the city. Most buildings had terraces on the high roofs, tiny spectacles of people walking across all of them. 'It's dinnertime, so they are all at home. Dinner is a holy thing for the people of Trad, who once starved here, in the War of the Lost Sibling. Thousands of years ago,' Cosia said and continued brusquely, 'and that is where we go.' She nodded across the street towards a white and brown wooden building, many stories high, and the yard lit by poles of pink marble with magical lights on top. It was a suspiciously modest building, with stables on the other end, but clean and prosperous people were walking in and out.

'Those are humans,' I breathed. And they were. I saw two men enter, wearing expensive jackets, yellow and golden, swords on their hips, their hair short and beards trimmed. One would not be able to tell them apart from our people, save for the dress. My eyes wondered at their pants, for they were tight and I blushed as Cosia snickered.

'Yes, fine looking men they are. Perhaps I shall have one if I am given time,' she grinned, and I was sure the man would not enjoy such a meeting to the end, though perhaps the beginning. She shook her head ruefully. 'But no. I am not allowed that. Come.'

We walked to the massive door, crossing a paved road of finely cut stone, pink, and red. 'What shall we do? In there.'

She shrugged, tired of my questions. 'Enjoy, but not too much. You are not to leave the room. And you will eat, drink and dance, and act when you must act. There will be a small commotion, and you will know what to do,' she told me savagely, and I grew alarmed at her ferocious tone.

But only for as long as it took to enter the room.

It was a tavern. Not like I imagined medieval inns to look like, with filthy hay on the floor, dark and smoky, but it was a happy, large room with many balconies reaching up and bathed in gentle lights and fires. Tables were scattered around, thick and well made, carved with intricate figures, dark wood mixed with lighter tones, likely magically crafted, the chairs enormous and cozy, the sort you can sink into and fall asleep as you smell the aromas around you. There were a hundred people feasting, enjoying their life, and an orchestra of flutes and violin-like contraptions were being played by women dressed in frivolous red and yellow gowns. A horn was also playing, but it was playing on its own. I saw an elf, a young male sitting lazily at the corner, concentrating and felt him exerting his will at the instrument, which blew embellished, blaring blasts that somehow mixed well with the band of females. I could only stare at the people, our distant kin and at the elf customers, many of them, somewhat aloof from the humans, pondering deeper questions, yet laughing raucously when they found something humorous, their thick, long hair and ageless faces, their bright and sometimes colorless eyes.

'Wonderful,' I said, wondering at the lively tune, one that thrummed through the floors. Some women were dancing, their gowns mixing together as they laughed and held each other's hands, twirling around. A short man was carrying an enormous plate of cold meats and steamed vegetables, many I did not know, and I decided I was ravenous. 'Do we have coin?'

'Coin?' Cosia asked. 'Yes, of course! Do I look like a beggar?' she sniffled.

'No, I want ...' I gestured, and she giggled and pulled me along. I stared around in stupefaction and tripped on a sheathed sword.

'Pardon!' said a young man lounging on a seat as his hand shot out to steady me. He grinned widely, then happily, and I grinned back, for he was the most handsome man I had ever seen, a sturdy man with a short beard, dark and ravishing, his smile full and face broad. 'Ah, would you, perhaps, care to join me? My friend and I could make up for our frivolous carelessness?'

His friend, a tall, grim man with a trimmed mustache rolled his eyes. 'I did nothing. But indeed, welcome.' He nodded at their table, and I pulled Cosia along. She was hissing a complaint, then adopted a hurt smile, her elven hair bouncing as she tilted her head imperiously at them.

'Excuse me, ma tarish,' the grim, older man said. 'I did not notice ... excuse us.' They both got up and bowed to Cosia, whose face took on an arrogant look as if a noble considering dining with crude peasants. Which was likely exactly the scenario, I realized.

She breathed theatrically. 'It is fine, noble men of Trad,' she told them imperiously, her sing-song voice replaced by a haughty one. 'I'm not ma tarish, but hail from the north. I'll happily eat with you since you are so kind as to offer to pay for us.'

'I ... of course,' the young man said, apparently distraught as the grim one undoubtedly kicked him under the table. 'The pleasure is ours.'

Cosia leaned on me. 'Ma tarish are the nobles of the south. They do not tolerate humans to share meals with the elves. In the north, this is not a problem, for ...'

'Few humans are allowed in the north, I know,' I said. 'And there are non-noble elves? Right?'

'Yes, of course. Most, in fact. Still higher than humans, though,' she whispered and nodded graciously at the grim man who asked for a waiter to approach. 'Great warriors, the lot of the elves, quick and skillful and merciless. Humans are hardier, able to endure rigors and pains. That's the reason why only Ron is dead in the training so far.'

'Will you drink? Eat?' the elder of the men asked in a hopeless tone as a grinning redheaded lady stopped by the table, lifting her eyebrow.

'Both!' I blurted, and the men smiled fixedly, their eyes going to the elf.

'My servant,' Cosia said sternly, 'is an idiot. But she speaks for me as well, and for some reason, before me. Bring us Mereidan Wine, roasted pork with Master Green's Sauce and assorted vegetables. Some fish, carp? If you have it?'

The two men were looking at each other in mortification as the waiter nodded with eyes full of respect. The younger man stuttered and nodded at the waiter. 'Yes, bring us ... Mereidan. You heard the mistress and some meats for us as well. Ale. Red Ale.' The two wiped their brows gently and attempted to chat about their households.

Cosia leaned on me again. 'Mereidan Wine is of golden color, tastes damnably expensive and will cost more than their horses' pet bottles. They took Red Ale for it is cheap and nearly tasteless and all they can afford now.' She giggled, and I could not help but join her.

'What brings you to Trad, ma tarish?' the younger man asked. 'Ah, I am Count Elor and this is my uncle, Lord Commander Maxam. We are of Duke Greyhelm's house, subject to ma tarish Glamir Tarnis.'

'I said I am not from the south. I'm ma narith, of the north. Stop quaking. And mistress Glamir is known to us,' she said as the poor humans bowed their heads in supplication. 'They are the fifty-fourth house to the Regency, are they not? House Tarnis?'

'Fifty-third,' Elor said with some pride. 'There was a war last year and two houses were left with so few nobles they were combined to their victors.'

Cosia grinned. 'I am Kalas Rimith, of the House Rimith. The tenth house.'

They bowed immediately, low and nearly banged their foreheads to the desk. 'An honor, it is,' Maxam said happily.

'I will speak to the mistress Glamir with high praises of your manners and goodwill towards weary travelers,' she said. And leaned to me, whispering. 'Most of the first twenty houses are housed in the Freyr's Tooth, clients of Houses Safiroon and Bardagoon. Of course, Coinar and Daxamma, and Vautan have their place in the top five, but ...'

'How does one measure the worth of a house?' I hissed softly as the two men were discreetly counting their coin.

'It was set so by Freyr, the lines of nobles by the purity of their hearts and blood,' she said. 'There were games and good deeds expected from those who would rule. That time is gone. It is so because he is gone, and so what was discreet in his time, is now the norm. A house must be able to overcome another in battle, in a challenge approved by the Feast of Fates. Of course, they might just surprise a house without any such agreement, but must win utterly with no survivors. Of course, it is easier to wipe out many houses in a larger war. Often when the great houses go to war, the real victims are the lesser ones, usually left crippled and victims to those who did not take part. Often, if a house is left too weak, the nobles renounce the house and join their conquerors or those who will have them. Or go and live as commoners. Few maa'dark are allowed to, of course, and ... ah! Our wine!'

'Indeed!' Maxam said with small panic, and I turned to see people staring at us, for a fabulous bottle of green inlaid with gold and emeralds was being carefully carried by what was apparently the most steady-handed servant. She was frowning at the bottle, and a male child with a happy, freckled smile followed her and then grinned at me happily. He was carrying goblets. They ended up at our table, and a small chorus of claps could be heard.

'Need a loan, Elor?' yelled someone from the back, and the young noble grinned at us, his face white.

'I'm sorry,' Cosia asked, looking shocked. 'You cannot pay for this? But you invited us to your table?'

'I can pay,' Elor nodded bravely. 'By next year, I should be able to eat again. I'll eat my horse in the meantime, so don't worry, dear lady.'

I giggled, Elor quaffed, Cosia roared, and so, we had a fine evening. We sampled the wine, which the servant always rushed to pour, the boy with her. It was rather like what Euryale had served me though that had fortified me, this made me uncannily happy. Didn't Anja also tell how she drank to excess? It certainly made misery flee for a while, at least. I frowned and shook such thoughts away as I leaned back. We ate well, the men told jokes about their lords and Elor of his mistress, even risking dirty gossip about mistress Glamir and their duke, for Cosia seemed a most relaxed elf.

'Care for a dance?' Elor asked, slightly drunk, half pushing himself up.

'Me?' I asked, stupefied. I gazed at the floor, where people were holding hands, their feet thrumming the floor in a nearly magical cadence. 'I have not ...'

'He was not asking me,' Cosia said with a grimace. 'Go on, fool. You won't get a chance soon.' That was true.

Elor got up, pulled me with him, his handsome face looking like a pirate with a golden chest of loot as he pulled me along. 'Your cloak, drop it,' he instructed, and I did, over the chair. He swept me along to the middle of a throng of people enjoying themselves. The wine, the food, and the ale I had stolen from Elor and the thrumming, heart-beating, near barbarous music hitting the floor, the ceilings and the smiles around me? It all made me dizzy with happiness. He twirled me, I knew absolutely nothing about what I was doing, but soon, and very soon I fell into the rhythm and surprised myself with a huge laugh. He laughed back, and I was so happy. Lex's gallant face swept by my thoughts, surprising me, but I cursed him. Something inside me was trying to spoil the evening for me as if I had no right to dance with Elor, but I forgot Lex soon, forcing myself to let go.

In the swirl of the dance, I noticed a party enter the tavern.

I frowned for a second, for there was something unusual about them. They held themselves alert, straight, and their faces were hidden in heavy cowls. There were ten of them; four of them dressed better, in modest dark and red colors, with rich twirls in their sleeves. One was lithe and small, a female perhaps and had a pale green cloak with a rampant, dark beast sewn on it. Though the tavern keeper that sauntered over to greet them did a commendable job of acting like they were frequent guests, it was clear they were not. Some were armed heavily, swords, axes, two had shields with a figure of a pale, red star.

Then I knew what was wrong.

Three of them were holding power, touching the Shades. Two of those were tall males; white and yellow hair peeking under their hoods, and one was the woman. My eyes settled on the tallest of them, wide of shoulders as he gently pushed along a slight figure, a female who was not touching the Shades. He was holding onto some sort of a spell, one to … defend himself? Perhaps. It was made of cinders and fires and would take a lot of power to hammer through, I thought for some reason. Almheir? The Regent?

The others held similar defensive spells, eyeing the room carefully. Then, suddenly, they moved upstairs using a broad staircase by the door. Some of the hooded figures stayed on the stairs, and others on the next floor, eyeing the floor warily.

Elor leaned on me. 'Some high elf. Here to set deals for the Feast of Fates,' he whispered. 'Ah, the star of Bardagoon and the Beast of Safiroon. Northerners. Like you. Your lords, in fact, rulers of your mistresses' house.'

'Yes, I think so,' I told him, and the music eased, a small thrum running through us, and the dancers around us smiled and relaxed, wiping sweat and leaning on each other. Elor looked surprised but gestured me closer. 'Might as well. I'm not married. And you ...'

'I'm not, no,' I told him and stepped into his arms. 'But you just praised your mistress, did you not?'

'I lied,' he told me sheepishly. 'It was something my friend told me about his, and likely he lied as well.' I giggled as he led me around slowly; his footwork gentle, and I let him, twirling in his arms. I let the music, wine, and Elor take me around the floor, and in my mind I forgot Euryale, the Ten Tears, the Dark Levy and all my commitments. I considered running to the city, escaping. I shook my head in sorrow.

The Rot.

Dana.

The others? Yes, them as well.

Elor's eyes were glowing. 'I'm a soldier, and I'm supposed to be brave. So, let me take the lead here. I think you are beautiful. I mean, I know nothing of you. You are with a ma narith of the north, yet there are no humans in the tenth house, for the tenth house live near Ljusalfheim, the forbidden continent. I'm confused. By that. By your eyes and lips. And ...'

And I kissed him.

There were snickers around us, apparently aimed at us as the music gently let us love each other, just for a moment. It was a long kiss, and enjoyable, and I felt it to my toes as his tongue touched mine. He stopped the dance, I allowed him to, crushing myself to him, and then the music stopped.

He pulled away; his handsome, strong face blushed with happiness.

'I ...'

He died.

I felt it. I felt Cosia draw in power, harnessing a spell of Fury, heat and fiery flames. Two pillars of flame shot up in the middle of the room, angry fingers of molten fire, the whole house was rocking in its roots. One rushed up to the air, tearing Elor with it, strewing him about in burning bits before me. I whirled to stare at Cosia while rolling away from the flames. She was grinning, her face an unholy mask of sadistic wrath, and I saw Maxam was bleeding on the floor, his grim face astonished as he held his slashed belly. The flames thrust higher, hit the ceiling with a roar, and a fiery rain came down, like a fountain of death, spreading and spitting angry white flames that burned holes in the people and furniture. I ran and dodged as the fierce, arrow-like fires splashed on the floor, amidst bodies. People and elves, formerly happy and now terrified ran, those who could. They ran but were scorched and mauled by the thickening, dropping fires, the insidious flames igniting their clothing and limbs. I stared in horror as a dozen revelers danced around in fire, holes in their clothing and bodies. Cosia giggled and pulled another spell together. She let curl a fiery whip and faced some elves running down from the stairs, wielding swords and axes, their faces full of wrath. They moved fast as wraiths, looking for a culprit, and Cosia hid the whip behind her. The musicians and the elf who had controlled the horn pointed at Cosia, and four armed elves faced her, and then rushed her. She danced away, lashing her hidden flame across two, cutting them in half, their bodies falling heavily against tables. The two remaining ones dodged falling fire, but only one managed it. One caught some on his back, turning him into a screaming pyre. The last one thrust at Cosia, but the wicked woman danced under the savage sword, grabbed the elf and breathed fire on his face. He died in an instant. Cosia laughed savagely and let the corpse fall.

Wind tore through the room, igniting more flames, and I saw Cosia flying around to land heavily on the floor, but she sprung up like a cat. On top of the stairs, the three highborn elves stood, two in armor of black and red, one with the green beast embroiled on the chest. It was a woman who had cast the wind, and she pulled again at the Shades, and I felt and saw the wind spell taking form again as Cosia struggled upright, grinning. The elven males moved for the stairs. Cosia grimaced at that, fell again with the wind, and as she rolled, she was calling for ice and water, so much frigid water. That water bubbled from the cracks of the stairs and then she snapped her fingers. The stairs broke as the water turned into ice, the mortar holding the stones turned into liquid puddles, and the whole thing crashed down with an enormous rumble, all the way to the basement and perhaps beyond.

The elves retreated back to the balcony and faced her, calling for spells. Spears of flames were flicking across Cosia's dress as she dodged a firewall. Then she stepped away from a gout of blue flames and finally, acrobatically, incredibly smartly she rolled away from a force of wind that threw around burning furniture.

'Your turn, Shannon,' she hissed.

She turned her eyes on one of the humans left untouched in the terrible hell of the tavern, likely due to her skill. It was the boy. His hair was long, blond and his face was one of shock as he stared at one burning lump of flesh. Perhaps his mother. Father? I sobbed. 'No!' I screamed.

'Yes,' Cosia hissed. She summoned a small, fierce ball of fire and it flew in the air, hit the boy in the shoulder and with an evil sizzle burst through it.

'You bitch!' yelled a high, imperious voice. 'Die!' The building rocked as the tall elf on the balcony jumped down, landing heavily. A fiery circle of fire protected him, and Cosia retreated from his wrath to the shadows where she melded. I prayed she would die as the elf summoned a blade of red flames, invoking powers to pull at Cosia, to find her from the dark corners. She flew to her face, her fingers scraping at the boards, and she grimaced as she was dragged towards him. She snapped her fingers, I felt and saw the Shades, and at that time, she rolled to the dark portal that appeared between her and the fierce elf.

I saw the Shades.

Euryale. She was around as well. Where was she?

I ran to the boy, who was sobbing his life away, a fist-sized bit of meat gone. The elf lord was near me, staring around in horrified anger, spitting at the sight of the burning bodies, summoning mist that was moist, trying to douse the flames. 'Help me!' he yelled up at the two others.

I ignored them and pulled at the healing power. I filled myself with it, feeling I would need every ounce of it and then, finally, breathed it to the boy. His flesh turned pink, then red, and he shuddered in stinging pain. I did it again, praying I could and cast my spell. I was feeling dizzy, the ice flowing from my being to him, and he cried weakly as he lost consciousness, the skin folding over the hole, his shoulder forever hurt, but he would, perhaps live.

I fell over him, then onto my back on the sooty floor as a hand dragged me up.

There was the elf lord staring at me in stupefaction. His eyes scoured my eyes, still keeping a hold on me. His mouth made incredulous sounds as he crouched next to me. He was handsome, his chin wide, his hair hugely thick, white and curly, framing his ancient, nearly colorless eyes. 'You healed him? How?'

'I'm the Hand of Life,' I told him slowly.

He shook his head at that and turned to look up. There, the two elves were whispering, apparently having witnessed the same sight.

But Euryale was not done.

There was a scream. A terrified, long cry of female horror. The elf lord got up in panicked haste, the sword of flame quivering in his hand. 'Aloise!' he yelled. 'Save her!'

The two elves turned to look up. From the stairway upstairs, elven bodies tumbled down, the guards slashed and ripped apart and then, thin, mocking laughter could be heard. I saw the fourth of the nobles; an elven woman of exquisite beauty, and Euryale was holding her by the throat at the top of the stairs, high and evil. Time froze. I heard her voice, a sing-song thing of spiteful mockery drifting down at us. 'Come, Regent, come and save your wife. And she is pregnant?'

He ran to the broken stairs, and climbed the remains with an uncanny ability, screaming at Euryale, incoherent with rage. Euryale laughed, tore the clothing off Aloise Bardagoon and sunk her fangs into her neck. I felt an ache hammer at my own shoulder as Aloise screamed. She let her go as the Regent reached the top of the stairs, full of rage, harnessing a spell.

I thought they would fight. I hoped he would prevail.

Instead, I saw a shadow moving across the walls, swift as

lightning and then, a twirl of darkness as Euryale grabbed me. I saw her face, her mouth smothered in blood, and I knew she had given the wife of the Regent the Rot. She pulled me in, her mocking, dreadful eyes meeting those of the powerful elves staring down at her. The Regent turned to look at us, his eyes haunted with fear and rage. She grinned. 'Sorry, Shannon,' she said apologetically and slapped me so hard things went black for me.

I woke up in her chambers. She was pacing back and forth, staring at the ceilings. I came to, not saying anything, noticed I could no longer see and feel the Shades. She stalked around for a time until she stopped and stared down at me. 'Well, Shannon. Thank you. You did fine.'

I sobbed and noticed I had been holding my breath. I rubbed my face, not wishing to see her. 'You killed all those people.'

'*We* did. We did that to make the Regent take note. He knows there is a Hand of Life. He knows I hold her. And he will not mind she is a human.'

'Because you gave the Rot to his wife?' I asked in misery. 'And while I cannot heal myself, I can heal her?'

'Yes. And soon, very soon, I will give you to him. During the Feast of Fates, he will be a desperate elf. Desperate enough to make mistakes.'

'Why then? Why not now?' I asked desperately.

She shook her snake-ridden head. 'A bit of wine, kisses and

happiness, and you are so ready to leave us. I sense there is a part of you that desires power and control, just like I do. Those who have always been without it, often do. But you were happy, and all you can think of is a joy of freeing yourself from us, not the longer game with great rewards. And now you also hate me.'

'That boy? His mother? I ...'

'You are allied with me, Shannon. You made a pact with me. For your sister. Think about that. What are the humans to us? Even to you, for we are maa'dark, and they all fear us, and race has nothing to do with that. You will learn this. Do not feel sorry for the elves, either. Nor their servants. If you don't see how cruel life can be and blame me for all the violence in Aldheim, at least think of Dana.'

'I will,' I told her miserably. 'Will there be more children getting slaughtered before this is over?'

'Yes,' she answered instantly. 'Many more. Is that clear?'

I swallowed my fear and repulsion and stared at the ceiling. I forced myself to answer. 'Yes, mistress.'

She smiled cruelly, staring at me. 'You did well under pressure. However, I think we have to take some of the innocence away from you. That way, you will be more useful to us.'

'I won't kill anyone,' I told her resolutely.

'Yes, you will. You will if you have to, for did I not say there is a speck of selfishness in you? Enough to force you to fight to stay alive, I think and later, perhaps you will find an appetite for power. You will be tested soon. I'll let you take part. I had thought I would spare you from it. And Dana. Now, I think I have to see you motivate yourself to my cause. What I did yesterday is a red path for me and for my people, a way home through our enemies, one that leads to what will make us happy again. Those who died are my enemies. Therefore, you will find your path the day after tomorrow, in the morning. With Dana. Fight well. I think you won't be so arrogant after that.'

'Yes, mistress,' I said again and grimaced, helpless. She nodded at me and clapped her many hands.

'I have no energy to pull you anywhere now, so walk,' she told me, and indeed she was exhausted. The travel had left her haggard as she settled into her seat, closing her eyes.

'Was she sweet, this elf woman?' I asked. 'His pregnant wife.'

'Her terror was, Shannon. They have laughed over the corpses of my followers, human girl. Her terror was a fine, addictive drug. And so was his fear,' she smiled.

Cosia entered, and I hissed in anger. She pulled her whip. I hesitated, straightened my back and went past her. We made our way down the stairs, the endless amount of them, and I was grateful to finally make it to our chamber's door. Cosia looked away as she opened it, her face neutral. Was she sorry for the people she had murdered? No, she had enjoyed it.

'Do you have anyone you care for?' I asked her.

'I ...' she began, her snakes twirling hypnotically. 'No. Not now. The Dark Clans are lost to us. I had love once, girl. Perhaps one day again if I shut my heart down.' She closed the door instead and left me with the dark room, where the Ten Tears saw me. Lex came forward.

'Where have you been?' he asked. 'Dressed like that? Torn, beautiful clothes! There is a bruise on your chin!'

'You all right?' Anja asked, climbing up to stare at me. 'Are you hurt?'

'I'm not all right,' I said and fell into Lex's arms. He carried me to the corner and even Alexei and Dmitri came to comfort me. Cherry hovered protectively, scowling at me, hoping I would smile. Albine sat near, staring at me, nodding at me, and so did Able. Ulrich stood far, looking down, his mood mysterious and hard to read. Dana stayed put until the others withdrew. Then, she held me as I cried.

'Remember, Shannon. For us,' she said. 'My poor sister. I told you this would be hard. Didn't want you to come, for you were right to fear this place. And now you are at the forefront of it all.'

'Yes, sister,' I said as I fell asleep before Nox came to feed us, dreaming of fiery deaths and many dead eyes blaming me for not being able to heal them. There were limits to my powers.

And my patience.

THE DARK LEVY

CHAPTER 13

Next day, we rested. Nobody came to fetch us, there was silence. We sat and waited until Alexei stirred. 'The year is up and so they are brewing some devilry for us. No?

'Going hungry today,' Dmitri said. 'First they made us sober, now they will make us cannibals?'

'Shut up you two,' Anja said, stretching next to Ulrich after having lain curled on his side. His hand caressed her neck gently, and I felt envious of their feelings, thinking about the dead Elor I had kissed in Trad. She was a gorgeous woman, and I hoped Ulrich would also appreciate her wits. Gods, I thought. What did I know? She saw me looking and nodded briefly, then looked away as Dana was also staring at them.

'He has a weakness now,' Dana said softly, and for a moment I thought it was Euryale speaking. But no, it was Dana, speaking of Ulrich.

'Shut up,' I told her and stalked around the room. I held my head, feeling hurt by the powers I had released on the hapless boy. I stopped by the dusty ball of robes, Alexei's rag ball. I toed it and then saw Able grinning at me. I kicked it his way, but he didn't bite.

Albine, on the other hand, was lying there next to him, scowling at the ball until she kicked it back at me, lazily, but she did.

'Too early for this, Shannon?' Anja asked with a laugh.

'We have to work together soon,' I told them.

'What if they actually plot us against each other?' Dana asked.

'Then we won't.'

'No, I doubt it. We have to work together.' I attempted to kick the ball to Dmitri, but I was a terrible player, and the ball ended up in the middle of Anja and Ulrich. 'Tomorrow, they will test us. It will be deadly,' I added.

'And you know this?' Ulrich asked brusquely. 'Tomorrow?'

'Yes,' I told him. 'I know it. She said. Tomorrow morning. It will change us all.'

'I saw my brother burn, girl. That changed me,' Ulrich grunted. He picked up the ball and hesitated. Anja tried to take it, but he shook his head. 'Here. Tomorrow, or as long as we stay here, I will work with you lot. All of you. No matter your sister's cruelty,' he nodded at her venomously, 'or your strange issues.'

'You fear when I speak to myself?' I asked.

'Who told you?' Dmitri grinned. 'It's creepy as hell. So, truce it is.'

'Will you work with us?' Ulrich asked Dana. 'Until we are all free?'

Dana got up with a shrug, running her fingers through her hair.

'Yes I promise you this. Together unless they make us fight each other. I'm on your side.'

They stared at each other for a while and then Ulrich nodded. As if that was their cue, Dmitri got up with a whoop, his brother following him. Soon, we played a mad ball game, did so for hours, save for Dana, who stared at us in a strange mood. I ignored her.

Night came, and there was no sign of Nox. Something was up indeed.

'They're keeping us hungry, bastards,' Lex growled before we fell asleep. 'Probably trying to make us hungry enough to kill. They'll have us fight some poor bugger next to a delicious feast and only the winner gets to take part. That might work.'

'I think so,' Anja agreed. 'I want that slop now. So badly.' Her belly churned loudly and even Ulrich chuckled.

'We will do what we must,' Dana said softly. 'No matter what they ask.'

'Whatever to survive,' Albine added. 'Gods help us.'

'They don't care,' Dana grimaced. 'Not one ounce. The gods.'

'They cannot hear us,' Albine said. 'If they did, they would.'

'You going religious on us?' Dmitri quipped. 'Say a prayer for me as well. I think I won't survive this place. The monsters will kill me.'

'Shut up,' Ulrich growled. 'Gather strength.'

And we did. Yet, in the night, I was startled by a shake of my foot. I shot up, terrified as I had dreamed of Euryale, but it was not her. It was Anja.

'Come,' she whispered.

I looked around. Ulrich was asleep, so were Dmitri and Alexei, the latter snoring thunderously. 'Where ...'

'Shush,' she said, her blonde hair brushing my knees. 'Come.'

'But ...'

'They are all asleep,' she said softly and impatiently. 'Come or go to sleep.' She got up and walked away. For the door. I saw Able was sitting up, and I stared at him. He shrugged curiously, and we both got to our feet. I detangled myself from Cherry's arm and checked that Dana was deep asleep. Anja went to the door. She closed her eyes, leaning forward. Then she pushed the door open, looked at me and grinned.

She went out.

'What the hell ...' Able said.

'I'll go and see,' I answered.

I slipped up, went out cautiously, peeking through the door. She was there, Anja, leaning on the wall, she gave me a curt nod and an impish smile and gestured downstairs. She began to walk that way, the stairs icy with rime though it did not bother me with my boots on.

Anja came to the foyer. She waited for me. 'There is never anyone about at this hour. They likely feast somewhere. Or sleep. Or torture puppies.'

'Surely they guard the tower?' I breathed, my teeth chattering a bit. 'And what do you mean, never anyone around? You did this before?'

She grinned, blowing her blonde hair aside. 'Yes, I have. You lot are usually all asleep at around three in the morning. I'm a bit of an insomniac.'

'We don't have watches,' I complained

'I'm smarter than I look,' Anja said with a hint of pride. 'I've developed a method ...'

'Fine,' I told her, rubbing my arms. 'You know the days and birthdays as well. Nevertheless, how do you do that burglary bit? They don't actually lock them? Or does Nox leave them open?'

'Where would we run?' she smiled but shook her head. 'But they do. You can heal. I can open locks. It's a skill like they told us.'

'The healing is not a skill. It's a spell. Can you see the Shades?' I asked her, bewildered.

'No, it's a skill I said,' she told me as she moved to the main doors. She pushed at them, not budging them. She grinned, closed her eyes, and pushed again, and they swung open effortlessly. 'I did this accidentally at first. I tried to run that first night and came here. Thought the door was open. I understood this was a skill when I was trying to open Ulrich's robe. He makes this knot on the belt and ...'

'I got it,' I told her, wondering at her casual skill.

She walked out.

There was a bout of winter whirling around the Grey Downs, and she retreated back inside. Anja shivered as we stared at the horizon. A strange, dark front of clouds was rushing over us, racing from the north, billowing snow filling the sky, heaping fine white particles around the Fanged Spire. 'Must make the gorgons think of home,' I muttered.

'Really?' she asked, surprised. 'They hate the cold. When I have sneaked around the tower, they are always hovering by furnaces and fires.'

'You said there is never anyone around,' I told her with chattering teeth.

'Not in the foyer,' she grinned, and I stared at her, now admiring her bravery.

'They come from Niflheim, their clans are native to ice and frost,' I told her casually.

'Hmm So much you know, and so little we,' she said unhappily. 'I'll leave the door open, nonetheless. Makes them miserable in the morning. They've been going crazy with the open doors.' We giggled at that, and indeed, snow was gathering on the floor of the main foyer, decorating the railings and the stone steps with a blanket of brilliance. I turned to look over the island, white patches dotting the craggy valleys. Apparently, it did not get cold enough for the sea to freeze, but the winds were bitter enough to make us take shelter in the doorway. She folded her arms under her ample breasts and cocked her head at me. 'No questions?'

'Have you gone down there?' I pointed to the tower.

'No,' she answered. 'I'm sure to get lost.'

'But you dare to come here?' I lifted an eyebrow at her.

'I come here to think,' she shrugged. 'I figured if I get caught, all I have to do is spill the beans about my ability, and they make me a prized burglar to be sold at a higher cost.'

'I see,' I nodded. 'I'm not sure why you asked me here? Is Ulrich coming along in a bit? Ready to pummel me for Ron? Finally?'

She shook her head empathetically. 'No. He sleeps soundly at this hour, as well. He and Ron, they were not very close. But Ron was his brother.'

'Dana is my sister, and I don't wish to …'

'I know,' she told me. 'I know very well. I'm bored with this ghost haunting us. Yet, blood is important, and he won't forget. I see that. And Dmitri and Alexei are my brothers. They are idiots to boot, and I used to dread every morning one of them would be dead. We drank a lot ever since we were fourteen. We had no prospects at all. None. They were going to go to prison. The law would have dragged them off one day. Perhaps they would have ended up in the army. Does not matter. They are not really evil, just … stupid. No, not that either. They are careless. Now, ironically, the boys you know here are not the boys I knew back home. I like them more than I did. Moreover, Alexei likes you. More than Dmitri does. You know what I mean.'

'I ... like him. And Dmitri,' I said neutrally. 'Is this intentional? Their fondness.'

'That they like you?' she asked me incredulously. 'I told them to be careful with you, but they are also so free and happy, not troubled like they were at home. I cannot stop them from making friends. Even with the one who is dangerous to us. And you are. Or were. Seems your sister does not have to protect you at our expense anymore.' Her voice softened. 'And I think you should have a higher opinion of yourself. I see it's been hard for you, as well. Life.'

'It's been confusing,' I agreed. 'But more sheltered than yours. Now I know I speak to myself. I never know when I do that, and I just have to endure the snickers. Difficult to have a high self-esteem when you keep seeing the looks people give you. Not fun.'

'Ah, that,' she said and looked troubled. 'You speaking to yourself is ... interesting.'

'See? You are doing it as well,' I said. 'Pitying me. Or finding it funny, at least.'

She nodded. 'I was doing it before, pitying you for that problem, but not now. For a reason. Wait for it. As for the two dolts. They've had some six broken bones since they turned ten, and Alexei had a near-deadly bout with fever disease. I took care of them since I was eight, Shannon. Eight. They were seven. We ran the store with the relatives, but I ran the brothers. I've done things to keep our family going, despite Uncle and Aunt nominally looking after us. They were drunks, and so were we. Now, they are different. So am I. While I took care of them, I never worried about the future. Now I worry about that, as well.'

'Dana took care of me. Still does.'

'Really!' she said too loudly, and we went silent for a moment, trying to figure out if we should run. 'Fine,' she went on, quieter this time. 'You have lain in her lap for all your life. This lack of the ... Shades ... made you weak, Shannon. Weaker than she was, no doubt. Here, despite your obvious issues, you are strong and just like anyone else. Here we all found out who we really are. Back home, we were all pretending.'

'So,' I said hastily, 'your're saying Dana's care was not real? Or is not now?'

'I'm saying she lies a lot,' she told me frankly.

'She killed for me,' I reminded her.

'She did. Alternatively, perhaps she wanted the one ally she was sure would always follow her around,' she said spitefully. 'You don't see her as we do. She lies. A lot.'

'You said that, yes,' I breathed, holding back anger. 'Albine said that the day we met. Back home, she had a dozen popular, beautiful friends, handsome boyfriends, admiring teachers and family, and nobody ever doubted her.'

'Did she have any ugly friends?' Anja laughed.

'I … no,' I said.

'She did what she thought she had to do. Here, she is no longer crippled by the absence of the Shades. Here she is Dana, and by burning Ron so publicly, she cannot hide and pretend. Perhaps that was our blessing, after all. She can't manipulate us. So all she has is you. She sees you have grown into a new Shannon and seeks to manipulate the old Shannon, who is still lurking there, very close to the surface.'

'I'll not stand against her,' I said. 'And I have no idea why you think she is dishonest.' My voice broke a bit on that.

She tilted her head. 'Yeah. However, you do have an idea why that is so and still won't share it. For you have that old Shannon there, whispering you need her, at any cost. And that cost is high, Shannon, if she is evil. I think there is a great part of her that is strange, uncaring and evil. If Alexei died, you would suffer for you like him. She would not. But she could pretend to if she wanted.'

I shook my head. 'I … perhaps.'

'We are worried; can you not see that? Have been since day one. I'm not worried about Ron. He seemed like an asshole. First he thought Albine would go, and then he pointed you out just like that and had he done that to Dmitri or Alexei, I would have loved to roast him. But your sister smiled. You didn't see it?'

'I saw it,' I told her hollowly.

'I would not have smiled. I would have thrown up,' she added. 'And now, soon, we are to be tested. You and she have a deal, no?'

'We are sisters. As you said, you love your brothers and that's the deal,' I agreed.

'And there is a lot that is taking place, things we know nothing of,' she added with frustration, stepping forward and running a finger across my burnt sleeve. My skin was pinkish under it, and I realized I had been hurt. She saw my face. 'What is going on?'

'Cherry?' I said as she came into sight.

Anja stared at her, displeased. 'I'm speaking to Shannon,' she hissed. 'Can you give us some space?' Cherry hesitated, looked at me, and I nodded, indicating she should stay put. She sulked, apparently, but did not leave. Instead, she sat down on the stairs, staring at Anja like a sullen dog.

'I just don't like her,' Anja complained. 'She is stranger than you. I have no idea who she is.'

'I speak to myself, and she speaks not at all. We complement each other,' I grinned, and Anja shrugged with a wry smile. 'Why did you call me here?' I asked. 'To convince me to let Ulrich kill Dana? Because you think she lies?'

'Because your Dana is right, in some small way,' she said. 'She is right in protecting you, even if I think she is actually protecting herself. She is right in thinking we must all change and forget the past. Yet I won't turn inhuman, whatever being human really means, and I won't murder people unless I have to.'

'We will have to, I think,' I told her frankly.

'We will see,' she said heavily, shaking her head. She looked away and nodded. 'Ulrich will take a shot at Dana when we are free. If we are ever free. He expects me to help him, for we are ...'

'Lovers,' I finished for her.

'Love,' she said with a sad smile. 'Imagine finding one here, but never a proper one at home. An Austrian, no less! Yes, lovers. We are that. In love. But if you make sure my brothers survive,' she told me calmly, articulating each syllable carefully, 'both of the idiotic chimps survive, I shall not help him, when he makes his move.'

'How is this different from Dana's deals?' I asked her sadly.

'It isn't,' she said. 'And I don't lie. If Ulrich asks me to help him, I will tell him no. For them.'

'How can I help them?' I spat. 'I'm nearly as helpless as you.'

'I think you have been promised something, something that only involves you two. And your sister is the hostage.'

'No,' I told her, looking away.

'A lie,' Albine said softly behind me, and I turned to look at her in surprise. Cherry shrugged from the stairs. Albine was staring up at me. 'You are not speaking the truth.'

'Everyone coming here?' I asked, exasperated. 'We should

probably just stay here until morning comes and then ...'

'I asked her to come here,' Anja told me.

'She came here to accuse me of lies? Hardly ...'

'She wanted to talk to you in private, but she is here for another reason, as well. As I said, Dana lies. When we made the deal to work together, she lied.'

'And she knows this?' I asked her angrily.

Albine nodded. 'And she has lied so many times. And you just lied about you and a deal you have to set you free. With her.'

'It's her skill,' Anja said grinning.

I stared at them, uncomprehending until it came to me. I rubbed my forehead. 'To know when someone lies?' I asked, cursing the small Albine. 'When have the others lied, Albine?'

'Many times,' she said uncomfortably. 'The boys especially.'

'I see,' I said and looked carefully at Albine. The dark face grinned for a moment, and then she shrugged as she visibly calmed herself. I continued. 'And she is a liar?'

'She is,' Albine said. 'But you are not, not usually. No, you lie when you say you don't know if she is dangerous, for you think she is. Something happened when you came here and so, we know without a doubt she is not to be trusted. While the boys lie about their girlfriends, she lies about her past. And the future. She is not to be trusted. Not even by you, new Shannon. The old one had no choice.'

'And I am trustworthy, even if I am mad?' I laughed bitterly.

'Yes,' Albine said, 'and you are not mad. Not really.' There was a tear in her eye, and I stared at her.

Anja hugged me briefly, shocking me out of my scrutiny. 'She says you are not, told me the reason, and so I believe her,' Anja smiled. 'You will be shocked. I was. Am. And freaked out.'

'Can she hear us?' Albine asked and looked at Cherry.

'She can't,' I said and shrugged at Cherry, who was looking worried. I thought about it, looking at their eyes, and decided not to lie any longer. I shook my head. 'I have been promised something, yes. The prize is high. Yesterday ... But what are you asking me? That I give up on this promise by our damned, hell-spawned mistress? To do what? To keep Alexei and Dmitri alive? I will do that as well as I can. I promise that.'

Anja pulled me close. 'I think it's better to be a slave Ten Tear than sell your soul to that thing. I'd rather die fighting altogether than save my chops alone. I think Dana would not agree, but do you?'

'I am not sure,' I told her softly. 'To fight?'

'She lies,' Albine said in a bored voice.

'I know Dana would not agree,' Anja stated, and I kept my mouth closed, doggedly. She nodded, finally. 'You know what I am offering. I say all or none. I think you are a good person.'

'I'm not always sure I am,' I whispered.

'True,' Albine told us, and Cherry looked down, smiling. She could hear us.

'Fine,' Anja said. 'But think about this. If she gives you what you want, freedom, Dana, we will die. You know this. The thin-faced runt, Albine there, my brothers and I, Lex even? Your happiness and freedom will taste like shit in your mouth. If you are even given it. We have to help each other.' She leaned forward. 'Let us agree to try to escape this very night. Before they test us.

I stared at her incredulously. 'How?'

'I don't know,' she said. 'But there is something we possess that will help. Something that might ...'

'We cannot go now,' I said in a panic. I was thinking about the Rot and about Dana and the fact the Bone Fetters tied us. 'Just like that? These Fetters tether us. We have no idea what is out there. We are helpless.'

'We have a secret,' she said with a whisper. 'I told you. Something that might help us flee. Will you trust me? We will go, find a way to freedom, a way to shed these shackles. But we should go.'

We stood there for what felt like a long time. I opened my mouth to say yes. Then I closed it, and her face was clouded with doubt.

'Very well, old Shannon. You need time.'

'I do,' I whispered. 'New Shannon might as well. What is your secret?'

'It's a weapon, a chance to fight,' she said. 'At least if we are not faced with too many foes.'

'Sounds very dangerous. Very unlikely to succeed. They told us there are no boats on this island,' I said, my mind whirling.

She nodded sadly. 'Fine. It is a long shot. Perhaps we have to endure the test, then, and I'll keep our secret until I know you will help us. That you are one of us. Not just Dana's sister.'

'I need ...'

'Yes. Nevertheless, here is advice for you. If we survive what she has planned for us, and you decide to be a Tear, you will be our second secret. It is up to you to get close to the mistress of this Fanged Spire, tower of hell. Find ways to her confidence. Find ways for us to escape. To be free. Albine can help you. Let me know.' I opened my mouth, thinking about Euryale's words about my enemies pretending to be friends, asking for favors that will doom me.

I struggled. I thought of agreeing with her, and then I hesitated. Finally, I turned to the small girl. 'Albine?'

Anja sighed, left, and pulled Cherry with her. Cherry fought her, ripping her arm free, and I shook my head at her. 'Please. Let me speak with Albine. Alone.'

'Come, imp,' Anja hissed. 'She does not need you now.' I gave her a long look, and she got up and went with Anja, sullen as a child.

Albine came to stand before me, staring up at me. She placed a hand on mine. I crouched before her and whispered to her. 'We should go. They might come by and then we are in for it.'

'We can tell them we are sleepwalking,' she giggled.

'You have not told us any jokes this past year and now you begin?' I asked her incredulously. 'But we should go, indeed.'

'Yes, in a bit,' she agreed. She took a long breath and then spoke. 'Do you see my brother?'

'Able? Not now, no,' I told her, craning my neck to stare at the darkness. 'Is he lost?'

'You could say that,' she told me with a sad smile. 'It's been a fascinating, terrible year. When they sent us on our way, it was to spare us. I was so angry I cursed them for the past year, but I know Aunt was dying of some lung disease indeed, and we are the last ones, you see? They thought this would be the last chance for us.'

'I see,' I told her with a smile. 'You were beautiful kids. But you seem much older now, though it's been but one year. This place changes all of us.'

'I began to grow the night we arrived.'

'We all did,' I said. 'Anja said you can help me? To help you?'

She grinned. 'Yes. I know what your skill is.'

'What?'

She poked me. 'Perhaps you have others and this healing is a fine, fine thing, apparently, and, of course, it is. You are a miracle amidst miracles. You are also kind, compassionate, and I often think when two people make a family, and the kids arrive, there is a bucket with this … this soul.'

'Bucket of soul, eh?' I said.

'Don't mock me!' she said unhappily. 'Bucket of something. One kid is kinder than the other, the other one has the brains.'

'You saying Dana has the brains, and I'm the kind one?' I poked her back with my finger.

'No! Yes, I mean you certainly have all the kindness in your family.'

'You never saw Dana when she was holding me when I was crying and miserable,' I admonished.

She agreed. 'That is the old Dana. Sorry, but I do not like her. And I think they gave brains to you two in equal measure. Moreover, she got all the cruelty and vanity.'

I held my face, so tired of the topic. 'You don't really know her,' I said. 'Grandma told me she is not all evil.'

'That would mean you are not all kind and then we are both right,' she said and sobered. 'Perhaps so. What do I know? Yet, for one year I have seen you trying to get Able to help me, to make me and him both take part and you are so worried about both of us.' She sobbed suddenly and took deep breaths, holding her hand over her face. 'How is he?'

'How is he?' I asked, totally confused.

'Is he happy?' she asked, clutching my hand.

'What the hell are you talking about? You're scaring me,' I said, but she did not relent, squeezing my hand until the blood was not flowing. 'Is he fine? No, he's brooding and unhappy and ...' I raised my face to look over Albine's shoulder and saw Able standing on the stairs. 'Able? Come here and deal with this. Finally.'

Albine stiffened. She glanced behind her and then looked at me. 'You have a skill. Perhaps it has something to do with this healing gift. Perhaps not. Perhaps you have other skills as well, as I said, for you are different, as we all know. You should find out what they are. In addition, I think he might be able to help you and all of us. If you choose to try to help the lot of us get out of here.'

'I don't understand, Albine,' I told her tersely. Able was walking towards us.

'You don't?' she said. 'Touch Able.'

I did. He was cool and clammy, and I held his hand. Albine's eyes followed my hand, my fingers stroking Able's hand, and she burst into tears. Ever so slowly, she moved her hand towards Able and grasped at him.

Her fingers went straight through him.

I let go of Able and took staggering steps back. I hit my back on the door, fell on my ass and stared at them.

'All through your years, Shannon, you have probably had that ... skill. You walk somewhere between heaven and earth and talk to people who are going away or staying for some reason. Did he stay for me?'

'I ...' I sobbed, staring at Able, who seemed suddenly sinister to me. He shook his head and said nothing, unable to explain.

'He wore the robe we all wore,' I told her incredulously. 'He wears it now. He sat with us, slept with us.'

'You have been speaking with him for one year. Passing that ball of rags to him. Probably you did this back home with people, at your village and they all called you crazy but never told you why,' she said with a small voice. 'People are like that.'

'He wears the same robe we do!' I said again with a small panic attack making me sound hysterical.

She took a deep breath and shrugged. 'I don't know about the world of the dead, but it certainly has to be different from ours. They might mimic things we do, just to amuse themselves? Just because the things are familiar. Perhaps they do things they don't ever realize? So he slept, ate and wore whatever we did.'

'He ate with us!'

'Did he?'

'I ...' I began. No, he had never eaten with us. He had sat with us but never held the ladle.

'You can actually touch him?' she asked, her voice breaking.

'I can. But ...'

'This is your skill. You mind does not understand the differences between the dead and living. You might have people in your life you never understood were gone. Did he stay for me? You see, the night we arrived, he fell on a stalagmite. He was pierced and bled in my arms.' I nodded. Albine had had blood on her. 'He was a sweet boy who used to play soldiers with his friends and he loved practical jokes, like the Russians. Now, he either waits for me or is worried about me.'

'Able?' I breathed.

He shrugged. 'I ... worry for her. And wait for her. For I doubt you will make it,' he said. 'I dream of a dragon, Shannon. Every night. It eats you. Tortures you.'

'What did he say?' Albine asked as she stared at the emptiness.

'He waits for you,' I told her hollowly, not telling her about his dreams. 'He thinks we will die.' I got up and staggered for a moment, holding my head. 'My God, I cannot ever know who is gone, and who is not. They think ... they thought I was crazy. The people that approached me in our village? In addition, I spoke with them. While everyone looked on.'

'I loved and love him,' Albine said, sitting down and hugging her knees. 'I wish I could go with him.'

'You must not,' I said. I took off my shirt and approached Able. He looked at me curiously and stood his ground as I approached. I hesitated and pulled the shirt on him, tugging at it until his cold face emerged and the shirt fell around him though not on him. 'Do you see? He stands here.'

'Yes,' Albine said, holding her hand to her face.

'Why didn't you tell me he was dead? You had one year to do so,' I asked her, without looking at her.

'I didn't wish to lose him,' she said. 'If ... I don't think he should wait. He should go to ...'

'Hel. Hel's kingdom,' I said bitterly. 'That's where the mortals and even some gods go, those who die of disease or old age, or accident, I suppose. The gates are closed to the other planes. And we all go to Hel.'

'Is it a dangerous place?' she asked as she got up.

'I doubt it's worse than Aldheim,' I said sourly, seething with anger and sorrow both. 'For a human.'

Albine approached the specter of her brother, and she reached out to stroke the boy standing in the middle of the fabric bunched around his invisible legs. I walked away from them. I went to the stairs, and Albine stayed there, whispering to the unseen kid. I walked away, covering my breasts against the cold until I came to our room. I avoided the looks of Cherry and Anja and settled down to sit in the corner. I waited until Albine appeared and came to me with my shirt, and I was half surprised to see Able follow her.

She stood there before me. Anja's eyes were boring holes in me.

'We wish to survive,' Albine said.

I nodded.

'He might be able to help you,' she added.

'We are fettered,' I said, hopelessly.

'Yes,' she agreed. 'I think you are right to refuse to leave this night. We are helpless. Therefore, we must be unfettered. Or just leave this night. If we stay, we have to find out their secrets.'

I stared at Dana, asleep. My family. They had never told me I speak with people they can't see. Never. But I had made a promise. She was my sister. My blood. I took a deep breath. 'Give me time to think.'

'We don't have much time,' Anja whispered in the dark and stroked Ulrich, who was stirring. 'Hopefully it won't cost us too much.'

Next day brought death, and the price for my reluctance was heavy indeed.

CHAPTER 14

Cherry crept close to me as I tried to get some sleep. I put my hand on her cheek to see if she was cold and clammy, but she was there, curling next to me, very much alive, and the others saw her. I ran my hand through her short hair. She was my friend, probably half mad as were the lot of us, but alive. I traced my finger on our chess game, wondering at my life. I felt both relieved and terrified and laughed out loud. I gazed at the ceiling, wondering at Able, who was lying down, apparently asleep, or perhaps just thinking he was. I decided the knowledge that death was not final was somewhat relieving, and terrifying both, for Able was real, lingering, not really alive, not really dead. He saw nightmares.

He might be able to help us.

Able might be able to do that, indeed. He would stick around until we either died or something changed. He had dreamt of a dragon eating the lot of us? Hopefully, that was not part of our test. A dragon. If such things existed. Surely they did.

Ten Tears.

They wanted me to help them. I wanted to. But what if that got Dana killed?

Euryale had promised us. She had promised us freedom. More. Power. I thought about Albine's words about buckets and traits and thought there was a part of me that had thought about more than freedom. Power for the one who is powerless, has been forever?

How could it not entice one?

Dana would find it strange, but we could be equal, happy, sisters, and rulers of our destiny.

Or dead.

Especially if I grasped at the mad schemes of the Ten Tears. They had a secret that might give us a small chance, Anja had said. Small chance? Bah. The Dark Levy was just that, a levy of people unwilling to be there, and I was sorry for them. But to risk all for them? The Rot and Dana? I could not ignore these things.

Then the memory of death Cosia had spread in Trad came to me. The bits of the lovely man I had kissed raining down. The dead dancers. The boy.

I fell asleep, dreaming of Elor.

Early that morning, Lex woke me up and I nearly shrieked, for I thought Elor had come back from the dead, like Able. Lex was very close, on his haunches, and his eyes scourged me as he was shaking me. 'Shann?' he hissed. I bolted up, staring around me in bewilderment. I saw Able still, and he was lying on his back. It had not been a dream. In fact, I had dreamt just for an hour, likely. 'Come on,' he said and we got up. I groaned softly for my back was aching. Cherry was still snoring, holding her knees in a fetal position. 'Today's the day, eh?'

'I don't know,' I whispered to him. 'Perhaps?'

'It's been an exciting year,' Lex told me, rubbing his face, moving his blond beard aside. 'Come over there, please.' He nodded towards the far wall, near the door. I shrugged and followed him, braiding my hair as I did. He turned towards me and took a deep breath. 'How you holding up?'

'I've been fine since ...' I sputtered. 'This night. I'm not mad, you see.'

'Oh?' he asked strangely. 'You and Anja and Albine, Cherry sneaking out earlier to chat cleared this? And she opened the door. And there you found out you can speak with yourself and that's just fine and very healthy?' he grinned. 'I don't mind a bit of crazy, mind you. You gonna tell me about it?'

'No,' I told him gently. 'But I appreciate you for accepting me and my strangeness when I thought there was something wrong with me. While it appears I'm not strange but only stupid, your friendship means a lot. You honestly didn't care if I was ... appeared mad. You stood up to me since day one.' It was true, I realized.

'Look,' he began and stammered. 'I ...'

'Yes?'

He cursed. 'We will be doing something dangerous soon. Well, all the time, of course. Waking up is not safe here. And I wanted to tell you something.'

'I stink? Or have something between my teeth?' I asked him, a bit nervous for his intensity. 'Look, I've had a lot on my plate lately. And you don't know what is going on. And we should sleep and rest!'

'And you will not tell me what's going on,' he stated, blithely ignoring the part about resting.

'No,' I pouted. 'I'm tired. Later, you will be the first to know.'

He looked exasperated. 'When they drag me away to be tortured? OK. I don't need to know. Not really. Never was the type to lead folks nor to care to know stuff not meant for me. I loved to have a nice long sail with my boat to get away from all the shit. I loved sunsets, nights out with my brotherhood and damned bastards they were, but honest bastards. Not many of those around.'

'You woke me up to tell me about your boat and the honest, damned band of criminals you ran around with?' I asked, tired.

'Damn. Shannon. Come on. A smile would be nice?' he said with a mischievous grin. 'One smile? Just to break the ice. It will hurt, I know, likely tear some skin.'

'You woke me up to see me smile?' I asked him, getting angry now.

He stared at me and sighed. 'Yeah. Actually yes. That's it. No smile? Fine. I'll show you how well I can dance for I have seen Cherry there teach you. And since you can't dance worth a damn, I'm sure you can appreciate these fancy steps of mine. I cannot do it for shit either, and you are sure to smile after.'

'Don't,' I warned him sternly, but he lifted his robe, hung his long, blond hair down over his shoulder as he tried to look at his steps. He whirled, stepped to the side, shook his hips ferociously, and I giggled. I put a hand to my mouth and bit my lip. 'Please stop!'

'No, here, look ...' he said and tried some sort of a sailor's dance move, stepping forward, then backward, and he fell on his ass quite ungraciously as he stepped on his robe. 'Shit. That smarts!' he complained.

'OK, I'm better than you,' I said, hysterical now and pulled him up. 'Cherry can teach us both.'

'Feels strange without music. And beer,' he added, and we laughed as softly as we could.

'So, you wanted to show me your dance moves?' I leaned on a pillar.

He dusted off his filthy robe. 'No, I wanted to ... I don't know. Speak with you? About some things. Yeah.'

'As long as it's not your damned boat, I'm all ears.'

'God, damn I miss the ... okay!' he said. 'It's been an exciting year.'

'Yes. You said that. Albine did as well. We all think it's been that and more.'

He waved his hand around. 'I miss the earth. The Tenth. How could I not? It was shitty as hell out there, with no money and few prospects other than eventual jail time. Perhaps there was to be some sweet, fat, amorous husband to share the cell with, but at least we did not have to fear so much. Did we?'

'I suppose not. I miss Mother and Father,' I told him and noticed a tear coming. 'And my small sibling, Rose. But it was still driving us crazy. All of it. Not hearing, seeing the Shades.'

He nodded. 'Funny that. We are shut off from it, but it's not half as bad as it was at home. Probably we could just barely feel and hear it and it drove us crazy. Here it's either gone or on. Yeah, I miss it when they take it, but still easier this way.'

'I miss it all the time,' I said softly and felt more tears come.

He waved his hand around. 'We don't know what's out there, do we? It might all be worth it. We have this small obstacle to deal with, the Fanged Spire and mad serpent women looking for every excuse to cull us and then sell us.' He stepped forward, and his finger came forward to wipe the tear off my cheek. I grabbed his hand, and it trembled. I took a deep breath and let it go. He thumbed away the tear, gently. He eyed it and smiled, sucking it off his thumb. 'Can't waste any sustenance.'

'I guess not,' I allowed and placed a hand on his chest. He did not look shocked, nor did he grin in his customary way. 'Dana and I are close,' I stated, 'and I cannot promise you anything. Besides, she has been speaking with you a lot. I think she ...'

He shook his head tiredly. 'Yeah. She has shown some interest. I've been listening, but she does not say much, really. She can make you feel really special, but when I thought about her just now, I realized I don't know her. I know she loves her powers. She smiles like the sun when we speak about that. Dana, I think, is much more into survival and beating this challenge than anything else,' he told me softly, caressing my hand. He was bearded and scruffy, but handsome as the devil. 'And so I'm lonely. In addition, I like you. I think I know you better than I do her. You just told me about rose, your folks and in one sentence you feel more human than she. I ...'

'Am I the last available woman? If Dana only loves the Shades, Anja has the mad, bloodthirsty Austrian and Cherry is ...'

'Devoted to you, as I am,' he whispered. 'And she is mute. And not my type anyway.'

'Not pretty enough?' I chided.

He shrugged. 'I could lie; it does not matter. And I can't say I would like her nonetheless since she never says anything. I don't even know how old she is. Anything from twelve to twenty.'

'Albine will grow up in a few years.' I said.

'She is too smart for me, probably, but you are not,' he told me drolly, and I slapped him playfully. He smiled and shrugged. 'The only woman I think about is you,' he said. 'And the only one who makes me smile, even if she is a bit out of sorts, a tad crazy. No matter if she claims it's all fine now.'

'Bilac liked you?' I asked him mischievously. 'Called you beautiful. She would show you some good time, I think. I bet she would. Would make dice out of your balls and a napkin from your beard,' I chortled, and we burst into painfully subdued giggles.

'Oh, she is a darling, but a bit too ferocious, perhaps,' he said. 'I do like you. So, I think we will face something horrible soon and just wanted to let you know.'

'So I could miss you?' I asked sadly. 'Perhaps you'll hang around with me anyway.' I giggled and shook my head at the thought and his shocked face. 'Never mind.'

He looked at me strangely and laughed with me dutifully. 'Just felt like it was important. I won't leave shit behind me. I wanted to leave you with that memory,' he said uncomfortably.

'Of you dancing?' I asked and nodded. 'Thank you. For your dance and words. Graduation to the second year will not be pleasant. I'm sure of it,' I allowed, remembering what Euryale had said. She would test me.

'And knowing these creatures, that is an understatement. It will be like swimming in burning tar. Perhaps we will be swimming in burning tar, actually. They did say we would not all survive two years here ...'

'Yes, they did.'

'And you,' he said in a determined voice, 'have nothing but the healing spell. So I will keep an eye on you.'

'I ... thank you,' I told him, blushing. 'But I do not think ...'

'Yes, you will need help,' he said huskily, and I shook my head but gave in.

'I do thank you. I shall keep an eye on you, as well.'

'We shall,' he whispered, 'conquer what they throw at us. You and me, the little strange girl and Dana. Not sure of the frog eater, but we will see.' His eyes found Albine staring at us, and I shrugged. 'And hopefully they will work with us as Ulrich promised. And your sister did, as well.'

'Perhaps she lied,' I said angrily. Did she? On the other hand, did Albine lie to make me change my mind? I waved the thought away. 'We shall see,' I told him and turned his face to me. 'Nobody's fought for me before. Save for Dana. You have and will, and it makes me happy. Jubilant.'

He blushed, smiled uncertainly and leaned forward. I pulled him to me and kissed him gently, thinking of my first and latest kiss, the dead nobleman of Trad and hoped it would not happen again. I kissed him more forcefully, then passionately, and it was a great kiss, full of promise, playful and severe at the same time, leaving me dizzy. I did not resist as his hand went around my waist, his lips on my throat, and I even forgot about Albine's probing eyes.

'Look, Shannon,' he stammered after a while. 'I've not been entirely honest.'

'First you kiss me, and then you tell me something terrible?' I said, looking incredulous. 'You are really a girl? No, that's not it, I've seen you taking a piss with that ...' I blushed. 'Well, what is it? You just wanted a kiss and didn't like it?'

'That is the one thing I would never lie about,' he said earnestly. 'So help me God, gods. Shit, I swear by anything that could flay me skinless.'

'Euryale could,' I told him with a giggle. 'Easily.'

'I'll not invoke her name,' he pouted. 'Listen. You know I am a smuggler?'

'Yes,' I agreed. 'What does that bit of news have to do with this?'

'I belonged to a criminal organization,' he told me reluctantly. 'A big one. Did more than smuggling.'

'What?' I grimaced.

He looked away. 'Some had part in that. We were a pretty diverse lot. We are pretty spread out. Had stuff going on all along the coast. Some distasteful stuff as well.'

'Slaves?' I asked.

'Some did,' he agreed. 'Not in Boston, though. I was too young to be trusted with any of that more sinister stuff. Our uncle often got his orders from the boss, but I knew shit about anything. We all committed similar sins, and I guess that was enough for me. Made me feel like part of something better. I ran things to the hideout with my boat and that was a good enough life for me. I wasn't the type to clobber folks who didn't have it coming. Nor did I ever see what they packed in my ship. Sometimes I did help break some bones. Yes, got into a row or two for the team, but nothing heavy.'

'I see,' I said. 'A smuggler and a ruffian.'

He didn't deny it. 'Perhaps I was. And you know the outfit has connections overseas. In England, in France. And we came from Austria to the Unites States. Cyburns did. Some still live in Austria.'

I stared at him as he squirmed.

He nodded heavily to my unasked question.

'Ulrich and Ron were your brothers?' I asked incredulously.

'Cousins,' he agreed sheepishly. 'Never met Ulrich before. He is family yeah, and they live in Austria, but I knew Ron and hated his guts. A year older than I was but a big shot already in the higher circles. Shithead. But family is family and so when Ulrich asked me to get close to Dana, I kind of obeyed.'

'You got close to me, instead. Sneaky,' I sneered at him.

'And I'm telling you this for I love you and will not play their game anymore. *His*.'

'You love me?' I asked, stunned.

'Yes, I, the damned fool, love you. Didn't you feel it in my kiss?

Sometimes you are so vulnerable, other times funny and clumsy, then strong as an old oak. Ulrich respects you as well.'

'He asked you to ...'

'No, he wanted to keep me as an insurance. I resigned today. He didn't throw a fit either, so I guess he trusts you.'

I stared into his eyes, trying to fathom if he was lying. I got up and tentatively pulled him to me. He said he loved me. I smiled at him. He had just made me more vulnerable.

Then, the door flew open.

We separated lightning quick, and the sleepers were roused as the gate banged against the wall and our jailers entered. Bilac was staring at the door balefully and then hissed something at some other gorgons, all of whom denied having forgotten to lock the door. Dana was eyeing them and then at Lex and me, curiously and then with some incredulity, which hurt me. Soon she turned away, rubbing her eyes, and I found Cherry was scowling at me. She was. She knew what had happened, and I resisted the temptation of apologizing to her. I forgot about her as our jailers came to the light. They stalked in, and there were many of them. This time, they were heavily armed and armored. Glittering gorgets of steel adorned their throats, their chests and arms were smothered in leathery chainmail guards. Skirts of stiff leather and high, leather and steel meshed boots clapped on the tiled floor. They held shields of dull silvery radiance; the customary whips on wide belts and some had spears of deadly make, thin and tapering. All had swords on their hips, practical and simple, long and short both. Bilac stepped in front of us as her eyes traveled our eyes. 'Today, you will be tested. You have spent a year learning to crawl, and some of you have built your stamina significantly. Others are fast and skillful in their weaves. Some are both.'

Cosia waved her hand and weapons were brought to the room. They were of strange wooden make and supremely heavy. There were swords of many makes and spears, heavy maces, and brutal axes. 'Toys?' Ulrich asked. 'What do we do with these? Build a fire? Pick our asses?'

'If you are not careful, I will have you fight your woman,' Bilac snorted and pointed at a

blanching Anja, and we knew she was not joking. 'You will be fighting for your lives. You will fight a second class. Survivors will go forward, the losers will not. Simple.'

'Second class?' Dana spat. 'They are much more skillful than we are! You have been teaching them for a year longer!'

'No, child,' Cosia grinned. 'We hold the auction every two years. You misunderstood if you thought there are classes above you. Instead, there are nearly forty of your kind here this year, new as wet lambs in the tower, four teams altogether. Some are dead already, of course. They know as little as you do. It will be brutal but fair.'

We stared at them in stupefaction. 'You mean we will fight other humans. Saa'dark?'

Bilac nodded at the weapons. 'Yes, of course. Don't be dull. Take your pick from the weapons. You will fight the Twisted Necks. Guess how they got the name?'

'We can guess,' Lex spat.

Cosia warned us. 'Don't lose too many. The graduation year's fight will not be fair nor exciting if only one of you breathes after today. Today, those who survive will all be killers. You might be the ones to make it to the end. We taught you well. At least give us good sport.'

'I do not wish to fight,' Able growled. 'It is wrong.'

'You won't have to,' I reminded him and ignored Dana's and Lex's long looks. Anja smiled while looking around, trying to spot Able.

'Have to what?' Cosia wondered. 'Never mind, mad one. But you have to fight, indeed.'

'What if there are family or friends we know?' Dmitri demanded. 'There are not so many families who were given this gift. We have to ...?'

'You decide what you will do,' Bilac said, bored. 'We have built you up for this. We cannot force you to wish to survive. However, you will fight. Most will. Most always will.'

'And if we do survive and make it through the years? When we

340

are auctioned, what shall we be then?' Lex asked tiredly. 'Beasts.'

Bilac grunted and waved her hand to the west. 'You will be owned by the elves, and they will wish for beasts. Especially the southern lords. Some are great, generous lords, others less so and guess who will buy you? Not the noble ones, for they have their honor. Fight for the bastard elves. Alternatively, you just die here today. Up to you.'

'Take your weapons,' Cosia said.

We gathered to look at the blunt, wooden things. 'They have no edges,' Anja growled.

'They are deadly, nonetheless,' Bilac grinned. 'Just takes some more effort to kill something.'

'You are cruel bastards,' I said spitefully. 'Cruel and dull.'

Bilac's whip lashed around my neck and arm, and she pulled me to her. Her yellow eyes were clear and bright with few kind emotions. She nodded viciously. 'We are different, slave, from you. And you will benefit from our lessons if you are to survive.'

'I think your mistress told you not to hurt me,' I said to her spitefully.

'One day, I might not care,' she hissed and pushed me away, the whip uncoiling. 'Well?'

Resentfully we rifled at the pile, pulled at the wooden mockery of killing tools, hefting them, testing their length and ability, and found they were likely as deadly as the real things. Alexei and Dmitri grabbed round shields and maces. For some reason, they suited them just fine, both suddenly looking grim and deadly. They had a ruffian-like look about them, which they really were, of course. Anja and Ulrich were sifting through weapons and Dana, looking distraught, grabbed a short spear, hefting it, unsure if she had made a good choice. I shook my head at the ludicrous thought of fighting for our lives. Lex grimaced. 'Can we do this?' he asked us. 'Can we honestly kill some other group of damned unfortunates like ourselves. Really?'

Anja pulled him close and whispered. 'We have no choice now.' She glanced at me, and I cursed her. I could not just agree to her plans, not without thought and at least a greater chance of success than some thin secret and the paltry hope it gave. But she was right; it was too late then. Ulrich gazed at me with a strange look on his face. Albine fingered a long spear, and Able was forlornly staring at the pile, looking down. Anja crouched before the weapons. 'What options do we have?'

'If there is someone lying in a pool of blood before you, begging, can you ...' Lex began but shook his head. 'I don't know if I can.' Damn Euryale, I thought. I would not. 'But I will try. For you. You are a great boon to us, Shannon,' Lex said and glowered at Ulrich, who had snorted. 'She can damned well heal. She can keep us alive, perhaps.'

'She does not have the heart of a killer,' Ulrich said heavily. Anja put a hand on his biceps, and he shuddered and spoke, reluctantly but honestly. 'That is fine. I don't know if I have one either. Neither do the poor bastards we are to fight.' He visibly forced himself to act, and he grabbed at a very tall and heavy wooden long sword with a slightly curving edge. 'Don't be useless, Shannon.' Dana was scowling to herself; apparently upset, and I thought she might be, for they were relying on me, not her to keep them alive.

I picked up a long, sturdy sword I had wanted, much like a longsword, and I loved the way it felt in my hand. I missed Father's training with the blade. Anja grabbed a shield and an ax, complementing her brothers. She grunted at us. 'Remember, we are allied. In this we are, and to fail at that, will condemn all of us.'

'I've never wanted a fight with anyone,' Albine spat.

'We don't,' Ulrich grunted, 'but today we will work together.'

Lex grabbed a simple wooden axe, Cherry took a thin sword, and we were nearly ready, save for Albine. She picked up a hammer. I nodded at Able; I would try to help her. All of them. In the fight if not in escape.

'Come then,' Cosia told us, waving at the door.

And so we went. Imagine that if you can, marching from the doorway, in a similar manner you have done for the past year, but this time at the end of the road, you will be fighting for your life. We were all solemn, but Dana was still walking out the front, brazenly holding her weapon, and casting eyes around the dark recesses of the stairways as we went down the stairs. Her eyes met mine, she smiled, coldly, nervously, scourging me, and I nodded at her. I would not fail her, either.

But how could I not? To kill someone? Impossible. Perhaps Ulrich was right to doubt me. I was useless, even if I was not mad, after all.

We were herded to the main foyer. I stopped in the doorway, clutching at my shoulder. The sun was shining and that would make the Rot happy. My shoulder had been numb, but I felt a tickle, a nudge in it. I fought the instinct to look at it, and Cosia nudged me with her armored foot. 'Don't get shy, girl.' I stepped out, imagining my skin crawling with the strange stick figures, uncannily, terribly hungry, thirsty for the flesh beneath. The light bringer Mar, the strange star was just raising to the morning sky, chasing the two moons, one red, one white across the golden dark horizon, and we shivered in the cold air. Bilac and Cosia pointed us towards a spiraling stairway on the edge of the high tower, and we took it, walking precariously down the old steps. The snow had melted during the night into cold puddles, and the other Ten Tears were staring at my boots enviously.

We came to an old street, once broad and very beautiful, that much was obvious. It was littered with pillared shops and marble fronts. It was now missing roofs, and buildings had collapsed onto the street in many places. We marched up that street, where the bones of humans were evident. Then, amidst a burnt building, a giant skeleton's foot in rusty armor could be seen amidst the rubble. Our eyes were wide at the sight as they herded us toward a ruin at the end of the street.

It grew as we approached it, and we guessed it had once been an important building in the capital of House Timmerion. 'Look at that shit,' Lex wondered. 'Fit for a dozen presidents.'

'For the King,' I whispered. 'And richer than ours.'

'Kings and politicians,' Albine said. 'Emperors. That's what it's fit for. Bonaparte would love it.'

'He would,' Lex murmured.

Dmitri spat. 'Didn't we just drive him from his throne? He has a cottage now, in some island?'

'He escaped,' Albine said.

'Silence!' Cosia yelled, 'It is no palace. It is a tomb.'

It was a domed, marble building of formerly gilded walls, burnt and crushed in many places. We climbed the rubble and the cracked stairs and got up to the edge of the main building, hovering near doors that were twenty feet high. We were herded inside by Bilac's savage pushes and Cosia's impatient growls and there, after a short, dark hallway that had been stripped clean of anything valuable, we faced an arena. Cosia grinned as we gazed over the thousands of dusty seats at the labyrinthine, round bottom with crumbling walls, shadowy corridors and pools of water, miles wide.

'That is what remains of Lion's Maw. A great theater once, the floor is gone and only the vast underground rooms and storehouses remain. A dangerous place, to be sure, even without the Twisted Necks lurking inside. It is oval shaped and near three miles wide. You will go down there and face your opposition. Some might come back if you work well together.'

'Where is the opposition? These Twisted Necks,' Alexei asked nervously, his shield banging on his mace. You cald how left

'Shut up. They are coming,' Bilac growled. 'Listen up. Do not waste your energies. Use them when you must and only when you are sure it will have a suitable ... *effect.* Waste is death. You might go into a panic and gather too much of the Shades, then release it too soon and too sloppily, the weave imperfect, and that will be doom for you. You might release spells of Fury until you burn up, even after there is only work for a simple sword, finishing the wounded. Do not waste your power. Use only as much as you know you can hold. Keep your heads. That is as important as your power.'

'Here,' Cosia said, pulling Dana to her. 'Look.'

Opposite us, in the bottom of the labyrinth, our foes appeared. Humans like us, most young, apparently, they were a nervous bunch. A tall brunette girl was gesturing at us, perhaps their leader, exhorting them. Most were boys, three were but kids. Bilac grunted. Cosia was whispering to Dana. 'See them. Kill them.' My sister was nodding.

Bilac smiled at us. 'Dana will lead you. You will obey her.'

'What the ...' Ulrich began, and Dana turned to mock him with her eyes.

Dana smiled nervously. 'They don't have a chance.'

'They do,' Bilac warned. 'Do not underestimate them. Some of them discovered particular spells when they arrived. Just like some of you did. Perhaps they have humble skills, as well. And speaking of which, I will find out why the doors are open so often.' She glowered at us briefly, and I bit my lip to stop from giving Anja away with my eyes.

A horn blared mournfully, the flat tone rising in note and then it ended abruptly.

'There is no more ceremony to this than that,' Cosia stated. 'When the horn sounds again, the battle begins. Go and fight. I bet against you, by the way, so do not bother coming back. If you do, you will be killers the lot, with scars you'll carry for the rest of your miserable lives.' She snorted and pointed at an archway to the side, one leading to the labyrinth. Bilac snapped her fingers, her ring glowed briefly, and we gained the access to the Shades. We caressed it for a moment, enjoying its stunning wholeness; the mystery of the filling Void, and we saw the Twisted Necks moving to where we could not see them. Cosia cursed at us, and we roused ourselves and walked for the way down, stumbling through the small incline that had once been a marble-laden stairway with fanciful paintings of winged lions. Alexei cursed profusely as he stabbed his heel on some sharp stones. A stub of a statue was guarding the ominous door below.

We entered it and reached the darkness, the tunnels running whichever way. Our Bone Fetters were glowing in the dark. 'Stay together?' Dmitri asked.

'And get tried all at once?' Ulrich said, 'Teams we shall do teams.'

'I suppose I know the teams you have in mind,' Dana smirked. 'You and the rest together, Shannon and I alone at the front. No. We have no way to keep in touch. It's a maze. We don't know it. And you will do what I tell you to do.' She faced the big man with a cheerful smile. Ulrich shuddered in violent anger, but Anja again calmed him with a soft whisper.

'You got better ideas?' Ulrich grunted, pained with humiliation.

'Sure,' Dana grinned. 'Tear your robes and wrap up the fetters. All save one. You.'

'What do you mean? Save for Ulrich?' Dmitri asked. 'For what?'

Anja slapped his forehead. 'To be a damned decoy while the rest will be invisible in this murk. I'll do it. The dangerous part.'

Ulrich squared his shoulders. 'No. The bitch is in command, isn't she? I'll do it.'

'Very brave.' Dana said, as she knew he would not lose face by refusing. 'Don't get hurt.'

'I'll make sure I don't,' he spat.

We tore at the robes and wrapped up our forearms tightly so there was no light emanating from the Bone Fetters. Albine gave me a strip of hers. We stared at each other in silence. Ways were branching right and left and a tight one just ahead. 'Let's go forward,' Ulrich said. 'Grab them by the throat.'

'Lead on, bait,' Dana grinned. 'That way.' She pointed right. 'We'll burn them up, all right.'

'The horn has not been blown,' Alexei said dubiously, but shrugged. 'But yeah, I suppose we should move. It was not against the rules. There are none, just the way we like it.' He pushed Dmitri, who laughed back, sweating in fear.

Ulrich hefted his heavy blade and walked forward. The water was dripping, and above us, the walls glistened where ancient bits of masonry and heavy timber hung broken. 'It's incredibly like earth this place,' Lex was whispering. 'They build stuff just like we do.'

'This is prettier. Some buildings have not been built by manual labor,' I whispered. 'They used magic. Spells of Gift.'

'This could be in Rome, much like the Coliseum,' Albine said. 'We visited it once with the family. On business. Some old buildings can be seen, stabbing out of dust.'

'Well, they built here first, then on earth,' I said. 'Our ancestors came from these lands or some other place. No wonder so many things remind us of home.'

'This is our home now,' Dana hissed. 'Or grave, If you mess up. Give them no quarter unless you wish to take their place.'

'We know how to fight,' Anja said with a warning. 'Not to kill but to fight. Perhaps you shall teach us how to take lives.'

'Yes,' Dana whispered.

The horn blared, and the note ended, ringing in our ears.

The echo of it went on and on, and we stood still, not quite comprehending we were now all potentially in danger of dying.

'Go,' Dana growled at Ulrich, who nodded despite his apparent anger at the imperious demand. Allies for now, he would have to be watched. We walked on, trying to stay quiet. In the shadows, a large snake slithered, and we took the time to avoid it. I was sweating in terror. Surely, Euryale would not risk our deaths. Mine and Dana's? No. However, she might fail to protect me nonetheless, and perhaps she was mad enough to enjoy gambling away everything she had hoped to gain for such a long time, whatever that was. Her sister, even? Possibly. She was a First Born, and such creatures find logic boring, perhaps. We walked on, trying not to make too many distracting noises, but the slashes and scrapes echoing in the confines made it sound like an army was dragging its feet over the gravel. The way zigzagged many rooms opened up to the left and right, water dripped, a bit of wind buffeted the dark corners. A pack of rats ran down one way to the right.

Ulrich passed it and followed a long corridor cutting left, walking for what I thought was the middle of the arena, but I gazed at the tunnel with rats.

Light. I saw a red light burning at the end of it. I bobbed up and down, and there was another. They disappeared. 'Wait!' I hissed. 'Out there.'

Ulrich stopped and came to me. He stared down the passageway. Then he gazed at me, very close. 'You sure?'

'I'm bloody sure. They ran to the left,' I hissed at him.

'Follow me,' Ulrich said heavily. 'The healer's got a hunch.'

'I saw them,' I insisted as they filed after Ulrich, giving me uncertain looks. 'I damned well did,' I added. I was walking and trying to fathom how far it was to the passageway ahead. I was grasping at the healing spell, briefly, and then letting it go. I felt the others holding power as well, saw their spells in my mind and then, suddenly, a bit further off, two others. I felt them, just like I felt my friends' magic and those of the gorgons. They were not too near though not far either. Previously, I had known there were other saa'dark in the tower, but now I could feel they were very near, and then I sensed their whereabouts. They were holding onto spells like ours, the familiar firewall weave. I stopped. I felt them moving. To the left of us, two of them, definitely. Then, behind us. 'Ulrich!' I hissed. He stopped, looking at me incredulously.

'What now?' he hissed back. 'You have to pee?'

'I think they saw your glow. They're coming from the tunnel we just left. I think. I … feel them.'

'You sure?' Lex asked. 'I feel nothing but the Shades.'

'You feel them?' Dana asked, perplexed. 'We all feel there's something happening with the power, but you are saying you see individual spells?'

'You are not seeing things again?' Dmitri asked, turning me around, and I ripped my hand from his grasp.

'I am not! No!' I said. 'They are coming. Two? More perhaps, but two, at least.'

'She is special, is she not?' Alexei smirked and clapped my back. 'Sucks at rag balling but knows stuff. Where are they?'

'I said behind us. Some are right over there, soon,' I said with fear thrumming in my voice, turning to stare back at the corridor we left. 'Get ready! Put the weapons away, or they will burn up.'

'Good thinking,' Anja grinned nervously, and Cherry smiled at me, nodding in appreciation I found briefly annoying. We turned to stare up the tunnel, a huddled bunch of people unsure of what to do. We slowly put down our weapons, and I held my breath, feeling foolish. Was I wrong? I turned to look back in the other direction, and Ulrich was about to explode. But he didn't. Instead, he froze. A step echoed in the tunnel we had vacated. Then, lights, whisperings.

'They are coming,' Dana said. 'She was right. Line up.' They did.

'I told you,' I said darkly. 'Should we speak to them first?'

'No,' Dana said quietly.

'Hold,' Ulrich added.

The enemy rounded the corner.

The enemy was young and scared.

One was a boy, with freckles and a quick, smart face, an astonished look on it. One was a girl, tall and gangly, with a scarred forehead. Her eyes were slanted and she looked like she was from far away. They were holding power, the same fiery spell we all knew. They took a tentative step forward as if wondering and doubting their eyes as they saw us standing there. I saw they were reluctant.

'Wait!' said the boy hurriedly. 'We ran away because we don't wish to ...'

'Kill them,' Dana hissed and fire spewed out from her hands. That somehow ripped open the gates of hell and the Ten Tears; tense to begin with did the unthinkable. Screams were heard as my friends sought to bury their fears with fire, to survive, doubts pushed away by Dana's initiative. Strings of flames danced from the outstretched hands of my compatriots, and I saw three rip through and engulf the boy's torso. His face betrayed horror and surprise as the flames cut holes in him and then exploded around him to engulf the corridor and the floor. Water hissed and evaporated, rats died with brief squeals in hidden holes, and so did the boy, dropping to his knees in a terrible inferno, and then falling on his face, his hands gone. It all happened so fast it was hard to understand. He was but a child, and then he was dead. The girl had fallen onto her belly in the water and now she shrieked as the flames licked at her back. She shot up amidst the spreading flames, her hair on fire, and she ran off screaming.

'Cut the spells,' Dana shrieked. 'Well done,' she added.

'He wanted to …' I added in terror and saw Anja's face, with a told-you-so look scourging me.

'Die. He wanted to die for that is the only way for us out of this,' Dana told me with bitter tones as she pushed me. 'Down here, sister, I'm the one who makes miracles. I just taught the Ten Tears how to survive. In addition, we have more to do now. We will do it too. We know how.'

'I …' Lex began; his face shocked as he stared at the flaming corpse, but he did not finish as Anja pushed him.

'She is right. We have to finish this and wonder about our souls later,' she said hollowly. Dmitri and Alexei were picking up their weapons, and Dana was walking forward.

'You feel anything else out there, sister?' she asked.

'Nothing near,' I said with a trembling, angry voice, about to explode with emotion. Rage? Fear? 'She is still holding the spell, but she is running.'

'Let's go, then,' Dana hissed. My sister nodded, giving me an unsympathetic, challenging look and went forward. Albine beat her to it. Her face was ashen, and a bit mad, sweating in terror. She was whispering, and I caught what she was saying. 'Able. Wait for me.'

'Sister?' Able said. 'She is ...' *Suicidal,* I added in my mind.

'After her,' Albine said suddenly, her voice high-pitched and scared as she dodged past Dana, leaving her weapon. She jumped over the charred corpse, running after the burning girl. Able took after her.

'Wait!' Ulrich hissed as we grabbed at the wooden weapons. 'Gods damn it!'

We ran after them, cursing as Dmitri spilled into a pool of slippery mucus, hindering us, but finally we scrambled after Albine and Able. We all stared at the dead boy as we passed him, and Anja was wiping tears off her face. His death would change everything. So far, we had been the victims. Now we had made a choice.

Perhaps I had to make a choice as well.

Perhaps the Rot did not matter.

Perhaps I should accept death rather than help Euryale. Even Dana's. Anja was right. Perhaps I would not truly be alive after surviving the Spire? I would be a husk of Shannon, neither the old nor the new one, but a living dead. Euryale claimed she wished to return the gods and justice, but there was no justice in the Fanged

Spire. I had seen the Regent. He had seemed wise and kind.

However, I had no time to think about it.

We splashed after the still shrieking girl until we reached a long, spacious corridor with a rounded ceiling that was moldy and glistening with moisture. We could hear the girl sobbing in pain as she tore forward, and we smelled burning, a horrid stench of scorched meat and hair. We saw a pillared doorway, and Albine, Dana, and the Russians entered a cellar with many sets of stairs running down and glimpsed heaps of rotting benches. Most of the Tears jumped down to left and right, dropping down to the dark for the burning girl was running crazily across the room, the burning Bone Fetter and flaming clothing weird in the dark.

Then, she fell in the middle of the room with sparkles, shuddering and dying, the flames claiming her flesh. I was following Ulrich as he was entering the cellar, but he stopped. He was peeking through the doorway, and I was trying to get past him. 'Go!' I hissed.

'Something is wrong,' he complained.

He was right.

'I cannot see them, Isabella,' a panicked, strange boy yelled ahead, and I felt many people harnessing spells of the Fury.

'Beware!' I screamed, for they had been waiting there, ambush ready, and had used their renegades as bait. And Ulrich entered the room, his hand ablaze with a flaming Bone Fetter.

'There!' a female shrieked, and Ulrich stopped on top of the stairs, hesitating. Flames lit up in the darkness and coils reached for the large man who blanched.

I reacted. I saw the spells, and somehow I reached out. I tore at the weaves, ripping off bits and pieces of them and some of the spells simply died, others changed direction to scorch the ceiling and the walls. One turned to fiery flowers, others stopped in midair.

However, one went on.

I cursed and ran, fighting the speed of the flames as I threw myself at Ulrich without thinking too hard about the consequences. Below, I dimly noticed Dana, Albine, and the Russians also harnessing spells of Fury. Fires flew back in the dark, thick or thin, exploding to reveal parts of the room, weaving for the unseen enemy casters. Yet, for Ulrich and me, things got hot. The spell missed us but hit the doorway, the flames exploded. I clawed and pulled him back as the heat tried to envelop us, igniting his robes. Ulrich screamed as a nearly living, bluish gout of flame was clutching at his shoulder, the skin growing dark, then peeling. I gathered the healing power and released it so fast I could barely understand it, the icy, frigidly flowing energy ripping from me, and it healed him. The flame went out as he rolled in a filthy water puddle, his flesh still singed and charred in places from the stubborn magical fire. There was an inferno roaring at the doorway, and we backed away, seeing but glimpses of what was going on beyond. I approached him tentatively while cursing the roaring flames.

'Don't use more of it!' he hissed, getting up and rubbing his pained shoulder. 'Move to the side, in case they decide to hurl something through the flames. He pulled me to the side, and we stayed there. The doorway was blazing, old wooden frames burning with an odd, sizzling sound, maggots popping out of holes they lived in, bursting in the heat. Stone veneer was falling into molten puddles off the ceiling. The sea of flames was wavering, and we could see something of what was going on. We heard Albine shriek, whether in anger or pain, I knew not, and an enemy, a boy actually, could be seen running from the dark room towards the stairway, flames leaving his hand. Apparently, Albine was alive, for the wind she had summoned the day we arrived, hot as cinders blew out at the boy, but this time it was deadly and controlled. We saw Anja spilling to the floor with a curse, and the boy who had been charging caught the brunt of the cinder wind, tearing him from the ground, spiraling him madly head over heels to the dark, his flesh ripped and flapping.

'My good God,' I said.

'Jesus,' Ulrich agreed, trying to edge past the flames. 'The kid's got some pending frustrations, it seems.' His voice was breaking as he saw Anja was hurt, holding her head. Several figures could be seen skittering at the far side of the room. A tall girl was pointing at something I could not see. Several of the enemies turned to look our way. They were gathering spells.

Then Dana showed her mettle. I saw her walking forward.

'Dana!' I shrieked.

I felt an enormous, terribly potent spell being gathered by my sister. I caught a glimpse of her face.

She was laughing, her eyes glittering with fury and mirth both. Lines of fire sprung from the enemy for her and I cried, for I forgot what I had done for Ulrich. It was too late to interrupt the spells. Dana would die.

Instead, she ran forward and rolled under the flames. A thick set of flames tore from her hands, ripped to the dark figures and an inferno erupted as she ignited a tall boy on a sort of a balcony, his body curling crazily, and then falling broken amidst the floor. 'We must get back in there!' I shouted, terrified, for I saw new strands of fire rip from the dark for Dana.

'Impossible, not through here we can't!' Ulrich grunted, slapping at the flames. In the room, Dana stood in the center, incredulously laughing like a maniac as she sidestepped some of the fiery spells. Her hands pushed out another set of high fires, and she screamed as she let her spell explode in front of her, cutting off several thick streams of light coming for her. Instead of a simple firewall, her exploded spell shot madly for the far wall and pulled along the spells of the enemy, growing hers to an enormous wave of fiery death. She shook her hands wildly, and the firestorm slammed like a breaking wave across the room. That end of the room was alight. A girl was flapping on the ground, dying as she burnt up. Another was but a whitened heap of bones, and others were scrambling for a stairway, trying to breathe.

Alexei and Dmitri dragged at Anja, and the three Russians linked hands and stepped forward, their spells weaving mad, bluish flames in a net-like way to cut off the enemy from the stairway. Two of our enemies were caught, their hair burning. Some escaped up and spread on a sort of balcony, temporarily out of trouble. 'Four or five left?' Ulrich asked darkly, swallowing bile and then looked back. 'Come, let's find a way out of here and over there, fast as you can!'

We ran back, trying to find a way around. We took a passage right, running in water to our knees, Ulrich's robes dragging him down until he tore his clothing off. Somewhere close, we heard the roar of battle. 'Here!' I shrieked, pulling him with me to a cracked hole in the wall, then through a small, musty room and a tunnel leading up a bit.

'Hurry,' he panted and we did rush, rushed madly, little heeding the rubble and a potential broken leg. Up ahead, the corridor filled with fire, just briefly and figures were running. Three people, one the woman who apparently led them, waved at two burly boys and stopped. She waited, grinning like a demon, her hair in tangles.

She harnessed a spell of Fury and released it, lightning fast. Fire was shooting out back the way they had come from. A shriek was heard, first panicked, then loud and inhuman as she held the spell, tottering a bit, exhausted. Someone was hurt, badly hurt. I heard Lex scream a challenge and felt a pang of relief he was alive. Then a wall of fire burst across the hallway, but the woman stepped back from it, her face smiling maniacally, still embracing the power, even if she was trembling with the effort. She flicked her fingers, and I felt she was doing something unusual, weaving something strange, and pulling at the roaring primal fire, twisting it with cinders and hot winds, a uniquely different spell from the spell we all knew. It was likely something she had discovered the day we all arrived by accident. She suddenly hefted a fiery, magnificent spear of fire, and she threw it deftly. We watched in horror as Alexei staggered into sight, his chest and side horribly burned already, his mouth open, skin melting as the spear burned through his innards. She weaved a wall of fire over Alexei's smoldering body and rolled away as Lex screamed in anger. He was throwing more light and flame above her. She was giggling, but our friends were blocked.

We were not.

'Alexei!' Ulrich screamed, and then calmed himself. 'Can you heal him?'

'I cannot raise the dead,' I said hollowly. 'What shall we do?' I asked, horrified.

'What?' Ulrich spat. 'Avenge Alexis, before more die. Three? We shall kill them and cry later. I want to get the hell away from here.' Out there on the right, some kind of a fight was still going on. Dana laughed, and apparently someone died, for a voice shrieked in terrible agony.

'Three,' I said, terrified. 'We are but two.'

He turned to me, grabbing me by shoulders. 'You can do this. I know it is hard. Keep calm. Fight with me, for me, and we shall survive.'

'I will,' I said softly, trying to gather courage, and we went on.

We sneaked past the burning wall, dimly seeing Lex cursing on the other side. Our eyes met briefly, and he looked at Ulrich in horror and ran off. Ulrich snorted. 'Thinks I will behead you, likely.' I shook my head as I wondered the same and saw he was eyeing the corridor ahead. The Bone Fetters were bouncing up ahead, we took after them stealthily, and Ulrich hid his hand behind his back. Then, suddenly, the lights stopped, milling in some confusion. 'Softly, tread lightly,' he said. We did, checking the ground carefully. Ahead were two hulking boys. Both were nodding dutifully at the girl who was gesturing around the room. They were setting up a trap again. 'I will scorch the bitch. Then we will take on the other two. Can you charge one with the sword?'

'Sword?' I asked, looking down at it. It felt strange and heavy in my hand.

'You have nothing else, do you?' he hissed. 'I shall do all I can, but you have to pull your weight. For Alexei.'

I nodded, and we sneaked forward. Perhaps if I swung the blade at the head, it would just knock them out. Let the gorgons decide what will happen to those who are wounded. I nodded at Ulrich, shaking in near-crippling fear. 'Go,' he mouthed, and so I prayed and ran forward in the dark, hoping the way would be clear, then imagined a hole I might drop into and break my neck. Ulrich harnessed the spell of Fury; I felt it and the streams of flames danced from his fingers, reaching for the woman. One of the boys next to her blanched and pushed her aside instinctively, and Ulrich's fierce fires burned through the boy in an eye blink, bizarrely looking like a snake writhing inside him, the flames exploding on a wall behind, flames flicking from his mouth, ears and nose. His remains fell to the stones with little ceremony. The other boy turned to face Ulrich in shock as the woman was struggling to get up, her face a furious mask of surprise and rage. I was close now, rushing as fast as I could, all the lessons gone from my head, and the eyes of the boy widened at the sight of a scared, sword-wielding girl rushing him. The boy blanched, fumbling with a wooden ax, but he was too late. I had done this before. I loved swords fighting, its practices, and the exertion. Now I would be tested. The blade went up with strange familiarity and came down. It hit. It hit hard. I could see his face caving in strangely, and he fell on his back, trembling and vomiting. The woman, Isabella, got up next to me, staring at the death in shock, and I waited for Ulrich to do his deed.

Nothing.

The woman glanced at the empty corridor. Her brown eyes were burning with the joy of battle, her angular face sweat stricken.

'Well,' she hissed. 'You have an enemy, I think. In addition to me.' She did not hesitate as she gathered the power of Fury and threw fire at me, skillfully entwining it around my feet. I fell away, rolling, hollering in fear, so close to her as the flames licked at my boots, my calves, hips and long hair. It burned horribly, and I felt my skin and flesh getting seared, my fine clothing burning, even my boots. I understood Euryale's lessons of pain more clearly. As naturally as an otter ducks under water, I grasped at the healing power, the supreme Gift, touched the healing springs and released them with icy, frigid relief while rolling, then again, and again as the flames still licked at my torso and then again, feeling senseless with exhaustion. I briefly saw Isabella's eyes, confusion playing on her features as I should have been a dead and charred bit of darkened bone, but I was not. I rolled and rolled, throwing myself away, my shirt in stubborn flames as I tore it off. Isabella's face was glistening with exertion, her body trembling even, but she pushed the fire still further, trying to cut me off from two directions. I scrambled back and dodged to the corridor. 'Ulrich!' I screamed.

She laughed and let the fire go, apparently too tired to hold it. I felt she was summoning the fiery spear again, her face growing gray with fatigue, and yet the weapon grew out of her hand, simmering and deadly. She held it, her face gaunt from exhaustion as she walked toward me. I dodged to the room, holding the sword, eyeing the thin, utterly deadly blade aimed my way. I tried to break the spell, but nearly fell from fatigue. I could not. My breast hurt. She spoke to me ferociously. 'I'll kill the rest yet. I'm sorry for it, but perhaps not sorry enough. I love this, in some strange way. I'll geld your boys and roast the girls, and I'll start with you.'

'I doubt you can beat them all,' I said with growing anger for she threatened Dana and Lex, all my friends. Suddenly I was too angry to fear, perhaps so also for Ulrich's betrayal. And for poor Alexei. 'There is nothing more to this, then. Come,' I told her venomously.

'No, nothing more. Hope your silly wooden sword can handle this thing,' she grinned as she lunged, dancing close though clumsily. She had not trained in such a sport. Few had.

But I had.

I was going to have to kill the girl if I could. I kept moving, sword at the ready, and tried to remember how to move my feet. Footwork, footwork, like Father had said and taught. Sword at the ready, pointing at her head, no, knee. I stumbled as she tried to flank me with a small rush. No, sword beside the right side of the head. I raised the sword away from her, the blade up in the air. Then, legs. Go back, step right, and keep the sword at the ready, I swore, staring at her eyes. I felt so clumsy. I tried to imagine the training, the ways of disciplined fighting. I was to beat her or die. I cursed myself, swearing aloud as Isabella smiled, thinking I was about to crumble. Instead, I was gathering strength.

I was the master of this rotten, shit filled room. I was the master of her.

She grinned, and I knew she was going to attack. I could see it in her eyes and the small tensing of her muscles. That too is something learned in training.

She shuffled forward, the fiery blade aiming for my face. She was thrusting as quickly as she could, but it was not really all that quick. I stepped aside, trying to forget the fiery blade and performed a thrust with all my strength, my foot slapping the ground and my arms pumping forward so the wooden sword point aimed for her throat. The thrust was enough, the result of weeks of tedious practice. She yelped, the spear disappeared in ashes as her mind let go of the spell of Fury, and she flew on her back, trying to breathe, struggling to get up. Her eyes were huge with fear, disappointment, and anger. I felt she was trying to cast a fiery wall, at least she was harnessing the Shades, and so I moved forward with tears in my eyes and struck down with all my energy, and hit her throat again. She jumped into the air with the power of the hit, gagging, gurgling, and crying, and then she died, her eyes losing the luster of life.

I dropped the sword, nearly gathering the healing power, but I was too horrified and tired to do so. I cried next to her, my long hair matted with the blood streaming from her mouth, and I realized she had bitten her tongue in pain.

The boy I had struck had not died, after all. He stood up behind me, cursed me thickly, and he called for the deadly spell that would leave me in a heap of bones, for I was beyond tired. I would die and I did not care, for I had deserved it. The boy's eyes went large as saucers, and he snarled. My muscles were screaming, my mind whirling, and the boy was going to get his vengeance.

Something moved behind the boy. A tip of a small wooden sword exploded from his eye. He fell.

Cherry popped out of a cindery, smoky spell, trembling with fatigue and smiled at me.

The horn blared forlornly.

We had won. I stared at the corpse Ulrich had burnt and I saw his heart blazing between a ribcage. I passed out.

PART 4: FINDINGS AND FAILURES

'Those who demand the Devourer for favors often end up unhappy, their souls broken, just like a ship's keel in a storm. We have a deal and do not ask for more.'

Euryale to Shannon

CHAPTER 15

I dreamt.

I saw Isabella's face in flames, her arms reaching for me as she died. I dreamt I reached for her, trying to help, but could not, for all I found were flames. Her hand shot out from the inferno, clutching me by my throat. The hand did not burn. Indeed, it was not painful in the least, but it was choking me. I felt I was losing consciousness amidst fires, blades, and the last thing I saw was my sword on the ground, flaming to cinders. Isabella's hand crumbled to dust.

Then, nothing. Shades, movement. Whispers, shouts, and a strange wailing noise.

I suddenly felt alive again. Sort of. I stared around and found I was seated on a sturdy horse. I lifted my arms and stared at an ornate, silvery armor, guarding all of my body. I realized I was wearing a mask, chiseled silver covering my face, a white fox framing it, and I pulled at the thing to see better. My sleeve was caught by a pair of twisted spears set on the saddle, a sad pennant of red forlornly flapping from each, and then I understood what the wail was.

I had seen this dream before. Before even we came to Aldheim. As a child. Many times. It was the dream I had been happy in, carefree and with a purpose in my life. Except this dream was much more real. I glanced around at the surroundings, and the horse reacted to my sudden movements by taking a small step. I was in the middle of a snowy landscape. It was a harsh, primal landscape, and I should have been cold, but I was not, and I felt nothing. I stared at the land, wondering at the ancientness of it all and somehow knew this was the land my powers were born in. Niflheim? Euryale's home. How could it be?

I placed a hand on my hip and noticed a magnificent sword. I was clutching it. It was as long as my foot; bright as a star, so bright it was hard to see the sword's edges. I stared at the blade, it was reddened and glistening, the carved metal bloody. I furrowed my brow and pulled on the helmet clumsily, and the horse shuddered as I struggled.

I froze. In the periphery of my sight, I saw slight movement. I turned my head that way, lightning fast and saw there were wolves not far from me. They were white and gray, grizzled yet oddly clean, not the sort of animals you would see in the wild typically, but somehow pure and pristine and very calm, with a purpose. They were not threatening, and for some reason, I thought I knew them. Both of them.

'Able?' I said.

I froze. My voice was breaking. Something was wrong with it. It had sounded like a rasping crow, and I put a hand on my armored chest. The armor was rent. I was sure it was and I looked down. There was a ragged hole in my heart, and my finger flickered into it and came out bloody. I panicked and sobbed, but again my voice was strange.

I realized why. I was not breathing

I woke up as Lex was shaking me.

I glanced around in panic, but I could breathe now. The snow was gone, so were the wolves, and instead, I saw the Ten Tears, some sitting listlessly in a new, round chamber. 'You OK?' Dana asked, concerned, gliding to sit next to me. 'They said you are just exhausted. You spent a lot of power saving yourself.' Her hand touched my hair, and I noticed some of it was dry and burnt. Most of it is still there.'

I tried to focus, concentrated on breathing.

We had been shown a different room in the Fanged Spire. I had been laid down on a fluffy bed and wore a dark, blissfully cumbersome and warm dark robe like the others did. I noticed there were no dead students staring down at us with their stone eyes. I looked around. The rest were huddled near each other, except for Able. He was seated near a door, unhappy as usual, holding his knees as his dead face stared at me. Then I noticed the sounds of misery and loss. Dmitri was weeping. Anja was holding him.

Alexei was dead.

I remembered that now. He had been speared and burnt, and I had seen it. I sobbed for my friend, holding my head as Dana stroked me. So many had died. The opposing team had had no chance. None. Thanks to Dana. She eyed me as I looked at her and smiled briefly as if she knew what I was thinking. She did, for she spoke. 'You did well. None can deny that. Took out that Isabella.'

I was shaking my head.

I had killed.

She had died for me, brutally suffocating on her own blood. I jerked up, holding my head and face. Her name had been Isabella, she probably had family someplace wondering if she was happy, and now she was gone. We had all done things to change us forever. I sat up on a bed next to the door. Cherry dropped on the bed next to me, looking concerned. I wept and cursed, and she rubbed my shoulder. Dana was still hovering nearby and crouched next to me. 'It is fine, Shann. Had to be done. And you did very well.'

'She couldn't breathe,' I told her softly. 'She was flapping there like a damned fish, dying and gurgling, and I had no choice.'

'I know, Shann,' Dana said. 'But now we live on.'

'For what?' I hissed. 'Anything they promise us is a cruel joke. There are neither words nor pacts they will ever keep. Euryale ...'

'Lex and Cherry, can you give us some room. Please?' Dana asked and lifted an eyebrow as the two lingered. They left, reluctantly, but they did leave.

I grabbed her face and pulled her close so only she heard. 'I think we should escape.'

'There is some plan I know nothing of?' she said, with some pity and spite. 'A tunnel dug across the seafloor? Or perhaps a giant bird to lift us to a paradise island somewhere? You and I, we have a plan. Remember? And we have invested our souls in it.'

'Just surviving is not enough for me,' I whispered urgently, 'I doubt they will ever let us escape this place. Why should they? They think us maggots. They cheer and holler happily as we die and dispense of our lives carelessly like they would the remains of an unappetizing dinner. And if we do get out of here with their blessing? We will be monsters. Let us try to get our friends out.' I nodded at Anja and the weeping Dmitri.

She scoffed. 'We have no friends, and I shall have to remind you again there is only you and me, sister,' she said somewhat desperately. 'We will forget all of this. Trust me. One day it will be a distant memory. Like home is. Earth. We have not betrayed these people. They have their destiny, and we have helped them survive this day. Did we not? You and I. We did it. Not they. Do not betray me, sister, I beg of you,' she said resolutely and hugged me. Then she got up to stalk the chamber.

I disagreed with her. She wished to run down a road I feared and distrusted, and I thought she was wrong. Alexei was dead. He was gone. It was my fault. Perhaps it was. Yet, Dana's will was so strong, she was so confident and overpowering that I actually nodded, blushed with anger. The old Shannon did. She eyed me carefully, her beautiful face motionless, and she was wondering about my thoughts. To hide my turmoil, I glanced at Cherry and smiled at her encouragingly, gesturing for her to come over, grabbing her arm.

'She saved my life,' I told them and hugged Lex as he sat next to me. 'Happy you made it as well.'

'It was kind of wild,' he said morosely, wiping his face. 'I killed someone, I think. In the large room. There was a shadow; someone running, and I set someone ablaze. He fell into a hole. It is better to die like that, I guess. I mean with fire. When you use the spell of Fury at a person, I suppose it's cleaner than a knife in the gut, perhaps. I am sorry you had to ...' he hesitated, and then rubbed his face again, more aggressively, whimpering to himself. 'They were damned kids. Many of them younger than us. Like Albine.'

I took a deep breath and gently stroked his shoulder. 'Grandmother said we were old enough. I wonder if this is why she

375

did not wish to send us here earlier. So we could be stronger and wiser and could weather this place. She didn't know anything about it, but she had seen the summoning before and thought nothing benevolent was waiting for us here.'

'I feel pretty lost, girl,' Lex said, his eyes haunted. 'This will not end well. I am losing hope.'

'I am too,' I said. Dana was still staring at me as she walked around, gauging my reactions as Lex cursed, got up and he leaned over and kissed me. I saw Cherry's eyes pop out and then she grinned, fidgeted and blushed, looking very bothered. She got up, walked over to the other wall and dragged a bed next to me, and Lex was still kissing me until she poked him. I smiled at her and shrugged at Lex, who scowled.

'She meaning to guard you?' he asked self-consciously as Dana was also staring at him with an unreadable face.

'I think she is. She did already,' I told him and got up. I searched and found Albine and walked over to her, sat next to her and pulled her to me. She let me, and she sobbed there, Able hovering nearby. 'You OK?' I asked the kid.

She shook her head. 'It was dark, so dark. I released the spell I tried to use the day we arrived. Did you see? It was horrible.'

'I know, I saw it,' I told her. 'Did you hope they would kill you?'

'What?' she asked.

'When you ran off. Did you hope they would …'

376

'Perhaps,' she allowed, leaning on me. 'I just thought it might be for the best.'

'Tell her she is an idiot,' Able said.

'I won't tell you what Able said, but he did not agree with your plan,' I said and stared at Anja.

Anja lifted her face toward me as if expecting my look.

Was it my fault? Anja's face did not say that. There was no anger there; only deep loss, and I wondered what she thought about. Had I said yes the night before, agreed to try to escape that very night, Alexei might not be dead. Likely, they would all be dead, and I a prisoner, but perhaps not. We could have built a raft, perhaps. I shook my head at the absurd notion and then looked at Able. I thought of Dana, I thought of myself, and the new Shannon took over.

I nodded at Anja, and she looked away, but there was a look of understanding on her face.

I would do what I wished to do, not what Dana hoped for. I would decide later what to do with Ulrich. Would I let Dana handle him? Or try to help her? I looked at a large shape sitting all the way across from us, in the shadows of the room, staring at Anja and Dmitri. Ulrich. His eyes met mine, cold and brutal, and there was not an emotion there I could possibly read. In the battle, he had seemed like a friend. Then he had abandoned me. I nodded at myself. He would face Dana one day. Anja expected me to let them fight it out. I felt a demon whispering in my ear, a devil tugging at my heart. He would pay. Anyone who betrays me should pay for it. From now on.

'Can you help us?' I asked.

'Huh?' Albine said, drowsy.

'I asked your brother,' I said softly. 'I asked him if he could help us. For we have to escape and to do so, we have to be rid of the Bone Fetters.'

'Oh,' she said. 'You agree with Anja, then?' Albine said, her voice full of hope.

I stared at the dead boy looking in my eyes, scared. 'We have to be rid of the shackles. Or find ways out of here ...'

I thought of the magnificent mirror in Euryale's study. That was the way. I knew the spells. I had heard them, and I had felt them from the day we arrived. I had not attempted any of them, for I had had no chance, but I remembered the spell Euryale had used to open it, and then I stiffened.

She had said something to it. There was more to it than the spell. Gods, it was not easy to escape the hellhole.

I took a hard breath and whispered. 'Able, listen up.'

'Yes?'

'You wish to help your sister?'

'I would like to help the lot of you. I'm happy you do as well. Though perhaps you should have tried to leave yesterday.'

'Shut up,' I told him impatiently and softened my tone. 'And thank you. There are books in her study. There was a glowing one. Perhaps others.'

'I am dead. Only you can touch me,' he said with incredulity.

I nodded. 'There are thousands of books there in her room. She collects them. Try to find something that looks promising. Anything that might offer a chance to do something about this situation. Attempt to find a clue to the Fetters. Something that might help us escape. Find this one book. It is glowing, as I said. Can't miss it unless there is a library of such things somewhere.'

'That will take forever! Perhaps longer!' he complained.

'You have forever. You don't actually sleep, dolt, so …'

'Do it, Able,' Albine said irascibly and then smiled. 'God, like old times.'

'He called you a turd,' I said while scowling at Able.

'Tell him, I'll switch his rear if I die,' she said with a giggle.

'It's dark and scary out there,' he complained. 'But I think I can, yes. I've been dreaming.'

'Dreaming? Of our death again?'

'He dreams?' Albine asked.

'He saw a dragon eating …'

Able shrugged. 'Yes, I saw that. Strange dreams. I have seen a beast in the dreams. A dangerous one, but not a gorgon. I think it was a dragon. Thinking about it makes me nervous. I … I shall look around. Hopefully, they won't grab me.'

'They cannot see you,' I hissed so loud the others stared at me. I shrugged apologetically.

'And if I do find something? This book?' he complained. 'And you cannot get to it?

'I have a plan,' I said. He looked skeptical, but finally Able got up and went. He walked through the door, and I begged the gods to grant him luck.

I would meet Euryale soon. That much I was sure of. And I had something of a plan.

Sort of.

CHAPTER 16

We went to bed and waited. There was a small window high up on the wall of this room, and we all stared at it, seeing the golden light replaced by the Two Wolves, the red and white moons. We had had no food, again, and so it took time to fall asleep.

'Think Nox is lost or just drunk? Or tasted his own lard and died?' Lex complained, and I tittered though the mood was still somber. I waited, and soon the others were asleep, in troubled, nightmare-filled slumber full of burning students and lost friends, but sleep nonetheless, save perhaps for the devious Anja, who was an insomniac. Deep in the night, I felt the familiar call in the shadows and got up, my hair standing up at its ends. I nearly fell on my face, for Cherry was curled at the end of my bed, anchoring the blanket, sleeping with her mouth open. I glanced around, hugging myself, and I noticed Dana's eye was half open. I shook my head at her and went to the door where the shadows were deepest. Then, a tingling and dizzying touch of wind and tumbling ice, and a portal opened, and I was grasped. I fell in the shades and shadows, feeling slightly nauseous and stumbled painfully on my knees onto a carpet. Euryale stood in front of me, regally gazing down at me, her face swathed with a scarf, the light of her eyes barely showing through the cracks. I bowed. 'Mistress.'

'Yes, it is your mistress, and you did well, indeed,' she said and ran her long, cold fingers through my hair. 'Brilliantly, in fact. Could not have done it much better myself. I think you might have a chance to dance with the ghoul.'

'I killed, mistress. I am not happy about it and cannot share the joy of it,' I told her dully. 'And we are starving.' I stared around her study. I noticed the mirror was uncovered so she had likely been using it not too long ago. Her eyes sought mine and saw what I had been looking at.

'Indeed. I traveled to the elven lands to set up a deal,' she said. 'We will be ready for the Feast of Fates.'

'With the elf whose wife you hurt?' I asked her.

'Don't worry about these plans,' she said with her singing voice, her hands tugging at my hair savagely. 'And change your tone.'

'I worry, for I know nothing of elven manners, my mistress,' I told her with a wince and then brightened as I spied Able amongst the furniture on the far wall. His dead eyes were scourging Euryale as the beast held onto my hair. Euryale's eyes sneaked that way, but she saw nothing and turned back to me. 'If I could learn some more of it, instead of suffering Cosia and Bilac, it would be for the best, no? Mistress? Perhaps seated right here, studying about the people and the places, it might be beneficial to our cause?'

'I doubt the Regent minds if you can curtsy like a human should to an elf since his lovely wife is afflicted,' she said suspiciously while thrumming her fingers on the desk. She let go of my hair.

'I would know of the world, mistress. I will deal with other elves than his highness and do not wish to die swiftly simply for omitting a gracious word or a humble bow. Especially to a southern elf? To a ma tarish?' I said carefully, for it was a dangerous game to manipulate her.

She smiled like a ghost, no emotion, and the twitch of her lips fleeting and cold. 'I see. And you would learn, no? Curious, curious,' she breathed, turning to the covered mirror. 'No doubt you would like its name as well, no? The mirror. Just because you are curious no doubt. However, I find knowledge dangerous. You were in Trad for five minutes and nearly forgot your sister in that time.'

'I shall not do that again. In addition, if we gain our freedom, one of us has to know the ways of the land,' I told her.

She snickered. 'Go to Himinborg or any city of the House Vautan. Especially Trad. These two cities and their Houses give humans rights. Do not go to the south, or the north. You know this already.'

'Won't I still be the Hand of Life, even after I rescue Hel's Eye? And be welcome in the north?'

She grinned and hesitated. 'That depends on my plans and how they will work out. And as I said, you need not worry about *my* plans, Shannon. No. Nevertheless, you will be free, perhaps, even if there is no more Regent and things will be different in Aldheim. There will be changes. The gods will return, won't they?'

I stayed silent, trying to decide if I should push her more, for she hinted at her plans. She was planning for something big. Perhaps to get her due from the gods. Perhaps something more, Or something else. She seemed in a dangerous, ferocious, and fey mood, and there was emotion in her eyes I had not seen before. It was anticipation, murderous anticipation. She was swallowing and grinning to herself, and I knew she had waited a long time for me. 'I see, mistress,' I told her. 'But I do wish to learn. And you are the most learned creature one might humbly learn from, older than men and ancient elves.'

She smiled with pleasure.

My gods, I thought. She was susceptible to flattery.

'Yes, I am,' she agreed and walked around me. I stayed still as she leaned to gaze at my neck, then my shoulder. 'It has advanced. I feel it. But I will be able to remove it, shortly after the Feast of Fates.'

'I thank you for reminding me,' I said hollowly. The Rot. I had forgotten it. I would die if I betrayed her. A terrible, horrible death. Would it matter if the others lived?

Yes.

I was afraid to die. Gods be cursed, as I did not wish to go to Hel.

She walked around me. I shuddered in fear as she drew a finger across my cheek. 'My pleasure.' She stopped before me. 'You fought like a battle maiden of Dark Waters, kept your calm and did very well indeed. You even killed. It will get easier, and so I think you grew into a more useful, less innocent creature yesterday. Perhaps I should reward you with this request. For I sense you love such stories as can be found in my library.'

'My sister is dear to me and I will not let you down,' I said, happy as she took her hand away, turned to sit down after dragging a chair to face me and was soon leaning on her knees.

She spoke happily. 'The Rot is there to guard and tether you, and so is your sister. Do not worry, Shannon, as I traveled today in northern Aldheim I succeeded in finding us opportunities to finish our collective pact, I can tell you I did. Yes, I did. I planted a seed, Shannon, which will bear us dark, thickly delicious fruits. It will be well, my love. You will stay here, I think, for months only. I am in a hurry now, for the seed I planted is growing impatient quickly, and the Feast will be exciting, full of new opportunities, previously missed.'

'Is this fruit made up of poison, treachery, and death?' I asked.

She nodded. 'Indeed. I planted that kind of a seed, girl, and it was delicious and deadly, and it will bring you freedom, no matter its nefarious nature. And to your sister as well. Never forget that. And yes, I have decided I shall let you study. I have precious little time for questions, but I will choose books for you to read and you shall come here each morning. It is a sacrifice for me, human girl, for I value my privacy and the pristine mornings spent in contemplation, but then, perhaps I can yield just a bit on that. You were betrayed yesterday?' she cocked her head.

'Ulrich,' I said.

'Ah, it was the vengeful boy who betrayed you? Did he, did he? Did I not tell you so?' she chuckled. 'I will train you, you shall learn, and like sisters we shall be in this study. Then, one day soon, we shall travel. You will learn about some lands of ours as you wish. However, it is no task for weeks. I do not care to teach you the history of the bygone houses, no, nor of the lands no longer there, but you shall study the minds of the houses that rule this day. You will enter a dangerous world of conspiracies and need to know that smiles do not always mean friendship. Or perhaps you learned that yesterday.'

'And such conspiracies are the bread you enjoy and eat, no?' I said with a smile.

'Careful, Shannon, even if that is true. Do not disrespect the hands that can strangle you,' she hissed with laughter. 'But essentially, yes.'

'The Hand of Life is a hard commodity to come by,' I retorted foolishly and went silent, letting that small jab sink in. 'How many houses are there of the elves?'

She shrugged, her manner nervous, anger playing in the undercurrents of her beautiful voice. 'A thousand. There are some millions of the bastards in the east. More than fifty million humans are living in these lands. Other creatures, plenty of them. You will never learn of them all. The rest is wild. There are millions and millions of elves and humans living past the Carrion Peaks to the south, islands we no longer remember and lands we never visit to the east. But the north is where the power lies. Never forget it. They all vie for one thing.'

'The Regent ship?'

'That and you,' she snickered. 'You will fetch the Eye of the Crow and then we are done. This one deed is all I require.' She had a strange, wrathful look on her face for a moment, but it quickly disappeared.

'Will you teach me new spells?' I asked.

'You are the Frigg's Gift. Whatever it is you must do there, elven hands have failed at it before. I trust the prophecy; the one claiming an awkward fool is to succeed. You will do this deed and succeed. Worry not. I doubt battle spells of Fury will destroy old Cerunnos Timmerion and his risen court. Those who have tried it before are dead. They were taught spells all their lives. There are old elven scholars in Colleges of Adapted Arts, White Halls and Spell Hold and mighty maa'dark who devote their entire lives to the discovery of spells. They study the Fury for violent applications of the power and the Gift of utility and comfort. Moreover, all such spells have failed against Timmerion. You will be different because *you* are different.'

I shook my head in disappointment. 'Yes, I understand.'

'Even if they disdain your tools behind their backs, Almheir will beg you to save his child and what is left of his wife. Therefore, he will let you enter the Hall of Freyr. Now, hush.'

If I escaped, I would have to get my friends to safety. To foil Euryale's plans, I needed the Regent. I would bargain for his wife's life, his child's life.

However, I would be lost.

'I'm impatient,' I told her resolutely, pushing back my terror.

'Patience, precious one, is not something either of us possesses.' She grinned. 'But I have waited many lifetimes of a human for such as you, so I have a good reason to seethe.'

'Am I precious enough to make demands to you?' I asked.

She laughed. 'And they have indeed begun to fool you, have they not? Your enemies are making demands on you. Fooling you. And in the end, they will be the death of you. I told you to look out for them. I told you to pretend to be weak and then nip them. Instead, perhaps you are weak indeed and ...'

'They are not my enemies,' I said carefully.

'They are if they would try to use you to get them free as well. Have they asked you for this? This is your opportunity to slay them. If they are asking to be free of their mistress, I should know.'

'I would like them to be free, no matter if they ask or not,' I told her with pride and went silent for a while. Had they indeed used me? No. Feeling compassion for them was not a weakness. 'And they have not asked me.'

She gazed at me intently. Then she pointed a finger my way. 'Very well. One can always make demands, human girl. That is not forbidden. Demand away, Shannon. Then you shall look at my galleries of stone corpses and think better of it, for I can give you my word and pledge indeed, easily I can. I can make you salivate with beautiful promises and hints at hidden treasures. I can guarantee you all salvation, set free all the sad little humans from this tower, for that is what you hope for. You will pray that I will spare your scrawny pet and the boy who wishes to be your lover, as well, spare them their pain, humiliation, and even death. Yes. I can promise all of that. However, know that dealing with one of the Three, you should curry favor and not cause resentment. I am ancient, girl, and have made and broken many ruthless slaves before, even centuries after fulfilling pacts with them. Perhaps you will go free with all you wish for. Perhaps, one day, I shall remember your arrogance this very night and hear willowy voices call for revenge, for I am petty and resentful and a great lover of tragedy. Perhaps you shall have a child by that time, and I will take her? I am cruel, and so you shall suffer eventually, should you insult a First Born, one that is above queens and just shy of gods. Instead, be my … friend, Shannon, and demand little. Those who demand the Devourer for favors often end up unhappy; their souls broken, just like a ship's keel in a storm. We have a deal and do not ask for more.

I looked away, swallowing my disappointment. 'So, mistress. I shall demand little and learn? And cannot free my … friends?'

'You have a sister. Nevertheless, I see you never had friends before, and so you suffer, even if they are using you. Beware of them. Make new friends later, human girl. What you have now and what we have agreed on suffices. You shall learn of the families of the continent. The others will continue their training. They will train hard. They should if they wish to survive the bout next year, especially if you and Dana are free.' She rose to stand, her muscled legs glistening in the torchlight.

'You will not consider releasing them?'

'I have a need for them.'

'Money?' I asked her scornfully.

She leaned over me. 'Much has to be risked in life, Shannon, for friends. But I said I have a need for them so be quiet now. You lot will rest a week, enjoy your life, and relax, all of you. You will have some freedom from the training and the pains and ails of the Fanged Spire and the demands of my house, but after this, you have a grander purpose, my precious student. Remember your place, and do not threaten me.'

'Is there anything,' I said morosely, 'that can threaten you?' I stared at her intently, hoping to be rewarded.

I was. Her eyes wandered to the bookcase. Just for a moment, but they did. Able saw it, *his* eyes running over the bookcase.

She laughed. 'Few things, Shannon. Very few. None you shall learn of.'

She disappeared, and I flinched as she appeared behind me. She held onto my arms, and I whimpered and prepared to feel her fangs, but did not. She jerked, and I plummeted back through the portal.

I fell on my bed, Cherry moving reluctantly as I bumped heavily on it. She was growling, giving me room, and I stared at the ceiling, casting glances at Dana. Thus we lay, looking at each other that night. She smiled, and I smiled back, knowing I had left our shared path. She was my sister and I loved her, but I would do what was right. It was a lonely feeling.

'Are we still on?' she whispered.

'She still trusts me,' I told her.

After she had fallen asleep, I turned to stare at the ceiling.

I was terrified.

I would die of Rot, even if I succeeded in our plans. Even if Able found a way to help us. Was there any way to force her to heal me? Euryale had not denied there were things that could threaten even her. Gods?

Could a god heal me?

Hel?

Should I get the Eye for her, perhaps? Without Euryale and after my friends were safe?

She could, surely, remove the Rot.

I stared at Dana, who expected me to obey the demon. However, I would not.

For I did indeed have friends. But perhaps, I thought as I stared at Dana, I needed still more.

I needed a goddess to help me. Only one was available.

Goddess of the dead. She wanted her eye back.

CHAPTER 17

We rested for a week. They marched us through the town to a small river, a beautiful stream of glistening blue and green, and there we stayed, blissfully unaware of anything but the food and calm. To Cherry's obvious annoyance Lex stayed with me, and I sat there, in a silken tent wondering about the future. I occasionally ventured out to swim with Albine and to fish with Dmitri, who did not blame me for Alexei. I walked the trees to speak with the birds, strange, colorful, and happy, and I envied them.

In a week, it was over, and we walked back to the tower, our new rooms.

And every morning, the training commenced. They would resolutely take the others down to the training hall, where they spent much of the day gathering power. They were taught other offensive spells, ones more delicate and subtle. Albine nearly died as they taught the Tears the spells, and Ulrich had a splitting headache that made him near comatose for a few days. We spied a body being dragged in the hallways, one of the other saa'dark. He had died of the teaching. Yet, learn they did, the Tears. They learnt to weave whips of flame, to use the spells while blindfolded, to run and to be hurt while holding onto the power, releasing portions of it and then weaving new ones on the fly, and they became deadly, or so Dana claimed. In the evenings, I played rug ball with Dmitri and half-hearted Albine and Anja until Nox provided us food. His spells were gentle, and the result a bit better the than the slop we had endured that first year, his fingers summoning meat and bread. And occasionally, wine, although we believe that was his own contribution to our fare for his eyes glinted mischievously.

As for me, when they were taken out each morning, I stayed behind.

I waited each morning for a curiously long time before I was summoned, and I no longer traveled with Euryale's spell but walked the steps, escorted by a young gorgon with bizarrely innocent eyes. I was passing many strange doors of the tower, some silvery and in good repair, then others ruined and abandoned. It was a terribly long climb, and I was always exhausted as the strange gorgon showed me the door to Euryale's abode, an onyx-plated door full of twisting serpents carved on its surface. Inside her lavish, strangely gothic apartment she was often busy with whatever she was doing at a desk near the covered window and the mirror. I was guided to a table in the far corner of the circular hall and told to sit down in front of a hulking wall of tomes.

Euryale would come and sit near me, staring over my shoulder.

And Able was there, hovering miserably. He dared not speak, though Euryale would not have heard him. But his eyes ventured up to the bookcase, and there were so many. He shrugged, and I despaired. He pointed at one spot in the bookcase, looking uncertain, but there was a thick blue tome there and whatever he had found was behind it.

I had no chance to rummage in the bookcase.

Instead, I had other books.

On the desk, there were but three tomes. One of them was with filled maps. A great many maps. So many maps I could only wonder at them, old as time. In that book, I found the Grey Downs, running my finger the length of it in the middle of a wildly strange bay. Timmerion was a faded name on the island, once an apparent paradise and my finger traced the map to the west. Around the Grey Downs were the waters of the Dancing Bay, and so I stared at the vast land stretching around us to the west. My finger ran across to the northwest from the Grey Downs, ending up in a gilded hall of great majesty, and that must have been Freyr's Seat, the hold of Almheir Bardagoon, the Regent of the land. Or was it? I gazed at the faded letters; I stared at that northern shore, where the land rose, perhaps, majestically above other lands, a cliff area for a god to gaze over his dominions. There sat an old city, Ljusalfheim, with a dull, iron crown painted on top of it. Yes, it was the Freyr's Seat. To the south of it, four great elven nations rose, each perched on the shores of the Bay and separated by rivers and forests. Great woods and ponderous mountain ranges separated the land of Ljusalfheim, a land of lush fields and numerous people and the land of rivers, those of House Safiroon, lords of Himinborg, Heimdall's Hold. Together they comprised Freyr's Tooth, an island or a continent, as Euryale called it.

Then to the south of Himinborg, a vast continent, like a green, jeweled coat dotted with what I took to be rivers and counties and cities. Other nations, houses were scattered around it, an enormous one to the very south, bordered by vast mountains, the dominion of Houser Daxamma. To the coast, House Coinar and more modest ones, but likely rich in holdings. Then Trad and the House Vautan, just across a strait from Himinborg. There were ancient maps of the east and south as well, so old few of Aldheim indeed knew about the distant lands and times. I had no idea how large the continent to the west was, but whatever its size, it was sure to be wondrous.

'It is beautiful, though there are different kinds of beauty all across the Nine,' Euryale said behind me, and I froze. 'My home of Niflheim is cold and brutal, where strength and wits are what you need to survive, but you must be very lucky, as well. In our lands, few weaklings survive. Maa'dark are the rulers there, as well, for the giants know spells of Fury and Gift both. They have taken men to serve their many needs in those lands also. Ah, the glaciers and the ice-filled valleys. Like diamonds by millions.'

'It must be wondrous, mistress,' I told her hollowly. 'I am surprised you appreciate beauty. You have usually only spoken about the thrill of hunting for blood and your lust for murder.'

'Yes, human girl, yes, but we appreciate the beauty of the hunt like the beauty of the wealthy lands, the riches and slaves they bring. Beauty is what makes any realm worth coveting and conquering,' she told me, laying her warm hand on my shoulder. 'Get to know the lands. Know, there will be a great war in those areas soon.'

'War?' I asked timidly.

'War, yes,' she answered.

'Why do they fight?' I asked, fingering the map, feeling her close presence, terrified of her touch.

'In general or soon? It's the same answer, I suppose,' she said languidly. 'The south is overly religious,' she sneered. 'The south thinks the Regent is not doing all within its power to recall the gods. They are likely right, for who would want a master to return when you sleep in his bed? The north thinks the Coinar and Daxamma and the houses supporting them are after power, not gods. All of them claim to do all within their power to recall the gods. So far, Houses Safiroon, Bardagoon, and Vautan are allied and have like mind, their hundreds of minor houses support them, intermarrying to keep the south at bay. I think,' she whispered, and leaned on me, 'that the elves are just plain bored. They enjoy the game of houses and the Race and the Feast of Fates. They love war and glory, and all the elven maa'dark compete in rank. Almheir is the First Light currently, all the way down to the least maa'dark.'

'What light am I?' I wondered.

She hesitated. 'In some way, the second? That is customary.'

'The second light of Aldheim,' I mused, 'and a helpless little mouse.'

She giggled. 'Indeed. They also raid the east. What they cannot do freely at home, they do in the east and south, wage wars against the people of the Wild's Coast especially. One led an army against us, some years past. It was interesting. But not dangerous.' She grinned. 'I punished the impudent Safiroon Lord, who was after something I took. I think I mentioned this before.'

'Are there any spells to create, perhaps of the Gift you know of?' I asked, for, like Albine, I yearned for beauty and utility rather than destruction.

'Ah, you desire calm rather than to hear of the ferocious elves. You desire fulfillment of the soul. You humans were all created to admire what the gods loved, and so you wish arts. Yes, there are spells that allow one to create wondrous things, and I know many. Here, let me show you.'

She harnessed the power, and I felt the roar of fires as she wove a spell of flames, and I was tempted to tamper with it, but could not, for the Fetter was shutting me off. Then, I was startled as some of the spell she released touched me. I felt it, like a cat licking my skin. Nothing happened, though, until after some time, tiny men and women grew from the desk, fiery and gentle, like a candle's flame, they were dancing to the flute, the sound haunting and old. Some were large, muscular, others slender and delicate. 'Your ancestors, before they left this island for the Tenth, your Earth after the greedy elven adventures. Thus they danced, the workers and brutes, the seers, and the leaders, not knowing their fates. It's a memory blaze, one to celebrate old times. Perhaps some were your ancestors. This is your memory, Shannon, torn from your being.'

I stared at the people. They were just like us. Old and somehow happier, people enjoying music, laughter, and I wondered if Odin had truly created them to be slaved. Midgard was their ancestral home, and I yearned to see it. 'Can you take any such memory and make it so?' I asked.

'No, you won't know what it is until the spell is cast,' she told me, caressing the flames by my head, her hand ending up on my shoulder. 'Ah, you think you could create your own. That you could alleviate your loneliness. Or are you making new memories, Shannon? This boy? Lex?'

'Yes, mistress,' I told her, hoping she would not be cruel and produce Lex's head in an eye blink. However, I needed no memory of Lex for he was there for me. I missed Father and Mother. Grandma. Rose.

'He is a beautiful human if scruffy and ill reared, is he not, and your first, no?' she smiled benignly, making me shudder. 'Ah, sorry, the boy in Trad had that distinction, no?'

I kept still, swallowing my rage. 'Yes, he was.'

She grinned. 'I have ever mulled about such love you humans have for each other. Fragile and dangerous, fleeting and killer, yet you would make a thousand such dancing fires of the love you once felt and would gaze at them endlessly in your old age.' She ran her fingers across the dancing figures, making them lose shape for a moment. 'Don't make a mistake, Shannon, now that we are so close. Be right to your mistress. If you fail, I shall make more than flames. I shall make artworks of pain and tears of the lot down below. You have seen the ones who have failed, in your first chambers. That was merciful. The release for the suffering Ten Tears would be years from now after a million tears have been shed. After the torture of loneliness, madness and pain. And your sister?' She squeezed my face painfully, her point made. I nodded slowly. 'You shall learn now. I will teach you, Shannon. You shall not heed your actual enemies, and it will be fine. And one day you will be free. All you need to do is think about the Eye of Hel and freedom, and it shall be so.' She stared at me, and her manner betrayed sudden lust, desire, and she tried to say something.

'Mistress, no, please,' I whimpered.

She shook her head, ripped my robe open and sunk her teeth into my neck, near where the Rot was already festering, the snakes entwining around me, holding me still. The pain was excruciating, savage, and painful, and my shoulder twitched and pinched as the Rot responded to its mistress, the plague giver.

I suddenly saw Able, standing by the table, his eyes moist as he witnessed my pain and horror, then he was grinding his teeth in anger. His eyes probed my pained eyes, his hands clutched at the desk, and I shook my head at him, smiling through the pain. He grimaced and shook the table.

I stared at him. He had left marks on the desk. His eyes betrayed the shock of it. Then they grew dark, and my eyes turned to the shelves.

He growled and hit the wooden structure. He clawed at the shelves, his hits passing through them. Then, his eyes grew enraged as he saw my face lose color. He was shaking and shrieking at Euryale. He slammed his hand on the shelf. It connected. The shelves shook, the books were trembling and some fell.

One was the blue book.

Dust billowed up into the air. My eyes went to slits as I stared beyond the dark hole where the blue book had stood. A glow. Able had been right, perhaps. The dust was still blocking much of my sight.

Euryale noticed nothing.

I shook my head at Able, and he calmed slowly, alarmed by his rage, and my eyes begged him to relax. I endured the pain. While my mistress was feasting, the dust was growing less, and then I saw it. Behind a fallen cookbook, there was a book in shadows, one with a cover made of skin, elven, or human, I know not, but there was a closed eyelid in the middle of it. More, it sparkled with strange power, stranger colors. I grunted and cursed in agony, feeling my strength ebbing, and the bitch was not giving up. 'Are you going to kill me?' I winced as the excruciating pain throbbed in my side and head.

She stroked my neck, shuddered reluctantly as she finished her meal, rising to her full height. She shook her snakes back and sat down with a sigh. 'I am sorry, child. Sometimes, my better judgment runs away with wings of rage and hunger. But it is fine now, and I am sated. Yes. Heal yourself.' I did, as I felt the power surging through me, and I gathered the icy and frigid energy and released it, feeling the familiar, bitterly freezing gust around me and the instant relief as my wounds closed, leaving me weak. I placed my head on the tome, trembling with silent agony and fatigue. She crouched next to me. 'I can devour anything and anyone, girl. I can creep through the night and shadows to rip open a warrior's throat. I can nip a mighty elf in his war splendor from his warship while he eats at his table; I can snub a baby's life as quickly as I would rub off a stain of dirt. I am the Night Slayer, and they sing sad stories of my deeds. And sometimes, I act impulsively. We have time; the Rot is not too terrible yet. Cheer up. Do you think you could have beaten Isabella Colbert, for that was her name; had I not trained you well? She scorched you, and the pain of that should have killed the Shannon I grabbed from her miserable existence in the Tenth. Thanks to my training, you are able and fierce, girl, and can take the pain like a saa'dark should. With pride and purpose. You did well. I knew you would. You will be ready.' She grasped my face. 'You have been a victim all your life, Shannon. Now, you have grown past that.'

'I'm still your victim,' I said as calmly as I could.

'Yes, but in that, you are in a large company,' she laughed hollowly, her teeth red with my blood.

With that, she did not touch me for a month. Curiously, the blue book stayed on the desk, but the desk was cluttered, and such a high being as she was, likely noticed nothing strange about the books stacked on the desk and the ones that had fallen. Happily, she had no need for the glowing book either. She would train me each and every day. She would force me to hold power, brutally, desperate for me to grow and learn, ever more and more power, sometimes while hurt, other times not, sometimes while reading. When that part was over, she let me study.

However, never alone.

I saw my quarry but could not touch It. Able stood there, every day, his face frustrated.

Therefore, I read of the high elves and magnificent lands of theirs. They were first of the beings gods created. True, there were plenty of beings older than they were, giants and gorgons, likely, spirits and beasts of many forms, but the elves were supposed to be perfect. Noble and wise, the gods had made them caretakers of their finest jewel, Aldheim. I snickered. Judging by what Euryale told of the creatures, they were nothing but a failure. Yet, apparently, despite their wars, intrigues and games, spectacles of art and of blood, the elves were balanced. They might be bored, the author of the book surmised, bored like the gods themselves, driven to petty power plays and bloody murders, devising a system of houses, one climbing over the other, hoping to sit in the first five houses, but there were limits to their self-destructiveness. They had laws, strict honor, and to fail in upholding one's honor, meant the loss of face and death.

Moreover, she was to thrust me into the middle of such a race? I felt the weight of the responsibility push down hard on my shoulders.

I abandoned that book, and I read of the gods' gates. There were eight gates in each world and in Aldheim, the holy gate, Asgaard's Pass, Heimdal's gate was in Ljusalfheim, the City of

Spires, the home of the Bardagoons. The book told of the gate to Niflheim in the lost east and the one to Svartalfheim in Himinborg, though Himinborg itself meant Heimdal's Seat. One was in Breidablik of House Daxamma, apparently. There was no mention of the others. I knew where the gate to the Tenth was. In Grey Downs. The rest were all closed and some, possibly lost in the east, Wild's Coast. I gazed at the text, trying to fathom the words of some ancient scholar. *Time passed fleetly, noble elves fell into oblivion, generations of long-lived kings lay down in their mounds or sought death in war, hoping to avoid the Enemy. The scholars were forgotten in their towers and caves and few cared for gods, whose absence was soothing to some, disturbing to others and gates were lost, forgotten amidst the mortar of fallen palaces and houses. Woe to lose these relics of old. But the nobles care not.* I shook my head, sometimes forgetting the glowing book, fascinated by the study.

Yet, then Able's presence would remind me and so did the glow. I despaired.

In the evenings, I sat in my bed, listening to how my friends spoke of their days. They held together, and I felt alienated from them, except for Cherry and Lex. They were changing, turning into jaded, practical weapons, for, in place of freedom, they had the growing power. Bereft of that, they had nothing. They would be weapons indeed, only that, but tenacious, strapping and proud and, of course, useful to their masters.

However, in Anja's face, I could still see the desire to escape, and we both knew we should do something soon. But, I had not yet summoned the strength to reach for the book. Nor did I have an opportunity.

I would have to, soon. Or betray their hopes.

CHAPTER 18

S trange weather was once again plaguing the island. That day, the tower was frosted over, and we huddled under out blankets when we could. Lex was sharing warmth with me, having ushered Cherry away for a while, and I lay next to him gratefully, giggling as he was groaning in lust we could not take advantage of. It was strange for a boy to desire me, but I decided perhaps not so much, after all. And Ulrich and Anja did, of course, many things in the shadows of the room, but we did not. Not yet.

Dana crept next to me, smiling at Lex, who stirred, and cursed softly for she nodded him away. He left to tease Cherry, who endured the big, blond man with infectious smiles. She sat next to me, ogling the tall boy. 'He being good to you?'

'Exquisite, sister,' I told her, missing him already.

'Have you learned much?' she asked suspiciously and then added. 'I have. They say I'm probably the most powerful maa'dark they've ever seen.'

'Saa'dark, for we are their slaves,' I reminded her.

'I think of myself as maa'dark,' she grinned.

'Congratulations then, sister,' I said and smiled, and she bristled. I raised my hands. 'Bilac and Cosia still train you?'

'They do, though they do not beat us nearly as much as they used to while we practiced harnessing the Shades. We also train with weapons. Swords and spears and shields. It's positively medieval. There they make up for missing the beating part. My arms ache,' she giggled. 'But you did not answer my question. Are you getting practice, anower? I want you to share, you know. We should be free, one day soon, no? You fulfilling your contract?'

I nodded. 'Euryale tells me it will be time soon. There is a thing called the Feast of Fates, an elven celebration, and there many things will change.' I rubbed my shoulder, terrified at the things crawling under and over my skin as if answering my words of the Feast. Her eyes traveled to my hand and she nodded, a brief look of uncertainty filling her face. 'But she is secretive and only lets me know so much,' I told her unhappily. 'Dana, I think we should consider something else.'

'Something else?' she inquired, her head twisted to the side. 'What else is there? She promises you freedom ...'

'After threatening your life and infecting me with the Rot,' I growled. 'Twice.'

'The Rot?' she asked.

'I ... She has infected me. She did it to motivate me. After all, it might have been so I did not care for your life.'

'Is that why you are always holding your shoulder?' she whispered and placed a hand on my shoulder. It tingled, and I had a hunch the Rot did not enjoy her touch. She pulled her hand away, her eyes wide in shock. 'I felt something.'

'Don't,' I told her, clutching her hand. 'It's pretty terrible.'

'What ...'

'Devouring illness. I will be cured if I obey her.'

'There you have it,' she told me softly, her eyes betraying rage. 'No option but to obey. There is nothing else.' She wiped a sudden tear from her eye. 'I am sorry, sister. Best do as she says, and it will be okay.' She looked around as if Euryale was near, lurking in the shadows. 'But perhaps, if you are careful, don't play it blind with her. Try to find out more of her plans.'

'I am trying.'

'You are?' she asked. 'Don't risk ...'

'She is ill at ease with me, keeping an eye on me. I have a hard time finding answers, even if I might know of something that could possibly help me. A book.' I bit my tongue, for I had spoken too much.

She considered me and finally took a deep breath. 'Be careful, sister, not to ruin everything. Yet, there is one thing you never practiced, Shannon, in your closed little world. The thing to make a creature like this love you? Want to know?'

'What?'

'Suck up to her,' she told me as she leaned towards me. 'Of course. All the relatives you hated, all the people that made you feel uncomfortable? Even Mother and Father, sometimes, when they ignored your issues and unhappiness? You were too wrapped up in your problems to try to make things work for you. You never attempted to please those who could make life easier for you, no matter how hard it was. I always did. It works wonders. Admire her, worship her, and hang on to her filthy words. I bet she would love that. I think she does not have anyone who truly calls her ... I don't know. Pretty? Smart? Brutal? Give her a foot massage?'

'What?'

'I don't know!' she giggled. 'You got a technique for that?'

'No! In addition, I don't wish to touch her cruddy feet! But I see what you mean,' I told her as she shook with mirth and then took a deep, hopeless breath. 'I ...'

'Suck her bottom, Shannon. I would if I could,' she laughed and squeezed my hand. 'You promise us freedom. Make sure you can deliver. See if you can find ways to make sure she keeps her words to us. Call her beautiful. Fawn on her. Tell her she smells good. Admire the carnage she has caused. Bed her!' she sighed and shook her head. 'I don't like this, but make sure we will find a way for us to escape in case she betrays her promises. As for the disease, we will find a cure, but we must survive to do so.' She leaned on me. 'I love you, Shannon. Nevertheless, I have always pulled our sleigh. Show me you can too.'

'I will sister,' I told her and hugged her fiercely. 'But I won't bed her nor massage her.'

'Flatter her. She is not a god, but I bet she would like to be one,' she grinned. 'You and I if none else. Remember, sister.'

The next day, I flattered her.

It is easy to flatter monsters. I already knew she was susceptible to flattery. Despite their distinct powers, it is not possible for them to garner real adoration from their slaves. And even evil beings, I suppose, need some form of acceptance from those they terrorize. Dana was right. When I entered her abode, I found her cowling herself, the snakes dancing heavily around her. Her powerful arms were smoothing a bodice around her beautifully sculpted body, covering her high breasts, and her shapely legs were carrying her to the side, trying to find a pouch where she likely stored many powerful artifacts. She was moving for my seat, ready to guard me.

'Mistress, I rue I cannot see your face,' I said softly as I kneeled.

'What, child?' she asked, apparently deep in her thoughts.

'I said, I rue I can never see your face. Your daughters are beautiful, in a dangerous way, but I have never seen you, mistress, and it saddens me.'

'Humans should not harbor a wish to die, child. Their lives are short enough,' she laughed. 'Longer here than in your home, but short as love. And you did see my face when I bit you. Briefly. That first time.'

'Yes, mistress,' I told her and bowed. I took a deep breath, shaking in terror of what I was about to ask her. 'I did. But there is beauty in that face when it's not hungry. Speaking of that. Do you wish to feed?'

'Feed?' she stopped. 'I thought it terrified you?'

'Your needs, mistress, should not be subject to my terror. I hope to serve,' I told her. 'I have found myself changing this past month. I feel no great urge to be free of the Fanged Spire. All the knowledge and your wisdom ...'

'I thought you hoped to be free of me, one day?' she chuckled with a hollow voice. 'No, I cannot speed up your Rot anymore, Shannon. But thank you, my little human girl. I'll feed on something else. So what else are you thinking about?'

'I have been reading about the lands and thinking about this freedom you will grant us. Perhaps it is not so desirable. Perhaps I might have a home with you?' I felt claws rake my soul at those words, for they might come to haunt me one day.

'Excuse me?' she asked, astonished. 'You honestly think like this?'

I went on hurriedly. 'When you are reunited with your sister,' I blurted, 'you will surely have plans beyond the sad business of slave trading. You have implied it. Perhaps you will free the gods and get your due, but that will not stop you, a First Born from reaching out for more. When we are free,' I added, 'perhaps we shall not have a clue on what to do with such freedom as you promised.'

She glided to me and stopped before me. She lifted my chin to gaze at her glowing, covered eyes. 'Humans do tend to waste their lives trying to find something that is not there. Perhaps you are wiser. The day I have Hel's Eye in my hand, I shall consider your request. You might be very useful indeed, Hand of Life, and we do have plans beyond enjoying each other's company, Stheno and I, and even the gods would not stop us, for they owe us. But you would have to serve us. You might not be a prisoner to my Bone Fetter, nor subject to Rot, but you would be subject to my will. Even to my sister.'

'Yes, I understand,' I told her reverently, the intense, shadowed glare painful as I looked deep into her eyes.

'And that, Shannon, might mean you will have to be like us. Like our brood,' she mused as she rocked on her heels. 'With different … morals than those of your kin. You will be like us.'

'Like Bilac and Cosia, you mean?' I asked her, wondering about their origins.

'No, not like them. They are from the darkness of Nifleheim's caves, lesser than we are, clans of warriors only, and you will never change to a demi-gorgon. But what I do mean is that you will be driven by a bloody purpose. It might mean you will be a slayer rather than a lover for that is what we are. We strive for ...'

'Power,' I added, and she nodded curiously.

'That, and chaos and glory. Riches and fulfillment. When the time ends, the gods will measure the deeds one has performed. We intend to rest high on the scales of glory in the Midhall and be shown our places in the afterworlds of the time beyond, rulers of many. To do this, we have much to accomplish. We love the thrill of a hunt, a pure pleasure of murder, and a grand war of conquest as you said, and we will do so in the future. If you stay with us and serve us, this is what you will serve to our enemies.'

'Yes, mistress, that sounds acceptable, perhaps even pleasing to me, though still beyond my powers,' I said, feeling her voice's seductive thrum move me in ways I did not think possible. I tried to deny it, but there was the desire deep inside me, hidden perhaps, but not unseen, one to let go of the weak, human values I knew were hampering me. There was a drop of Dana inside me, I thought. With Euryale and Stheno, there might be absolution from my fears in ways I never suspected. I pushed the thought away.

'I see,' she said with some amusement. 'I saw it in you, I think. There is a very dark side to you, hidden, but there nonetheless, like there is to your sister, with whom it is more obvious. I am happy we had this discussion, Shannon. We shall see. Many things will be asked of us soon enough.'

'I only wish to find a purpose that suits me,' I told her huskily.

'Yours is likely a worthy one.'

'You do not yet know what our purpose is. Nor do we. Did I not tell you we are perilous and chaotic?' she smiled. 'Come.' She raised me up and led me to my study, and she sat me down. 'Read of Cerunnos Timmerion, who once held Grey Downs.' Her fingers flipped open a gray tome full of history. 'Read, for you will meet him. Here. He was Odin's appointed Lord and held this island in Hel's war against the hordes of foes. It was ripped apart, his family destroyed, his daughters, mighty Yrenia, and Araste falling ahead of his household armies right here. I killed both, but that's another story.'

'A mighty endeavor, slaying high elven nobles,' I agreed with horrified awe. 'Didn't Hel's armies attack this place, not ...'

'It's a long story,' she said with a fond smile. 'They knew a hundred spells, the fine ladies,' she said, pleased with the memory. 'I knew more. And I have a secret.'

'A secret I shall not ask about,' I giggled and laughed with her, feeling foolish.

'Good, right, child,' she agreed. 'A wise policy. The Fanged Spire holds many not meant for you.'

The Fanged Spire. My eyes glanced at the book glowing on the desk, now gathered in some dust for it had been exposed for a month.

She hesitated next to me. And then she left and went to stand far from me, near the mirror where she sat down to write, leaving me alone for the first time.

'What, mistress, is the seat of Bardagoon like? Ljusalfheim.'

She described the halls of the north. 'Golden, much of which was delved in the Underworld and some even in your land. They covet gold, they eat it with their eyes, loving its sheen. They yearn for it with all their heart. Imagine mighty pillars of golden and silvery radiance, finest details everywhere, the industrious smiths ever at work, adding to the porticoes, the walls, and the floors, the seats and the shelves. Rich, richer by war, I doubt Freyr would recognize the elegant hall he built. It is much the same in all the capitals of the Dancing Bay and the Spell Coast.'

'Do you covet it?' I asked carefully. 'Gold. You said you did, for the measure of success it gives you.'

She licked her lips. 'Gold, silver. Wealth is powerful, in many ways more so than the maa'dark, Shannon. Even in here. In Asgaard, yes, as well. All the creation covets it, humans not the least,' she smiled. 'One day, we shall sit on a pile of skulls, covered in gold and silver. One must measure one's success in the great game, Shannon, and gold and silver, platinum, and even jewels are a fine way to do so.'

'We'll have to move. This tower won't accommodate all of it.' I smiled, and she laughed heartily.

'Indeed, indeed so!' she agreed with a smile under her hood.

'Read.'

And so I studied while eyeing the slightly glowing book gathering dust. I read of Grimhold of the south with ebony towers of leaning rocks. There were wondrous stories of Bellow Hold, the house Simmiron's home with golden woods full of larks and its High Harbor of mighty fleets and merchants. Dragon's Maw was the sibilant pass full of piled skulls separating Ljusalfheim from the south.

'Ask her of dragons,' Able whispered in my ear, and I nearly shrieked, for I had not seen him.

'Why?' I asked him so very softly.

'I think of dragons all the time,' he explained. 'I think it's ...'

'Are there any goblins or dragons? Giants? In Aldheim?' I asked as I skimmed the book in front of me.

She stopped her writing.

'Dragons?' she inquired sweetly. 'There are plenty of strange creatures all over this world, Shannon, but most are in hiding. After Hel's war, the elves and men tried to purge all their foes from the world. I do not know, sadly, what took place in Midgard or Jotunheim, for example. Do you yearn to see a dragon?' she grinned. 'I would not advise it.'

'Really? Are they like the stories say? Rumbling, huge, carnivorous? Dreadful and brutal?'

'They are ... difficult,' she said. 'Yours are in hiding, in the

Tenth.'

'We don't have any! Certainly not?' I asked.

She laughed with a knowing voice. 'Indeed. Indeed so. You think you know your entire world so well, so very well. You are but infants.'

'They love treasure, don't they?' I asked.

'They covet it like any other creature of power,' she agreed. 'They are older than us, First Born to the olders even and perhaps as old as the gods. You do not wish to learn of them. No.'

'Yes, mistress,' I said and gazed at Able, who smiled weakly. His eyes wandered to the glowing book. 'When,' I asked, 'is this Feast held? Where the elves gather.'

'It is held in a week, Shannon,' she said happily if nervously.

'A week?' I asked rather weakly, for that meant I would have to act.

'One week,' she affirmed. 'I shall keep a close eye on anything that might change during the time. Do not worry and be ready. Read all you can today, brave human girl. Tomorrow, I shall be gone for the time and this is our last day.'

With that, she began to write again.

I stared at her back and noticed Nox sauntering in the room, the vast tomte near unseen in the shadows. He hefted a flask of oil for some lamps and filled them, and left the oil on the corner. He noticed me staring and flashed me a wide, wrinkled, toothy smile.

His eyes went to the glowing book and then at me, an unreadable expression on his face.

He wanted freedom as well.

I cursed my timidity. I would have to act. I shrugged and read and enjoyed a moment of solitude, even if I noticed Able's ghost lurking in the shadows, nosing at things he likely should not. Now that I knew what he was, I felt somewhat uneasy about him, his dark, dead face strange and sinister, but I did flash him a smile when he was looking. I saw the terrible gorgon was meditating on some problem, leaning over a desk, her pen quivering in the air. Her head was swinging as she contemplated some harsh choice, and I shook in terror at what I thought I would do. I flexed my hand, got up slowly, reached out and grasped the book of glowing covers ever so slowly, glancing at Euryale, who was still deep in her thoughts.

But clumsily I dropped the book.

Nox appeared and grabbed it. He glowered at me, left it on the desk away from me and disappeared in a blink.

I shook in terror for a moment, cursing myself profusely. Then I grasped the book, fearing a flash of searing, burning light but instead, the glowing book made of skin was light as a feather, soft as silk and cool as a winter's kiss. I pulled at it, trying so very silently to open it up. I was sure to die. Or someone else at least. My hands shook, and I forced myself to think happy thoughts. I didn't find any, even Lex's happy face brought fear, for I was going to fail, I was sure of it, and they would suffer. The book moved as I pulled at it with my finger, light and cold to the touch, it came towards me, moving under my hand, slowly, but resolutely. Then the chair creaked as I was straining myself. I froze.

Nothing.

I nearly screamed in fear and noticed Able gesturing for me to calm down, eyeing Euryale. I turned my face that way and saw she was no longer writing, but staring past me, far, very deep in her thoughts. I moved the book in front of me. Able was whispering urgently at me. 'Act cool. She needs you. Remember that if you get caught. And I like your new bedside manner with her,' he grinned. 'She swallowed it whole.'

'Ass licking is a skill I find hard to learn,' I whispered.

Able blanched, and I turned again. Euryale was staring at me. 'What did you say?'

I licked my lips, leaning on the book. 'I said; grass digging is a thrill hard to enjoy. Despite that, I think the elves could do some of it, farming instead of waging wars and plotting.'

'They do not touch the dirt, girl,' she agreed with a shake of the head. 'Never will.'

'They would if they were starving,' I mumbled and heard her snicker.

I let her mull over her thoughts and stared at the cover. The fair luminance of the dreadful, leather and stitched skin cover was sort of hazy, bright at one point, then at another. I let my thumb fly over the leather, feeling the fringes and imperfections of it, perhaps made so by age or wounds of the persons whose skin had been used for it. The lid was closed, happily, but the eyelashes looked strangely fine, and I shuddered as I touched the pages. I opened the book. Inside it, words were dancing across the brittle, yellowed page, though just briefly.

Then, nothing. The page was empty.

I turned the next one, also empty. Then another. I skimmed the book, and it was all blank.

'The hell,' I sniffled very softly, and Able was shrugging.

'Sorry, it was hidden, so I thought it might be hugely important. You asked for a glowing book, didn't you?' he told me morosely. 'It's a blank one. It looked promising, but it's just useless. A month is gone! Useless thing. Like I am!'

'Nothing. Nothing about the tower?' I complained so very softly, yet bitterly. 'Nothing useful indeed. Useless.'

Able shrugged, nervous. 'I found it. It must have something useful.'

'You found it by accident,' I hissed. 'And I helped you, remember?'

'Still found it! Ask it questions,' he urged. 'It's magical.'

'Questions?' I scoffed.

'Ask about the Fetters,' he said impatiently.

I sighed so softly, like a breath of a ghost. 'Might as well ask about dragons. Are there any? No? See ...'

Then, the book responded.

The pages filled with information. There was so much information I could not keep up with the text as it scuttled across the pages. Able smiled like an imp, and I stared at the pages. The gorgeous script spoke of the ancient dragons, Memorrix the Grand Agornator the Golden. I read of their history and cities, lands far and near the great dragons had sacked once. I thumbed page after page of the dragon lore, wondering at it and the book. I was whispering as softly as I could. 'It's magical all right. Probably can answer anything, no? Or is it just the history of the Fanged Spire? Or Grey Downs?'

'It's more,' Able said. 'Yet, the island is famous. See, many visited it at one point. Usually to wreak havoc. There, Agornator attacked it once and left after razing parts of the city.'

'During Hel's war? Would make sense,' I whispered.

'Did she write it?' Able asked. I turned to look at Euryale, hunched over an ancient scroll.

'Not sure,' I said softly, my hands running across the pages. 'More dragons?' I asked it, and it replied. Nidhogg, the deadly serpent was often mentioned in a very attractive, overly ornate page, the mighty dragon and a foe of the balance, striving to topple the gods, even to snuff out the Shades itself. I nearly forgot about Euryale, utterly fascinated by the book, and then I despaired as I skimmed the pages.

Able nodded in agreement. 'This does not help us, though,' he sniffled.

'Unless …' I thought, 'there is one nearby.'

'One what?'

'A dragon,' I whispered.

'I think we would know if an eradicator of life was around,' he smiled. 'They are enormous.'

'There are no pictures of them here,' I told him very softly. 'They might be small, in fact.'

'I dreamt of one. I saw a maw. A huge maw. It ate you. And what use would we have of a dragon?' he wondered.

'She told me not to think about them. It would surely be stronger than she is,' I ventured, as I made a barely audible whisper to Able. 'Perhaps there is a spell to summon one? I'm worth a lot. It could sell me for gold to the elves and slay this beast, and let the rest of you go.'

'Great plan,' he rumbled. 'Perhaps it would slaughter the lot for sport? And selling you to the elves puts you exactly where you don't …'

'I have to go to them anyway,' I told him. 'I will need to attempt the deed she asked for me to perform, so I can treat with the goddess for my life.' Euryale began singing and soon the song was thrumming through the air, soft and vibrant at the same time

We sat still until I remembered to breathe again.

'Ask then,' he said dubiously.

'Where is the closest dragon to Grey Downs?' I asked, and the pages went blank. 'Is there a dragon in the Fanged Spire?' I asked and thought I had failed again, but then the text began running again, filling the page.

'In Grey Downs,' I breathed, 'there is a dragon. In the Fanged Spire, indeed. Below.' The text spoke of a dragon called the Masked One. It was a dragon, near fallen in the war, terribly hurt, lost to its kindred. 'A Pact he made, a thrall he became,' it says. 'That is Euryale's secret?'

'Below? Dungeons?' Able said in wonderment. 'I should go and see. We have a week.'

'I know who to ask if you cannot find it, though I'm not sure he will tell me,' I breathed softly, thinking about Nox. He had saved me and now let me skim the book. I glanced at Euryale, and she was still hunched over her table, now scribbling something furiously as her song had turned into a soft lament of loss and mourning. It made me stop for a moment and, staring at the monster, I wondered what her long history had done to her, how it had changed her? Surely she was a ferocious, dangerous beast, but perhaps she had smiled once for something that had been happy and pure and without malice.

'You going to ask something else? What are the weaknesses of the gorgons, for example?' Able interrupted my thoughts, but I shook my head furiously.

'I dare not,' I mouthed and closed the book, trying to find strength and courage to put the tome back. I shuddered and gazed at the hole in the bookcase from where the book had fallen. It was a hard, supreme effort to lift the book, sweating all over as I did, but then I put it back down.

I opened it with a small curse.

'Can a gorgon be killed?' I asked in the softest whisper. Text began sprawling on the pages.

The book slammed closed.

The sound was so loud my ears rang. The eye opened up, a dark orb staring at me. 'Mistress, say the passphrase,' the book whispered, and I fell back to the seat. I turned but too late. Euryale had a hand on my shoulder.

'Well, human girl, what is the passphrase?' she asked laconically and then continued viciously. 'Only some questions or commands are allowed without one, that is all. It's my diary, after all, though it, like Nox, once belonged to another. I have not filled it for a while. And I wonder what you asked it about? Curious you are? Or treacherous?' She placed the book on her palm, her eyes gazing at me intensely from under her hood. 'I think the latter?

Yes?' she whispered. 'I did not give this book to you. How is it in your suspicious little hands, my lovely friend?'

I gathered myself, knowing there was a fixed, terrified look on my face I could not shake off. She would punish me. She would punish the others. 'It fell to the desk when you last fed on me. It was glowing, and I was intrigued. I asked about the dragons. I know you commanded me not to delve into the dragon lore, but there are legends of them on Earth, of the gigantic, terrifying things as you said, and the book was glowing, mesmerizing,' I told her as casually as I could while trying to stifle the terrified shake in my leg. 'I am sorry.'

'Sorry?' she asked softly. 'You should be sorry. And I will see how sorry you are.' She whispered to it, the lid closed and her eyes scoured the book. 'Ah. Not very sorry, not sorry enough to speak the truth, at least. How to kill a gorgon? Our deal is thus changed.' She touched the Shades and her hands flew to the air as she gathered power. I saw she grasped ice and wind, and my hands flew to the sides as I whirled painfully out of the seat to the floor. I could not move nor even twitch a muscle, and I spied Able's infuriated, desperate face gawking at my pain. I spun in the air, going around and around, cursing bitterly as she grasped me by my hair and we flew to the doorway of shadows and darkness. We came to stand before the familiar speaking door, the one leading to the Timmerion's War Hall. The door burst to life with a surprised shriek as if it had been napping on duty.

'Welcome, mistresses, to your delicious dinner,' it greeted us happily.

'Shut up, you pile of confused lumber,' the gorgon spat, and she ran a finger across it and cast a complicated spell. The door's happy mouth changed into brooding black, dead lips. 'Come and mourn in the Chambers of Flaying,' the ominous voice from the ugly mouth proclaimed. Euryale pushed me through the door into a large, circular hall with a curving roof and ornamental, rib-like arches decorated with leering skulls. Pennants of yellowed skin hung from the walls, shivering in some moving air, and there we stood on a dank, mossy stone floor, and there were magical lights set haphazardly around the walls. Around us were cells, most open, filthy and abandoned, but some were closed and apparently in a good condition, adorned with glittering locking mechanisms. 'This is what you were looking for?' she asked spitefully. 'The dungeon below? The dragon?'

'I made a mistake,' I whispered. 'I was curious, just curious.'

'Well, you of the Tenth have a saying about the cat and its curiosity,' she whispered. 'You were pouring honey in my ears, and I, the fool, my heart moved by your false words, outright lies and the spec of darkness that is truly inside you thought you would worship us like you would a goddess. Like you should, indeed, human girl. As soon as you were allowed some trust, you betrayed me, like a mean, petty little child. These are the Chambers of Flaying as you heard my door just proclaim, the dungeons where the Timmerions held their most reluctant guests. Up there, the skulls of those who would not follow the way of repentance and find a way to their master's graces. There, the skins of his enemies who were never expected to change their hearts. Some are Cerunnos's former friends, and even relatives are amongst both the skulls and the skins. Come, sister, until her where his folk flayed those who would not bend a knee,' she laughed and pushed me across the room, the spell around my limbs hurtful, clutching. She was pushing me on and through a massive, ironbound door, slamming me into it with force. I was not terribly hurt, for the gate flew open quickly, the lock falling away like a puddle of skittering crabs, flowing molten and golden on the glistening floor. I hurtled downstairs, not painfully, but I was terrified, for we descended into darkness that was only cut by the Bone Fetter in my arm. The lock was repairing itself until it was glittering iron once more, I noticed. Euryale followed me, running in shadows across the floor and the walls, wraith of the night, and as I stopped, she dropped from the darkness above, lithe like a stalking demon before me. She grasped my face as a light snapped into being above. 'You read the book, and you saw the lines about the Masked One? Yes, you did. You were seeking power over me, were you not? Matters not, Shannon. You shall perform the deeds I asked for, and Hel knows

428

if I will let you go free, after all. And sadly, the Masked One has no power over me. I have power over him, you see. His power is mine and that was my secret, clever little one. The beast made a Pact for his life, and I am the mistress of the wyrm's powers. And now we have to think of a price for you to pay.'

I felt the tears come. 'And why should I help you, then? If there is no deal with a reward?' I spat as bravely as I could as she raked a fingernail across my chest. I saw Able gawking at me from the doorway, his dead eyes enormous and white, anger playing on his young, childish face.

Euryale's eyes were burning under her cowl. 'There will be a price, not a prize. Ah, still you worry about your friends and always did, despite my warning. You have no dreams of freedom and power for you and your sister, no. You let them seduce you, and I tell you now, Shannon, one day, if you had made it out of here with them, you would have regretted it. But now you are here. How the masks fall. The Dark Levy is ever tricky, with vagabonds and wastrels of the Tenth, full of the foulest creatures, but you have not learned your lessons back in your former misery, no. Instead of growing and being sensible, you developed a conscience. Sad it is, that you have more promise in these lands than most of the mighty maa'dark elven nobles, the mistresses of high houses and lords of the guilds. Sad, as the Second Light of Aldheim worries over a simpering, foolish group of humans. You are willing to shed your life rather than let the scum go. And no doubt you think you are so precious, I cannot do without you?'

'Yes, that is true!'

She giggled madly. 'But you do not truly understand me, Shannon. Sometimes I waste what could be supremely useful to me, just because it thrills me. Didn't I let you fight the other team? Dangerous! But I am a gambler. And I know my theory was right. There will be others, perhaps. Here ' she flitted in the shadows and grasped something in the dark. She appeared before me. In two of her hands were goblets of dull, simple make. She placed them to one side and slipped off her leathery garment, exposing her magnificent, nude physique. She extended her remaining two arms to her sides, suddenly holding thin daggers. I flinched, but she was not going to flay me.

Instead, she wounded herself.

She made a thin wound on each of her sides, and thick blood came forth. She grimaced and held the goblets under each injury, letting the liquid flow inside. Her eyes were gloating at my distress. She smiled malevolently under the hood as the cups filled. She took a sip of the cup on her right side and grinned.

'When the Void filled with the frigid ice and eternal fire and the dice were thrown for all of us, the first creatures of the worlds, as old as the Fates and the gods, the wondrous things that were born thus were given gifts. You have yours, Shannon, the gift of healing.

Others of the Ten Tears have theirs, the lesser ones, but while you are unique in your ability to heal, the gorgon's blood, my little flower, is a thing of many uses, and one is nearly like your power, only more powerful still. This one,' she shook her right hand and the liquid sloshed inside the goblet, 'is wondrous nectar, bled from my right side, and can resurrect even the dead, perhaps. You see, I could save the Regent's wife easily, but alas, you are the only one who can enter the damned hall. This was your salvation from the Rot as well.'

Her wounds closed.

'This one?' She sloshed the liquid in the other goblet. 'It does the opposing,' she giggled hollowly as she mulled the wine-like liquid on the other side, 'let us see.' She twirled her hands and the cups were enveloped in lingering dust and shadows as they spiraled to the floor before me, and I could not say which one was which. Dreadful suspicion and fear hammered at me as I gazed at her, and she enjoyed every moment of my torment.

'I'll have a sip of what you had,' I told her spitefully.

'Ah, but let us keep the Rot at work in you.' She pointed a long, white finger at me. 'Wait.'

She cast a spell, pulling at ice and winds, the dark, swirling portal appeared, and she disappeared. I stared at Able, who looked helpless and sorry, and I shook my head at him, trying to reassure him. Whatever Euryale was going to do, would have to be borne.

It took some time, but she reappeared.

She was not alone.

She had Ulrich, Cherry, Albine, Dmitri, Dana, Lex, and Anja with her, all held by spells, their eyes huge with fear and surprise. 'Shannon! What the hell did you do?' Dana shrieked, and I looked away in shame. Fear ran up and down my back, I could feel its presence in my spine, making my knees weak. She wove some more icy spells and the lot went quiet, their eyes surprised. Furyale stepped between her victims, their faces glistening with sweat and confusion, and she hurled me to the floor before them. She ran a finger across Anja's face, drawing blood. 'Choose a drink for her. Select a drink for her or one for your sister. Choose which one shall drink and what.'

'No!' I said, horrified. 'No!' I screamed.

'Choose a drink for your friend or for your sister,' she said again and laughed dryly. 'Do it. Perhaps you are lucky?'

'I will serve you and aid you, mistress, and shall not question you again,' I pleaded, and she giggled. 'I read a damned book!'

'Yes, you will aid me and will read no more,' she laughed. 'Indeed, you shall do as I say! But like a child, your period for fair warnings is now gone. A child gives their word only to turn renegade at the first possible moment for selfish reasons and must know it burns to fail so.'

'Selfish? I want my friends to …'

'Shh. Selfish, for I am your mistress, the one who dragged you from the misery of the Tenth. You plotted against your mother. Now you pay for such an affront. Since you love them better than you do your sister, or me, one shall suffer. Fool girl, they hate you both, yet here we are. They must giggle at the idiot Shannon, who could have been free and rich, but who listened to their whispers, the simple girl who never had friends. But one won't giggle shortly. Choose!'

'I don't wish to choose,' I begged her.

Euryale disappeared and appeared at my side, pulling my face to stare at Dana's face, then at Anja. 'Do you take me for the type to play games? Do you? Choose.'

I eyed Anja and Dana, my eyes traveling across the lot, all held magically. Dana was defiant, her eyes fierce as she regarded the terrible creature gazing at me with perverse excitement. Lex's eyes were begging me to choose him, but she had not asked for him. I shuddered in anger, cursing Euryale bitterly. I took a deep breath.

I spat and cried, staring at them. 'I am sorry.'

'They cannot answer you, love. Choose,' Euryale said softly.

'This one,' I told her, taking one cup randomly, and then I stared down to my knees. 'Give it to ... Anja.' I hazarded a glance her way. The Russian's eyes smoldered in anger and then she was nodding bravely.

'That one?' Euryale giggled, the goblet flying to her hand. She stalked before Anja, her cowl the only clothing on her, gliding with animal-like dexterity. She grasped her face. 'Speak. And resist at your own peril.'

'No need to pry my mouth open, see?' the blond woman said dourly, suddenly able to speak. 'I'm rarely reluctant for a proper drink. Let me have it.'

'Yes.' She tipped the goblet in front of her eyes, which were round as plates. Ulrich turned pale and sweated, but the spells holding him stood fast. He opened his mouth with a quiver but could not speak. Euryale kept the goblet up before the tall, blond girl for so long she had to close her mouth and malignantly she snapped her fingers and her mouth opened impossibly wide. She groaned in pain. She trailed a finger across her face, making another long cut, and she was whimpering.

'Taste it, my sweet girl, the fomenter of discontent, and let us see if you are in luck,' Euryale hissed and leaned her body on hers and poured the liquid into her mouth. 'Swallow, little one.' Anja's eyes filled with tears, and she swallowed.

The wound on her face turned pink, then closed, and I let out my breath.

Euryale turned to me, enjoying my relief. 'Lucky, very lucky,' she smiled, and I knew she was not done. 'But things will change now. The Ten Tears are no longer training, Shannon. The class is dismissed. They will linger here, guests to my creatures. All of them. They will have cells until they rot there. That girl,' Euryale told us with spite and pointed a finger at Albine, 'and the one called Cherry and the dolt,' she pointed at Lex, 'shall sit and share a cell with something to keep them on their toes. Nothing deadly, of course, unless madness and hunger will drive them to suicide on this thing. Your sister, Shannon, I shall chain to the door of the dragon you sought to find. She will be near the monstrous thing, and must endure his whispers. He is a master of manipulation and schemes, lonely as an ugly cripple. He is cruel, much like I am and so close to him, she will be nude, bared and flayed in spirit and mind. Perhaps she will endure his lies and whispering, perhaps not. Perhaps she shall last for the remaining week? If not, she will be one of the mad ones. So you will have to hurry and obey me. The longer she stays near the thing, the more it will … change her.' Dana's eyes betrayed fury, as she stood there, shaking, unable to do anything. The air holding her still apparently tightened in response to her anger, for she grimaced in sudden pain.

'But you, Shannon, shall wait here. In this cell.' I saw she was still not done by the gleeful slap of her hand on her nude thigh.

'I read a book,' I whispered. 'That is all.'

'You read a book you were not supposed to read,' she hissed. 'You asked it questions you should not have. You shall have company. Ulrich will share this cell with you.'

'And Anja?' I asked heavily.

'She,' Euryale grinned. 'is a rebel. She shall share her cell with the mad. You shall hear her begging for mercy, and they shall not be merciful. They lust for entertainment. I doubt you will know her if you ever see her again. I doubt you will, anyhow.'

'No!' Ulrich forced himself to scream, even through the spells holding them silent.

Euryale stared at him, confused. 'My, but you are furious. Enough so to break my spell. Here let me redo it.' She cast air and ice, and Ulrich's face distorted painfully. 'Thank her!' she grinned and pointed at me. 'And as for the mandatory death that is required in a situation like this, he will pay the price.' She turned to Dmitri. She removed her cowl with a flick of her wrist and a glistening sea of snakes flew to either side of her head. I caught a glimpse of her formerly beautiful, smooth face, and now it was haggard, a ropy face, with terrible, burning eyes, huge and fierce, and she flew to the helpless Dmitri. The snakes shot out around him, pulling him to Euryale, and his thin scream ripped the thick air of the dungeons, making unseen creatures yap in fear. His eyes burned. They melted. They burned in flames and shrunk in his head as Euryale pulled him closer and kissed him, apparently through the lips as blood flowed profusely. His face turned white, then grayish, his hair shed, and skin turned to ash, his legs were twitching and hands shaking violently.

'Dmitri!' Anja screamed, and she was free of her bonds, for she rushed the demon. The snakes twisted in the air and slapped her several times, entwining themselves around her throat, leaving her shuddering, her fingers just barely touching Dmitri. Euryale's hand shot out and grabbed her by the throat, holding her away, cruelly letting her see her brother dying. Ulrich was fighting the spell, I saw that much, but he was helpless.

Dmitri died.

He died slowly, his sister staring at him. He died whimpering, his face turning to stone as her eyes probed into his sunken, stony holes, and it was a gruesome, painful death. The prolonged kiss went on, and blood was flowing from the cracks in the stone-like face of our former, happy companion. Maliciously, she cut off her kiss, turned her face away and let him crumble to the ground, feet and arms half flesh, half stone, dead, or dying, shuddering in hazes of pain. He was gone, nonetheless, lost to us. She shook her head, and the cowl flew from the ground to her hands. She garbed herself and held onto Anja. She turned to look at me. 'Soon, girl, you will leave this place. Serve me with the Eye, and your sister and you might survive, yet.' She moved her hand, and Ulrich flew to the wall. She walked over, dragging Anja helplessly after her and latched a chain around Ulrich's foot, leaving him staring at the long iron coil keeping him a prisoner. The Austrian sat up, freed from the airy clamps and stared at the terrible beast, his face ashen with anger. Euryale petted him like she would a dog and got up and turned to me. 'Penitence is a long road, Shannon. One must truly suffer to feel sorry. So you shall. Stare at your nemocis, Shannon. He does not like you. Especially after he hears his woman suffering. You will stare at him for a week, sitting there, shackled and starving, his eyes and words accusing you of your silly failure. Terribly unfortunate this is, but it is so nonetheless.' She smiled with bloodied fangs and disappeared, pulling the rest of the Tears with her to her portal.

I slumped to my knees. Anja screamed, in terrible fear, a long, ululating scream of terror.

But something was wrong.

Ulrich's hands moved. His face had a demonic look as he gathered the chain until it was taut.

And then he gathered a spell of Fury and released fire on it.

He was not shut off from the Shades. The fire poured on the metal until it heated to orange, then white, and he pulled at it, snapping it. He screamed in terrible anger and rushed to the door. He beat it and shook his massive shoulders as he tried to tear it open. He summoned fire, so much fire and poured it at the door. Nothing happened, the color of the wood turned dark, but that was all. The lock glittered mockingly. Ulrich spun and fell on his fours as he crawled for Dmitri. The boy was shuddering as Ulrich's fingers ran over the stony flesh, the quivering fleshy parts, and he wiped tears off his face.

Ulrich got up and harnessed another spell of Fury.

'How?' I gasped for Euryale had left him with his powers.

He spat, his face burning with fury. 'How? It's my skill. The ability to see the Shades without interference! It is the secret we had! We would have tried an escape that night Anja spoke with you. But you hesitated!'

'You should have told ...'

'Ah yes! And trust you not to tell her about it? Euryale? This murderess. I'm sure you would have trusted me not to murder Dana when I had my powers and she did not! No, we could not tell you before you were committed! And now you failed!'

'I did, I ...'

'Failed!' he roared. 'Lex, my cousin is gone. Now she is suffering! Anja! And they are dead! Both Alexei and Dmitri! You piece of shit! You and yours are our bane!' He summoned fire and released it across Dmitri, so long and harsh and hot the remaining flesh burned to cinders, leaving blackened bones. The smell was terrible, and I gagged and looked away.

Somewhere, Anja screamed again.

It was a terrible, long cry full of horrified fear and pleading. A chorus of cackling voices could be heard, pleased by her arrival, an imperious voice could be heard, thin with madness. 'Surround her! Grasp her! Do it!' It was a mad male voice, full of commanding force, and Anja was shrieking in absolute horror. She begged and pleaded, and so I saw madness entirely claim Ulrich.

He turned to me. His eyes were bitter and hopeless, lost and resentful, full of pain and terror.

He harnessed Fury and a thin, fiery whip danced in his hands. 'You and your bitch sister. Always due to you, we suffer. People die. People I care about!'

'Why didn't you attack her?' I yelled at him, backpedaling as he stalked closer. 'Before he killed Dmitri.'

'I ...'

'Failed! Coward!' I spat.

'They are doing things to her. God knows what! She is lost.' He was sobbing and shaking his head. 'You two were born to torture me. One less, soon, and say hello to the shit Ron and the two merry brothers!' The whip came down and touched my side, burning my flesh terribly, and I screamed and tried to get away. I fell, hitting my head. I sensed he was coming closer and soon felt his hands around my throat. He bent over me. 'Drink from this cup, you cunt.'

He had Euryale's other cup, the deadly one. She had forgotten them in the cell.

He grabbed my face with a terrible force. I fought, but he slapped me and pushed his knees to my arms. I gasped and shrieked, but he grasped my mouth with his fingers, making me gag and sloshed some cool, vile blood in my mouth. He kept me down, forcing my mouth closed, and I finally swallowed. Then he jumped up and away, staring at me as I curled on the floor.

The liquid burned. It burned with bottomless, excruciating pain, and I felt it touch and melt my innards, the agony was raking me head to foot.

The last thing I saw was Ulrich's face above me, studying me like I was an animal he hated. I thought I saw Able cursing him, trying to hit him in his helpless undeath, and I knew I would join him soon.

PART 5: SNAKE DANCE

'You hare-brained idiot. You ate her.'

Shannon to Thak the Giant

CHAPTER 19

cy white swirls and fierce wind buffeted my frozen face. I was crawling through the familiar dream, the one with a snowy, ethereal landscape. A horse neighed and the weight of cool armor touched my face, but then, something rocked; a rumble and explosion shook the ground I was lying on.

I woke up sputtering and dust was coming down the walls and ceilings. People were shrieking in fear nearby and howling like animals. I screamed and took deep breaths, turning to my side, vomiting blood and stomach fluids violently. I was on my hands and knees, gagging, clutching the ragged, ripped robe, molested by the fiery spell of Ulrich. I suddenly remembered him and wiped my mouth as I turned around and around, sure to see his dead body and Euryale mocking me.

However, what I saw were two cups of gorgon's blood.

Ulrich was crouching next to them, his face haunted. His eyes were feverish as he stared at me, rubbing his forehead with his massive hand. 'She did not come. I saved you,' he told me with a desperate voice. 'I'm not sure what the explosion was.'

'You killed me,' I said softly. I did not see Able in the room.

He grinned weakly. 'I think I always wanted to kill you, Shannon. We've lived a rough life, and when you lose a brother ...'

'In your criminal gang?' I asked as I slowly stood up, feeling very wobbly. 'But you were from Austria?'

'The gang? Oh? Lex told you? Yeah, I figured he would. Lex and Ron moved to America, when I was ten. We shared a father. Cyburns all. They called me over to join them for this ... mistake two years ago. I traveled and made it to Boston. Joined their outfit for a while. I always thought of myself as Austrian, not American. They called me that, in the gang, Austrian. Ron's business was killing. Lex was just a smuggler. I did something else. I ... I have never killed anyone. Except for the boy in the trial, yes, but that was not ... the same. I thought I could nip your life, but I could not. It was not ... what I thought it would be like.'

'Good. I am happy,' I told him, rubbing my throat. It felt strange but not sore. 'I cannot believe I was gone. Did you bring me back so you could kill me again when she screams again? Then resurrect me and ...'

He shrugged. 'You died. No breath and eyes lifeless. I suppose witnessing that took the edge off my yearnings, and I did not want to live with that on my conscience. I hate your sister, I do and you made Anja drink that shit over there,' he said bitterly and stared at the cups of blood, 'so I suppose that pushed me over.' He hugged himself as if deathly cold. 'It was not as pleasurable as I hoped it would be.' He picked up a goblet and whirled the contents around. 'Potent stuff this blood of hers. So this is the bitch you have served?'

'She promised me and Dana freedom. I tried to help Anja and the lot of you. But Dmitri ...'

'They are dead,' he said heavily. 'The idiots. I loved them.'

'I loved them as well,' I said painfully.

He opened his mouth and shut it. He shook his head mournfully. 'You were right. I should have stopped her. I've been pretending about my skill for a year, but Dmitri died, for I hesitated. Then it was too late. It's my fault.'

'She is immortal,' I told him. 'You would have failed. I loved him. Both of them. And I feel at fault as well.'

'Now we have to love each other,' he said with a small chuckle. 'I don't want to die hating so much.'

'I love even you,' I told him, leaning against the moldy, wet wall. 'Even if one day we might have to finish what began with Ron. Moreover, I am sorry for him. I always was, even if he thought I should be the one to die.'

Ulrich grunted and lifted his head. Anja's weak scream could be heard, and he looked down, balling his fists. 'Anja,' he whispered. 'Gods curse this place.' His fists tightened as he massaged them on his forehead. He shook his head forlornly. 'We will settle things one day. Now we should get out of here.'

'You can see the Shades,' I told him enviously. 'Always could.'

'Yes,' he grinned weakly. 'It's been damn hard pretending to have the same, silly and blissful look on my face as you lot when you were given access. Damned hard. Damned hard not to roast Dana when she was blocked. When Cosia dismissed that fiery thing I accidentally summoned that first day, I nearly summoned a firewall immediately after. Happily, I did not. I could have killed your sister any day.'

'There is good in her as well,' I said weakly.

He hesitated. 'Yeah, she loves you enough to kill. She could have just let Cosia take you and be done with looking after you. But I cannot ...'

'I know,' I breathed.

'Matters not, Shannon,' he agreed. He played with fire, bouncing it in his hands, from one to the other. 'You are not crazy? Truly?'

'No,' I told him.

'And yet you speak to Albine's brother. And he died the day we arrived,' he said carelessly, the flames running between his fingers and scattering to the floor. 'Anja told me.'

'We all have some unique gifts from the day we arrived. Albine can tell truth and lies apart. I see the dead. Should they stay around, that is. And no, Dmitri and Alexei didn't stay. Neither did Ron.'

'Creepy skill that. Both, in fact.'

'I also see and hear all the spells others cast around me,' I confided in him. He was all I had.

'Really?' he asked, stopping. 'Do you see how I do this?' He ran the flames around him in small circles. 'Can you fathom the level of control and the skill I show? They taught us the whip and this thing this past week. It was painful. And you can learn it like that. Just like that?

'I see it,' I said, and I did, wondering at how he pulled at the fiery inferno and twisted it just so, adding heat, and even the crackle of flames to the mix. 'But I cannot do it. I cannot touch fire. But I can see how it is done.' I decided not to tell him I could meddle with the spell. Perhaps that would be useful one day with Dana's life at stake. Though, of course, we would not be leaving.

'Impressive,' he mumbled. 'Even when you cannot see the Shades?'

'Even then,' I agreed. 'And I can heal, but that is useless now.'

'Yes, we all know about that,' he said with a withering smile as Anja screamed again, asking someone or something to be quiet, to leave her alone. A cackle of a crowd answered her.

I tried to distract Ulrich and myself. 'None else can do that. Not even the elves. Therefore, she has a plan for me. I'm the Hand of Life and carry the favor of a goddess.'

'Elves?' he grinned. 'And a goddess. Ah, you have seen a bit of this world whereas we have been stuck here like cows in the pen. This gorgon can resurrect people with her blood. Are you saying she cannot cast such a spell?'

'No, only I can heal with magic,' I whispered. 'At least so she claimed. She had a plan. I am apparently something the elves respect and revere, the Hand of Life, and I was supposed to serve her by fetching something belonging to a goddess. She longs to return the gods to us. And her lost sister. And she has many other plans. Most involve inflicting pain on some poor innocent soul, no doubt.' And so, I told him everything about Hel's war and her stolen eye, and the shattered gates. I told him of Euryale's plans and what she expected of me. Ulrich stared at me nearly emotionlessly until I was done.

Then he laughed hugely, wiping tears.

'What?' I asked him, irritated and hurt.

'Killing you would have been no punishment, just a premature release, I think,' he smiled, wiping his face on his palm. 'That is mad. Elves and an eye of a goddess? And you have to meet the lord of this keep. Cerunnos? A ghoul? You mean, some sort of an undead?'

'Millions of elves,' I agreed. 'They rule Aldheim. And yes, I'm to challenge the one dead lord, who caused the Sundering of the worlds.'

'You think very highly of yourself,' he breathed in wonder.

'I am unique in this world, Ulrich, so I don't think too highly of myself at all,' I spat and bristled. 'Unless she lied. But I do think the deeds she expects of me are beyond me.'

'Right.' He looked skeptical and then massaged his shoulders helplessly. 'So, what now?' He arched an eyebrow at me.

The tower rocked. We glanced up, worried.

'You think it will come down?' I asked him nervously as the walls crumbled.

'Might as well,' he pouted. 'We are finished anyway.'

'No,' I countered. 'Didn't you just say we should get out of here?'

'Yes, I did,' he glowered at me. 'But then it occurred to me I can't think of a plan.'

I grinned. 'You have your power.'

He shook his head in disgust. 'You think I could take her down, even if I surprised her?'

'No, but I was reading ...'

'God's sakes, reading. That's why Anja is ...' And she was screaming again, begging and crying, and we went quiet for a moment.

I went on, trying to forget the terror in her voice. 'What now? She controls us, though, not you. She is powerful, yes. Apparently much more powerful than she should be, but still a primal, ancient creature. But I think she is much more a ... I don't know.'

'A bully and an assassin,' Ulrich grunted. 'A nightmare more than a god. She makes mistakes?'

'Yes, she does. Didn't she leave the cups here? She is a slayer and stalker of the night. She is a maa'dark, sure, but perhaps she is not omnipotent. She said she has a secret, and she refused to speak about the dragons, and I know she holds a beast prisoner. She said she holds its powers. And it's down here, somewhere.'

'Dragons?' he asked, incredulously.

'Yes. I tried to find a dragon, for they come from Nifleheim, I think. I found Naricirrax the Seething ... many others. And I found one in Grey Downs. The Masked One is supposedly a prisoner of hers. In here, somewhere and she took Dana to it. I wish to ...'

'Speak to a dragon? I think we should skip the dragon and just get out of here, but there is no way to do that.'

'I said it has my sister,' I cursed him.

'Could this dragon help us?' Ulrich asked carefully.

'Possibly.'

'I doubt it's interested in anything we have to say. And if she has its powers, then it's likely only going to gobble us up instead of casting swift, deadly spells at us,' he insisted. 'Sounds unpleasant.'

'Look, Ulrich. It's the closest thing to an escape we have. Actually, I know a gateway out of here, but it is locked, our powers are barred and that thing might ...'

'If she holds its powers, then it has no powers, Shannon!'

I slapped my hand on the stone. 'She says so, but is she

honest? Or a liar?'

He banged his head with his fist. 'Fine. And you say you might, somehow be able to spring us from here?'

'Possibly. Likely, even. If I find out some secrets,' I said, thinking about the mirror and what she had spoken to it. Whether I could cast the spell, was a mystery. The mirror had a name. I clawed at the silvery Bone Fetter. 'I need to be free of this in order to do anything. And hence the dragon might know something to help us.'

He banged his head with his fists again and looked like a forlorn kid. 'Yeah, yeah. I said okay. You have to unfetter yourself and learn some secrets. Then we rescue the others. And you think this beast will help you?'

'Yes,' I told him plainly.

'Why?' he demanded.

'Because it must detest Euryale. It's a prisoner.'

'And what can a prisoner do? Give us prudent advice?' he despaired.

'I could use even that!'

'Right,' he growled.

We stared at each other, and I gazed at Dmitri. 'I wish they had not died.'

'Even when they bullied you in the beginning?' he noted with a small smile.

'They were funny and liked me despite thinking me crazy,' I

noted. 'So I liked them just fine, most of the time. They were as lost as I was.'

'I liked .. *like* Anja.'

'Do you love her?'

His face darkened. 'Is that a word one dares to utter in this place? No. One should not love here, Shannon,' he warned. 'Do not love Lex if you value his life. Just do not. If we manage to get rid of the bitch and this sodden, sad, ruined island, then they, and I mean anyone will use him to hurt or enslave you. Even if we escape. You don't honestly believe these ... elves are noble? No, they will be ruthless as she is.'

'So I have been told,' I agreed.

'There,' he nodded. 'They think we are less than they are. You said you have read their stories. Is there anything in those books about human kings?'

'They have no rights in the south of the Spell Coast. In the north, they are not allowed. In Himinborg? Trad? They have lords but ...'

'Do they rule?' he articulated. 'Decide their own fate?'

I shook my head. 'No, they rule nothing unless in the names of their elven masters,' I agreed. 'But, as I said, I am special. I am the Hand of Life, and that title has a touch of a goddess in it. It will make a difference for us, perhaps. And if I will love someone ...'

'You don't yet?' he asked and sniffled with some disappointment, for Lex was his family.

'I don't know, Ulrich,' I told him patiently. 'If I do or will, I shall not let anyone stop me.'

'Not let anyone ...' he mimicked me insipidly and then Anja shrieked in a bottomless fear, somewhere near. He rested his hands on his face, and I saw the tears come. I hesitated and walked over to him. I sat down next to him, miserable as hell and placed a hand on his. His face shot up, startled, and for a moment that stubborn, hard face was like a scared small boy's face. He looked down. 'Aren't we just a miserable lot?'

'Yes. I never thought to comfort my killer,' I told him and leaned on him. He shuddered as he drew a huge breath and put his arm around me, keeping me close. 'I dream of Isabella.'

'The girl? The one we fought?' he asked.

'Yeah,' I told him. 'She ...'

'I can see how the boy died,' he told me softly. 'His eyes, nose and ears on fire. And he was snuffed out just like that. I'll never forget it.'

'My sister lied to me,' I told him hesitatingly. 'She is dangerous.'

He nodded and swallowed a sarcastic retort. Instead, he waved his hand in a conciliatory manner. 'I'm sorry for that. I wish ... I had intervened when Ron indicated you should be the one to die,' he said huskily. 'About your sister ...'

'I know. Let's cross that bridge when we get there,' I told him reluctantly.

'That will be a long day and a bridge of pains,' he told me.

'The door won't burn?' I asked him.

He shook his head, eyeing it. 'It's resistant. Now, I have another special skill, as well.'

'You do?' I asked, hopeful. 'Can you summon food like Nox? Some roast or stew?'

'You look like you only eat apples,' he grinned as he let go of me. 'Skinny.'

'The slop we ate the past year would cure anyone of apples. What is it? What can you do?' I asked him.

'I can open locks. Not like Anja, but something similar,' he told me as he got up and walked to Dmitri's corpse.

The tower rocked again, and we tried to steady each other as the dust billowed. 'What is going on up there?' Ulrich cursed as many living things moaned in fear nearby.

'I have no damned idea. You were saying?' I coaxed him as I ran after him, thinking Able had been angry after I died and had probably done something irreversible somewhere.

'No, I was the burglar in the outfit, back home. In America, that is. A second story man. Useful skill. I can open locks. And Dmitri here can help.' He stared at the corpse of the boy, charred, stony, with smoldering bones exposed in his thighs. He stiffened.

'What?' I asked him.

'I ... I,' he began, shaking.

'What?' I asked him again, worried.

'Would that stuff resurrect him? I mean, before I ...'

Had roasted him. I shook my head and pulled his face to me. 'No. He had no mouth, even.'

'But ...'

'No,' I insisted and held on to him as he fought his conscience. 'How?' I asked him, 'how can he help us?'

Ulrich wiped his face with the back of his hand and gathered himself, his voice coming in forced gasps. 'He kept a fishing hook from our holiday. Under the nail of his toe,' he said sadly and fondly.

'Why did he keep a hook?' I said as we scrambled to look at the charred remains of Dmitri. There, amidst his toe bones was a sooty hook, peeking from under a scorched toenail. 'You don't look like a burglar. Perhaps a thug like Ron was.'

He grabbed the hook and eyed me curiously. 'He kept it for me. Anja can open anything, but I insisted. Never know what is going to happen. Prepare for everything. Austrians are like that. Have you ever seen a burglar?'

'I cannot be sure, I suppose,' I allowed. 'Fine. I'll give you the benefit of the doubt that you might not be a clumsy thug or a knuckle-dragging brute. Of course, you could be all those things. You climb walls like a spider, no?'

'I can climb just fine,' he said as he vigorously twisted the hook.

'Do I look fat?'

'You looked a bit big when we arrived,' I said softly.

'That was muscle,' he growled. 'And your sister mocked Ron like that and look where that got us all.'

'Sorry. The lock is magical,' I told him. 'And Euryale is sure to watch us.'

'She didn't save you. I think she is busy. Something is happening out there. Now, I used this kind of a hook once. I broke into this elegant country house that looked wealthy as hell, and we thought it would be an easy job. The guys were waiting outside, and ...' he grunted and cursed as he pricked his finger on the hook and continued, 'and I sneaked in, climbed to the second floor balcony and opened the door's meager locks with something like this. I went in and this woman accosted me, nude as the day she was born. Wasn't supposed to be anyone in. Bastard Tom had scouted it and claimed he had seen the owner leave with bag and a woman. Well, she had come back all right, taken a bath, and there she was. Not a bad looking one either. Entirely unclad. Except she had a shotgun.'

'I suppose you seduced her?'

He looked at me curiously. 'Yes. I think she had always fantasized about something like that. A handsome Austrian burglar gawking at her breasts. Later on, she wanted to marry me,' he said, twisting the hook vigorously.

'Really?'

'No, she shot at me,' he laughed. 'Flew to her round ass, and I cried for a week. My back and ass ... shit. Now, I think our Euryale loves chaos. Let us give her what she loves.' He eyed the twisted hook turned skeleton key in his hand appraisingly and nodded.

'Can you see the Shades still?' I asked nervously

'She can't cut me off,' he assured me. 'But little good it will do if Losia and Diluo are on the other side of that door. Or some others of the filthy cows.'

'I wish I had a sword,' I mumbled as we hiked for the steps towards the door.

'I wish that as well,' he snorted. 'You seemed pretty deft with it.'

We reached the door, and he leaned to look at the lock. 'The bitch opened it how?' he asked.

'She cast a spell, and the lock sort of skittered on the floor. Apparently, it fixed itself.'

'Skittered,' he grunted and put his finger in the lock. 'This shit is magical. No mechanism I know. Might as well stick my dick in there.'

'If that helps, do it,' I growled. 'Though I don't know if I or the blood can heal something like that if it fails.'

'Funny, but the hole is too small. Here, let me see if the key is useless.' He entered the skeleton key into the lock. He cursed and tugged and turned the key. It took some time and then his face screwed into a grin. 'It's been a standard lock sometime in the past.' The lock crackled, burning softly, the spell holding the steel lock snapped, bluish symbols ran around the steel and the wood, and the whole thing melted into red, molten ruin as the door opened. 'Well, that worked nicely,' he said and pushed open the door.

There stood Bilac, looking confused, grasping at her whip, her fine chain armor glittering dangerously. 'Get back in!' she demanded.

'No,' Ulrich said savagely and charged out, and I followed him. At the same time, I felt Bilac's ice, frost and wind buffet us, toppling Ulrich and gaining intensity, icy shards thrumming at the doorway. Then, cold hands grasped the big man's hands and legs, drawing blood from his side. I screamed and rolled clear, crushing a hand trying to grab me and ran at her, gathering satisfaction from the surprised look in her eyes. I grappled her and we rolled on the floor, cursing, I tried to choke her. Even her snakes looked shocked and none bit me, for some reason. I saw Ulrich hovering nearby, the spell holding him lost as we rolled on the floor. She was weaving a spell of Fury, kicked me off and then she was sitting over me, her short armored skirt cold on my ripped robe and chest beneath, fire playing in her hand as she stabbed down with a fiery, molten dagger. Her eyes were intense and victorious, and again I thought I would die, as Ulrich cursed her. Her eyes turned his way and grew large in shock.

A burst of fire hit her chest It was Intense, harshly hot and was followed by a whiplash that tore several snakes off her head. She screamed, music to our ears. I was pushing at her as Ulrich charged and tackled her pain-wracked body off me. They rolled on the ground; Ulrich grunting as he was punching her, flames were running wildly across the floor as his fire whip dissipated through lack of concentration Bilac, and her snakes recovered, and Ulrich howled as the serpents' bites raked him. Bilac, despite her sturdy frame, was lithe as a cat, even armored, and she sprung up, powerful arms pushing her up from the ground. She grabbed Ulrich, grasped his foot and elbow and threw him aside. She again wove a spell of Fury and her left hand held the dagger of molten fire again. Ulrich cursed, half paralyzed by the snake venom, tried to kick her unsuccessfully, and I moved and so Bilac lost.

For while wrestling with her I had grabbed her sword from her belt and held it beneath her chin.

She went silent and still and slowly stared up at me. Her snakes slithered across my arms and chest. 'Let him go, you death-faced bitch,' I said thickly, getting ready to butcher her.

'Do you not think I would die for my mistress?' she asked acidly.

'I doubt anyone would be willing to do so,' I retorted. 'She is a worthless thing. Let him go.'

'Saa'dark,' she chuckled. 'Fool. What will this accomplish? Go back to your cell. You'll die out here anyway, should I help you.'

'Release the Bone Fetters,' I told her brusquely, the blade hovering near her throat. Her eyes were bright yellow, angry and surprised.

'Release the damned Fetters, you worm-haired pile of shit,' Ulrich told her, near unable to move.

'I cannot,' she said with some trepidation, her eyes scouring my face. 'I must not.'

I smiled at her coldly as the sword drew blood. She flinched. 'Do it, girl. You told me that one day you might not care if you died for slaying me. Now you can show me. Or take the chance she might spare you.' I grinned at her and slashed at a snake getting too familiar. The head flew off to the dark corner, spilling thin blood, and she grimaced in pain as the sword blade rested on her neck. 'Let me free. You'll live. For a while at least.' I pressed the blade on her neck, and so she crumbled, the defiance flying away from her face, replaced by hopelessness.

'The Rot will eat you, and I shall dream of it,' she whispered.

I smiled and then whooped in happiness, for I had not realized something. 'I was just cured of it, Bilac! It is gone!'

'How?' she whispered, eyeing my shoulder carefully. 'You will regret this,' she said, shaking her head, and then closed her eyes, the ring in her hand glowing. Suddenly, I saw and felt the frigid tumbling of the ice, the tumult of freezing ages passing somewhere near, and I screamed with joy. Ulrich was smiling as well.

'You got it?'

'I got it,' I told him and gathered the healing powers and released them at him. He was gasping for breath as he rolled on the floor and got up laughing.

'Thanks,' he told me. 'Though I'm unhappy about that.' He nodded at Bilac's severed snakes and the healed stumps. 'You healed the ugly monster as well.'

'Sorry about that,' I grinned and leaned over her. 'Undress, you cruel vermin,' I told her.

'What?' she asked, confused, and at that I clubbed her with the sword, so quickly and hard she had no time to block me. She went to her knees, and I struck her again, brutally hard. She fell, twisting in agony. I kicked her over, and she did not move. 'I'll take this sword and armor,' I said and started working on the buckles.

'I should use the armor, actually,' Ulrich complained. 'I'll be doing the fighting.'

'No, I'll fight all right. And it's cut for a female.'

'Fine!' he said as he turned to gaze at the cells.

I nodded. 'Find which door holds who.'

He watched me incredulously as I tugged the armor off the unconscious gorgon. Then he moved to stare at the various doors. I pulled open Bilac's belt, then tugged at the chain armor, cut to allow movement, with a very low and immodest metal skirt and long, thick boots. Finally, rolling her down the steps, it came off the creature, and I pulled off my ripped robe and pulled on the chain mail, cursing the cold metal that seemed supple enough to be worn without anything under it. I grasped the belt and skirted myself with it, hefting the sword. Ulrich was going from door to door, staring at each. He turned to me, running his fingers across the wood of one door, carved with ghostly hands and a skull-shaped lock. 'There are twenty doors, at least five are locked. The stairway goes down over there on the left. That looks ominous. How do we find anyone here?' he asked as he stared at me pulling on Bilac's dark, strange runed boots. 'You do look excellent in that, I have to admit,' he said with a blush, and I grinned and wiped my hand across the wonderfully crafted armor.

'Thanks,' I told him, feeling spectacular, victorious for some reason, free of Rot and full of Shades. I stared at the doors. Then I eyed the main door, the fanged one, and the speaking freak of a barrier. I walked over to it.

'Exit, mistress, from this morass,' it declared and began to open.

'What is your name?' I asked it, and the mouth stopped moving, the fangs shuddering in indecision.

'Exit, mistress ...'

'Shut up!' I told it.

'Yes, mistress,' it agreed somewhat reluctantly.

'What is your name?'

'Call me Baktak,' it said. 'A spirit of the door, nothing more, just that, mistress. Nothing really. Something they bound to this gate, once.'

'You are a liar, Baktak. You know everything around here, don't you?' I cooed at it.

'Well ...'

'You are an ingenious little door, are you not?'

It had no face, but the lungs disappeared and a feminine mouth took form instead, pursing lips. 'You see through my varnish, mistress. How can I help you?'

'We have a bit of a problem, you see,' I told her happily. Anja shrieked somewhere, a tired, long scream, and Ulrich was running about, desperately trying to figure out where the cry came from.

'A bit?' It giggled, white teeth flashing. 'Grand serpent is going to be back anytime soon.'

'Where did she go?' I asked, intrigued. The lips started to whisper. I could not make it out. 'Louder, please,' I demanded imperiously. Ulrich was hovering behind me.

'There is the ghost. You know the one. Runt, dark-skinned male child. Loves pranks. Now it was mad as a beat badger. He pushed over a pint of something up there. There was a fire. Some magical explosions. Nasty business. They are salvaging her treasures and some are still exploding. Heads are rolling. Soon, she will begin to wonder at the coincidence of this business of yours and that fire.'

'He can sometimes push at things while enraged,' I told Baktak. 'And I'm grateful to him.'

'The dead can do that indeed, young, pretty mistress when they are terribly upset or terrified. They can grab things, nudge them, definitely. And he was afraid for you. No, he was angry. Thinks you are dead.' The voice was resentful, and I could imagine it staring at Ulrich with grave disapproval.

'It's blaming me, isn't it?' he asked.

'Yes,' I agreed. 'Is the fire under control?' I turned to Baktak, fingering the sword. 'How much time do we have?'

'That blade won't help you against the Devourer,' Baktak said sadly. 'Soon, the time is up for you. Very soon.'

'Soon. Thanks, I guess. So, Baktak, we will need to know ...' Ulrich asked.

'Tell this ape to be quiet,' the door said morosely. 'He kicked me once, didn't he?'

'He did, and he is damnably sorry for it, Baktak,' I tried to assure it.

'What do you need?' she or it asked, hardly mollified.

'We need to find our friends,' I grinned.

'You are mad to think this sad excuse for a barn door knows anything,' Ulrich crumbled.

I slapped my hand over his mouth to silence him. 'And we need to get out of here.'

'Gods,' Ulrich moaned softly. 'We are so dead.'

Baktak pursed its lips. 'She brought two girls and a boy to the fourth cell, the one with a skull lock and that ridiculous coat of hands. Terrible taste the Timmerions had, a horrible house, not to mention the drinking. There was the cute black girl with a huge bundle of hair, like an elf, and a strangely ugly, thin-faced girl, and one hulking ape of a boy.'

Albine, Cherry, and Lo",' I agreed. 'And Anja? The ...'

'Large-bosomed blonde?' the door said lecherously, smacking its lips happily. 'She is behind the red door, young mistress. Right next door to the skull lock.' It lowered its voice. 'And your sister is with the beast.'

I slumped and shook my head. 'The dragon? The Masked One?'

The door tried to speak but went quiet. It smacked its lips again. 'She is chained to the gate. Down the steps, and the thing is as dangerous as your ape thought it might be. Across the worlds, few things frighten the living as much as a dragon. The gorgons perhaps, terrify the weak in the night and creatures like it prowl the shadows and lands to harvest lives, but your sister was taken to a dragon. Moreover, I do not know how you aim to save her. You cannot get in to speak with it. It was part of the Pact that the door is closed to any, but those Euryale allows opening it. Yet, I know you will go and try. It hurt her and won't release her unless you do.'

'I have to,' I told Baktak weakly.

'You do not,' Ulrich said.

'Is there a way to enter the lair of the beast?' I asked the door, ignoring Ulrich. 'Any damned way?'

'She will fry me, she will make shavings of me and chew on my lips,' Baktak complained.

'There is a way?' I asked Baktak.

'Yes, there is a way,' the door said with resignation. 'I said ...'

'Speak!' Ulrich said.

The door brooded. 'I will tell you if that ape gives me a proper kiss.'

'He will,' I agreed. 'Purse your lips, Ulrich.'

'I will not! Kiss a door?' He looked horrified. 'It's got fangs!'

'Anja won't mind, and I shall heal you if you lose something,' I chided him. 'Kiss Baktak.'

'Is it even female?' he asked weakly.

'Does it matter?' I asked him with a sneer. 'Come now, be a man.'

'I won't bite,' Baktak teased, pursing its lips, wet and amorous.

'For God's sakes,' Ulrich grunted and bent to kiss the lips. Their lips met, and Ulrich's eyes popped open. He vaulted away, retching. He pointed an incredulous finger at the door. 'It put its tongue down my throat. Deep in my throat. That was damn disgusting. I shall ...'

'Thank Baktak for a sweet kiss,' I finished for him. 'Now, tell us.'

'Delicious, my happy man, very much so,' it cooed, and I thought it a bit mad. It went on. 'I said the door won't open to anyone but those Euryale allows in. The dragon had a servant when it fell. I remember the day. She took the servant, and the servant is a very useful thing.'

'Yes?' I said, and it brooded quietly. 'Nox? Yes? She told me he belonged to Stheno ...'

'She is a liar, mistress,' the door laughed. 'As for Nox, he cannot speak against his mistress. Remember that as you deal with him. Call Nox when you reach the door. Only he can open the door and keep it open.'

'And the thing up in the tower? Do you know it? This tunnel of the crow?' I asked. 'There is this thing ...'

'What? No crows here, none. Never was,' it said angrily. 'They shit everywhere. Can't abide bird shit.'

'The mirror in her hall,' I told it patiently. 'With crows on top. I don't know its name.'

'Ah! I see what you need,' Baktak grinned. 'She is a bit of competition for me, but I manage the tower, it takes people elsewhere. I have forgiven her. Dark Prayer it is called.'

'Dark Prayer?' I asked.

'Old artifact, Gift created,' Baktak said happily. 'That thing can take you far away from here with this name uttered in its presence and a spell cast. Where? I know not. Certainly not to the other worlds, but perhaps elsewhere in Aldheim.'

'I know it,' I said. 'Is it still intact?'

It thought about It for a moment, the tongue traveling the lips, and Ulrich gagged. I gave him the evil eye and then the door was happy. 'Yes? Yes, it is. The bastard. I don't mind the competition, but I'm stuck here, being kicked at and Nox shines it every day. So ...'

'Thank you Baktak,' I told it. 'Well, let's get to work. We will enter the lair of the beast last. I can travel there,' I said weakly, terrified of going against her.

'She is called the Devourer,' Ulrich said, turning me. 'We need a better plan.'

'We need to take our chances,' I told him. 'Let us free the others.'

'I would be careful in those rooms,' Baktak said. 'Very careful. In addition, I would open the one with the skull lock first. Might help with the second room. Just might if you play your cards right.'

'Gods are humping us,' Ulrich said miserably and moved down to face the door with the skull-faced lock. Ulrich pulled out his skeleton key and inserted it into the lock. He tugged and pulled and filled our ears with his soft curses. It took time to wheedle the lock open, but finally it opened, and I pulled my blade, afraid of what we might find behind the door. Ulrich pushed at the door carefully. 'Stubborn bastard door,' he said. 'Keep behind me.' The door was hugely thick, like a trunk, and we had to push it, both of us. It opened silently.

Silence inside as well.

It took time for our eyes adjust to the murk and while we saw there were figures sitting on their haunches down below, it was not easy to make them out. Finally, we saw there were Bone Fetters glowing down there. Then I saw a face. Albine looked up towards us. Cherry was on her knees next to him, and I was before them, eyeing the shadows carefully.

I walked down, holding the sword. 'Lex?'

His eyes glanced my way, brilliant and happy for a briefest of seconds, and then he shook his head in a terrified warning. Puzzled, I walked towards them. Cherry was not moving, only staring at the darkness, and I stopped at the bottom of the steps. Ulrich came to stand next to me, leaning on my shoulder, fatigued, and I had not realized the poison of Bilac had left him so harrowed. Albine shrugged and spoke gently. 'You would not, by any chance, have access to the Shades?' she asked weakly. 'We need some careless applications of the Fury.'

'I ...'

A voice, deep as mountain's hole spoke from the shadows. In fact, it was one shadow, and it moved.

'Deep as night, old blood, as old as blight,

grimy to touch, with a terrible rasp,

you shall heed Thak and run from his grasp.'

The creature was huge, as big as a small house, entirely black of skin. It had a vaguely humanoid shape, though thick as many elephants and a head as large as a small vehicle. It walked forward, shackles pulling behind it, strong and thick, and it was halted short of us. The shadow went to its knees, and we saw it was wearing blue, faded pants. Its hands reached forward as it went on all fours, the face emerging from the shadows. Its hair was thick and white; beard long enough to hang to its waist, and its physique impressive, a rippling mass of muscle. Its eyes were deep and brown, and it sniffed at us, a few feet away.

'What the hell is that?' Lex whispered. 'It's been mostly sitting there, giggling, and there are damned bones strewn on its side.'

'It can't reach us,' Albine said. 'But as the bitch said, perhaps people eventually rather let it eat them than suffer pain and hunger.'

'Perhaps,' I said. 'It is a jotun. A giant. Thak?'

'Jotun?' Lex asked, noting Ulrich. 'Anja?' he mouthed at me, and I shrugged, shaking my head. He nodded, staring at the huge man with unbridled suspicion, family or not.

'Giant,' Ulrich said incredulously. 'A damned giant.'

'Thak,' said the creature, grinning happily. 'Thak of the Scorched

Hold. Presently and lately a prisoner of the Betrayer.'

'Mistress Euryale?' I asked. 'She did tell me she has many names. All appropriate, no doubt.' I was moving carefully next to Albine as the creature shifted its massive weight.

He rumbled and scratched his armpit, a feral smile on his face. 'Mistress? Offal I call her in my loneliness. She is a harsh one, is she not? But I do not have to tell such stories to you, the simpering fools of the Dark Levy'

I shook my head at him. 'Indeed.'

'A whole class?' he grinned. 'One of you must have dropped a hot coal on her toe, eh?'

'I tried to ...'

'Free the lot?' he asked with pity. 'Well, well,' he grinned and roared suddenly, stretching forward, his huge, clawed fingers burrowing stone before us. He cursed and grinned, like a mad thing.

'He keeps trying,' Albine whispered, shaking in fear. 'Though as Lex said, mostly it just stares at us.'

'Hungry, girl. That I am. What I would not give for a feast of the jotuns,' Thak grimaced. 'Oh, I would love to chew on a fresh whale if I could.'

'I suppose I won't free you,' I told him. 'Seeing we have no whale to occupy you.'

'She is going to come back, girly,' Thak said with a muttering voice. 'There is something peculiar about you. Matters not.'

'You would slaughter and eat us if we freed you, you starving bastard,' Lex told him bravely but blanched as the thing grimaced at him.

'What makes you think I wish to be freed?' he rumbled.

'You wish to stay here?' I asked him.

'Do I wish to stay here?' he mouthed. 'Oh, let me see. What choice do I have? Yes, yes! I can come with you and run around the cells, playing hide and seek with the mistress of pain until she finds the lot, flays some, and breaks the others. Perhaps me! Yes!'

'You are entirely negative for a jotun,' Albine grumbled.

'What do you know of jotuns?' it asked back.

'We are learning they are morose cowards,' Lex added.

It pulled in a huge breath. Albine nearly fell forward with the power of the inhaling wind. 'I! Coward! You bastards. Fine. What shall we do with this thing?' He showed me the manacles, vast and forbidding. Ulrich and I both looked at his skeleton key and both shook heads. 'Indeed, you runts,' Thak said with a miserable huff.

'Look, we have a plan. It's a terrible idea, but if you help us, perhaps we can free you and take you with us ...' I told him and considered his size. He would never fit the Dark Prayer.

'You don't know the spells, do you?' Thak complained. 'Spells she uses to travel the Fanged Spire. You will have to leg it, and there are a hundred gorgons in this tower. All maa'dark. Casters.

Fury Whips of the Dark Clans.'

'I know the spell,' I told him. Cherry and Albine turned to look at me, and I took a long breath. 'I can hear and see what spells others cast and learn them.'

'Oh?' Thak said, suddenly intrigued. His eyes took on a calculating, excited look, and for a moment, his orbs were on fire, flaming and so were the ends of his hair. A fire giant? That's what he was, I decided. 'I know you have more people to rescue,' he said finally and grinned, looking like a smiling mountain. 'I doubt you will escape here. But what the Hel. I shall try to amuse myself a bit. Will be hard. After all, I'm still chained.'

'We shall get our friend. She can open any lock, and ...'

'No no,' Thak rumbled. 'You will die in that room. It holds an army of would-be rescuers.'

'Rescuers?' I wondered.

'Tried to rescue this poor girl once. Now mad as hell the lot,' he said. 'The mistress has a habit of slaying elves, you see. Most often she hunts for the Hand of ...'

'Life,' I added.

'Indeed,' the thing said softly, eyeing me from under its eyebrows. 'One she captured once and brought here to play with. So, the brother of the poor girl came after her with an army. What remains is there.'

'And Anja is there with them?' Ulrich said with desperation.

'What have they done to her?'

Thak looked at him distastefully. 'Nothing but terrorized her. Not a thing more. They could not, even if they wanted to. There is a host of mad elven sailors there, some women. The army is not important, no. But the captain is. Her brother.'

'An elf maa'dark,' I stated.

'Red Rooster,' he told me. 'His name is something fancier, of course, but he favors red and looks like a bloodied rooster. A deliciously tasty morsel he is, but still powerful. He could beat you raw. Free me first.'

'And if we free you?' I asked suspiciously. 'Though I don't see how without Anja.'

'I'll take on the Red Rooster, the scrumptious little pirate,' he confirmed, 'I'll eat them all. And shall not share. No.' He looked suspicious.

'What kind of a jotun are you, anyway?' Albine asked suspiciously.

He brightened. 'How many kinds do you know, my little snack? Fine! I come from Muspelheim, young lady. Land of thick fires and soot-black foes. Do we have a deal?' he asked with a feral grin.

'What can we do to free you, beast?' Ulrich asked.

'You cannot,' he said sullenly. 'But you can give me room to run around in.' He nodded at the doorway, and there was a lever by it. 'That will give me a lot of chain to drag around. They use me to clean the cells, the bastards.' That curse came out so murderously It shook us.

'I can burn the lock, perhaps,' Ulrich mumbled. 'But not sure it is a very good idea. It seems as chaotic as Euryale.'

'It's not, and I am,' Thak said happily, 'but do you have a choice? No. And you cannot burn this lock nor the chain.' He rattled his chain. 'It's been made to resist fire. Fire is what I'm made of, after all. Oh, it will hurt me, but I shall need you to release the chain, and if your lady is still alive, she will free me.'

'What do you think?' I asked everyone.

'I say we take our chances without the beast,' Lex told me sternly. 'That thing …'

'Is needed,' Baktak yelled hysterically from the top. 'Free him.'

'Fine,' I said and ran up the stairs.

'You asked us! Not the lecherous door!' Ulrich complained, but I gazed at the intense eyes of Thak and imagined him striding through molten pools of fire in his homeland. 'There is a lord amongst you, Thak. Surtur. Swear on his honor, you will obey us.' I had read of Surtur with Euryale. He was a giant who was a mighty lord of Muspelheim, his sword molten fire and one day, he would slay Odin. 'That you will follow me.'

'You know Surtur, perhaps?' he asked carefully. 'Few humans find Muspelheim hospitable.'

'I …'

He thumped his fist on the ground so hard our ears rang. 'Fine! I so swear,' the thunderous thing agreed, raising himself up to his knees. In the dark, his eyes and hair seemed alight with fire. 'I swear on Fire Pants himself I will do your bidding, and I shall feast very, very well.'

'So be it,' I said heavily and pulled the lever.

A rattle of chain. It ran free of some holes in the walls, and more and more of it heaped around the giant. This had a remarkable effect on it. It whooped and jumped, landing in the middle of our group, scattering the lot. Its hand flew for me, and it grasped me up, leaving only my head free inside its huge, dark fist. It brought me level with its eyes. 'I shall tell you, young one, a sad fact. There are a thousand lords of the fire jotuns, and Surtur is my lord's enemy.'

'A liar and a traitor,' I said in his tight hold. 'Like Euryale.' I felt Ulrich gathering strength for the flame whip, a pitiful weapon against the thing.

'Do not, boy,' Thak said, pointing a thick finger at Ulrich. 'Do not make such a mistake, for you cannot harm me. Fire is useless, did I not tell you so?' He shook his head at us, his mane of hair sweeping the floor as he roared. He tossed me down on my rump. 'But I shall humor you and myself, little ones. Red Rooster is the lord of the lunatics, and I shall deal with them. Why? Because I love battle, and I doubt I am going anywhere after her vileness kills the lot of you. I want peace, and the Rooster's wailing idiots keep me awake. Follow and fight for yours.'

He got up and ran for the door, swift for such a large creature. He dived for the doorway and went through it in a surprisingly agile way, leaving us blinking, and the rest of us could only stare at each other as we ran after it, avoiding the rattling chain, which managed to trip Cherry in any case.

'What the hell did you do?' Albino asked dubiously, 'It's like a gigantic, evil child.'

I spat. 'I tried to get us out of here.' I grinned as we followed Thak. 'Still am.'

'Well done,' Albine said.

We found Thak, and he was staring at a red door. He was yanking at the chain, gathering lots of it as he licked his lips. He seemed slightly smaller than he had in his room. Then, when he was happy with the amount he had gathered, he roared so hard our ears thrummed.

'Gods, be quiet, you fool!' I yelled.

'Gods are quiet,' Thak rumbled. 'I'll make up for their timidity. Let me have my fun.' Then he kicked at the door. It exploded into splinters with an enormous boom. Only the magical lock stayed in place before falling to the rubble.

'Mad thing, mad, mad,' Baktak the door complained. 'Make your prayers.'

'This was your idea, Baktak!' I screamed.

Thak entered the room, shrinking to fit the doorway. He could alter his size. We followed him and stared at a bizarre sight.

Anja was unshackled in the middle, sobbing, her face buried in her arm. She had freed her locks and chains, but she could not move.

Around her were many creatures. Elves, possibly, for some had the remains of thick hair.

They turned to stare up at us.

None had arms. None had teeth. Nor tongues. All were clothed in red rags, huddling around her, others speaking to her sweetly, some venting vile, slobbering threats and some just asking her name, repeatedly, their words barely comprehensible. They were all mad, their eyes full of terror, envy, and hate. Across the door of the circular cell stood a throne made of small bones. A figure was sprawled on it. Thak smiled wickedly as his size increased swiftly. 'That is the Red Rooster. A pirate and a maa'dark, elven lord and mighty caster of spells. A lord of the second house, Malikar! Maa'dark noble and a fool who tried to challenge Euryale to release his sister and rob her of the island. These are his followers. And my dinner. Here, Rooster!'

The figure on the throne stood up, chained to it. He wore red all across his thin body. His crimson boots and pants were worn and dirty, and he wore a curious, pink feather-crested hat. We could all see he was very, very fair, sort of ethereal and strangely angular, his eyes silvery white, hair dark and hugely thick und long, and his piercing voice made a kind of surprised, fateful oath. 'Intruders!' He was mad, crazy as his men.

'An elf?' Ulrich breathed and then things began to happen.

The elf cursed, and Thak jumped down in the midst of the hundred strong throng of maniacs like an angry hill, burying some. The elf lord grasped a spell of Fury with both hands and a sort of a fiery shield surrounded him, similar to what I had seen in Irad, leaving a circular, vague figure in sight, dancing and casting more spells. Thak took no note of him as he stepped on the maniacs, sweeping his claws across, tossing remains of the helpless, handless enemy around like broken toys. A sizzling hot wind tore across Thak's chest, ripping at his hair, but had no effect on his thick, fire-resistant skin. The giant grinned at the elf's mistake. He grabbed a handful of charging, handless maniacs, crushed them into pulp and picked up Anja and tossed her behind him. We ran down to retrieve her.

'Ulrich, drag her away!' I yelled.

'You'll need me!' he complained.

'We need you later,' I said and stepped forward, not sure what to do, how to help Thak, who was apparently having an enormously happy time.

'Where are you going?' Lex asked desperately. 'You have no

spells against such as them!'

But I did.

The elf was dancing on his throne, the fiery shield moving back and forth as he tried to break free of his shackle, muttering madly, his mind broken even if his spirit for a fight was not in any way cowed. He was gathering spells, this time of frigid wind and ice, and I saw what he was doing. Suddenly, ice spears grew up from the ground, splitting the room in two, impaling the mad elves by the dozen, their stubby arms flailing in the air as they rose up, spilling blood on the ice. Thak was still gleefully kicking the mad, skittering crewmembers of Red Rooster around and seemed oblivious to the caster. 'Thak!' I screamed, and the giant turned to look at the impending doom of the spell, blanching. He moved, but too late. A dozen such spears rose from under him, spilling madmen and stones, and one impaled his foot. He screamed and fell, cursing at the sharp weapon lifting him up by the wound, leaving him hanging upside down. I ran to him, slicing my sword across a hollering madman running heedlessly at me, leaving him dying and kicking. I did not give it more thought as I went forth.

'Shannon!' Lex screamed after me.

'Get back here, you stupid, red-haired idiot!' Ulrich agreed, having dragged Anja to the doorway.

Thak was squirming in pain, tearing at the ice holding him and managed to break the icicle, spilling him to some squirming madmen, flattening the lot. Thak was rolling and trying to get up, but he was in trouble. The elf was apparently laughing happily inside his sphere of protection. A dozen madmen, their handless arms flailing, turned to me. Lex was next to me, grasping at my shoulder, but I pushed him away. I remembered what Cosia had done to push and pull us around and I harnessed the Fury and felt I overdid it, for I felt weak as I pulled at tumbling ice and whirring wind. I pulled the April, the winds barely tossing my hair around. The elf was releasing another spell, one Bilac had used, and a dozen icy hands protruded from the ground and grasped at Thak, tearing at his sides, and some even held him doggedly down. The giant bellowed in incredulous anger. I grunted and mimicked the elven spell.

I wove a similar spell he had and then released the power. We saw misshapen icy hands grasp at the madmen, clawing at them, all of whom fell, shrieking in pain, blood flying as the hands kept gouging at the twitching foe. The elf turned to look at me in surprise, and the ice spears reappeared, grew, and changed direction for me. They were cracking, becoming thinner and sharper as the elf perfected his craft, and the dangerous spears looked near sentient as they raced for me. I released the spell of the icy hands, and in my mind saw the intricate spell he had used, and knew what to do.

I touched his spell and unraveled it.

I tore at it, interrupted it and left it in ruins, and a chill wind was all that remained and the elf flew on his back as his icicles stood sullen and silent, still for now. It was an enormous effort, but surprisingly successful. It left me exhausted, however, and on my knees. The elf moved to a seated position, his face hard to see through the guardian spell, but there was likely an acute look of disbelief on his features.

'No matter how exhausted, no matter how hurt,' I stuttered, and I mimicked his spell as I saw him climb to his feet. Many weak, crude spears grew around him, and I thought I would fail and die, for he started to gesture, touching fire this time, but one final spear thrust up from under the throne, pushing the rickety, mocking seat to fall on the elf's back. The shield apparently burned it to near cinders, but enough remained to topple him forward with a shriek, and he lost all his spells at that moment. He tumbled down the steps from his throne and the chain yanked him to an abrupt stop, and he lay there, pushing up painfully. His colorless eyes were probing at me from under his cascading, hugely thick dark hair. I was gasping with exertion and tried to gather more power to attack the now cursing, horribly angry but beautiful elf, and knew I would fail.

Thak did not.

He finally ripped out of the grasp of the now idle icy hands, leaped up, fell like a cat on his feet and charged, his fist wrapped around his chain, about to use the man-thick shackle as a whip.

The elf's eyes opened wide, he began to roll aside, struggled in some bony remains of his throne, and the chain smashed into his chest like a huge hammer. Blood flew thickly around and Thak giggled painfully. 'Bastard shit walker. Uppety damn thing. I'll taste its sweet blood, I will.'

'You are hurt,' I told him, looking up at him. His foot and sides were bloody and wounded.

'Not enough to upsill my foot.' he grumbled as he picked up a wounded madman and broke him in his fist. 'Now ...'

'Here,' I said, gathered some healing power and released it at him, smiling at the frigid, refreshing wind.

His eyes shot open as his hurts grew pinkish, then gray as scars replaced the ragged wounds. 'What in the name of a sooty goat's ball hairs ...'

'I'm special,' I confirmed. 'The Hand of Life. Anja?' I yelled at Ulrich.

'You are a damned human,' Thak wondered, running a thick, gory finger over his former wound.

'She is alive,' Ulrich confirmed, eyeing Thak. 'Sort of sane as well.'

The giant was playing with a head as he stared down at me. His eyes were curious rather than feral. 'What does she wish with you?'

I shook my blade free of blood. 'They were elves?' I asked him, not bothering to answer.

'They were Red Rooster's servants. Sailors. Oaths men. Lords and commoners following him to war. Elves only, for the humans died years ago of old age and malnutrition,' Thak said impatiently. 'What does she wish with you?'

I gazed at him for a moment and then shrugged. It did not matter. 'She wants to regain the Eye,' I told the huge thing before me, who flipped the head into his mouth, crunching it like a peanut, his eyes never leaving me. 'To trade for the Horn.'

'You are to regain what was lost?' he mused.

'Yes,' I said softly.

'And you will bring it to her? This bitch?' he asked, dragging his chain after him, pulling the dead elf up by its foot and pushing the corpse into his mouth with his finger. 'Silence, finally. Imagine living with this lot for hundreds of years. Of course, my hearing is much better than yours. Terrible cacophony. They fart too. Nasty business. So, how do you propose to get out of it?'

'What?'

'This puddle you have landed in, girly thing,' he grinned. 'How can you get out of the Dripping Dark? I call it that. Everything is dripping. I said I have good hearing.'

'I have to get my sister, and then we go up to her tower,' I spat. 'I told you I can. I just mimicked his spell.' I nodded at the bloody patch by the throne and saw something propped behind it.

'Terribly, but it did the job, yes,' he said. 'You healed me.'

'I am special, I told you,' I said with a pout. 'We have no choice,' I said. 'And we need my sister.'

'Where is that one?' Thak inquired while choosing a fat corpse on the ground.

'My gods,' Albine whispered and threw up as Thak ate the body.

'Weak belly, eh?' the giant asked. 'Where is she?'

'Dana is with … this dragon,' I told him. 'Chained to the door.'

'The Masked One?' he asked with a raised eyebrow. 'No. That is … bad. Or good. I know not.'

'I'll get her,' I said, 'or die doing.'

'Oh.' He gazed down at me. 'I tell you what. If you manage to convince him to let your sister go, and if you do, by some odd chance make a Dragon Pact with the critter, if he thinks your word is worth it, I shall come with you. Promise.'

'You already promised to follow me and my commands!' I told him.

'But you didn't tell me you are really special,' he said, his eyes strange.

'I am not sure if I can afford to feed you,' I said somberly. 'But it's a deal. Again! What is a Dragon Pact? He is powerless, I hear.'

'You will see, flower,' he giggled with a rumbling voice that shook the hall, shaking the corpses. 'Think hard on if you wish to give it. Dragons are as evil as she is. Or I am. And while his powers are with this skirted queen of turds, the Pact is not a power you cast. It's something all dragons possess, a part of the very soul of a dragon. You know. A ...'

'Skill,' I added. 'Yes.'

'And you will let me come along?' he said suspiciously. 'Not that you could stop me.'

'You don't seem too bad,' I told him with some doubt. 'Aside from your dinner manners. But I will.'

'Down the stairs then,' he grinned. 'Out the cell and to the right. If you fail, I'll just go back to my solitude a happier prisoner. Full belly as well unless Euryale makes me puke it out before it's all digested. Will the busty one open this chain?'

'My friends are blocked,' I told him as I turned to go. 'But she can open it for it is her skill. Anja, can you, please?'

'Free it?' she asked with horror, shaken to her core by what she had endured.

I nodded. 'Then, Thak if you would help the rest get their access to the Shades?'

'Shades? You mean so they can drink from the Cauldron?' Thak asked. 'All of them?'

'I care not what jotuns call it, we need their powers!' I shrieked. 'Don't be tedious!'

'So you want me to free them? I cannot overcome the Fetters,' he complained. 'That is Euryale's device. No, not even hers, in fact. But certainly not mine!'

'There is a gorgon kin laying out there in the foyer, perhaps ...'

'She is still here, mistress,' Baktak confirmed with an echoing voice.

'If you convince her to let us all see the Shades and weave spells of Fury, I would be happy and grateful,' I told him patiently.

'You should be grateful already, you mad little thing,' he grumbled, 'but since the gorgon is one of hers, I'm happy to comply. But know and understand you off quickly enough, She grants her servants these powers to control you with the Bone Rings, but she is the mistress who owns the curse.' I nodded.

'You are not going to go in there alone?' Lex asked.

'For once I agree with my cousin on something,' Ulrich echoed him, and the two stared at each other in confusion.

'When did you begin to care for her?' Lex asked suspiciously.

'Since I killed her,' Ulrich told Lex.

'What?' Lex asked, his fists balled. 'No, she is not going alone.'

'I cannot agree more,' Albine said, her small child's face screwed in a disapproving grimace. 'Take one to help you. We will need Dana. She is powerful. A powerful liar, but powerful still. Get her and then let us go and surprise the bitch up above.' Lex was nodding at that, and I waved them off. Cherry stood aside, her face listless, and yet she gave me a small smile.

Thak smiled at Albine, who looked at the giant suspiciously. 'I like the little one. I'll not eat her,' Thak whispered to Anja as she approached him, hugging herself.

'I'm going. It's my sister. And as for you lot, stay here. It's a dragon,' I said. 'I would not tempt it with anything more than one skinny girl.'

'It's a dragon,' Ulrich spat. 'You don't even know what a dragon is. Nobody knows. You only know some throat-wrenching names and that's it, really. We go and get eaten together.'

'You killed her?' Lex asked in a daze.

'He feels sorry about it,' I told him and took a tentative step towards him. 'I'm sorry.'

He looked bothered and grasped my shoulders. 'You cannot carry her if she is hurt. One has to come, at least. And no matter if Ulrich seems friendly now ...'

'He is. We have to trust each other now. Fine. Someone has to follow me. Then let it be someone other than you?' I told him softly. 'I care for you.'

'She says the truth,' Albine nodded seriously as she made her way out of the blood-spattered room, looking sick.

'Do you love me?' Lex asked. 'I love you.'

'He speaks the truth,' Albine said. 'The fool.'

'I ...' I began but swallowed. Did I?

I played my finger across his chest. 'Ulrich said something,' I told him. 'We should not utter such words here, for someone will use that against us.'

'She speaks the truth again,' Albine confirmed though the look in her eyes told me she knew I had hesitated on purpose. I thanked her with a small nod. I did not know what I felt for Lex. Affection? More?

'I agree,' Lex said with a small smile. 'But I can help you.'

'Not this time, Lex,' I told him. 'Please. I have to go down there.' He was left there as I turned to Ulrich. 'Will you come and help me? If I have to carry her?'

'Into the maw of a dragon?' he spat and shuddered. 'For Anja, I will. For now, I will help you with her.' He walked back and forth, holding his head, convincing himself. 'Your sister better be worth her weight in gold for this,' Ulrich growled from the doorway. 'And I have a bone to pick with her yet.'

'He gets to go?' Lex mouthed, and I put a finger over his mouth.

'I don't know what's down there, Ulrich, and I'm afraid of going alone,' I told him as I followed him. 'Thank you.'

'I don't get it,' Lex complained.

'She wants to get me killed and you'll be in one piece, cousin,' Ulrich spat and walked up the steps and turned to the stairway. Somewhere up the tower, something exploded again, shaking the walls.

I hesitated and turned to Anja. She was touching the lock of the shackles as Thak stared down at her, perhaps wondering what she would taste like. She concentrated; her face had a harrowed look and then, the chains opened up. I grinned up at Thak. 'There, you big lummox. Probably a mistake, but happy to see you free. As free as you can be.'

'I …' the giant began and then went quiet, staring at me. It did not look hungry, but stunned.

I turned to Anja. 'Thank you. I am …'

'Sorry?' she asked me with bone-chilling anger. 'I lost Dmitri and Alexei. Just like I was afraid I would. Nearly died myself. The creatures wanted to make me lose my mind like they had. I'm not happy; Shannon, and I don't want to be reasonable. Had you agreed with me that night before the battle, gods know if we would have been free already.'

'I could not decide then. And I didn't know Ulrich had his powers,' I told her.

'I think I hate you,' she said plainly. 'Let's get out of here.'

And so she became my enemy.

I turned to go, but Thak stopped me. He pointed at the throne. 'If you are the Hand of Life, you should look at that. She wore that armor last.'

'What armor?' I asked him, confused.

Thak shuddered and crumbled. 'You understand the Vanir and the Aesir are our foes. No jotun loves the gods and their wicked wives. They claimed our worlds and our lords are First Born, some as old as they are.'

'Yes, of course,' I told him as he squatted before me.

'Fine, so this is no favor to them, just so you know, but it could be for that armor is of the gods. I should go and piss on it, but I think I'll endure seeing it on you.'

'I have no ...'

'Time. But this is worth it. Frigg gave elves this gift of healing. Well, apparently not the elves, since you are there, healing away, but that is moot. That whose there is the Rooster's sister. Miralian Safiroon was the Hand of Life for Almheir Bardagoon two hundred years past and a hated enemy of the Devourer. She challenged Euryale to a battle though the Bardagoons did not approve. She was a Safiroon and a proud warrioress and heeded no one.'

'She is there?' I asked him, softly. Something was hunched behind the throne mound.

'Yes, she is,' the jotun said, his eyes glimmering with fires. 'She thought to end the Devourer and so she met her, nonetheless, eluding the Regent and dismissing his wishes, dressed in the Silver Maw, the magical armor of Frigg. Dwarven-crafted, doused in the deep spells of Svartalfheim it was and the armor given to the First Hand of Life by the goddess. But despite the high grade armor she lost, of course, for Euryale trapped her by treachery. She lost the armor too, a hereditary regalia of the Hand of Life. Miralian was a fool girl and thought to fight her with Frigg's sword, Nerug, like some bloody human knight, with honor and rules and graceful mercy at the end. Euryale took the girl and her armor, but the sword she could not touch, our slithering mistress. Here she tortured Miralian with hunger and then, the sufferings of her Safiroon brother. He went mad when he found her here, suffering before his eyes, and Euryale let her starve slowly. She died miserably over the years as his brother looked on.'

'You seem much less brutish when you speak like this, instead of eating the corpses,' I told him, wondering at Miralian and her brother.

'I'm a crude creature of the Muspelheim, girl ...'

'Shannon,' I told him with a smile.

He faltered, and smiled back. 'Shannon. But even I respect bravery. And beauty.' He got up and left me there wondering.

'What does the armor do?' I asked his back, gazing at the shadows.

He walked away. 'It enhances your powers. It makes them more powerful and your force lasting. In addition, it is, of course, armor. Dwarven-given gift,' he rumbled. 'Hurry.'

'I don't know how to wear one!'

'It's crafted for you,' he whispered as he went up the steps, changing his size while booting the thick chain in spite. He also pushed Ulrich back as the boy had come to ask where the hell I was tarrying. 'Where is the snake woman?' I heard him rumble. I felt sorry for Bilac.

I walked into the shadows and found a dust-covered corpse with glimmering, blonde hair billowing from a holmet. I kneeled and wiped my hand across the armor, and it shone dimly. I took a deep breath and wiped some more off the face. I breathed in, terrified. I found a slit of an eyehole, framed in gold. It was a fine helmet, silvery with intricate symbols of dragons and griffins, and it was gleaming in the light of the room.

I had been wearing the armor in my dream, I was sure of it.

Moreover, something magical happened.

The dust burned off. The magnificent greaves popped off, laying on the ground, leaving skeletal, small feet bared. Faulds of scaled silvery metal fell to the floor and the plate and chainmail slid aside, splaying on the side, exposing a small female skeleton of brown bones and dust. Then, the helmet rose up.

For the skeleton sat up.

I fell back as the slitted eyehole stared at me. I was groping for a spell, but the skeleton lay a warm bone hand on mine, the forearms magnificently armored. She took her hand off and lifted the helmet until I could see her yellowed teeth, then the empty sockets, and I felt sorrow for the creature, strangely like a sister to me. I hugged my knees as I stared at the thing now wondering at the helmet, and then it turned to stare at me.

It handed the helmet to me, silvery fur lining on the crest ruffling in some breeze going through the room. I took the helmet and hesitated until I thought the dead elf woman nodded slightly, the bones creaking, and I lifted the mask and pulled it on.

The rest of the armor fell off her. Then it skittered towards me, and I backpedaled furiously. The armor practically flew in the air, straddling my feet first, then covering my thighs with plates and my hips with the faulds. I felt gauntlets, supple and durable cover my hands, and then I was embraced by scaled armor skirt and finally, the cuirass encased me. I felt the rush of ice so keenly my ears thrummed. I tried to lift the helmet and found I could, but then I let it back down, breathing, feeling one with the Shades or Glory, as the elves called it. I stared at the silvery golden magnificence around my torso and limbs. 'Silver Maw, sister. I shall carry it with honor,' I told the skeleton, but it was not moving. I kneeled next to her and lay a hand on the skeletal hand. Sister, like Dana. 'Farewell,' I told it. It was dead.

The tower rocked again, dust was billowing.

'Thank you, Able,' I said, and I walked out. Thak nodded at me as he was reviving Bilac and the others stared at me in disbelief.

'Where is she?' Ulrich bellowed as he stepped forward.

'It is her, you dumb mule,' Thak told him as he was waking up the unhappy Bilac with brutal slaps, and I smiled inside the mask. 'She truly is the Hand of Life,' Thak added.

THE DARK LEVY

CHAPTER 20

We walked down steps that had not been used in ages. Apparently, Euryale did not allow her cohort down there, or there was some other way to reach the downstairs, a safer way. Thick layers of dust and fearful cobwebs covered the tall, dark walls and moldy stone statues of once beautiful make. Fearful, for I did not wish to see the spiders that could weave something like that. I felt somehow exposed in my bright armor but waved the thought away. The steps spiraled down and down, and I hoped not to break my foolish neck on the slippery way and thought the armor would probably save my neck anyway. At least I would make a dazzling corpse. Ulrich was following me, mumbling. I hiked down as carefully as I could, running my hand along the wall to my right, wiping it on my armor when the mold got too thick over my fingers, until I reached a room with a burning light on the ceiling. At the end of it were two old doors, heavy and thick with old timbers and they had rungs of chiseled iron.

'Is that ...' Ulrich held me back. A featureless shadow was hanging from the door's lock. I gasped. Dana was crumpled in front of the door, her wrists chained to a rung.

'Dana,' I breathed and rushed forward. 'Dana!'

'Shh!' Ulrich hissed as he struggled to follow me. 'Is she alive?' I reached her and pulled her up, trying for her pulse and cursed, for I wore a gauntlet, and I could not. Yet, I noticed mist forming on the gauntlet's silvery surface.

'She seems alive, yes,' I told him finally as I raised her head. She was pallid, her face screwed in a smirk of pain as she mumbled something incoherent. 'Though what happened to her, I know not.'

Then, something found us.

Our hearts were suddenly beating harder, much harder. Some strange form of panic seized us. I fell on my knees, whimpering, and Ulrich raised a hand as if to ward off a blow. 'What the hell is that?' he blurted, trying to breathe.

'The dragon,' I uttered with fearful reverence amidst the horror. 'It is seeking us. It knows we are here. It did this to Dana. Hurry. Get her free.'

'Good, for I'm beyond tired of fearing for my life,' Ulrich said with trepidation. 'Let me see the chains.'

'Magical as usual,' I spat as I fingered a small, round lock with a bluish surface. 'The key?'

'Sure,' he said drily. 'But I don't like this. None of it.' He took out his skeleton key and inserted it into the lock. It changed color from blue to white, and then angry red, and again, the meltingly magical metal skittered apart, breaking into a shower of half-sentient pieces. 'Quickly, before it comes back together.' I pulled at the chains and dragged Dana free.

The dragon spoke.

A voice slithered around us, dangerous and curious while somehow careless as the wind. 'The young folk at large? Touching the Cauldron? You found your kin, no? Come in, sweet ones, and I'll make her hale again. Be quick! For your hostess is becoming organized and is gathering her minions. She is not daft, no.'

We stared at each other. 'No,' Ulrich mouthed. 'I know you said we should, but …'

'It might be our only chance,' I argued. 'I have to revive Dana. And find out if it can break the Fetters.'

'It can break us with its voice, Shannon,' Ulrich answered. 'It is as unpredictable as …'

'An army of gorgons?'

'Lex is good with the ladies, ask him to charm the lot?' he retorted. 'This is madness.'

'Children,' the voice uttered, and our hearts nearly burst with fear, leaving us breathless. 'Come in here or she shall never wake.'

'Let us, then,' I agreed with a pained voice.

'You know how?' Ulrich pushed the gate. It would not budge.

'Nox?' I said.

The tomte arrived, grinning hugely. It shuffled from the shadows, and it bowed at us gracefully, its ruddy, wrinkled face full of mirth.

'The master of frights must I feed, its gentler side, I have never seen,' he chortled.

'It is your former master. Perhaps still is?' I asked him.

'I serve both, that is my oath,' he told me with a sad smile. 'But my master I have not forgotten, for my service is rotten.'

'I shall see, Nox. Will you suffer for this?' I asked him.

'I shall suffer, perhaps get killed by that elf stuffer,' he said with rumbling spite. 'I care not for her anger, and if I catch it hot,' he added as he walked to the door. He smirked and then pushed at it. It was open and swung into the darkness silently, an enormous thing like a cathedral. A cold, musty wind blew across from us, and the door swung back in.

'Take Dana, Ulrich,' I said.

'I shall hold the door, but do hurry and we shall avoid the whore,' Nox chortled, eyeing the dark. 'Also, avoid making a mess and do not push him to excess ...'

I leaned over him. 'You told me I would call you one day. How did you guess I would one day be here?'

'Nox is not stupid, and his thoughts are fluid,' he grinned. 'Go on.' He jerked his head to the darkness.

I took a deep breath and stepped in. Ulrich followed me tentatively.

It was not as dark as we had thought, for there was a strange luminance around the columned space, and we realized there were torches burning far, far away. The vast hall was set with dim fires, and shadows sputtered across the room as we entered. Some of the shadows looked alive.

'Charming,' said the pale Ulrich. 'Let us go, then?'

'Perhaps you should stay here with Dana,' I told him hesitantly. 'Thank you for coming down here with me.'

'Nah,' he said and walked in before me. 'The dinner is served, and there has to be an appetizer, a main course, and a dessert. I doubt it will be happy without the full deal. Seems like a pushy bastard. And I don't wish to go up if her vileness has returned to inquire about the fools sitting around the foyer, wondering why they are not in their cells feeling miserable.' I grinned at him nervously, and he struggled a bit as he hefted Dana over his shoulder. He walked on and then I followed him, cursing as my steel-shot boots made hollow, echoing sounds on the dusty floor.

Dana was breathing harshly and was incoherent, rubbing her head occasionally, uncertainly as if having suffered a severe concussion. She would not wake unless the dragon willed it. I tried to keep calm, but could not, and rushed forward past Ulrich, my mail clinking and my boots clopping on the floor. I skidded to a stop in the middle of a sea of massive pillars, feeling hopeless. Ulrich stopped and lay Dana down and took a step back. She was pale, shivering and coughing, her robe sodden, 'Dragon Masked One!'

Silence.

I screamed in frustration, the scream echoing around the dark pillars. 'It's playing with us. Can you make fires around us?' I asked Ulrich, who took a tentative step forward, weaving a spell of Fury for the firewall spell, but then he hesitated and stopped. He took a step back. 'Ulrich?'

He shook his head and pointed beyond me.

I turned.

A short man with powerful shoulders was standing at the edge of the light. He was dressed in a simple, unadorned tunic and pants of dark velvet. His boots were high and black, with silvery edges glimmering softly. He seemed to shift as he stood there, seemingly ethereal, then solid again. Most disconcerting was the dark mask of hanging velvet, the eyeholes empty.

He looked like a man. Nothing like I had anticipated.

Yet, there was something else there.

Evil emanated from him. It was strangely evident. Evil, or perhaps a casual attitude for cruelty, as flippant as a tornado leveling a town. While Euryale occasionally felt almost human, with a past that might not be all evil, this one had no such past. The air felt stuffy, thick, and when you tried to look at the man, you could do so only for a short time. Ulrich shook his head and croaked something, and I dragged Dana back, keeping an eye on the odd creature.

It laughed softly. Where the gorgons had a weird, sing-song voice, the dragon had a hollow, faraway one. 'You need not worry, little sister. She will be fine,' the man thing said, his voice much like an echo. 'She is upset and stunned, for I forced myself deep inside her mind, Shannon. I still hold her. She put up a brief fight, the fool, and so she is more hurt than she should be. It was delicious, girl, your sister's fight. But in I went, like a devious peddler sneaking his way past a guard in a noble's house, and in the end her spirit was kneeling before me, open and helpless.' I saw Dana was shaking her head half-consciously at his words, and I was also sure he was staring at her, shaking his head back subtly. They were struggling still.

'You shall do no such thing to me,' I grimaced and squared my shoulders.

'Yes, I shall,' he said casually. 'She is released, and you are next, for I have to know what you are, don't I?' Dana jerked, her face blushed, astonished, her eyes opened wide. A dark shadow whisked away from her, traveling the floor and columns into me. Then I felt him knocking on the door to my mind, his empty eyeholes probing me.

I was standing there in the dungeon.

Then I was walking along a dry road, wind buffeting me.

It was so cold, freezing and I was lost, not knowing which way to go. Suddenly Lex was walking next to me, his lips blue from rime. I grasped his arm instinctively, and he smiled at me inanely, thankfully, full of love. He put his arm around me, giving me support and love, and I leaned on him, seeking shelter from the dread and the cold, the hunger, and the hopelessness, and he pulled me to him. He leaned over and kissed me, his lips like fire, and then I shuddered, for his face was not Lex's any longer but the masked face of the square-shouldered man, and I tried to pull my eyes away, but it was impossible to refuse him his kiss until he let me. He quit the kiss and spoke to me like he would to a child. 'Don't fight it, girl. It is a gift to be visited by a dragon. Stand still, and let me see into that silly mind of yours or fight like she did. It nearly broke her.' The wind around me rose to a whirling firestorm, and the dragon held me in a fight for my mind. He held me in his paws, his grip incredibly strong, and I whimpered as he lifted me, my head pained like a giant was standing on it. I realized I had half let him enter already by trusting the lie of Lex, letting my guard down, and I breathed and wept and fought and then his face shifted to that of Grandma's, her face pained and lost.

I broke for just a moment, giving a shuddering breath at the sight of her, and I felt his mind slither into mine.

The eyeless man disappeared, and I fell to the ground, clawing at my temples. I knew this was what possessions felt like. I felt him staring at my memories, my wishes, and my deepest fears, rolling his hands across things most precious to me. I grasped at the air, screamed, trying to push him out and for a moment, I saw the pillared hall, the dark masked man standing there.

'No!' I cried and wove a spell of Fury, growing the ice spears around the man, but it was no man, and the spell broke as it touched him. I felt his presence inside my head tighten its grip, and I fell on my knees, clawing once again at my temples, the helmet hampering the effort. I fell forward over Dana, trying to breathe, holding my helmeted head. His voice whispered into my mind. 'That dark-hearted traitor. She has mighty plans for you, does she not? Moreover, you are to dance with the twisted ghoul to recover the Eye? Hand of Life? Yes, yes, the armor would not have accepted you otherwise, no. Yet, a human Hand of Life?' he said with a note of amusement thrumming in his voice. 'Yes, I do see you are special. Nox is right. Very special. Unique indeed for Frigg only bestowed one such blessing on Aldheimers. Not the elves, apparently, but the maa'dark, those who can stir the Cauldron. And you are this esteemed thing. Until you die, of course.' He laughed softly. 'She is smart. She truly is. And my freedom is a dream of dust if she succeeds. Hopeless, as impossible as finding a cold drink in the Batha desert.' His voice was dripping with anger and desperation, and I felt my head cracking. 'Nox was right indeed.'

I pleaded. 'You won. Please.'

'Killing you, girl, would thwart her plans. They would crumble for the time. Then, perhaps not. Perhaps they would only be postponed,' he was saying to himself. His mind sought every last corner of my mind, and I heard him wonder. 'Such a boring, scared life you have led. Sad, sad. However, perhaps you can help me, no matter your past. You are here for your sister, no?' he said mirthfully and likely grinned under the mask. 'She is a strong one, she is indeed. But is she what you think she is?'

'She has her faults, oh ...' I began and then went silent, cursing the man. 'Thing. Dragon.'

'Oh mighty one, that is an appropriate way to address me, my friend,' he said with a robust laugh, dry and humorless as old bones, hollow as if coming from a pit. 'But I saw in your lovely head something interesting. You meant to visit me in any case, no? This is how you lot got into a trouble that likely will get most of your followers killed? Stop quaking, boy.'

He had released me and spoken to Ulrich.

I thrust myself up, swaying onto my feet. I saw Ulrich cowering in the shadows, his face listless. Dana was clawing at her temples, trying to recover. I spat at the thing's feet only to discover the helmet stopped me from doing the gesture justice. I reddened in shame, but the helmet covered that as well. 'Dragon horror? Terror?' I said with as much strength I could. 'You instill fear in your foes, and they fall helpless victims. I'll not let you do that again.'

He nodded slowly and snorted. 'I did already and can again. You have too many holes in your mind's fragile armor and are unused to such games. You have no choice but to fear, girl, when you endure my mind inside yours. Terror is in our nature. Like you see the dead and the Fury's and Gift's many wondrous weaves and applications, my kin are your bane, and well do you know it. Few things creeping forth from the mists of the Nine will leave you unimpressed and a dragon is the most impressive of these things. Yet, I see you are bound to fight many such creatures in the future.'

'I wish for no fights,' I said forcefully. 'I would like to be free of this!' I thrust forth my shackled hand, then cursed as the armor covered it. 'The Bone Fetter. It is what binds us to the bitch.'

He stared at my hand with little interest. 'Hel's toy that. Once made to hold in check the unruly dead, it is not something one removes easily. Euryale has ever used it to control her slaves. She stole them and the rings when she took the Eye.'

'Is there a spell?' I asked him. 'It was made in Helheim, I know. It is controlled by the First Born Euryale. And you are one, no? Mightier than she is?'

'You are grasping at very rotten straws, girl. It is an artifact,' he agreed, staring at it. 'A powerful one. And dear girl, you have to die to be rid of it. You saw the bracelet, when you came here, did you not? Before it changed thus? You chose then. For your sister, I know. For something more, perhaps for yourself as well. There is a speck of selfishness in you. I saw parts of it, just now.'

'For Dana,' I insisted.

'For freedom,' he laughed mockingly.

'I took it, accepted it,' I agreed, deciding to abandon my attempts of trying to reason with the madly terrifying thing. I remembered the bracelet I had taken willingly. I felt tears and tried to wipe them off my face, fighting desperation. The helmet once again hampered me.

The thing seemed to get some perverted amusement from that, for it chuckled. 'There are deeds that are impossible to undo, girl. Everyone knows this, even the gods. Yet, you humans are so half-baked, strangely brutal and soft at the same time, logical in one matter and then so foolish in another, as in love. It is no wonder your kin are slaves, unable to join forces for the simplest of purposes, enjoying slavery over freedom. No wonder it is, considering you were meant to provide, not to rule. Immature things, men. Here you weep for something you chose.'

'I'm a woman,' I spat.

'Even worse,' he said sourly. 'Half-baked and raw, just like men. Only more emotional and subservient and prone to unkindness and quarrels.'

'Half-baked?' I cursed. 'I am fighting the bitch, refusing ill choices she thrust on me. If that is immature and subservient, dragon-thing, then I'd rather be a senseless child than an ancient, cowardly prisoner, happy to linger here in a lightless, dung-filled dungeon, sharing air with rats, an amusement for a gorgon. You are a helpless, toothless coward.'

And at that, he showed his immature side.

He shifted, moving so fast one could barely take note, from shadow to shadow, growling, and I whimpered in fear at an oppressive hand that seemed to be pressing on my chest. 'Impudent, foolish toad! You think to mock me? The gorgon found me hurt, tricked me, lied to me, gave herself to me, and never shall I forgive her trickery. She has shackles on me as much as she has them on you, and that is disconsolate, for such as me to be compared to the rats.'

'You done raging, wyrm?' I asked. 'Wyrm. I always thought you would look different. Scaly, elongated lizard or a flying worm, but no, you look like a man with severe skin issues.'

He stopped and hissed, crouching in the darkness and then laughed. 'I'm the Masked One. Not an ugly specimen compared to any race, girl and bound to this form for now. As for Euryale, we were no friends. When mad Cerunnos Timmerion drove off the invading armies, she made a pact with me. One to save my life, perhaps, and I did drink her blood from her cursed cup to keep mine. Life is precious, even to a dragon. She made it so I had to agree to her terms. She made me a cursed thing as I swore a Dragon Pact. One favorable to her. I got a life, she got everything.'

'What's the difference between a Pact and a spell?' I asked.

'Ah, curious you are. A spell is woven by dipping into the Cauldron, one that comes out as Fury or the Gift, but the Pact is a treaty with the Cauldron, one only a dragon can make. We give our word and the Cauldron, Shades, Glory, whatever you want to call it, gives the dragon power to seal the deal. Break it and the Cauldron punishes you. There is more to this power of ours than maa'dark see. There is sense, evil, and good in the Cauldron. Perhaps there are beings in it. We call one such Tiamox. Our god she is.'

'I see,' I told him, not actually seeing at all.

He waved a hand in dismissal. 'It is our mystery, our skill. Make no pacts with a dragon unless you are in mortal danger. But I had to make one, and it doomed me. She made it so, human; that I cannot ever leave this cell so long as she is alive. It is not possible to do so, for the Cauldron would slay me if I tried. It would deprive her of my powers, but no dragon dies willingly. I am chained and helpless and cannot dip into the Cauldron for spells to amuse me, not even that, no. She took my powers, the Cauldron granted them to her, and she took my voice. Here I wither while she is made powerful by my strength and that, Shannon, makes her the most powerful creature in Aldheim. Maa'dark she is, one of the First Born, but with my strength, she is more than any mortal, just shy of a god. I'm starving, not unlike your fire giant out there, but starving of life, of pillage and gold. I am counting rubble on tiles, cracks in the pillars, and mold growing on stones until I know each imperfection by name. In addition, I do resent the rats, Shannon, oh Hand of Life. I hate her. She plans for many things. She hates the elves. Many do, but she does especially.'

'What does she plan for?' I asked him.

'No,' he said. 'I'll not help you with that. I have a hunch, but it might be it will benefit me not to tell you.'

'Fine,' I hissed. 'But we wish to leave.'

'Yes, I see. Wise, as no saa'dark ever leave this place.'

'What?' Ulrich dared ask. 'She is selling us to the elves.'

'Shut up, fool. You are saa'dark. That means …'

'She sells people to the elves,' I supported Ulrich. 'Saa'dark are like maa'dark, unfree, but useful. Maa'dark means the Gifted Hands. Saa'dark …'

'No!' he laughed. 'You fool! I am her power. She has me by the Pact. My abilities make her high. It gives her time to spin her plans, to achieve her goals. The powers keep her safe. In addition, they are vast, hugely vast powers. I am not modest, but it is the truth. Yet, even a dragon can starve.'

'What do you mean?' I asked, confused by the apparent change in subject. Then it came to me. 'She needs us to …'

He laughed. 'Yes. She needs you, girl and finally has you. But while looking for you, she has been harvesting food for me. She gives me flesh sacrifice. That is what saa'dark means. Dead Hands.'

'But what flesh?' Ulrich asked and blanched. 'Not us?'

'Yes, you. Dimwit. Dragons,' he said with some enjoyment, 'must feed every two years. I happily eat Nox's fare weekly, but to keep up my magical powers, I have to devour things that are more than flesh. I have to feast on the flesh of a magical being. Many, in fact.'

'What?' Ulrich breathed 'Un?'

He threw his hands in the air. 'Why, every two years she gives me the surviving, trained and powerful saa'dark. Anything from five to six of the most powerful survivors. I eat them. I remain strong, my powers renewed. So does she, by default, as she owns them. However, it seems she has been searching for a way to grow even more powerful. And she found you.'

'She has plans,' I confirmed. 'And we are not here looking for a place to take a piss at, are we? We want a solution to our plight. Will you, can you help? In any way?'

'Help?' he said slowly. 'I will be free when she is dead. Can you do this?'

'No,' I gritted my teeth. 'You know this damned well. She is too powerful. A First Born. Perhaps something that cannot be killed.'

He smiled. 'She can be slain by magic or blade, but not fully and truly. Her body will vanish, and she will reappear in time. No, she has to die a very final, very nasty death,' he told me. 'You will need a weapon of the gods for that, my little one,' he said unhappily. 'But now, it seems I need to give you some trust, no? So you would save your friends and one day, perhaps, me? Perhaps you shall stumble on such a weapon one day and then, with luck, slay her?'

'I would go and save my friends, all of them, yes,' I told him incredulously. 'And perhaps you.' I felt a heavy weight of responsibility weighing on my chest, sure the dragon was going to make it very hard for me to renege on any promise I gave. 'Finding you was very hard. We have very little hope. You are our sole hope.'

He shook his head. 'And you are mine. It's no coincidence that you, young mistress, are here. You are here because the dead boy led you to a book.'

'How do you know this?' I whispered.

'That book is called Markawion. It is a Gift created wonder, crafted by the dwarves of yonder age, and master smith Brokkr hammered the pages with a chisel of gold and the skin of a traitor. It is...'

'Your book?' I breathed. 'You ...'

He waved a hand. 'She took my servant and my treasures as well as my powers. Moreover, I see the dead as you do. I see them and hear them ...'

'Able was here?'

He denied me with a shake of his head. 'No. I sense the dead and knew he was about. There are others, hiding in the tower. The boy was confused and scared and would not let you out of his sight that first year. He yearned to go as most do, but the dead dream as well, and I visit those dreams. I gave him hints of your coming deaths and nudged him to stay with you until the day you asked him to help. He did not heed Hel's call for he was sure you would die soon. The dead are loath to travel alone, you see. Finally, in the end, he dared to explore the tower at your request. The book was not truly hidden, no. Nox knew where it was, and I think you found out as well, clever girl, by fooling the bitch. But I had a problem.'

'Problem?'

He nodded. 'Yes. My servant is oath-bound neither to speak of her secrets nor to show them. That was part of the Pact. Nor could the ghost touch the book. However, I sensed he loves you, in a childish, endearing way. Like he would a mother. Therefore, you were the key. And Euryale is a beast. She has base yearnings and feeding is one of them. I sensed the time was right, for she was starving, and you were there, so close to her. I pushed her.'

'She bit me again for you? You don't have powers, do you?' I asked him, my fist clenched.

'I can push, touch, strong emotions, girl, enhance them. The closer the person, the easier it is and so as she was far, it took me a supreme effort to nudge Euryale to bite you. A small suggestion sneaked into her thoughts when she was unwary. It worked. Then, the ghost got mad. I knew he would and made him even madder. I suggested Albine would suffer like you did. In the end, luck served us as he nudged the book into sight. Most ghosts can do this if properly motivated.'

'What if the book had not fallen?'

He laughed. 'Perhaps Nox had cleaned it so the books were unstable, but he did not break the Pact for the book was hidden before your ghost helped you. Cauldron forgave Nox his help there. My brave servant.' The tower rumbled again, dust fell from the roof. The dragon-thing looked up. 'As for the commotion? I think your Able caused something terrible up there. Good, very good.' The Masked One then shook his head, with a twitch of his hands. 'But if my treasures are gone? My book? I shall visit him in Hel one day and flay his undead hide.'

'What if I had never seen the book?' I asked. 'And we had tried some other method of escape? I only spied it that first time by chance.'

'Ah,' he said sadly. 'In that case, I would have had Nox tell you of me and all this charade would have been needless.'

'But the Pact,' I breathed.

'He would have died for me. Sad, of course, but there it is. The Cauldron would have punished him, hopefully after he managed to betray the Pact. I'm what you call evil,' he said steadily. 'I'm happy you saw the book, though. It is a thing to attract attention. It calls to you, in a way. She had likely been scourging it for information on silvery fetters before she called in on you.'

'I'll not forgive you the bite,' I told him sullenly. 'But you wanted us here and have been playing long enough. We have no time for such games. Give us any solution to this problem and...'

He ignored my arrogant posture with a dismissive gesture. 'It is a near unheard of thing for a dragon to hope to gain redemption from a mere human, but there it is. And I can indeed help you though perhaps not the way you would wish to be helped.'

'I would like to be rid of these bonds. She will never release us, never, even should I do her bidding,' I spat.

'Probably not,' he allowed.

'Hel can release them?' I asked. 'These fetters? Or the elders? Such as ...'

'A dragon,' he agreed. 'I said no, already. And Hel is not here, sadly.'

'Can you harness the Shades?' I asked with a shout. 'Dip the Cauldron? At all?'

'No,' he told me irascibly. 'She has my power. That was the Pact. Ah my, you are a fiery one,' he giggled. 'I am her slave. Her unwilling vessel. However, I can do something. I too hope the ... Eye returned and her slain, so I am no longer bound and gagged by my mistress. I will make a deal with you, and I also wish you to return the eye. I do think you should. The Eye to Hel. We shall have to make a deal. A dragon can make them, no matter their depravity and degradation.'

'A deal, a dragon ...'

'Pact,' he allowed.

'You want to curse me like you are cursed?'

'A curse and a Pact, the latter sounds more reasonable, girl, for it gives both something. And before you start to tear your hair out, or mine, remember where you are now. In deep shit!'

'What will you ask for?' I asked with a small, quivering voice. 'Is not setting you free enough?'

He laughed hugely. 'It seems we are in a situation where a dragon tells another: "I'm sitting at the summit." I can demand anything, for I have nothing to lose. In addition, it is in our nature to be greedy. Wouldn't have it any other way. I do not know yet what I will want for. Perhaps I lack imagination? I will know when I will know. Nevertheless, these two promises I ask for. Kill her and then, when I wish it, grant me my wish. Refuse and perish here.'

'This all depends on what you can help us with,' I shouted. 'Can you remove the Fetters?'

'I cannot remove the Fetters,' he sighed. 'I grow tired of repeating it.'

'Is this your idea of a joke?' Ulrich spat, and the Masked One's head turned his way. I heard Ulrich whimpering and cursing as he fell on his knees.

'Let him be,' I told the masked beast.

He waved a hand, dismissing my demands. 'I gave him a headache and some modesty, that is all. He dreamt of waking up as a girl, and it did not sit well with him. The Fetters. I can wrest them off Euryale by the power of the Pact. Ah, she will be unhappy!'

'You can ... take them?'

'They were forged on the Anvil of Brumal. They are magical and part of the Cauldron. If we make a Pact, they will obey me for the Pact can command things made of Cauldron.'

'But you cannot make them disappear by this Pact?'

'I might,' he allowed, 'but the Pact is a funny master. It might be too much to be asked for, for the Pact must be in balance. I was given life in return for my powers. It was fair, for life is a great gift. You would be given the freedom for the paltry, unlikely promise of slaying Euryale? I think the Cauldron would rebel against the Pact.'

'I see,' I fumed.

'And why would you be a better master than she is?' Ulrich asked painfully, not looking at the beast.

'One day, I might not be,' he allowed, 'it is so. You know this. Yet, is it not also so that in life one must take chances? No?'

'Yes,' I said with a small voice.

'Do you agree?' he asked.

'Wait,' Ulrich hissed.

'Silence, you gutless puddle of slime,' the dragon-thing said. 'Do you?'

'Whatever she does, we might not agree!' Ulrich spat.

'She decides for the lot of you, lout,' the Masked One said. 'Yet while your fetters will be mine, she carries the heaviest burden. You just dreamt of waking up without your toy. Shall I make it so it is no longer a dream?'

'No,' Ulrich said with a hiss.

I had no choice. I looked around, seeking for an escape. All I saw were damp cobwebs fluttering from once mighty and beautiful columns, and the flicker of faraway torches.

'Well?' the dragon asked, a hint of impatience playing in his voice. 'Shall we make a Pact?'

I breathed out, realizing I had held my breath. 'I agree to grant you your wish the day Euryale is slain, and you are free and in return you will wrest the Bone Fetters to your control.'

'So be it,' he grinned. 'You, worm.' Ulrich perked up. 'Fetch your kind. Leave the giant outside. I detest the lesser jotuns.' Ulrich stared at me balefully but went out, and I stood next to Dana, who was coming to, slowly. Her eyes had been open, but only now they focused. I waited for the others, sure Euryale would arrive any moment. I stroked Dana's face, wondering at her beauty and remembered all our history. She had been my only friend once.

She suddenly sat up, taking deep breaths. Her eyes widened at the sight of my armor. 'It is I,' I calmed her.

'What did you do? Shannon?' she asked softly.

'I got caught,' I told her.

'Caught? Why didn't you just leave the others? You only had to care for our needs? Why? Why did you ...'

'Silence, little lamb,' the Masked One sighed. 'They are here.'

And they were. Albine shuffled forward, her eyes lost. A kid, for God's sakes. Ulrich was bringing Anja forth, the blonde woman who had lost both her brothers and was thrust into a hall of madmen. She had a haunted look and clutched Ulrich's hand painfully hard. Cherry crept to me, her short hair bobbing as she came to stand near, considering the masked man carefully, and he stared back at her. Then there was Lex. He looked wild and upset and did not enjoy Ulrich's proximity. He sized up the dangerous master in the shadows, ogled at me, and I gave him a small, reassuring smile, and he answered it coldly.

Yes, I cared for the boy. Loved? Not sure.

But I loved Dana. Despite everything, she was part of me. She was sitting up, her thick, dark hair coiling down to the ground as she gaped at the supple armor I was wearing. 'We are here,' Ulrich said.

'What's going on?' asked Lex.

'He will take our Bone Fetters, and he will control them,' I explained.

'He will? What the devil is he?'

'No!' Dana yelled. 'I don't wish to …'

'Euryale will not let us go, ever, sister,' I said tiredly. 'Can't you see that? Moreover, we have to escape,' I said, and she stared at the Masked One, struggling.

'You damned snake,' Dana hissed at the dragon.

'Yes, Dana, that I am,' he answered her with a warning. 'Behave, or you will suffer, no matter what takes place.'

'I don't like this. I don't wish to be held by anything ever again,' Anja whispered.

'She is right,' Ulrich growled. 'I say we take our chances and force Bilac to help us along.'

'You didn't leave the giant with her?' I stated more than asked.

Lex shrugged. 'She gave us the Shades back. That thing, the jotun said he will toss her while he waits.'

'He will toss her head,' I complained. 'She is gone.'

'A giant?' Dana asked, confused.

'That is a dragon,' I told her. 'Therefore, a giant is a minor wonder. And I shall make the Pact. We will all pay the price if we cannot fight. He can give us what we need.'

'He is her slave,' Ulrich complained. 'If she tells him to cut us off, he will smile like a drunk being offered free grog and he will obey her.'

'Don't upset him, Ulrich,' I growled as the Masked One stared at us bickering. 'He has already said I will be the one to make the call.'

'Your call,' Anja spat, 'got my brother killed.'

'And nearly her as well,' Ulrich added.

I whirled on them. 'And it might get the lot of us killed still. We will all rot in this dungeon until I shall be used in her schemes, and you will be fed to this one, perhaps, or die in some other sadistic game of hers. There is no freedom here, There is no hope Without those letters gone. None! You wanted to escape. We tried it too late. Perhaps that is my fault, perhaps not and perhaps none of us actually trusted each other before the testing. It cost me friends and you brothers. Now we must act. He,' I thumbed towards the dreadful man standing behind me, 'can help us now.'

'We cannot trust him any better than Euryale, but it will be better to fight that battle later than die here,' Albine said with a childlike whimper. 'Do it.'

'Come, Shannon,' the Masked One said. 'To me. Ignore the fools.'

I walked forward, clutching the sword pommel. It felt cold and clammy in my hand. I stopped before him, and he raised a hand to stroke my cheek. It was a warm touch, a large, powerful hand. 'By Tiamox the Eldest, you shall enter into a Dragon Pact with me. You shall give me what I desire, and I shall aid you here today.'

'I will,' I said softly.

He grasped my face. 'You have been infected by the Rot,' he

whispered.

'I have,' I agreed. 'Many times. But it's healed now.'

He seemed doubtful but shrugged. 'You will slay Euryale and grant me a wish. I shall free you from Euryale's fetters now. Fail and the Pact will shrivel your heart. Say you agree.'

'I agree,' I whispered.

He pressed a finger to my chest, and I felt a brief ache there. 'Remember. One day, the day Euryale dies, I will wish for something. Or you shall die. Perhaps others.'

'I can hardly forget it. I'm hunted by Euryale the Night Devourer, my friends are to be fed to you if I fail, my sister is in mortal danger, and the world of elves I hope to escape to has never seen a human Hand of Life and detests the very race I belong to. And now this.' I massaged my chest.

'It is a challenge indeed,' he chortled. 'Agreed?'

'Agreed, by …'

'Tiamox, the god of the dragons,' he nodded, coaxing me.

'By Tiamox,' I whispered, and he grinned under his mask, the mouth's outlines showing. 'I make the Pact.'

'So be it,' he said and lifted his finger. My chest was pained again, briefly. There were no spells involved, but we all felt a burning in our arms and then blood was flowing thinly, curiously from the skin, with no apparent wounds. It was uncomfortable, then nearly unbearable for all, and then it was over. 'Here,' he said, snapped his finger, and we all lost the Shades.

'See?' Ulrich hissed. 'Betrayal.'

The Masked One snapped his fingers again, and we were restored. 'Merely testing the Pact. A dragon can be out of practice, and the Cauldron is unpredictable, at times, as I said. Now, none of them can deny you this birthright of yours, not the lesser things, nor the greater evil. Only I can. Or a god, perhaps. Go. And Shannon?'

I remember my oath,' I told him tightly.

'Of course you do,' he chuckled, 'it is the Pact. Not an oath. Binding beyond your approval. Fail, and you will not survive the mistake. Your friends will be hunted by my kind. They will hunt them for sport.' The Masked One nodded, hesitated, and his figure flickered away for a second. 'One more thing. I know you will go to the mirror. But to pass through the Dark Prayer, you will need a gorgon to touch it.'

'Will a gorgon blood do?' I grinned.

'Yes,' he agreed. 'We will see each other again, Pact Sister.'

'Come,' I told them and marched out, my mind whirling with the implications of the Pact. The Pact. It didn't look good. I squeezed Lex's hand and gazed at Dana. She did not look happy but scowled at the ceiling. We made our way out of the huge cell, walked up the dark steps and there, in the hall, Thak was arguing with Baktak. He noticed us before we could be seen, greeted us with a grunt, the massive thing sitting on the steps leading to the door. He was holding Bilac. What was left of her.

'You hare-brained idiot,' I said thinly. 'You ate her.'

'Mind your tongue, little girl,' he rumbled, pointing a tree-sized finger my way. 'They are dangerous. Best dealt with quickly.' He threw Bilac's head in the air and grabbed it. 'Can't eat it. Would make a terribly hard to digest lump of eels that one. You needed her?'

'Yes, I needed gorgon blood to open the doorway,' I hissed.

'There is blood in here,' he grinned, shaking the head so the snakes flapped grotesquely. 'It will do.'

'You ... fine,' I told him, hopelessly. 'We are going up there in a bit. They are likely waiting for us, but we have a surprise for them.'

'Made a Pact, did you?' he asked. 'I think you had to, but will regret it shortly. Or in the long run.'

'I made a Pact,' I told him, nervously. 'And I'm sure I will.'

'Met someone who tried to renege on one once. His heart burst, I mean, exploded,' Thak said absentmindedly. 'Gory sight, but cute.'

'We will have to fight soon,' Albine said, getting fidgety. 'What shall we do?'

'How many gorgons do you think there are?' Anja asked, surprisingly bloodthirsty as she was braiding her hair.

Thak grunted. 'Some hundred altogether, perhaps. Thirty to forty in the tower itself if you don't count Euryale. All Fury Whips of the

Dark and Deep Waters Clans. She, of course, is worth an army.'

'They have all the spells and power,' Dana stated dubiously. 'But we have the surprise. Some might make it.'

'Oh, possibly, some,' the giant said morosely and got up, eyeing the cells with a dangerous glint in his eyes.

Then, I felt a presence. Forty presences. Forty beings were grasping the Shades, and filling them with various forms of Fury. And they were close.

'Up!' I told them, preparing myself. They all jumped up in surprise.

I turned to look down towards the former red door cell, and there stood Euryale in front of her troops, spreading out from the cell. She too was wearing supple chain armor, decorated in dull silver and bright gold, cowled in the battle mail, her eyes swathed inside iron-laced silks. On her shoulders, there was a beautiful red drooping cloak. In her hands there were a curved bladed spear and a shield, both inlaid with serpents and flames. Behind her stood a cordon of gorgon blood, Cosia amongst them. They were all armored and armed, all harnessing spells of Fury, some carrying whips of ice, others of flame.

Euryale snickered as she walked forward, gazing at my armor. 'Well, you found the Silver Maw. Mighty fine it looks on you. Suits you well. Yet, we shall discuss the dead elves and the circumstances leading to their demise later. Now. You burnt my study. Many of my books and a number of irreplaceable artifacts are cinders and dust. You did this. Somehow you did. How did you do it? How did you even escape?' Her eyes traveled around the room, fixing on Ulrich's broken shackle. 'Where is Bilac?' she asked.

Thak slowly hid the mouth behind his hand and burped.

I was terrified though only momentarily. Had Able destroyed the mirror, after all? I wiggled my hair back from my forehead, deciding it did not matter. We would go up there anyway. 'My secret, you lying, murderous bitch.'

'You can still drop this foolishness, human girl and keep the ones you love. They will all keep breathing, if I will it,' she challenged me, her voice angered and nervous. She aimed the spear my way, the point quivering. 'I need you. But there will be others eventually, and I am a patient one. Spare your friends this trouble and submit quickly.'

'I am sorry, our filthy, dark-hearted mistress of sacrifices, but they will all die here, one way or the other. Saa'dark sacrifices to feed your power. They are like lumps of coal, useful but soon gone.'

'He told you this? So, you went down there? Inside? Nox will pay for it. I think he has betrayed me more than once. Shades will get him, if not I. Brave you are,' she stated with dangerous sweetness. She glowered under her hood, that much was clear for her anger was enough to make me turn my eyes away from hers. She spoke slowly. 'You do not understand, Shannon, what we have to go through to stave off the elven kingdoms. You know ...'

I slapped my thigh angrily. 'Stop right there. I don't care if you are the victim or the oppressor, disgusting mistress of pain and treachery. Elven houses do not like you? I don't like you. That is all I care about, you ugly wench. I care nothing for your hardships,' I grinned. 'I Will take us all away or none.'

'None,' she said, near bored. 'And what of the Rot, should you escape?'

'It's gone, dozy bitch, for you forgot a cup of rancid blood in the cell,' I said, and she froze. 'And as for more surprises? Here is one.'

Her manner turned cautious, taking a step back. The gorgons lifted their shields, making a wall of steel.

We all harnessed spells of Fury.

'I went down there and met your First Born slave in this damned dungeon, and I made a Pact with the slimy bastard, just like you did. He owns the Fetters now, and he is not here to cut us off, is he? He is stuck down there by your own Pact. Here!' I hissed, and we wove our spells. The enemy stared at us in shock. I gathered power, so much power I staggered. I summoned the ice spears from the floor in front of them, tall and thick, swiftly spreading to the left and right, before and amongst them, blocking their sight. They were massive and thicker than any I had seen as I added more and more, laughing with the wlld powor. I braided the weaves together, and even when my friends let forth flame walls, the flames sizzled on the massive block of ice.

'Shannon!' Euryale screamed from beyond the wall. Some gorgons were on our side of the wall, getting to their feet. 'Shannon, you coward, reticent little traitor. I shall ...'

'Feast on me no more,' I spat and grasped at the spell she had used so many times. It was a massively hard spell, and I gathered ancient ice and whirling wind, adding tingling bits of frozen waters, and the familiar dark hole blew out of the ground before me. The gorgons were scrambling around the ice now, some slipping and falling heavily, but I pushed my friends forward. 'Jump in! Quickly, don't tarry, dammit!' Thak grinned and went first, shrinking to man size. We had to dodge as a gorgon's crushed torso flew back out of the tunnel. Thak had met a guard. I begged he had not lost Bilac's head.

'Go!' Anja screamed as she went in, pulling Ulrich along. Albine jumped in with a shriek and so did Lex after I kicked him. Dana grimaced and hesitated, and then I felt her gathering force, a huge, huge amount of it, rivaling what I gathered with the help of the Silver Maw, much more than I could ever hope to hold without the armor. Smiling demonically, she let go of thick strands of flame that exploded over a pair of backpedaling gorgons, then the fire waved forward to erratically hit the ice wall. The fire and ice roared together so powerfully we all flew on our asses. Ice shards skittered about, flames licked across the room like cannoball shrapnel, and Baktak banged open, the door trying to shield itself. I nearly lost my spell.

Dana wiped sweat from her brow and glanced at me. She grinned, swaying next to me. 'You might be particular to Aldheim, sister, but I am powerful beyond anything. Don't forget it. However, I'm with you, now, love,' she told me with a grin and jumped into the portal.

I stared at the room.

Gorgons were staggering around, some tearing at smoking armor and a few were on their knees in the final throes of pain. Some were burning fiercely, others charred lumps. Others were frozen, unable to breathe, their snakes writhing on the floors. Over a dozen confused gorgons were still holding to the Fury in the smoky room. One cast a spell, and I noticed a lumbering thing made of stone rise from the rubble, a huge thing. It came to stand before the hurt ranks of my enemies, shielding them. Others were casting lights, one summoned freezing wind to clear the smoke away.

I saw her.

Euryale stood there, her legs spread, cheek bleeding. She tore at the cowl, trying to catch my eyes, and our eyes met for a brief moment, the pain ripping through me, the petrification and death of her ancient gaze creeping In at the edges of my eyes, making them dry and ill. I tore my eyes away from her and spat. 'You and I, you creep of Niflheim, are not done.' A feeble threat, really, but I had surprised her.

'No, we are not,' she grinned. 'Go then. I shall find you. And perhaps I shall call for your young Rose in a year? One day I shall have her, should you escape me.

I rocked my head at her in shock. She moved for me, fast as a shadow, but flames licked the ground between us, and Cherry appeared, pushed me through and jumped through the portal, and I let it close as I whirled away. I felt Euryale's portal opening up somewhere close, and I cursed as I stared at the faces around me, all anxious. The study was in simmering ruins. Books had been burnt indeed, great stacks of dark pages and leathery covers floating in the scorching air and perversely I felt a moment of regret. There were holes in the floor, and some featureless, darkened corpses were lying about, people, or gorgons who had fought the fires and explosions. By the far wall, something had shattered violently, spectacularly, leaving the wall open to the light of Mar.

The once magnificent study was gone, replaced by a terrible chaos all around.

Able was nowhere to be seen. By the miraculously spared bed, the dark, swathed mirror stood. I ran there and pulled at the dark thread for it was stuck. 'No time for that now,' Thak informed me and hefted Bilac's head. He stared at me, and I gathered myself, swaying as I did. I pulled at the powers Euryale had used to call on the mirror and whispered the name of the artifact. The crow heads turned to stare at me, the thing glowed, and I nodded at Thak. He pushed the gorgon's head through the velvet, and the heavy drape was sucked in. A simmering doorway stood open, glittering with light and promise, and I shook with fatigue.

Euryale's portal opened up.

'Go!' I screamed and cursing, Ulrich and Anja jumped in. Lex grabbed at Cherry, who shook her head and disappeared. Lex stared at me, and I pointed at the mirror. He hesitated until Thak grabbed him and tossed him through and kicked Dana along as well. 'Did Cherry go?' I yelled.

Albine dived in with a shriek, and Thak stared around, shrugging. 'I suppose so?' His eyes narrowed as he looked at the dark tunnel.

I turned to face the enemy. Euryale stood there in her war glory, grimacing in anger as she witnessed our escape. More and more of the enemy followed her, carrying fiery whips. She grinned at me. 'What, human girl? Afraid of the trip? Go on!'

'I don't want you to follow me,' I said with spite.

'Very hard to stop me,' she laughed. 'Very hard. Go on, I'll be along. Leave the giant here to fight for you.'

'I'd love to squat on your ugly skull and void my bowels,' Thak rumbled, but I shook my head at him.

'I don't think,' I told her brazenly and eyed the dozen or so enemy, now all harnessing spells of Fury, all carrying flaming whips, 'that I told you about my skills.'

'You have a skill?' she asked sweetly. 'What is that? Other than failing to become what few could dream of.'

'I can see what you weave,' I spat. 'What elven maa'dark, the First Born train for centuries, I learn just like that.'

'What?' she said as she took a step forward. 'That is how you had that ice wall spell?'

'This is what I can do,' I said and grasped at their spells. I yanked and tore at them and the effect was spectacular. Some of the whips disappeared. One exploded, spattering the lot of us with blood and intestines. Another grew wildly and lopped off a leg of another. Then I called the power Cosia had called in Trad.

I melted the floor of the Fanged Spire.

I pushed everything I had left in it, and the walls and the floor changed to ice, then it melted, and everything holding the stones in place just disappeared. The floor buckled crazily. It turned to mush, then to water, and the last thing I remember was Euryale hurtling for me, her face a mask of rage, snakes hissing madly. I felt I was falling and saw Thak pulling at me in midair and pushing me through the half falling mirror, the fancy thing spinning in the carnage as the tower collapsed.

'I bit you twice, love!' I heard Euryale screaming and with that, I fell into the vortex.

Twice?

Was I still infected?

We fell hard. It was not a magical fall, a featherlike, sweet thing of dreams, but a brutal and cold tumble and likely I had broken something in Dark Prayer for what I had done to the tower. The tumble ended quickly, and we were all exposed to Mar.

However, we were in the air, and below us was the Dancing Bay, perhaps. We fell into a sea, the fall was painful, for we fell on top of each other. I had barely time to draw in a breath as the gray and blue brilliance claimed me. We went in and under, deep, and all were bruised by the impact. I came up, sputtering, trying to draw a desperate breath. Cherry was coughing nearby, having swallowed saltwater. Lex was suddenly there, paddling like a dog, and Albine was trying to support him, and I saw Anja was swimming for Ulrich. 'Everyone can swim?' I yelled, finally spotting Dana's head, her hair over her eyes, struggling fiercely to see.

'I can't, not very well!' Lex panted. 'I know I like boats, but I never took the time to learn!'

'Well, this is great,' Dana spat. 'Just what real freedom tastes like. Salt. Shit cold salt and so we shall drown!'

I could not see well. I realized I was armored, and it weighed me down. Not like I would imagine a real armor would, for the metal was supple and light, but it was still heavy, and I wore Bilac's armor under the plate as well. Dana cursed and swam to me and grabbed me, treading water. She held me like she had held me when we grew up, and I stared at her and she stared at me. She shook her head at me and stammered. 'What?' I asked her.

'I suppose I shall thank you,' she said as if unused to being grateful. 'You disagreed with me, and it worked. Even for them, the dolts. I guess you don't really need me, not like you used to.'

'I still need you. I want you to need me as well,' I said with chattering teeth. 'And I'm not sure why you think I saved us. There are beasts in the seas, they said.'

'No, you saved us,' she grinned and nodded at Albine, who was treading water next to me. The teen yelled gleefully. 'Look! We are free!'

A ship of purple sails was sailing behind us, and on the deck, imperious faces could be seen, their thick dark and silver hair whipping in the wind, and some pointed at us.

The flag was a rampant beast on a green field. A House Safiroon ship.

Elves.

We would be safe. We were free. We had so much to do yet, but we were free of Euryale. I hesitated and gazed at my shoulder. It tingled.

Then I turned around, staring around at the sea. 'Where is Thak?'

EPILOGUE

So it was, that we escaped Grey Downs and Euryale. The Dark Levy, the cursed road so many had previously taken had not quite claimed our lives. Not all of our lives. Not yet, not then. We waited for the fabulous elven ship to make its way to us, and we would face many, many challenges, for the elves were not kind, gentle folk by nature, though there were those who were, of course. We would meet both kinds.

You ask what then?

Well, there is more. Much more.

I would meet Euryale again, and I would dance with the ghoul. I would deal with the Pact, I would learn of love, and sisterhood, and many things would change.

Many things indeed, for I would also meet Hel.

Wait.

- The story continues in the Eye of Hel, early 2016 -

Thank you for reading the book.

Do sign up for my mailing list by visiting my homepages. By doing this, you will receive a rare and discreet email where you will find:

News of the upcoming stories
Competitions
Book promotions
Free reading

Also, if you enjoyed this book, you might want to check out this one as well. It is related to Eye of Hel:

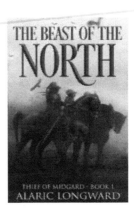

Grab them from my AMAZON HOMEPAGE